"*The Master Craftsman* is a fascin[...] spheric tale of the Russian Revo[...] generational story: What more d[...] us inside the enthralling world of Fabergé while introduc[...] us to deeply felt characters who must put everything on the line to discover the truth. Compelling, exhilarating, and richly imagined, *The Master Craftsman* is historical fiction at its best."

Patti Callahan, *New York Times* bestselling
author of *Becoming Mrs. Lewis*

"Artfully crafted and constructed, *The Master Craftsman* is the perfect blend of intrigue, suspense, history, and romance. This novel has it all! Lovers of transportive historical fiction will find all their delights met within these pages."

Susan Meissner, bestselling author
of *The Nature of Fragile Things*

"Every so often I want to fall into a story that takes me on an adventure. One with twists and turns that I don't expect and surprises that keep me engrossed. Kelli Stuart's *The Master Craftsman* was such a book for me. This novel was a delightful escape from housework, a lovely distraction from daily tasks. More than once I completely lost track of time while reading and took a break only so I could Google pictures of St. Petersburg and the particular Fabergé eggs that Stuart described so well. Grab yourself a copy of this book, then buckle up for an escapade you won't soon forget!"

Susie Finkbeiner, author of *The Nature of Small Birds*

"With in-depth research and a passion for Russia's unique culture, Stuart delivers a colorful and complex story that's sure to delight. Part contemporary, part historical, part treasure hunt, part mystery . . . this book is unlike any you've ever read. Sit back and enjoy being transported to early-twentieth-century Russia where nothing is what it seems."

Julie Cantrell, *New York Times* and *USA Today*
bestselling author of *Perennials*

the

MASTER
CRAFTSMAN

KELLI STUART

Revell

a division of Baker Publishing Group
Grand Rapids, Michigan

© 2022 by Kelli Stuart

Published by Revell
a division of Baker Publishing Group
PO Box 6287, Grand Rapids, MI 49516-6287
www.revellbooks.com

Printed in the United States of America

Library of Congress Cataloging-in-Publication Data
Names: Stuart, Kelli, 1978– author.
Title: The master craftsman / Kelli Stuart.
Description: Grand Rapids, MI : Revell, a division of Baker Publishing Group, [2022]
Identifiers: LCCN 2021041200 | ISBN 9780800740429 (paperback) | ISBN 9780800741150 (casebound) | ISBN 9781493435715 (ebook)
Subjects: LCGFT: Action and adventure fiction. | Novels.
Classification: LCC PS3619.T829 M37 2022 | DDC 813/.6—dc23
LC record available at https://lccn.loc.gov/2021041200

This is a work of historical reconstruction; the appearances of certain historical figures are therefore inevitable. All other characters, however, are products of the author's imagination, and any resemblance to actual persons, living or dead, is coincidental.

Baker Publishing Group publications use paper produced from sustainable forestry practices and post-consumer waste whenever possible.

22 23 24 25 26 27 28   7 6 5 4 3 2 1

St. Petersburg, Russia, 1917

He walked quickly down the narrow staircase, hand pressed against the cold wall to steady himself. On the last two steps, his foot slipped, and he went careening forward, catching himself just before falling. His hands trembled as he straightened and rushed into the next room. Glancing over his shoulder nervously, he ducked behind the counter and pulled back the rug upon which he'd spent countless hours standing. Beneath it, the wood panels showed only the slightest variation from the rest, expertly hidden, the attention to detail his most defining characteristic.

Slipping his fingertip beneath a slat of wood, he wiggled and pried until it released. The entire panel now sprung loose. He stared into the black space below and drew in a shaky breath. Lowering to his knees, he winced at the pain that nipped his joints, and reached his arm down into the hole. It was cool inside, but dry. He had made sure that the climate of this hidden space was perfect. His fingers brushed the metal box, and he wrapped his hand around it, pulling it up, then quickly replacing the floor panel so that it would be hidden to the untrained eye.

Covering the floor with the rug, he pushed to his feet, wishing that his back and knees would better cooperate.

"Did you get it?"

He gasped and spun around, still clutching the metal box between his hands. He looked in her eyes for a long moment, a thousand needs and instructions swirling through his mind.

"Yes," he answered quietly.

Outside, a loud bang caused both of them to jump. She put her hand to her chest while he gripped the box even tighter.

"Not here," she whispered.

"No."

He jutted his chin toward the room in the back and the two ducked behind the curtain. They slid through the shadows until they reached the small desk next to the wall that faced the alley.

"Dust and shadows," she murmured as they tucked themselves beneath the window.

"I'm sorry?"

"It's nothing," she replied.

He set the box on the table and pulled a handkerchief from his pocket, mopping at his brow while she watched with tender eyes. He tucked the handkerchief back into his pocket with shaking hands, then slowly reached forward and unlocked the clasp on the box. Opening the top, he turned it toward the thin stream of light coming from the upper window. She drew in a long breath and let it out slowly.

"It's stunning," she whispered. She leaned forward, studying the detail, the intricacies, her face etched with awe.

"It is my masterpiece," he said quietly.

"It is the finest you've created." She paused, straightening back up. "Why did you do it?" she asked.

He held her gaze for a brief moment. "I've felt it all unraveling for quite some time," he finally answered, eyes misting over. Another loud bang on the streets followed by angry shouts cut him short. He shook his head. "There isn't time to explain." He looked into her eyes with an imploring stare. "They cannot find it now. If they do, they will destroy it and they *will* kill me."

"I . . . I don't understand," she breathed. "Why? This looks so . . . ordinary."

"You haven't seen it all."

"The surprise?"

He nodded. At the sound of glass breaking, he leaned forward and removed the treasure with the hands of a master. Beneath it was a bed of blood-red velvet. He tugged on a small string sticking out from beneath the fabric and pulled out the top to reveal a hidden compartment underneath. Two more objects lay nestled in the hollow space below. She leaned forward and gasped, her hand covering her mouth. Looking up, her eyes met his.

"Bloody Sunday," he muttered.

"I'm sorry?"

His gaze glassed over as his mind wandered to that horrible morning when peaceful protestors were massacred on Nevsky Prospekt, St. Petersburg's main street.

"I was there." His words were a mist. He closed his eyes, trying in vain to chase away the images of the bodies and the sounds of the wailing. That was the moment when his allegiance had fissured. And this—he looked back down into the box that contained his secret—this had been his act of defiance.

"You have to take it," he said. His voice was stronger now, more sure and determined. He resettled the top shelf, covering the rebellion, then gently laid the treasure onto the velvet. Closing the lid, he clicked it shut, the sound echoing off the walls around them. "You must take it with you and go. And my dear girl . . ." He paused, searching her face. "You cannot tell a soul what you have until the time is right."

She was quiet for a long moment. "I will do this for you," she finally said.

The two held one another's gaze. Outside, angry shouts grew louder. They were getting closer.

"The tsar has abdicated," she whispered.

He nodded, then reached down and picked up the box that housed his masterpiece. He let the weight of it rest in his hands for the briefest of moments, like a father cradling his child for the last time.

"It's only a matter of time before it all disappears," he said. "All of the pieces, all of the beauty."

He reached over and put the box in her hands. "But not this one." He looked at her tenderly. "You must guard it well. It could be the only one left."

The sound of shouting grew closer. She pulled the box to her chest and looked back at him, her eyes widening.

"What do I do with it?" she asked.

He shifted his stare back to the box. "This will be my legacy, but they aren't ready for it now. I trust that you will know what to do when the time is right, and by that time I will be only a memory."

She shook her head, blinking back tears. "What will you do?" she asked, eyes shining. She reached out and grabbed his hand.

"Don't worry about me," he replied. "I'll be okay." He pulled her hand to his chest and gave it a quick squeeze before turning her toward the back door. "You must leave now. Find a place to hide it until you can get out of the country."

He looked around at the shop where he'd spent the last

years bent over his own worktable encouraging his employees and making his fortune.

"Not much longer now," he said quietly.

"Thank you for trusting me," she said, blinking back tears.

He nodded, leaning forward and placing a soft kiss on her cheek. "Until we meet again, my dear girl," he said. "And, Alma . . ."

She looked up and met his steady gaze.

"Don't ever forget the things I told you."

He turned and walked quickly through the room, disappearing behind the curtain.

----- ❋ -----

Alma heard him going back up the stairs to the flat he shared with his wife. His entire family was in danger now, angry rioters coming after anyone with a connection to the royal family.

She turned to the back door and flung it open, catching her breath as the icy wind smacked her in the face. Tucking the box beneath her coat and pulling it tight around her, she pushed out into the back alley. The metal burned against her chest, the weight of the secret thick. She would do what he asked. She would escape, and she would hide his masterpiece.

She turned the corner and ducked her head, pressing into the wind and walking quickly past the front of the shop on 24 Bolshaya Morskaya. The Gothic Revival façade of the building that had once been a source of pride now screamed of excess and begged to be targeted by the Bolsheviks. Out of the corner of her eye, she could see the gray Finnish granite of the outside of the building, and she pushed past the display windows that had once gleamed invitingly, but which now sat dark and despondent.

The noise of the crowd swelled in the distance, and she looked down at the ground, walking as quickly as she could without breaking into a panicked run. She didn't look up when she passed the door she'd walked by a thousand times before, and she didn't see the wisps of snow falling over the sign hanging just above her head. The sign that read K. FABERGÉ.

Present Day

Ava dropped to her feet from the rope and put her hands on her hips, her chest heaving as sweat dripped off her forehead. She squatted down and rested her elbows on her knees.

"Nice workout."

Ava looked up and nodded at Joe. She offered a fist bump to her workout partner and jutted her chin forward.

"You too," she said. She pushed herself up and shook out her arms. "That was a lot harder than I thought it was going to be," she added with a grimace.

Joe snorted. "They always are." He grinned. "If it's not hard, then you aren't doing it right."

She smiled back. "Word."

She walked to her bag, grabbed her towel, and mopped her face while offering reluctant fist bumps to everyone else in the class. She'd rather only talk with Joe, but it was an unwritten rule of CrossFit that you had to be best buds with the entire group of fitness buffs in each workout you attended. Ava much preferred anonymity.

Walking outside, she pulled her sunglasses from her bag and slid them on. The watch on her wrist buzzed, and she glanced down to see who was calling.

MOM

Ava reached into her bag and pulled out her phone and her keys at the same time. She hit the answer button.

"Hey, Mom," she said, fumbling with her keys and dropping them. She cursed under her breath as they slid beneath the car.

"Ava?"

"Hang on," Ava said, gingerly lowering on shaky legs to her knees.

"Ava?" Carol's voice called again through the phone's speaker.

"Coming!" Ava said, reaching under the car and grabbing her keys. She pushed back to her feet and put the phone against her ear. "Yes, hi, Mom." She unlocked the front door and slid into her car. "I'm here."

"Ava, honey."

Ava paused, her key over the ignition. Her mom's voice sounded tight.

"I've just heard some . . . news."

"News?" Ava asked.

Carol took in a deep breath and let it out slowly. Ava shook her head and started the car. It was her mother's calling card to draw things out longer than necessary.

Ava's car sputtered to life and the radio began blaring, causing her to jump and drop her phone again.

"Agh!" She hit the button to turn off the radio and grabbed her phone once more. "Sorry again."

"Good grief, honey, are you okay?"

Ava snorted. "Define okay."

"You didn't get fired again, did you?"

"Uh, no, Mom," Ava replied. "But thanks for the vote of confidence." She glanced in the rearview mirror as she slowly backed out of her parking space. "And I didn't get fired from my last job. I left willingly."

"After you argued with your boss."

"Didn't you say you had news?" Ava asked.

A heavy pause lengthened between them. "It isn't good news," her mom said, her voice strained.

"Mom, you're killing me. Can you just tell me why you called, please?"

"It's about your father, Ava."

Silence engulfed them both as Ava ingested her mom's words.

"My father?"

"His sister sent me an email this morning. You remember your Aunt Sylvie? She met you when you were little. She came for dinner after Christmas when you were . . . oh, I don't know. I guess you were nine or ten? Maybe you were seven. Anyway, she came and ate with us because she wanted to meet you, but . . ."

"Mom!" Ava threw up a hand in exasperation. "If I tell you that I do remember Aunt Sylvie, will you move on please?"

"Well, honey . . ." Her mom paused. "It seems your dad is dying."

Ava slowed to a stop at a traffic light. She sat silent, watching as cars crossed the road in opposite directions. She hadn't seen her father in ten years. She had been sixteen, and it was only the fifth or sixth time she'd ever been alone with him at all. Nick Laine wasn't a man for commitments, and his understanding of fatherhood was extremely limited. On that final visit, he'd spent most of their morning together tinkering with his motorcycle and avoiding eye contact with Ava. She told her mom later that day that she'd rather not go back to see him again.

"Ava?"

A car behind her honked its horn, and Ava jumped. She hit the gas pedal, her wheels spinning briefly before fishtailing her across the road.

"I'm here," she said.

"I'm sorry, honey," her mom said.

"Why? I hardly know the man."

"I know. But he's still your dad."

"No. He's my father. There's a difference."

It was silent for a moment before Carol continued. "In any case, I think it would be a good idea if you went to see him. We should both go together."

Ava hit her blinker and slowed as she rounded the corner toward her apartment. The Florida sun above dimmed as a gray cloud moved over, a typical afternoon storm rolling over the palm-lined road leading to her home.

"I don't know, Mom," Ava said with a sigh.

"Ava—"

"I know, I know. He's my father," she muttered.

"Well . . . yes. And he's the only link you have to that side of your heritage. There are things that you should ask—things you may want to know so you can tell your children someday."

"I'm not having children, remember," Ava said. There was a beat, and Ava could almost see her mother pinching the bridge of her nose—something she always did in an effort to control her frustration.

"I don't believe that."

Ava turned the car off and leaned her head back, staring at the stairwell that led up to her second-floor apartment.

"Why do you want to go see him, Mom?" she asked. "He left us, remember? He left you alone to raise me. Why do you care about him?"

There was no answer at first. Ava could picture her mother staring off in the distance the way she did when she was trying to formulate a thought. Where Ava was quick and impulsive with her words, her mother was careful and deliberate—a quality Ava appreciated, even if it drove her crazy.

"I loved him, Ava," she finally answered.

"Right, Mom. Loved. Past tense. But this is the present."

"We had a child together. My love for him now is different, but . . . well . . ." She drew in a deep breath and let it out slowly. "I can't let him die without at least thanking him for giving me you."

Ava shook her head and blinked back tears that pricked at her eyes. "Well, when you put it that way," she mumbled.

She shoved open her door and stepped outside just as thunder began rolling from the sky—a low, steady rumble that grew in intensity as it pushed over her head.

"Fine, I'll go with you," she said, tucking her phone between her ear and shoulder as she reached in the car for her bag.

"That's my girl."

Ava heard her mother's satisfied smile in her reply. She rolled her eyes as she slammed the car door, then rushed to her apartment stairwell, dashing upstairs just before the sky opened up and a sheet of rain dropped from above.

"I have to go, Mom," she said. "I have to get ready for work."

"So, you promise you haven't lost your job?"

"Mother!"

"Okay, okay. I'll email Sylvie and tell her we'd like to stop by and see him on Saturday morning."

"Fine." Ava drew in a breath. "Love you, Mom."

"I love you, honey," Carol replied gently.

Ava unlocked her door and pushed into her apartment. She dropped her keys on the entry table and kicked off her shoes, then padded to the kitchen. She yanked open the refrigerator and sighed. There were a couple of apples, some soggy spinach that needed to be tossed, a jar of peanut butter, and an empty carton of milk.

After grabbing an apple, Ava shut the fridge and turned around, leaning back against the countertop.

"So, Nick is dying," she murmured. She let the thought sink in for a little while, trying to dissect how she felt about it. She'd given up on the idea of having a dad a long time ago. She hadn't even missed him. But now, with the knowledge that he'd soon be permanently gone, she felt a new emotion swelling inside her chest.

Pushing away from the counter, Ava walked to her closet and pulled down a box from the shelf. She wiped the layer of dust from the top and sat on the floor, took the lid off the box, and sifted through the contents inside.

She pulled out a news article that she'd found when she was thirteen. She'd paid fifty cents to have the local librarian print it for her on their computer so that her mom wouldn't know what she'd been looking for.

"Oh, are you researching treasure hunts?" the librarian had asked her, and Ava had nodded, because in a way she was doing just that—only she was really researching a specific treasure hunter named Nick Laine.

She'd discovered her father's infamous treasure hunts quite by accident. She'd been snooping around in her mom's dresser, looking for a pair of socks, when she saw a letter her father wrote to her mom explaining how sorry he was that he'd had to leave her and Ava, but he needed to find what he was looking for.

Treasure hunting is my passion, Carol, the letter read. *It's what I do. I can't be the guy that stays home and provides for his family. I'm not that guy. I wanted to be him, but I just couldn't.*

The letter led Ava to the library the next day to search the internet for the father she'd seen only a few times in her life. She held up the news article and read the headline.

TREASURE HUNTER NICK LAINE UNCOVERS ANCIENT AZTEC ARTIFACTS

Beneath the article was a picture of her dad standing proudly at the top of a large hill, crumbled ruins behind him. He had one booted foot up on a stone and his hands on his hips, a wide grin spread across his handsome face. Ava had never seen her dad look like that—happy and relaxed. Every time she had seen him, his eyes flitted from side to side nervously, and he rarely smiled.

She dropped the article and pulled out another, this time hailing her father's accidental discovery of an emerald mine in Zambia. The one below that showed her father standing in front of the Smithsonian, the headline announcing an upcoming presentation by the famous Nick Laine detailing all his many adventures in seeking out lost treasures.

Ava leaned back against the wall and thought about all the dreams she'd had in her teens of someday reconnecting with her dad and joining him on his famous expeditions around the world. Together, they'd become an unstoppable force in treasure hunting.

"*I can't believe I wasted all those years without you*," she imagined him telling her as the two of them stood at the mouth of a cave, preparing to hike deep into its belly and unearth its secrets.

Ava would lie awake at night imagining all the places she'd finally get to see, an itch for exploration working its way into her heart. She and her mom never went anywhere besides a yearly trip to see her grandparents in Miami, and one time her mom managed to save up enough money to take her to a little cabin in the Smoky Mountains during spring break. But the weather was unseasonably cold while they were there, and as Floridians they were unprepared to handle it, so they mostly sat by the fire and tried to stay warm.

Ava wanted to travel, to see the world and discover new people and places. But she'd long given up on that dream. She let it go around the time she realized that Nick Laine was never going to change, and he was never going to invite her to be a part of his team. Still, as she stared at the articles she'd read so many times, she felt that familiar stirring wiggle its way back in. The longing for adventure was always there, bubbling beneath the surface, tempting her to let down her guard and tap into it.

She glanced back into the box. At the bottom, beneath all the news clippings, was a picture of her and her dad together. It was the only picture she had of the two of them. She was about two years old, and the photo was taken shortly before he left. Ava sat in her dad's lap, a large grin splitting wide her face. Her wispy blond hair had been pulled into two crooked pigtails, and she clutched under her arm a stuffed giraffe that her mom told her Nick had brought back from one of his business trips. Nick had his arms around her waist, and he was looking at the camera with a small smile that didn't quite reach his eyes.

Ava studied the picture closely. "Why did you leave?"

She dropped the photo back in the box, stood up, and pushed the box into place on top of the closet shelf. She glanced at her watch and winced, running to the bathroom to shower quickly. She hadn't lost her job yet, but her boss had told her that if she showed up late one more time, she'd have to start looking for new employment.

Ten minutes later, Ava dashed out the door, hair dripping wet and still trying to tuck her white shirt into her black pants as she yanked open her car door. With a twenty-five-minute drive to her job at a restaurant in Tampa's Hyde Park Village, she was cutting it close. She slid into the seat, jammed the key in the ignition and turned it. Nothing. She turned again and let out a frustrated growl as the engine sputtered and coughed but wouldn't turn over. She pumped the gas pedal a few times and turned the key again, this time the car making only a few clicking noises. She banged her fist on the steering wheel, then leaned her head back against the seat and closed her eyes.

A tap on the window startled her. Ava yelped and turned.

"Hey, sorry!"

She shoved open the door and shook her head as her neighbor Zak stepped back. Ava stood up and slammed the door behind her.

"You okay?" he asked. His jet-black hair was slicked to the side as though he were ready to have a school yearbook photo taken. Tall and lanky, Zak made up for his lack of girth in personality. His bright blue collared shirt was tucked into a pair of slim khaki pants that only made him look like a skinny Clark Kent. Zak pushed his thick-rimmed glasses up on his face and smiled.

"I'm fine," Ava muttered.

"You don't look fine," Zak said. "You look frustrated."

"Yeah, well, I guess I am." She kicked the side of her car. "Stupid car won't start, which means I can't get to work, which means I'm probably getting fired today. So that's awesome."

"I can take you to work," Zak said.

"No, you don't have to do that. It's totally out of your way."

"No, it isn't. I'm working from home today, so I have the time. Let me help you."

Ava considered his offer for a moment. It was no secret that Zak had a crush on her. Their apartments were right next door to one another, which offered a lot of opportunity for interaction. Their complex was forever throwing mixers and parties where she and Zak would make small talk. Several times, they'd joined up with a few of their neighbors to volunteer at the local homeless shelter, where Ava noticed Zak had an especially endearing way of conversing with people who were struggling with the hardships of life. His attention hadn't bothered her at first. Zak was quirky and funny in his own strange kind of way, and Ava had enjoyed talking with him, until it became apparent that he enjoyed talking with her for different reasons. Eventually, the attention began to annoy her, and she had purposely been putting distance between the two of them, but Zak wasn't easily swayed. He'd made it quite clear that he would like nothing more than to spend quality time with her. He was sweet, and he could definitely pass as handsome with a little bit of work, but not wanting to lead him on, Ava had turned him down as gently as she possibly could several times.

She glanced at her watch and then sighed. "I guess if it's not too much trouble, that would be fine," she finally answered.

Zak grinned. "Splendid!"

Ava fought to suppress a smile. It was one of Zak's calling cards to talk like a ninety-year-old grandmother. What guy said things like "splendid"? She reached into her car and grabbed her purse, then followed Zak across the parking lot to his little black Audi and slid into the passenger seat.

"Dude"—she looked around at the spotless interior—"your car is freakishly clean. Is it new?"

"Oh, no. I've had this car for five years now. This is the same car you rode in with me a few months ago when we volunteered."

"Yeah, I thought it was new then too." Ava laughed. "It even smells new! How do you do that?"

"How do I do what?"

"Keep it looking and smelling like you just drove it off the car lot!" Ava said, shaking her head in amusement.

Zak shrugged his shoulders. "I don't know. I don't eat in it, and I vacuum it out every couple of days. And I wash it every Saturday morning."

Ava gaped at him.

"What?" Zak asked.

She shook her head. "Nothing."

"So, do you like working at that restaurant?" he asked after a brief minute of silence.

Ava shrugged. "No. But it covers the bills, and it's all I've got right now."

Zak merged onto the highway and glanced at her from the corner of his eye. "But you have a college degree, yes?"

Ava sighed. "Yeah, I've got one. I majored in world history with a minor in sociology."

"Well, that sounds very interesting."

"It is! I just can't do anything with it. My mom tried to warn me, but if I was going to suffer through college classes, I wanted to at least be interested in what I was learning." She shrugged.

Zak nodded. "I understand that. I did not want to study business statistics and computer sciences, but my father insisted. It was terribly boring."

Ava turned to look at Zak. "I know you're in IT or something, but I don't know what that means. What do you actually *do*?"

"I do data analysis and statistical reconfiguration for a local marketing firm."

Ava snorted. "Uh, I don't even know what you just said."

Zak smiled. "It's okay. It is as boring as it sounds like it would be. On the side, I do web design, which I actually enjoy. I want to start my own business at some point, but right now I must pay the bills. You understand."

"Too well," Ava murmured.

They rode the rest of the way in silence. Zak pulled up to Ava's restaurant seven minutes before she was due to clock in, and she offered him a quick thanks.

"I'll get someone from the restaurant to drive me home tonight, so you don't have to come back," she said, pushing open the door.

"Oh, I don't mind! I can come get you, and maybe we could go grab a bite to eat." His eyes lit up, and for a brief moment Ava considered taking him up on it only because he looked like an eager puppy dog longing for a pat on the head. But she swallowed hard and shook her head.

"Thanks, but I'm usually wiped after work, so not tonight. But I really do appreciate the lift, Zak!"

His face fell, but he quickly recovered. "No problem, Ava. Anytime."

"Oh, and Zak," she said, leaning down to look at him across

the seat. "Try eating some french fries in here. It won't kill you." She gave him a wink, and he smiled.

"I don't think so," he said.

She laughed and shut the door, then turned and rushed into the restaurant. She tugged open the door and turned back to see Zak lingering at the curb. He gave her a big smile, waved, and eased his car onto the street.

———— ❁ ————

Saturday morning came more quickly than Ava would have preferred. She had spent the week juggling rides to and from work, several times opting to call an Uber rather than ask Zak for help again, even though she knew he would drop everything he was doing in a heartbeat and help her out. Ava stepped out of her apartment and locked the door, then turned and walked down the stairs. She glanced at her car and let out a frustrated sigh. She'd finally had someone come out and look at it yesterday only to learn she needed new spark plugs and a host of other small things that added up to a bigger price tag than she could afford. She was going to have to ask her mother for money.

Ava leaned against the trunk of her car and waited for her mom to arrive. They'd planned to ride together to see Nick and her Aunt Sylvie. Apparently, her father had gone to live with his sister in Lakeland a few months back when the cancer had begun advancing beyond what the doctors could control.

Ava jumped at the sound of a car horn and looked up to see her mom turning into the parking lot. She pulled up, and Ava opened the door and slid in.

"You look nice," Ava said, taking in her mother's perfectly styled hair and made-up face. "Red lipstick?" She raised her eyebrows.

"Oh, I just freshened up a little bit this morning," her mom said with a sheepish wave of the hand.

Ava tossed her a skeptical look. She reached out to close her car door, glancing up just in time to see Zak stepping out of his apartment. He made eye contact and waved enthusiastically.

"Good morning, Ava!" he called out. He wore a different polo today, once again tucked into pants that were just a little too tight.

"Hey, Zak," Ava said.

"Oh, is this your mother?" he asked, peering into the car.

"Yeah," Ava said with an impatient sigh. "This is my mom, Carol."

Zak quickly crossed over to their car and leaned forward, offering an awkward wave to Carol, who waved back with an amused grin.

"Well, hello there, Miss Carol. It is a pleasure to meet you," he said.

"And you as well. Zak, is it?"

"Yes, ma'am." He thrust his arm across the seat over Ava and shook Carol's hand. "So, what are you all up to today?" Zak asked, looking back and forth between the two.

"Oh, not much," Ava said. "You know, this and that. Girl stuff."

Zak nodded knowingly. "I get it." He stood up and stepped away from the car. "Well, have a lovely day, ladies! And Ava, if you need a ride anywhere at all this week, let me know. I'm always happy to help."

"Thanks, Zak," Ava muttered. She shut the door and leaned back against the seat as Carol snickered beside her.

"Well, he was . . . pleasant," Carol said. "And clearly smitten with you."

Ava groaned. "I don't want to talk about it."

Her mom laughed out loud. "What a peculiar young man. Does he always talk like that?"

Ava tossed her the side-eye and pursed her lips. Carol laughed again and pulled up to the stop sign, checking her hair in the rearview mirror briefly before looking back at the road and pulling out of the parking lot.

"So . . . ," she finally said. "Why would you need a ride anywhere this week?"

Ava shrugged. "I don't want to talk about that either."

"How much do you need to fix it?" Carol asked with a sideways glance.

"Seriously, Mom. We don't have to talk about this right now, okay?"

For a long time, the two sat in silence as the tension worked its way through the car.

Finally, Carol spoke up. "Are you nervous?"

Ava shrugged. "Are you?"

"A little," Carol said. "It's going to be difficult to see him this way. Sylvie said he's very weak and frail. We need to prepare ourselves for that."

They lapsed into silence again until Ava spoke. "How come you never talked to me about what Nick did for a living, Mom? How come you didn't tell me about the treasure hunting and the traveling?"

Carol was quiet for a long time. "It was . . . complicated," she finally said.

"How?"

"Well . . . you are so much like your father," she said. "You have the same itch that he did, and the same tendency to flit from one thing to another without settling down and being responsible. I didn't want to fill your head with some romantic idea of a life of adventure, when practically that's not how life really works."

"It worked for him," Ava said pointedly.

"Yes, but at our expense," Carol answered, her voice quiet. "He got to do all the things he wanted, but it cost him his family. It cost you your father. It cost me the love of my life."

Ava was quiet for a long time. "I've followed his adventures for a while now."

Carol nodded. "I know. I suppose that was right—you should have known about him and his work all along. I wasn't open about all this with you. Looking back, I could have done things differently. I'm sorry for that."

Ava glanced at her mom and watched as she swiped a few tears from her eyes. "It's okay, Mom," she said. "It wouldn't have changed anything. I know who Nick is professionally, and I know who he is personally. I get it."

Carol nodded. They drove a long way in silence, lost in thought, mulling over the past they couldn't change and the future that loomed before them without the possibility of Nick Laine being a part of it.

Finally, Carol pulled off the highway and glanced at her phone for directions. "We're almost there," she said softly.

Ten minutes later, they turned down a quiet street. Trees lined both sides, with Spanish moss hanging down and brushing the top of the car as they drove by. Down the hill, at the end of the road, a giant lake gleamed in the morning sun, the ripples dancing in the light like diamonds.

"It's pretty here," Ava said.

Carol didn't answer. She simply gripped the steering wheel and kept her eyes forward. Moments later, she turned onto a narrow driveway leading to a white house, its picket fence surrounding a perfectly manicured lawn. A giant oak tree stood proudly in the front yard, and bright flowers lined the walkway to the door. An American flag hung from the side of the house, waving in the gentle breeze.

"Sylvie was always good at making things look pretty and inviting," Carol murmured.

"I only met her the one time, right?" Ava asked.

"She came and visited several times when you were little, before Nick left. But yes, only once that you would probably remember."

"Why?" Ava watched as Carol checked her reflection in the mirror, fluffing her hair nervously.

"Sylvie is . . . different."

Ava turned to face her mom and raised an eyebrow. "Mom, I'm twenty-six now. You can stop sugarcoating things for me."

Carol smiled. "Well, I guess that's true. Sylvie didn't like me. She thought I was simpleminded, and she believed I would hold Nick back in life."

"So, she was a b—" Ava stopped under her mom's withering stare. "Female dog," she finished with an innocent smile.

Carol suppressed a smile in return. "I suppose you could put it that way. Sylvie is just a little . . . rough around the edges. She's six years older than Nick, and she has always felt a strong, motherly protection for him."

"Why? Where was their mother?"

"I never really got the full story. I actually didn't meet my mother-in-law. She died shortly after Nick and I began dating. All he said was that she was a woman who'd been disappointed in how her life turned out. I don't fully understand why."

"And my grandfather?"

"He died when Nick was young, but he'd been a treasure hunter as well. I don't think he was around much when your dad was growing up." Carol glanced at Ava. "Sometimes we turn out like our parents without even really trying."

Ava looked back at the house. "That side of the family is from Finland, right?"

"Yes," Carol answered. "Your grandmother moved to the States as a teenager and met and married your grandfather before she turned twenty. Your great-grandparents lived in Finland their whole lives. Your dad always said he wanted to take me to Finland." Carol sighed wistfully. "He said I would love it there."

Ava looked at her mother for a long moment, silently taking in the strong woman who raised her without ever complaining about having to do it alone.

Carol shifted her gaze to Ava and offered a thin smile. "Well," she said. "I guess it's now or never."

Ava was feeling particularly drawn to the option of never, but instead, she pushed her door open and followed her mom up the front walk and onto the porch. Carol knocked lightly on the door, then the two stepped back and waited for it to open.

Soft footsteps padded across the room inside the house. Ava swallowed hard as the front door swung open and she found herself face-to-face with a woman who looked to be in her sixties. She was short and stout, with thick, gray hair that had been pulled into a loose bun at the nape of her neck. She wore a floor-length dress that made her look wider than Ava suspected she actually was. Her mouth was turned up in a forced smile, but her eyes remained skeptical as she took in the sight of the two women.

"Hello, Carol," Sylvie finally said. She pulled the door open wider and let them step inside.

"Hi, Sylvie." Carol leaned forward and offered her ex-sister-in-law an awkward hug.

Sylvie pulled back and turned her gaze to Ava. "Well, you've grown into quite a lovely young woman."

Ava thought she sensed a note of gentleness in her aunt's voice, but she couldn't be sure, so she just offered a smile in return. "Hey, Aunt Sylvie," she murmured.

Sylvie closed the door and gestured them inside. "Nicky is resting right now," she said. "He wanted me to wake him when you got here, but I'm not going to do that just yet." She led them into the kitchen, a small room that was so neat and clean and white that it almost made Ava's eyes hurt. There were tones of black here and there in the cabinet hardware, two tea towels hung over the oven door, and green plants spilled from flower boxes under the windows, but otherwise, the entire kitchen was white. It looked like it came straight from a magazine.

"Lovely kitchen, Sylvie," Carol said. She sat down at the table and looked around admiringly.

Ava knew that her mother always wished she had a cute, picture-perfect home. "But I don't have a decorator's bone in my body," Carol used to say in frustration when the two of them would walk through home decorating stores looking for knickknacks to spruce up their space. Inevitably, they always left with nothing and went to get coffee instead.

"Thank you," Sylvie replied. She opened the fridge and pulled out a bowl of fruit, setting it on the counter in front of them. "I've made some scones, as well," she said. "And I have coffee or green tea. Which would you prefer?"

"Oh, um . . ." Ava let out a nervous cough as Sylvie stared

at her through narrowed eyes. "Coffee. I'll take coffee," she finally answered.

Sylvie shifted her gaze to Carol, who nodded that she'd have the same, and they both watched as Sylvie prepared two cups of coffee and set it before them, along with a plate of orange scones, lemon curd, and the fruit. They each got a dainty plate, and Sylvie led the way by piling fruit on top of her scones, then gesturing to Carol and Ava to do the same.

Ava had never eaten a scone, and anything with the name "curd" sounded questionable and disgusting, but because she found her aunt moderately intimidating, she grabbed a little of everything and took small bites in between gulps of coffee.

"How have you been, Sylvie?" Carol asked.

"I suppose I've been alright," Sylvie replied. Awkward silence hung between them for a beat.

"I heard about Hank," Carol finally said, hands gripped around her coffee mug. "I'm terribly sorry."

"Oh, it's fine," Sylvie said with a wave of her hand.

Ava noticed the way her fingers trembled, and she got the distinct impression that it actually wasn't fine.

"Hank died four years ago, and both kids left the state, so I've spent most of my time pouring into my home decorating business."

"Where do your kids live now?" Carol asked.

Ava watched her mom take a sip of her coffee and noticed the concealed grimace. Her mother hated coffee unless it was swimming in sugar and cream and looked more like a milkshake than anything else.

"Sarah and her husband are in South Carolina. They have three kids, so they're too busy to call, but they come down once a year for a quick visit and a trip to the beach."

"Sarah has three children?" Carol shot Ava a look. "How old is she now?"

"She's twenty-eight," Sylvie replied.

Ava shifted her eyes to her plate and refused to meet her mother's pointed gaze. So what if she had a cousin who was only two years older than her and already had a husband and kids? Ava took a large bite of her scone and busied herself chewing.

"And Jason . . . ," Sylvie continued. "Well, who knows what Jason is up to these days. That child can barely get his head screwed on straight. Last I heard he was living in Colorado and working at a ski resort. He can't ski, mind you. I think he's serving coffee in a lodge on the side of a mountain." She rolled her eyes and took a sip of coffee.

Ava smiled and instantly decided that she and Jason would probably have gotten along quite well growing up.

"And what do you do, Ava?" Sylvie asked.

"Me?" Ava swallowed hard, trying not to choke on the scone that she was struggling to swallow. "Oh, you know," she said. "I'm just working hard to pay bills and enjoying my twenties." She offered a tight-lipped smile, and Sylvie narrowed her eyes slightly.

"Well, then," Sylvie said. "Good for you."

Ava blushed and shifted her gaze away from her aunt again. "So . . . how is my father doing?"

Sylvie sighed and set her cup down gently. "He has good days and bad days. We've set up hospice care. They said he could have anywhere from a few weeks to a few months to live." She glanced at the door just off the kitchen, where Ava suspected Nick was staying, then shifted her gaze back to the two women. "That man is stubborn," she said, her voice lowered, "and he's got his mind wrapped around one last hunt that he says he must complete before he passes, so I wouldn't be surprised if he lasts a little bit longer."

"He thinks he's going on another hunt?" Carol asked.

"Oh, he's not going anywhere." Sylvie leaned back and crossed her arms. "He'll have to leave this house over my dead body."

Carol smiled as Ava's eyes widened.

"So how does he think he's going to hunt?" Ava asked.

"He's hoping to find someone to go in his place. He's looking for . . . oh, what's the word he used. It was a strange one from that *Star Wars* movie."

"He wants a padawan?" Ava asked.

"Yes! That's the word he used!" Sylvie threw her arms up over her head. "I don't even know what that means!"

"It's like an apprentice," Ava said with a smile.

Carol looked at her daughter with an amused expression. "How do you know that?"

"It's *Star Wars*!" Ava exclaimed. "How do you *not* know that?"

Sylvie shook her head. "Well, at any rate, Nicky thinks he is going on a remote expedition with a young pada-whatcha-call-it leading the charge."

"What is he looking for?" Ava leaned forward toward her aunt.

"He won't tell me," Sylvie grumbled. "Says I wouldn't understand."

A bell rang from behind the door off the kitchen, and all three women sat up.

"That's Nicky." Sylvie pushed to a stand. "Let me go tell him that you all are here. He's . . . he's anxious to see you." Her eyes settled on Ava when she spoke.

Sylvie left quietly. Carol and Ava watched her tuck into the room and close the door behind her.

"I haven't seen Nick in such a long time," Carol murmured.

"It's gonna be okay, Mom," Ava said, grabbing her hand.

Carol squeezed and offered Ava a tight smile.

A moment later, Sylvie opened the door. "Okay," she said. "Nicky will see you now."

St. Petersburg, Russia, 1904

Augusta Fabergé entered the room and scanned the tables, the rhythmic clinking of hammers clapping out a melody she'd come to love. The dark wood paneling that covered the walls gave the room a charming glow under the orange lights that hung above their heads. At each table sat men with heads bent over as they assembled and shaped the finery that defined her husband's name. Each of these men, some young and some old, had earned the title master craftsman, and they were the best in the world. Of course they were—her husband expected nothing less. She surveyed the room, an indiscernible expression on her face. One of the men at the first table saw her enter and laid down his small hammer. He stood and walked quickly to her.

"Can I help you?" he asked with a slight bow.

"Oh, Dima, hello," she answered with a nod of her head. "Have you seen my husband anywhere?"

"He was here ten minutes ago," Dima answered, looking around the room. "I'll go downstairs and tell him he's wanted."

"No, no. Don't stop your work on my account," she said with a wave of her hand. "I can find him myself."

He nodded. "If you wish," he said. He turned and returned to his workstation, picking up his small hammer and adding to the rhythm.

Augusta gave a little smile, careful to guard her expression from the craftsmen in the room. She turned and left before they could sense her pleasure. She wasn't one to allow her emotions to be so easily read.

She'd spent her life in the midst of artists and creatives. She knew well the beat of new creations, of the finest materials being sanded and bent and molded into something that left viewers in awe. Her father had been a manager at the Imperial Furniture Workshop deep in the city. When she married her husband, she traded the smells of pine and cedar and mahogany for that of fires burning and metals and stones being heated and made into precious works of art.

Though not terribly artistic herself, she had an eye for beauty, and she had made herself quite useful over the years as one who could spot even the tiniest of flaws in a creation, which pushed their employees to not only work to please her husband, but her as well.

Walking downstairs, Augusta glanced into the gleaming main-floor showroom where lit, glass boxes formed a semicircle around the dark, wood floor. In them were displayed the latest finery, from necklaces and brooches to paperweights and miniature porcelain carvings. A large, circular chandelier hung on the ceiling above, casting a warm glow throughout the room. Two men sat at the helm of the cases, bent over the glass as they wiped away any dust or streaks that may hinder the view of one of the pieces cased inside. They wore dark suits,

35

their silver-gray hair and beards standing out against the fabric, which gave them an air of dignity and wisdom.

They glanced up at the sound of her swishing skirts as she descended the final step, and both stood, bowing their chins slightly to the woman married to their employer. Augusta offered a thin smile and nodded back at them. Sergei and Evgeni had been manning the front table of her husband's shop since he'd opened this new store three years earlier. They were gentle and kind, both of them, and customers often commented that they enjoyed talking with the two older men as much as they enjoyed perusing the displays in the Fabergé shop.

Augusta turned and knocked lightly on her husband's office door.

"Come in," he called out from the other side.

She pushed the door open and entered the room. Karl sat behind his desk with pen in hand, head bent forward as he read over the paper in front of him. He glanced up and saw his wife, then pushed out of his chair and walked around to her.

"Hello, my dear," he said, giving her a quick kiss on the cheek.

"Hello," Augusta answered back stiffly. There was a constant strain between the two of them. A level of respect, and perhaps a measure of love, existed, but it had dimmed slightly after the death of their fourth-born son, Nicholas, so many years earlier. Despite the fact that they'd had a fifth boy, whom they also named Nicholas in honor of his deceased brother, the heartache of the previous loss had done its damage.

Augusta didn't say as much, but truthfully her husband's close relationship with a woman named Amalia, an Austrian actress who he insisted was no more than a traveling partner, did nothing to help bridge the gap that had deepened over the years. She maintained her emotional distance, but still remained a team with her husband, despite the strain. Proud and stoic, Augusta did what she felt was necessary to support the burgeoning business because she wanted to see it thrive for her four grown sons, each of whom had already taken over operations in some way, shape, or form.

"Have you heard the news?" Augusta asked, as Karl returned to his seat behind his desk.

"What news, dear?" he asked, leaning back in his leather chair and looking intently at his wife.

Augusta often wondered what he saw when he looked at her. Did he see the woman she had once been, before age and hardship had lined her face and bitterness had permeated her words? Or did he see something he no longer found desirable? She tried for so long to be the woman who occupied his thoughts, but somewhere along the way that had changed. It happened around the time that he was elevated to the position of Royal Jeweler to the Imperial Family, which had lifted his name and business to that of high respect throughout all of Europe.

That's when the travel really began. His new title required many nights away from his family, and every time he returned, she felt him slip a little further from her grasp. There was hardly time for the two of them to become reacquainted with one another before he had to leave again.

She'd finally broken two years earlier. She unleashed all her hurt and pain on him in one angry tirade, to which he had not responded. But he did shortly after that open the sales office in London and hand the reins of running it to their youngest son. A few months later, he opened the large operation here on 24 Bolshaya Morskaya, allowing him a little more time to focus on the creations that had given him his royal title in the first place. It was, she supposed, his attempt at remedying the damage caused by his earlier travels, but though his body had remained home, his spirit was still just outside her grasp.

"The tsarina has given birth," Augusta answered quietly.

Karl sat forward, pressing his elbows into his desk. "Yes, and?"

Augusta offered a small smile. "It's a boy," she answered. "We have an heir to the throne."

Karl leaned back and let out a long breath. "A boy!"

"The tsar has a son," Augusta said.

"At last," Karl breathed. He looked up at his wife and stood, clapping his hands together triumphantly. "Perhaps all this nonsense will calm down and the people will no longer feel threatened by the Imperial family. Children always bring people together."

"Not always," Augusta said, thinking of the son who they hoped would erase the wound of his dead brother, but who had only deepened the heartache they'd both felt.

Karl paused and looked at her for a long moment before clearing his throat and turning away. "I wonder what Hiskias would think of all this?"

Augusta smiled. "I imagine he would have some kind of commentary," she said.

Their dear friend and Karl's mentor, Hiskias Pendin, had died decades earlier but remained a constant topic of conversation. One didn't simply forget Hiskias.

"Yes, he would," Karl said. "I imagine it would border on indecent as well." He chuckled. "Do you remember the time he spoke with the old woman considering the purchase of diamond earrings? She was married to one of the wealthier merchants here in St. Petersburg."

Augusta smiled wider. "I do."

Karl shook his head. "When she told Hiskias that, after careful consideration, she decided it was too great a sum to spend on someone her age, he responded, 'But, my dear lady, just imagine what you will look like without earrings—like a cow without a bell!'"

Augusta laughed lightly. "He had a way with words," she said. "That woman wasn't even insulted."

"Not in the slightest! She bought the earrings!" Karl sat down at his desk and stared out the small window across from his desk, his smile fading. Augusta swallowed against the wave of sadness that washed through the room. The House of Fabergé would not be what it was today without Hiskias. Losing him to cancer had been a blow from which Augusta felt Karl had never quite recovered.

"Yes, well. I suppose we should begin making preparations then," Karl said, shaking his head and turning back to look at her with glassy eyes.

"I suppose you should," Augusta murmured. She clasped her hands in front of her waist and drew in a long breath, then let it out slowly.

"I'll leave you alone with your thoughts," she said.

"Yes, yes," Karl replied, leaning forward to pull out his sketch pad.

Augusta turned and walked soundlessly from the room.

———— ❋ ————

Karl put pencil to page and immediately felt a familiar comfort sweep over him as soft lines swept across the blank sheet of paper.

"My darling," he said, "do you know the new tsarevich's

name?" Karl looked up to find the doorway empty. Augusta's skirt disappeared up the staircase outside his door. He sighed and shook his head, then bent back over his sketchbook.

"An heir to the throne," he murmured as his pencil moved in soft wisps up and down in an easy rhythm. He paused for a moment and let his mind drift to the year he created his first egg for the Imperial family. He stood and crossed the room, pulling from the bookshelf the sketchbook that he used to design the original *Hen Egg*.

It had been a simple design, but the simplicity is what the empress loved most of all. Shortly after he gave it to Tsar Alexander III, Fabergé was given the official title "Supplier to the Imperial Court," and the tsar placed a standing order for a new egg to be given to the empress every year. The tradition of gifting the eggs continued with Alexander III's son, Nicholas, after he ascended to the throne in 1894. From that point forward, Fabergé had created two eggs each year, one for Empress Maria and one for the tsarina, Alexandra Romanov.

But they had all begun with the *Hen Egg*. Made of solid gold, Fabergé had decided to coat the egg in white enamel to give it the appearance of a real egg. The two halves of the egg came apart to reveal a solid gold "yolk" inside. But Fabergé, wanting to create something never before seen, had hollowed out the yolk and tucked inside it a golden hen, expertly molded and designed so that it looked almost real. And inside the hen, he'd hidden a gold and diamond miniature replica of the Imperial crown and a ruby pendant on a golden chain.

Maria Feodorovna was delighted with her egg, and a tradition was born. Tsar Alexander III had requested a few guidelines be set in place when they established the tradition: Each creation had to be shaped like an egg; each egg must contain a surprise; each one had to be an original, not a duplicate of anything else. Beyond that, Karl had been given full creative rein.

Karl ran his hand over the sketch of the *Hen Egg*. Nearly twenty years had passed since he began his relationship with the Romanovs, and his name had spread throughout the world. He was now officially the Royal Jeweler to the Imperial Family, and he outfitted most of the wealthy merchants and royals within the Russian Empire. And now there was an heir to the throne.

Karl slid the sketchbook back into place and walked back to his desk, slowly lowering himself into his chair. Life in Russia had been contentious since Nicholas ascended to the throne. The young tsar came to his position without strong convictions. Shy and feeble, he'd allowed himself to be swept up in the tide of advice from those closest to him that perhaps had the best interest of the throne in mind, but not of the people. Rumblings of revolution had steadily hummed over the years leading up to now. It was something that worried Fabergé more than anything else.

Head bent forward, Karl began working on the sketch again. Of course, the next egg he made would honor the birth of the young tsarevich. It would be evidence of his hopeful expectation that perhaps now the people could come together to salvage their great nation.

Present Day

Ava followed her mother tentatively down the hall. Dark wood flooring led them into a bright and airy bedroom. The walls were painted a soft gray, and a large white area rug covered much of the floor. Green plants hung from one corner of the room, and bright yellow curtains gave a much-needed pop of color. The room was fresh and inviting, and Ava felt her shoulders relax immediately.

She turned toward the queen-size bed that stood in the center of the back wall and took in the sight of her father sitting up against a tall, gray headboard. He was surrounded by pillows, his legs covered by a yellow quilt that matched the curtains. He had lost most of his hair and what remained was bright white. His face was long and drawn, covered in white stubble. He wore a blue flannel shirt over his gaunt frame, and his hands were folded tightly in his lap as he stared at Carol and Ava.

"Hello, Nick," Carol murmured.

He looked at her, and a smile parted his lips. "Carol."

His voice was the same—strong and warm like Ava remembered it. She wondered how he could sound so strong but look so weak. He shifted his gaze to her, and she shrank back under the unfamiliar tenderness.

"Hey, kiddo," he said.

"Hey," she answered.

"Yes, well," Sylvie said, looking back and forth between them. "I'll let the three of you talk and catch up. I need to go to the bank and the store, so I will be out for a little while." She turned toward her brother and tossed him a firm glance. "Nicky, as soon as you start to feel tired, you tell them, and they will leave." She turned and looked at Carol pointedly.

Carol nodded.

"Okay, sis," Nick said with a smile. "I think we'll be okay."

Sylvie drew in a sharp breath and let it out with a long sigh. "I suppose," she muttered before turning and walking out of the room, closing the door behind her.

"She hasn't changed much," Carol remarked when Sylvie had gone.

Nick let out a soft laugh. "Not a bit," he said.

Carol smiled back at him. "She still doesn't like me."

"Nope," he replied. "But Sylvie doesn't like a lot of people. It's not personal."

Carol's smile faded. "It's good to see you, Nick," she murmured.

They stared at one another for a long moment while Ava observed from the corner.

Finally, Nick cleared his throat and gestured to the chairs beside his bed. "Please, sit down," he said.

Carol slid into the first chair while Ava hesitated.

"Ava?" Carol asked.

Ava took a few steps forward and slumped into the chair beside her father's bed.

"So . . ." Carol paused, her eyes scanning over Nick. "How're you doing?"

Nick laughed out loud, shoulders shaking. He shrugged. "Been better, I guess," he answered.

Carol nodded. "Why didn't you call me sooner?" she asked.

Ava looked at her mother with raised eyebrows. Carol's tone had changed. She was using her "mad" voice. It was a tone Ava knew well.

Nick looked at Carol for a long time before clearing his throat. "Well, it didn't seem like this cancer thing was gonna be much of a problem until it became a problem," he finally answered.

Carol narrowed her eyes. "So, you didn't think that maybe your daughter would have wanted to hear from you earlier? You know, before you were on your deathbed?"

"Mom," Ava said. She reached over and touched Carol's shoulder.

Carol shrugged away from her and continued staring Nick down. "Well?" she asked. "What do you have to say for yourself, Nick?"

Ava dropped her hand in her lap and stared at her nails. The silence now hanging between them was uncomfortable. Nick shifted in his bed, turning to look more closely at Carol.

"I . . . I don't have an answer for that," he finally said. His voice was sheepish. Apologetic, perhaps?

Carol crossed her arms over her chest. "Well, tell me what's new then! Nick Laine doesn't have an explanation for his silence and selfishness? Goodness, that isn't something I'm familiar with at all!"

"Mom, easy," Ava whispered.

Carol turned to her daughter, eyes shining. "No, Ava," she

said, the fight leaking out of her words. "I've been easy for a long time. Now I'm just mad."

Carol stood abruptly, her chair nearly toppling over behind her. She turned and rushed out of the room. Ava sat back, stunned, as she watched her mother's retreating figure.

"Uh"—she turned back to Nick—"sorry about that. Mom's not usually . . . she doesn't . . ." Ava shrugged. "I have no idea what just happened."

Nick followed Ava's gaze to the open bedroom door. "Well, it was bound to happen at some point," he said quietly.

Ava turned to look at him. Did he have tears in his eyes? She couldn't tell.

"She never was good at telling me how she felt," he said, glancing at Ava. "She was always sort of passive."

Ava stood up. "I should go check on her," she said.

Nick nodded.

Ava walked out of the room and into the kitchen. Glancing out the window, she saw her mom sitting on a large, wooden swing in the yard, her back to the house. Ava pushed open the screen door and stepped into the muggy Florida air. Walking quietly through the thick Bermuda grass, she stepped up beside the swing.

Carol wiped the tears off her cheeks and glanced up at Ava, who sat down next to her mom.

"That was weird," Ava said, her voice soft. "I've never seen you lose it like that before."

Carol drew in a deep breath and let it out slowly. "I don't know what happened," she said. "I just—I saw him lying there and it suddenly hit me that he had to have known about this cancer for quite some time. Why wouldn't he tell us sooner? Why didn't he reach out to you? Why didn't he . . ." She stopped and covered her mouth, blinking back fresh tears. "Why didn't he love me enough to stay?" she whispered.

Ava leaned her head on her mom's shoulder. "I don't know," she murmured.

They rocked back and forth for several minutes, Carol reaching over and grabbing Ava's hand.

"I need to go back in there and apologize to him," Carol said. "That wasn't fair."

"Actually, I don't think you owe him an apology, Mom," Ava replied. "It's about time you let him know how his leaving affected you." She looked at her mom. "You don't always have to be so strong, you know."

Carol smiled and pushed Ava's hair off her forehead. "Thanks," she said with a smile.

Ava glanced back at the house where her father lay dying. Her heartbeat quickened as an idea took shape. She blinked several times before sitting up straighter. "Mom," she said. "Do you mind if I go in there alone for a few minutes?"

Carol shook her head. "No, I don't mind," she said. "I could use a little more time to pull myself together."

Ava stood up. "I'll come out and get you when I'm done. There are just some things I need to say to him. Privately."

Carol nodded.

Ava hustled back toward the house before she lost her nerve. She entered the back door and circled through the kitchen to the bedroom. Stepping inside, she saw Nick still sitting in the same position, his head leaned back and eyes closed. He looked so old.

Nick opened his eyes and focused on Ava. He pushed himself up straighter with a grimace and met her steady gaze.

"Mom didn't mean to go off on you like that," Ava finally

said. She stepped all the way in and closed the door behind her.

"I know," Nick said. "I deserved it, though."

"Yeah, you did." Ava sat down next to his bed.

"How you doing, kiddo?"

Ava shook her head. "No, don't do that. Don't talk to me like you've been around and know me. I'm not your kiddo."

Nick nodded. "Fair enough."

"What *do* you know about me?" Ava asked, crossing her arms.

"Well," Nick replied, turning to face her. "I know that you're twenty-six. I know your birthday is April thirteenth. I know that you went to the University of South Florida, and you got your degree in world history with a minor in sociology. I suspect you have no idea what to do with those degrees, so you're trying to figure out what you want to do with your life. And I know you love health and fitness."

Ava gaped at him. "How the . . ." She stopped herself, thinking of the admonishment she'd received from her mother for using "unnecessary language," as Carol liked to say.

"How do you know all that?"

"I check your Instagram every once in a while," Nick replied.

"You're on Instagram?" Despite her annoyance, she smiled.

"I only follow you," he replied.

"Why would you follow me on Instagram, but never reach out?"

Nick sighed. "I'm not great at communication."

Ava raised her eyebrows. "You think?"

He tossed her a wry smile. "Anyway, I started following you a few years ago, hoping that I could somehow connect with you. But I never knew where to start. And then I got sick, and . . . well, here we are."

"Here we are," Ava murmured.

"So, tell me. What are you doing with yourself these days?"

Ava leaned forward, pressing her elbows into her knees, and shook her head. "I don't want to talk about that. I only want to ask you a question."

"Okay. Shoot."

"Actually," Ava said, pushing herself up straighter. "I don't want to ask. I'm just going to tell you what I want."

Nick nodded silently.

"Let me be your padawan," Ava said. She leaned forward and stared hard into her father's eyes. "I want to go on your final treasure hunt."

The silence hung between them for a long time, thick and heavy, as Ava's words hovered between them.

"My padawan, huh?" Nick's eyebrows raised. "And just how did you know about that?"

"Sylvie told us that you want to go on one last treasure hunt and that you were looking for a padawan."

Nick shook his head. "Sylvie always was terrible at keeping secrets." He glanced back at Ava. "Sorry, kiddo . . . uh, I mean . . ." Nick shook his head, his lips pursed. "I don't need you to be my padawan."

"Why?" Ava asked.

"What I do isn't always the safest line of work. And this particular mission could be a little more dangerous because I'm not the only one chasing this item."

"What is it?"

Nick shrugged his shoulders. "I can't say." He looked at her apologetically. "I'm sorry. I wish I could tell you more, but I can't."

"Yes, you can!" Ava tossed her hands up in exasperation.

"Look, Nick—" She stopped as he raised his eyebrows. "Sorry, but I just can't call you Dad."

Nick paused, then nodded. "Fair enough."

"I'm twenty-six years old and I work in a restaurant. I guess you know that too, since you follow my Instagram."

Nick nodded again.

"Great. So, you know that I haven't exactly figured out what I want to do with my life. But here's what you *don't* know about me." Ava drew in a deep breath and let it out slowly. "I've been following you for a long time too. I've got a box full of articles and photos, and a head full of questions."

They were quiet for a long few minutes before Nick opened his mouth to speak.

Ava held up her hand and cut him off. "Sitting outside this house on a wooden swing is the woman who raised me. She did everything on her own. She sacrificed so much so that I could be successful, and I'm working in a restaurant. Why do you think that is?"

Nick leaned his head back and stared at Ava.

"It's because I'm like you. It appears that no matter how hard we try, we end up becoming our parents." She searched his eyes. "So, let me go. Let me have this one adventure."

Nick narrowed his eyes and studied Ava. "How do you even know what a padawan is?"

"Um, because it's *Star Wars*, and I don't live under a rock," Ava replied.

Nick smiled, a fleeting look of pride flashing across his face. Ava watched the smile slowly fade, and she wondered if he was thinking the same thing as her—so many wasted years hung between them. Nick opened his mouth, then closed it again, almost as though he were trying to catch the words he longed to say but couldn't.

"Look," Ava said. "I get it, okay? You didn't want to be a dad. You had a life to live, and sticking around with Mom and me would have held you back. It was a choice you made." Ava shrugged. "But here we are now, and you're stuck in that bed while there's one more—I don't know—*something* that's out there waiting to be found. Obviously, you can't be the one to find it, but why can't I?"

"It's not that simple," Nick answered.

"So, explain it to me!"

"Man, you look like your mom," Nick said.

Ava crossed her arms and stared back at him pointedly.

"Even more so right now," he murmured, a hint of laughter dancing through his eyes.

Ava pursed her lips, dropping her arms to her sides.

"Look, this sort of mission isn't glamorous," Nick said defensively. Ava blinked but didn't respond. "The news articles make it sound like it is, but it's not. And you're never the only one seeking something. There are always others who are trying to find the same thing you're looking for."

"So, it's a race, then," Ava said.

"Kind of. I guess. But it's a race with higher stakes, because you never really know who you're racing against, and there aren't really rules. It's every man for himself."

"I like competition." Ava leaned forward. "So, what are we racing for, then?"

Nick took a deep breath and let it out slowly. Ava could sense his resignation.

"What do you know about the Russian Imperial family?" Nick said.

Ava leaned back. "The Romanovs?"

Nick nodded.

"Let's see." Ava closed her eyes and tried to remember as much as she could from her unit on Slavic history in college. "They ruled for about three hundred years. Nicholas the Second abdicated the throne in 1917 when the Russian Revolution broke out. He and his family were exiled to Siberia and were later murdered in July 1918."

"Impressive," Nick said.

"History major," Ava replied with a smirk. "It doesn't come in handy often, but every once in a while . . ."

Nick chuckled. "Alright. Well, what is one of the things that made the Russian people most loathe the Imperial family?"

Ava shrugged. "It wasn't one thing. Nicholas Romanov was a terrible leader. He was weak-willed and intent on protecting the aristocracy at the expense of the people. He had no clue what was happening outside the palace walls. And then there was the grotesque display of wealth—"

Nick snapped his fingers and pointed at Ava. "That's it right there!"

"What's it?"

"The grotesque display of wealth. That was the visual representation of the Romanov family that the Russian people loathed. Do you know which items in particular were most unsettling to the people?"

Ava sat back and searched her memory for the answer. Her eyes widened. "The Fabergé eggs." Leaning forward again, she stared at him incredulously. "You're searching for a Fabergé egg?"

Nick nodded slowly.

"I don't know much about the eggs," Ava said. "Only that they never recovered all of them."

"Right. Fabergé and his master craftsmen created fifty-two eggs between the years 1884 and 1916, but so far only forty-one of them have been found."

"So, you're trying to find one of the missing eggs?"

Nick shook his head. "Not exactly."

Ava looked back at him, confused.

"I'm looking for the fifty-third egg," he said.

"But you said there were only fifty-two."

"Right. There were fifty-two official eggs, but Fabergé created one more that he never gave to the family, and this one was a bombshell."

Ava stared at Nick long and hard. She pressed her hands into the bed. "I'm in," she said.

She held his gaze without flinching. Nick drew in a deep breath, then nodded. Ava dipped her chin, then pushed to a stand. She held out her hand, her eyes still locked on his. He reached up and put his thin, frail hand in hers, and they shook.

"I'm going to go check on Mom," Ava said, releasing his hand. Her eyes softened and her mouth turned up in the smallest of smiles.

"Bring her back in here when she's ready."

Ava nodded, then turned and exited the room, hands shaking at the deal she'd just struck.

———— ❄ ————

Nick watched his daughter leave, then laid his head back on the pillows and studied the ceiling. His mind drifted back to the many years he'd spent traveling and digging and seeking for those lost artifacts that most people had given up on. Early on, when he met Carol, he'd thought that treasure hunting would be just a hobby—something he'd do on the side. He had every intention of settling down, but it didn't work out like he'd hoped. Maybe settling had never really been in his blood. He supposed his genetic makeup made sitting still too difficult. And once he made the choice to leave, he committed all the way because he couldn't see any other way. It had to be all or nothing.

He glanced at the door where Ava had retreated, and he thought about the look in her eyes when she told him she wanted to hunt. He knew that look. She had her mom in her, for sure. The pursed lips and crossed arms were all Carol. But *that* look? He knew it. It was a mixture of determination and stubbornness. It was a reflection of himself.

"Alright, then," he spoke into the empty room. "My daughter and I are going to find the fifty-third egg."

St. Petersburg, 1904

S itting back and pushing his glasses up high on his balding head, Karl rubbed his eyes. With a yawn, he began to gather his materials, packing up for the evening. The workshop was quiet, most of his employees having long since left. It was his favorite time to work, when he was alone with the silence, and the lights were off in the room with only the lamp at his desk to illuminate his creations.

The sound of footsteps drew his eyes upward, and Karl squinted as Albert Holmström stepped from the shadows.

"Hello," Karl said, the surprise in his voice evident. "What are you doing here so late?"

"I was upstairs finishing my own work for the evening," Albert said with a slight bow of his head.

Karl reached over and shook the hand of his friend and longtime employee. Albert had worked in the workshop since he was a young boy, apprenticed under his father, August Holmström, and was one of the most skillful jewelers Karl had ever employed. His design of the miniature cruiser that had been the surprise inside Empress Maria's egg in 1891 had been so breathtaking that Karl himself was mesmerized. They had named the egg that year the *Memory of Azov Egg*.

At that time, Tsar Alexander III and Empress Maria were thinking of their two sons, the future Tsar Nicholas II and his younger brother, George, who had been sent on a nine-month tour of southern Asia on the Russian naval vessel, the *Memory of Azov*. Empress Maria fretted terribly throughout the trip over her younger son. George had never been a strong child, and his health had declined with age. The hope was that the tour south would allow him time to heal and gain strength.

Likewise, Tsar Alexander was concerned about his older son's infatuation with Mathilda Kschessinka, the seventeen-year-old nymph who danced with the Imperial Ballet. To ease the concerns of his employers, Karl carved the *Memory of Azov Egg* out of a single piece of bloodstone, flecked with red and blue. He then decorated the egg with golden rococo scrolls.

But while the four-inch egg was itself a remarkable piece of art, it was the surprise inside that pushed the design to an entirely new level. Karl pulled August Holmström into the design, having trusted him implicitly with the details and vision needed to create something never before seen. August managed to craft a replica of the naval cruiser made entirely of gold and platinum. He used diamonds to create the portholes, then constructed movable riggings, anchor chains, and guns using pure gold. He rested the miniature model on a plate of aquamarine, shined to perfection and looking like a small body of water. It was not the first time Karl had felt a swell of pride in the art he delivered to the tsar and his wife, but he never quite forgot the delight that he felt in delivering that particular egg.

August had died just a year earlier, and it had been Karl's

supreme honor to pass on the legacy of design and creation to his son, Albert, who shared his father's keen eye for detail as well as his confidence to try new things.

Karl finished gathering his tools and brushing shavings off his worktable, then tucked the piece he was working on in the drawer beneath the desk, locking it with a key that hung from a ring on his belt.

"What keeps you here so late tonight?" he asked Albert.

"Well, I've been thinking. I wondered if I might bring my niece in to the design shop from time to time to show her the ways of our work."

"Do you mean young Alma?"

"Yes, sir. As you know, she is attending *Annenschule*, and she's very talented in design. She's eager to learn the business as a whole."

"Ah! I had quite forgotten that she was attending *Annenschule*, as I did." Karl smiled. "Well, of course that makes me want even more to bring her here."

Albert smiled in return. "Yes. She is enjoying her time there very much. She's even receiving some private lessons from Eugen Jakobson."

Karl nodded in approval as he thought of his former artist. "She will do excellently under his supervision."

Albert nodded. "I fear the girl has been lost without her father. When she finishes school, I'd like to apprentice her here, with your permission."

Alma's father, Oskar, was also a talented master goldsmith like his father-in-law and brother-in-law. Oskar had married Albert's sister, and together they'd had five children, each one artistically gifted. Oskar headed up the jewelry shop in Moscow but had died quite unexpectedly at age thirty-seven of blood poisoning after stepping on a rusty nail—a terrible tragedy that had affected everyone deeply.

"You say she has a talent for design?" Karl asked.

"Yes. I'm also told that she's a gifted artist and has a mind that dances with creativity."

Karl nodded. "Wonderful. I remember meeting her as a child. She was such a delight. I would be honored to have her here studying under you when the time is right. Until then, bring her in when she has some free moments and let me see her. It's been quite some time."

Albert bowed his head. "Thank you. I'll see her mother this Sunday at our weekly family gathering, and I will tell her then."

Karl nodded, then reached out and shook Albert's hand. "Go home to your family now," he said with a friendly wink. "You work too hard."

Albert smiled. "Thank you, sir," he said.

The two walked into the hallway. Karl turned and locked the door of his office, then gave Albert a nod and headed up the stairs toward the flat he shared with his wife.

———— ✾ ————

Albert hurried to the coatroom and pulled his coat off the hanger, anxious to rush home and write his sister to send Alma to live with him. He felt a swelling of gratitude at his boss and friend's generosity.

Karl Fabergé was known to be a wonderful employer. Anyone looking to find work in jewelry making and design wanted to be hired by Peter Karl Fabergé. He treated his employees fairly, and no one hoarded their creativity. It was a place where they all came to work together to create the finest pieces because they took pride in working for the Fabergé name.

Though kind, Fabergé had a high standard, and he demanded perfection from his craftsmen. Albert chuckled as he thought of the few times when Fabergé had strolled through the workshop, stopping to observe their work and offering critiques when he deemed it necessary. He was known on occasion to take a hammer and smash any piece that he didn't find satisfactory. But even in this, his people did not fear him or grow angry.

"You can do better," he would say when he forced them to start from scratch. "Start again and do it right."

And so they did. No one working at the shop on Bolshaya Morskaya was willing to settle for anything less than perfection, and this is what elevated Fabergé above all the others. It was this attention to detail that made every master craftsman want to give their very best, and this is why the Imperial family held the House of Fabergé in such high esteem.

This was also why his father had placed his full trust in the master craftsman. Working for Fabergé had become a family business, and Albert had long wanted to take in his niece and properly train her in the artistry of jewelry design. She was such a natural talent, and Albert felt full confidence that she could thrive under his tutelage and inside the environment of the House of Fabergé.

Pushing out into the cool night air, Albert began to whistle a sprightly tune of contentment. He turned toward the banks of the Fontanka River to begin his walk home. The sprawling city stretched out before him, the gilded spire in the center of the Peter and Paul Fortress glinting in the distance beneath the light of the full moon. St. Petersburg was a magical place to live, colorful and grand. Albert loved when visitors came to the shop, foreigners from America and Europe who stepped delicately into the showroom, wide-eyed and breathless.

"It is like a fairy tale," one woman had remarked earlier this week—an American who had recently married a wealthy European merchant. She had a lilt to her voice that indicated she came from a refined background, as refined as one might be, living in America.

"The buildings are so bright. I can hardly stop staring in wonder," she'd exclaimed. He had gone on to help sell her a pair of diamond earrings as her husband, clearly a man much older than her, looked on sternly from the corner.

Albert turned the corner and walked along the water. The air was cool and crisp tonight, winter having not quite settled in. It was quiet as he strode next to the waters, which gently lapped at the stones below.

St. Petersburg had been constructed by Peter the Great. The tsar had chosen the banks of the Neva River to build a city that would be set apart from the rest of Russia. Far from the typical fortifications that comprised other big cities, Petersburg had been purposed for refined civility. It was a city meant for royalty, and Peter's plan had succeeded.

Of course, the construction of such a city wasn't without its pitfalls. St. Petersburg was built on the backs of serfs—a city of corpses, a fact that few liked to mention when talking about the tsar's home. This had been his playground, and the neoclassical buildings that stretched long and wide made it a unique home for the rich and famous.

The buildings lined the riverbanks in a variety of colors from coral and pale blue to bright pink and honey brown. In the light of the moon, it seemed that the city itself glowed, as though the favor of heaven itself had been cast down on the gilt-trimmed façades. Truly, it was a delightful place to behold, though Albert supposed it was all just a mask, for beneath the watercolor exterior rumbled a less colorful truth: Petersburg was a false face on a failing body. Albert paused for a moment, standing before the Anichkov Bridge and turning to take in the row of buildings across the wide boulevard. He drew in a deep breath and let it out slowly, a familiar sorrow pressing down upon him and threatening to force out the beauty of this peaceful moment.

For the first time, he felt a slight lifting of his spirit. Taking over his father's place in the House of Fabergé had been a daunting task, though one he'd been trained and prepared for since his youth. His father had been a true Master of Design, his initials *AH* engraved into many memorable pieces of art throughout the echelons of royalty, but none more prestigious than those of the Fabergé eggs. The first time Albert had carved his own initials into a completed design, he'd felt the weight of the responsibility he bore. *AH*. Two small letters that carried great meaning. Albert had been determined to make his father proud, more so since August's death.

Bringing Alma into the fold of design only made sense. Her grandfather had always been smitten with the girl, ever since she was a cherub of a child with wide, inquisitive eyes and more confidence than perhaps was healthy.

"That one has an important future, you mark my words," August Holmström had said on more than one occasion.

Albert smiled. "Well, Papa," he whispered into the night air. "Let's see if you're right."

Present Day

Ava glanced at Carol and offered a small smile as her mom raised her fist and knocked lightly on the door.

"Come in," Nick called from the other side of the door.

Carol pushed it open and stepped into the room, her eyes still red, but the expression on her face showing the determination that Ava had come to know well. Her mother had control of herself now, and Ava knew she wouldn't lose it again.

"Nick—" Carol began.

Nick lifted his hand. "Carol, you don't have to apologize," he said. "I deserved it."

Carol cocked her head to the side with an amused smile. "Oh, I wasn't going to apologize," she said. "I know you deserved it."

Ava grinned and glanced at Nick, who looked sheepish.

"What I was going to say is that I'm glad you let us come to see you today. Maybe it was too little too late, but it was something, so . . . thank you." She squared her shoulders.

"I'm glad you came." He looked from Carol to Ava, and then back again. "I'm glad both of you came."

"Yes, well," Carol clasped her hands together in front of her waist. "Ava and I should probably be heading out now. If you need anything else from us, let us know." Ava heard the slightest tremor in her mom's voice.

"Oh, um, Mom?" Ava asked. "Would you mind if . . . well, I was, uh . . ." Ava paused and cleared her throat, glancing at Nick.

"I asked Ava if she would like to stay a few days," Nick said. "You're both welcome to stay if you'd like."

Carol's mouth dropped open, and she looked back and forth between Ava and Nick. A look of understanding shot through her eyes, and she took a step backward, shaking her head.

"Oh no." She shook her head. "No, no, no, no. Nope." She turned to Ava. "No," she said firmly.

"No, what?" Ava asked, her voice dripping with fake innocence.

"I know what's going on here. I see what you're doing." Carol put her hands on her hips and faced her daughter. "No way. You are not becoming his Paddington."

Ava snorted. "His what?"

"His pada-wampus. Whatever. His apprentice! I know what you're up to, Ava. I know that look in your eye. I've been fighting that look for twenty-six years now, and don't you even try to say anything to me right now!" she barked, turning to Nick, who looked back with wide eyes, palms raised in front of him in surrender.

"Mom, calm down. Nick and I are just *talking*. That's a good thing, right? You wanted me to talk to him, and here I am. Talking to him."

"Also, just to set the record straight—the term is *padawan*," Nick said.

Ava turned and gaped at him. "Really?" she whispered. "Now's not the time."

Nick shrugged.

"No way, Ava Caroline! No, no, no way! You are not going on some fanciful treasure hunt at the behest of your father who never bothered to bring you into his life before." Carol shot Nick a withering stare.

"Mom, nothing is being decided right now," Ava said. "We're just *talking* about it. And also, why not? What harm would there be in me taking on this project?"

"What harm would there be? What HARM WOULD THERE BE?" Carol stared down her daughter.

"Maybe your mom is right," Nick said quietly from the bed. "I shouldn't have said anything about it."

"No, my mother is not right," Ava said through clenched teeth. She faced her mom, squaring off with her, and watched as the fight siphoned out of her. They both knew Ava would win this argument.

"Why, Ava?" she finally asked. "Why would you want to do this?"

"Mom, you know why," Ava said, her own voice quiet. "You said it yourself—sometimes we become our parents without even really trying."

Carol closed her eyes and drew in a deep breath as Ava continued.

"I mean, obviously I didn't come here planning on this, and I'm not really even sure that I want to do it, but . . ." She glanced at her father. "I think I need to."

"I blame you for this," Carol said, turning to Nick.

"That seems fair," he replied with a sigh.

Carol tossed her hands up in the air. "Fine," she said, voice tight. "Fine, you can stay and talk. *Talk*. But I do not support you jumping in on some wild-goose chase."

"Actually, it's more like an egg hunt." Nick shrank back as both girls gaped at him. "Sorry. Goose chase is fine. We can call it that."

"And you're not leaving me out of this," Carol continued. "I'm not letting you just run off like I let him." She jutted her chin out toward Nick.

"Mom, I don't need you to protect me here."

"I'm not looking to protect you, Ava. I just don't want to be left behind again."

The tremor returned to Carol's voice, this time more obvious. Ava gazed at her mom for a long time, the two communicating back and forth without speaking a word.

"Okay," Ava finally said. She turned back to her dad. "I guess you've got two padawans."

"Oh, and one more thing," Carol interjected, holding up her hand. "Can someone please explain the whole 'padawan' thing to me again? Because I just don't understand the term."

Nick sighed from his bed as Ava snickered. "Okay," he said. "It looks like we've got the beginnings of a team here." He looked back and forth between the two girls. "I don't know how much time I have. So, if we're really going to do this, we need to move quickly."

"Ah, but remember," Carol said. "I said we're just talking. No one is doing anything." She looked back and forth between Ava and Nick. She sighed, her hands dropping to her sides.

Ava sat down next to his bed and gestured for her mom to do the same. "Okay, so go on then. Tell Mom about the egg."

Carol sat down warily. "You mean we really are going on an egg hunt?"

"Not just any egg hunt, Mom," Ava said. "We're looking for the missing Fabergé egg."

"Fabergé egg? Like the fancy eggs from Russia?"

"Kind of," Nick answered. "Only there's more to the story." His gaze wandered to the window.

Carol followed his eyes to the blue jay flitting back and forth through the branches of the tree outside. "There's always more to the story," she murmured.

St. Petersburg, 1904

Karl sat back in his chair, pushing his glasses on top of his head and letting out a long sigh of frustration. He glanced back down at the letter on the desk in front of him.

Dear Mr. Fabergé,

The Tsar regrets to inform you that he will not be commissioning eggs in the coming year due to the ongoing conflict with Japan. Your understanding is appreciated.

The Imperial House

"Sir?"

Karl looked up to see Albert standing in the doorway, thumbs looped into the front of his crisp, black suit. He stood straight-backed and tall outside the door. Karl waved him in, picking up the telegram and sliding it into the top drawer of his desk.

"Hello, Albert," Karl said. "How can I help you today?"

"Well," he began. "I wanted to let you know that my niece, Alma, has arrived for her first visit."

"Oh, excellent. I'm glad she was finally able to make it."

Albert nodded. "Yes. She wanted to come sooner, but her studies have been rigorous, and she felt she needed to focus on her exams before visiting."

"And where is young Alma now?" Karl stood up and walked around his desk.

Albert cleared his throat. "She's standing outside the door."

"Well, bring her in! Don't leave the girl standing out there alone." He shook his head and chuckled as Albert turned on his heel and tucked his head outside the door, motioning with his arm.

Seconds later, Alma timidly stepped around the corner. Her hands were clasped in front of her as she looked up at Karl with wide eyes. It wasn't the first time he'd met Alma. He had known her since she was a small child, ducking between desks at the Moscow design office. She'd been a curious little waif, flitting from craftsman to craftsman, peppering them with questions and watching with keen observation at the way they turned paper designs into real-life objects.

"Alma," her father would admonish when he caught her leaning too close into a craftsman's workspace. "You mustn't crowd them. Step back please."

She always complied, though Karl had seen the reluctance in her eyes. The child was destined to become a jewelry designer, and he found himself delighted at the prospect of having her here. He studied her closely.

She had grown into a young lady since the last time he had seen her. Her dark brown hair was piled elegantly on top of her head, framing her petite face. A single curl had escaped and hung down on her forehead. She pushed it self-consciously to the side.

"Master Fabergé," she said, her voice gentle and sweet.

Karl was instantly taken with her, a fatherly affection swelling in his chest. "My dear girl."

She looked back up at him and smiled. He saw the mischievous little girl she'd been, but something new was swirling in her gaze. There was an eagerness there, and a confidence that Karl admired. He turned to Albert.

"Have you determined the plan for her training?" he asked.

Albert nodded. "She'll visit whenever she has free time until she is finished with her studies at *Annenschule*. After that, she'll come here and begin as a draftsman trainee."

Alma grinned. "I'm so honored to join the House of Fabergé," she said. "And to be a draftsman—" She closed her eyes and put her hand over her heart. "Well, they are the ones who set this marvelous place apart from all the other design houses. To take on the responsibility of producing life-sized, detailed drawings of every item produced in this magnificent place for the archives . . . it's all just so exciting!"

Alma stopped abruptly and clamped her mouth shut. Karl watched her process all her emotions with gentle amusement.

"I'm sorry, sir," she said with a slight tilt of her chin. "What I meant to say was thank you for the opportunity. I am thrilled to work under the Fabergé name."

"And we are happy to have you," Karl said. "Now, Alma, tell me. How are you enjoying your time at *Annenschule*?"

"It's very nice, thank you. I'm learning so much."

"I imagine you would be! The instructors there are the very best."

"Oh, yes they are! And they are all so proud of you and all that you have accomplished. You are a hero at *Annenschule*."

Karl chuckled. "How unfortunate that I'm the best hero

they've got," he said with a good-natured smile. He winked at Alma. "I'm looking forward to having you start with us."

She grinned. "I'm thrilled to be here." She grimaced. "I already said that, though."

Karl suppressed his amusement. The tone of her voice was filled with unrestrained delight and excitement. Her eyes danced, and it seemed she was fighting to keep from bouncing up and down.

"Well, Albert," Karl said, turning to his friend. "I suppose there's no time like the present to begin showing her around. If you need anything, please let me know."

Albert nodded, then grabbed Alma's elbow and guided her toward the door. Her eyes were scanning Karl's office, taking in the sight of the tall bookcases, the framed drawings on the wall, the ornate wood paneling and golden light that bathed the room.

"It's lovely in here," she said.

Karl looked around at his office, then glanced back at the newest apprentice of the House of Fabergé. "Indeed, it is," he replied.

She offered him one more smile, then turned to follow her uncle back to his desk on the second floor. Karl turned back to his own desk, his smile fading as he thought of the telegram in the top drawer. Frustration swelled in his chest once more. He walked back to his desk and lowered into his chair with a sigh. He thought of the finished eggs already created for last year's Easter celebration. Time and resources had been spent on the eggs in anticipation of the yearly commission, and at the final moment they canceled the standing order. Now there was to be no order for the coming year as well.

Karl leaned back and clasped his hands in front of him.

There was a hum beginning to take flight in the streets of Petersburg. He heard his clients speaking of it when they walked through the front of the store.

Yesterday, a merchant passing through town had brought his wife into the shop, allowing her to browse the selection and choose any piece that caught her eye. Karl had assumed the man was paying penance for some indiscretion based on the way his wife narrowed her eyes and asked for the price of each piece of jewelry, then looked back at him with an air of accusation.

"I heard wind of a rising revolution," he murmured to Karl as his wife shopped.

"There is always wind of some kind of uprising these days," he responded politely.

"This sounded different," the man said. "I overheard two men on the train talking about it. They said it's going to happen, that the masses are assembling to rise up against the tsar and the bourgeoisie in control of the wealth in Russia."

Karl hadn't responded, mostly because he didn't really know what to say. He supposed he agreed with the stranger, but he wasn't entirely sure what the final result of this uprising would be.

"If I were you, I'd be careful," the merchant said. He'd turned to Karl then, offering a pointed look. "You'll be the first to go."

Karl rubbed his eyes and thought of the eggs that sat in the locked safe in the back room. They'd been ornately designed, one of them being the largest the House of Fabergé had made to date. The *Moscow Kremlin Egg* was to be a celebration and a commemoration of the tsar and tsarina's successful return visit to Moscow in 1903. They had avoided Moscow since Nicholas's disastrous coronation. Karl shook his head. It seemed the young tsar's reign was doomed from the start.

In 1896, after his official coronation, Nicholas had planned to open up Khodynka Meadow to the people of Russia. It was meant to be a celebration, much like the one his father had at his own coronation many years before. But, as with most incidents surrounding the new tsar, things did not go as planned.

Karl, of course, wasn't there at the time, but he heard the details as did most people throughout Russia. The rumors that Nicholas and his young wife were planning to offer extravagant gifts to all attendees of the postcoronation celebration spread rampantly, and by the morning of May 30, thousands of people were crowded together outside the large field—many more than the Imperial family had anticipated.

"They're giving out gold coins inside mugs!" the people exclaimed, jostling one another for position. In a land that was strained for lack of resources, the thought of food and shared wealth from their tsar produced mass hysteria that had reached its peak on that field outside the palace walls. How it all began was nearly mythical in explanation, but a rumbling grew in the crowd that there wasn't to be enough food for all who had gathered. Likewise, frantic news spread throughout the crowd that there would not be enough mugs to hand out to everyone, and in the ensuing panic a stampede began. The Imperial police force, entirely taken off guard by the amount of people and the massive rush for the field, was unable to maintain order. In the end, it wasn't known how many people died, but Karl had heard that it was many more than the official number released by the palace.

"Hundreds?" scoffed those who had been there that day. "I'd say thousands. Bodies everywhere."

The most unfortunate truth of the event was that there was never to have been gold coins for the people anyway. Karl only knew this because he was privy to the gossip of those closest to the tsar.

The memory of that ill-fated day had been both appalling and embarrassing to the newly crowned tsar. But last year, they had made a tentative trip back to Moscow and found themselves well enough received. The *Moscow Kremlin Egg* was to commemorate this triumph.

Inspired by the Upenski Cathedral in Moscow, where all the tsars were coronated and crowned, the *Moscow Kremlin Egg* was ambitious in both design and innovation. Using a variety of materials, Fabergé's master craftsmen had designed a work of art that was both stunning and meaningful. The egg was made using onyx, quatre-couleur gold, white and green enamel, glass, and oil painting.

White opalescent enamel comprised the egg, which stood regally on an enameled-gold stand modeled to look like the Spasskaya Tower. These turrets bore the coat of arms of the Russian Empire, and of Moscow, and were inset with chiming clocks. One could look directly through the windows of the egg to see the ornate details inside, designed to look like the inside of the cathedral itself using rich velvet and gold accents. Tiny, enameled icons hung on the side of the egg, while the main focus of the interior was the white-enamel High Altar, which stood on an oval glass plate. Topped with a golden cupola and flanked by two square and two circular turrets, the egg was a modern marvel in both its design and artistry.

The surprise of the *Moscow Kremlin Egg* was also different than any other. Using a key that fit neatly into a slot in the back of the egg, a small music box could be wound, resulting in the sound of two Cherubim chants, traditional Easter hymns, playing from the base of the egg itself.

On the base of the egg, a gold plate was attached with the date 1904 etched into it. Karl sighed as he thought of the hours spent and resources utilized to make the egg that now sat untouched and unadmired in the company safe.

The second egg waiting to be presented to Empress Maria was the *Swan Egg*. Karl preferred this egg to the *Moscow Kremlin Egg* for its elegant simplicity. This egg had been created by one of his most prolific designers and master craftsmen, Henrik Wigstrom.

Henrik had taken over the position of head workmaster the year before when Karl's partner and friend, Mikhail Perkhin, passed away most unexpectedly and much too young. Passing the title of head workmaster on to Henrik had been the natural choice, and Henrik had taken the responsibility on with pride as a means to honor Mikhail.

Henrik was more than capable of handling the many tasks associated with the position. With painstaking care, Henrik had overseen the design of the *Swan Egg* himself. It was much more traditional than the ornate *Moscow Kremlin Egg*. The *Swan Egg* was gold and covered in a mauve-hued enamel, giving it a very feminine appearance. It rested lightly on a platinum and glass base and was covered with rose-cut diamonds in a symmetrical design made to look like little bows across the surface of the egg.

The top of the egg opened, and inside there was what, at first glance, appeared to be a basket of flowers. When pulled from the base of the egg, however, one discovered that it was, in fact, a swan made entirely of platinum, gold, and precious stones. The swan sat on a thick piece of aquamarine, ornately

decorated with gold so that it appeared the swan was floating on a crystal-clear aquamarine lake lit by the sun above.
But Henrik didn't stop there, having been so well trained that
he understood that the surprise must contain more than just
beauty—it must also awe the onlooker. When pressed, a small
button on the left of the lake, barely visible to the eye, sent
the swan into a delicate motion, making it appear to swim on
the aquamarine. When displayed in the correct lighting, one
could even see the swan's shadow move on the glass lake, the
effect of which was breathtaking.

This egg had been designed specifically with Empress Maria
in mind, but it would remain locked away for another year until
they were ready to once again receive the gifts that had put
Karl Fabergé on the map in the design world.

Karl reached into his desk and pulled out the telegram with
a long sigh. He only hoped that the commissions would come
back in again, and that the two eggs wouldn't remain locked
up forever.

Present Day

Ava tiptoed down the stairs, her computer tucked under her arm, and made her way as silently as possible into Sylvie's kitchen. She froze as the floorboards under her feet creaked, glancing around the dark room to see if anyone came tearing out to catch her.

When Sylvie returned from the grocery store yesterday, she'd been obviously displeased at the change of plans.

"They're staying for a couple of days?" she barked from inside Nick's room.

Carol and Ava stood on the other side of the door, cringing at the obvious displeasure in her voice.

"Sis, isn't this a good thing? You told me to make amends before . . . you know." He cleared his throat.

"I said make amends, Nicky! Not invite them back into your life and play family. This will put enormous strain on you." Her voice broke. "And stress and strain will only bring about the inevitable faster."

Ava had looked over at her mom to find her eyes shining. She felt an unfamiliar lump in her own throat and swallowed hard.

"Sylvie." Nick's voice was softer now. "Sis, look at me."

Soft sobs from inside the room carried beneath the door. Carol retreated, tucking into the kitchen to compose herself, while Ava stepped closer to hear the rest of the conversation.

"I understand all of these things and how terribly difficult they are on you," Nick continued. "But I have a chance here to do more than make amends. I have a chance to know my daughter. And to have one last adventure, albeit from a different angle." He paused. "Please don't deny me this chance," he finally finished quietly.

Moments later, Sylvie had yanked open the door, startling Ava so much that she'd let out a yelp. Sylvie narrowed her eyes.

"So, it seems you're staying for a couple of days, then," Sylvie said.

Ava swallowed and nodded.

"Did you come prepared? Do you have toiletries or a change of clothes?"

Ava shook her head sheepishly.

"I do." Carol had stepped back into the hallway, her eyes red-rimmed. "I brought some things for us to stay for a couple of days."

"You did?" Ava asked.

Carol shrugged. "Just in case."

Now, in the still, dark early-morning air, Ava shook her head. Her mom had spent half her life reminding Ava to be prepared for the "just in case." "You never know when life might throw you a curveball," Carol would say every time Ava left the house. "Do you have what you need just in case there's a change of plans?"

Ava would roll her eyes, but this morning as she made her way into the dark kitchen, she was immensely grateful to her mom for her "just in case" preparation.

After slipping on her flip-flops, Ava slowly pushed open the side door and walked out onto the wraparound porch that surrounded the front and sides of Sylvie's little home. A wicker couch sat in the corner, fluffy pillows inviting her to snuggle in, and she pushed open her laptop, waiting until the soft glow lit up her face.

The Florida air was warm this morning, but it felt fresh and clean. The mugginess of the late summer was finally fading away, and they were entering the fall months, which were still painfully warm but less humid, and that was enough for a true Floridian.

Ava stared at the screen for a few moments, her fingers hovering over the keys. She shook her head at the change of events that had taken place over the past few days.

"I am Nick Laine's padawan," she murmured. Twenty-four hours earlier she'd been determined to say her goodbye and walk away from her father altogether. But the moment she saw him sitting in that bed, sick and frail, something inside had switched.

Drawing in a deep breath, she rubbed her eyes, then leaned over her computer and clicked a few keys, pulling up information on the Romanov family, and refreshing her memory of the details surrounding their final years as rulers of Russia. She then moved on to Peter Karl Fabergé, looking for the connections between the famous jewelry maker and the ill-fated family that employed him.

Ava studied the photo that loaded on her screen after clicking one of the links. It was an image of the inside of Fabergé's workshop on 24 Bolshaya Morskaya in St. Petersburg. The image caption read "Peter Karl Fabergé and his master craftsmen, 1914."

Ava leaned forward, squinting at the blurry image as she studied the faces of the people lined up in the photo. Fabergé stood to the side, his shoulders pressed back proudly, chin held high. His beard was white with some flecks of black sprinkled in. With one hand, he held the lapel of his dark suit. The image wasn't clear enough to make out his expression, but Ava sensed pride and contentment based on his posture.

The others in the photo stood with equal confidence. Most of them were men who looked to be varying ages. But it was the woman that drew Ava in. She leaned in closer to take in the small-framed female flanked by men. There was something charming about the figure. Her hands were clasped loosely in front of her waist, her posture relaxed. A soft smile turned up her lips. Ava tried to make out the expression in her eyes.

Pulling up a new tab, Ava typed into the search box, *Did women work for Peter Karl Fabergé?* She sifted through the links that popped up until she settled on one that listed the names of Fabergé's master craftsmen. Scrolling down slowly, Ava stopped when she landed on the name Alma Pihl. She clicked the name and read further.

Alma Pihl began her career as a design artist for Fabergé under the tutelage of her uncle, Albert Holmström. She became known for her attention to detail and her extraordinary talent. Her intricate drawings of snowflakes brought her up from the design floor and into the creation of jewelry. Alma Pihl was later responsible for the design of the *Winter Egg* presented to Empress Maria in 1913. Carved from rock crystal, the base was polished until it seemed to melt, while the egg itself was engraved to give the effect of ice. The design was so breathtaking that one almost expected the egg to be frozen to the touch.

Only upon close examination would one find that the egg was overlaid with over 1,300 rose-cut diamonds.

Visible just beneath the surface of the egg, as though looking through a foggy winter morning, was the surprise inside, a platinum basket of spring flowers made of diamonds, white quartz, and leaves designed from nephrite. When asked where she got her inspiration for the trademark snowflake design that came to define her, Alma answered that she saw it in the icicles that hung from the window beside her worktable. The *Winter Egg* would later go on to be described as the masterpiece of the House of Fabergé.

Ava sat back and rubbed her eyes. She looked out over the side yard and took in the sight of the lightening sky. Streaks of red and orange cut a line through the horizon over the trees. Inside the house, she heard a deep, rasping cough—the kind of cough that rolled through one's lungs and sounded as painful as it likely felt. Ava grimaced. She heard the pad of feet down the stairs, and she peeked into the window beside her to see Sylvie pushing open Nick's door with a tray in her hand.

Ava pulled back and slouched further into the couch. She tried to block out the sounds of Nick coughing as she turned back to her research. Navigating back to Google, Ava typed in a new search.

Who was Alma Pihl?

She read until her eyes began to ache and the streaks of orange and red faded into the golden hue of a perfect morning. Rubbing her eyes, Ava sat back and chewed on her bottom lip as she pondered what she'd learned.

Alma Pihl was known to have designed only two of the eggs given to the empress and the tsarina, yet both eggs were thought to be the most innovative of all of Fabergé's designs. In 1914, Alma created the *Mosaic Egg*, a design for which she was inspired when she took notice of her mother-in-law's embroidery one lazy afternoon. She went on to design an egg that, from a distance, looked like it was an elaborate tapestry or needlepoint. When one looked closer, however, it was discovered that the egg was made from hundreds of precious and semiprecious stones which were arranged in a flower pattern. The result was another stunning display of ingenuity and creativity from the young female craftsman in Fabergé's shop.

Ava glanced back down at the last line of the article she was reading.

> Alma Pihl's eggs could be described as the most innovative not because they were the most elaborate, but rather because they were the most elaborately simple, and that simplicity made them breathtaking works of art.

"Well, obviously that was because she was a woman," she muttered. She flipped her computer shut and stood up, stretching her arms over her head. Walking to the railing of the porch, Ava leaned down on her elbows and looked out over her aunt's garden. A small cluster of grapefruit trees stood in the far back corner, a ladder leaned against one of them, and a basket sat at the base of the ladder. The sunlight cut through the trees, shooting golden beams across the thick grass. A bird hopped from branch to branch, whistling a merry morning tune.

"Morning."

Ava jumped and turned to see Carol stepping through the screen door, two steaming mugs of coffee in her hands. She handed one to Ava, who accepted it gratefully. Taking a sip, Ava closed her eyes and swallowed, then let out a wry laugh.

"What's that for?" Carol asked.

Ava opened her eyes and looked at her mom, then shrugged. "It's just weird, you know?" She gestured toward Sylvie's yard. "She's been living here this whole time in this bizarre picture-perfect, magazine-ready house with her two children and grapefruit, and ridiculously delicious coffee, and I never knew her. She never reached out to see how we were doing."

Ava turned and leaned back against the porch rail, narrowing her eyes at her mom. "All of this has been here the whole time, while you were working two jobs to make ends meet, and we lived in a crowded apartment complex with a weirdo neighbor who cooked us tofu and carob-chip pancakes because she felt like we needed to take better care of ourselves."

Carol chuckled. "I loved Mrs. Tucker. She was sweet."

"She was weird, Mom," Ava replied.

Carol shrugged and took a sip of her coffee. Both fell quiet as they watched the world wake up around them. "You can't be angry with Sylvie," she finally said. She glanced through the window where Sylvie was bustling through the kitchen preparing the day's food and laying out Nick's medications.

"Why?" Ava asked. "She abandoned me too."

Carol turned to Ava and reached her hand out, smoothing Ava's short hair back from her face. "No, she didn't, babe. I asked her to leave us alone."

"You did? But . . . why?"

Carol sighed and gestured toward the couch. Ava sat on the edge by her mom. Carol sat still for a long time as Ava drummed her fingers on the side of her coffee mug.

"You were barely two when your father left," Carol began.

"He wrote me a long letter telling me everything I had always known—that he couldn't be the person who held down a nine-to-five job, he couldn't handle the pressure of being the provider, he had exploring in his blood, and he needed the freedom to be away as long as necessary to find what he was looking for. It was a conversation he and I had had several times, and I'd always told him that I would never hold him back from what he was made to do, but perhaps I wasn't completely honest."

Carol paused and took a sip of coffee. She turned back to her daughter, her face full of regret.

"I thought that having a child would make him stay," she whispered, the confession heavy on her barely parted lips. "I thought that maybe the adventure of raising a little person would replace the adventure of finding the next big treasure. I should have known better."

"Mom—"

Carol held her hand up and shook her head. "I know that I'm not responsible for your father's decision to leave. And I do not for a second regret what he and I created together." She reached over and grabbed Ava's hand. "I gave up that misplaced guilt and responsibility years ago. Nick made his choice, and in my opinion, it was a terrible choice, but he made the decision he felt he needed to make. I can't change or fix that."

"Okay," Ava said. "But why ask Sylvie not to reach out?"

Carol chewed on her bottom lip. "At first, I kept in touch with Sylvie regularly, hoping that I could somehow get information out of her on where Nick was and convince her to make him come back home to me. But, like I already told you, Sylvie didn't really like me from the start. After I let her come see us that one Christmas when you were young, I realized that nothing I did would measure up to her standards. I mean for heaven's sake, look at this backyard! It looks like a magazine."

"Yeah." Ava glanced again at the grove of grapefruit trees.

"For my own sanity and healing, I had to cut ties with Sylvie. I don't know if it was the right thing or not, honey. Because truthfully, while Sylvie never seemed to care much for me, she really did love you. She was quite taken with you that day she stopped by."

"I just don't even remember it," Ava said with a shake of her head. "How could I have blocked that out of my mind?"

Carol shrugged. "It was sort of a non-event, really. Sylvie stopped by for about an hour on Christmas Day. She had called me earlier in the week to tell me that she would be driving through Tampa and she had a gift for you that she wanted to drop off. I'd hoped it was a gift from Nick, so I said yes. But it was just a box of clothes that her daughter, Sarah, had grown out of, and she wanted to hand them down to you."

"Just out of the blue? That's so . . . bizarre," Ava said.

"I thought so too." Carol lowered her voice and leaned closer to Ava. "Truthfully, I think she was curious. She wanted to see the child of her beloved brother."

Carol leaned back and stared out into the backyard. "Anyway," she said with a sigh, "after she left, I dug through the box and saw all these beautiful clothes, expensive brands, and it filled me with such a sense of . . . I don't know, insecurity, I suppose." She took another sip of her coffee. "I called her and thanked her for the gift but told her that it was confusing to you to see her, and I thought it would be better in the future if we didn't have contact. That was the last time I heard from her until last week."

Ava sat back and the two finished their coffee in silence. They looked up several moments later as Sylvie pushed open the door and stepped out onto the porch with them.

"Nicky has asked to see you this morning. He woke early with a coughing fit, so he will need an earlier nap today, but he says he feels well enough now to talk and visit."

Carol and Ava pushed themselves up off the couch. Ava reached down and grabbed her computer, tucking it under her arm.

"Your porch is lovely, Sylvie," Carol said. "It's very peaceful out here."

Sylvie nodded and pursed her lips. "I'm glad you're enjoying it," she replied, her words clipped. "I don't get out here much myself anymore. Hank and I used to spend entire mornings out here in the winter when the weather turned cool. Now, I am just so busy with my volunteer work that I simply don't have the time to sit here."

Ava heard the noticeable shake in her aunt's voice, and she felt a tug of compassion.

"Anyway, it's nice to see the space being enjoyed again."

She turned and went back into the house with Carol and Ava following her. Carol looked at Ava, the same compassion masking her eyes. They followed Sylvie into the kitchen and deposited their mugs into the farmhouse sink, then turned toward Nick's room.

"So, you will leave him when it becomes clear he's tired, correct?" Sylvie asked as they approached the door.

"Of course," Carol murmured.

Sylvie pushed open the door and stood to the side, arms crossed over her chest, as Carol and Ava walked by her. Nick sat up in bed, propped against the pillows. He was dressed in a red flannel shirt today, and it was clear he had brushed the white wisps of hair he had left to the side in an effort to spruce himself up.

"Morning," he said, his voice raspy. He cleared his throat. "Did you guys sleep okay?"

Ava nodded, sitting down in the chair next to her father's bed. Carol sat on the other side of the bed.

"So, how are my padawans today?" Nick asked with a smile.

Ava smiled back as Carol shook her head. "I still don't understand the reference," she said.

"You don't need to get it, Mom," Ava said. "It's fine."

Nick grinned, then nodded his head toward the computer on Ava's lap. "You been working already?"

"I was up early this morning doing a little research." Ava opened her computer to the notes she had typed into a document.

"What did you learn?" Nick asked.

"Well, obviously there is no information on a fifty-third egg. Everything I saw stops with the mention of the *Karelian Birch Egg* and the *Blue Tsarevitch Constellation Egg* in 1917."

Nick nodded. "Yep. I've seen the same things. What else did you learn?"

"Fabergé was super innovative for his time," Ava said. "I mean his egg designs were almost prophetic, and they were certainly technologically advanced. But it seems to me that Fabergé was only as good as the people he employed, and he had some kind of magical ability to see talent in people and bring them into his fold. His master craftsmen were the very best at what they did. It's all pretty fascinating."

Nick clapped his hands together and looked at Carol. "She's a smart one, isn't she?"

"Oh, you have no idea," Carol replied, the comment falling flat and resulting in an awkward pause.

Ava cleared her throat. "Anyway, most of what I found surrounded the eggs themselves and their designs. But I didn't really find anything that might be a tip-off of a secret egg."

"Well, that's because you're focusing on the big details. The clues to finding something that's missing always lie in the little things that seem meaningless. That's where you'll hit the trail."

Ava stared at her notes for a long moment. "Okay," she finally said. "So, where do I look for the little clues, then?"

Nick narrowed his eyes and stared at her. While holding Ava's gaze, he spoke, "Carol, where does she start?"

Ava turned to her mom, eyebrows raised. A half smile tilted up the corner of Carol's mouth.

"She follows her gut toward the one thing that seems most interesting."

Nick turned to Carol and smiled. "You didn't forget," he said.

"That little bit of advice proved to be helpful for more than just treasure hunting," she said. "Turns out, it was quite useful in raising a child with a rebellious bent."

"Rebellious bent, huh?" Nick asked, turning back to Ava.

"Whatever," Ava muttered. "So, I follow my gut toward a detail that stuck out, then?"

Nick nodded with a chuckle.

"Well, there was this photo I came across that sent me down a rabbit trail. Most of my notes here are regarding that detail."

"Okay," Nick said. "What did you learn?"

"Fabergé employed several women as master craftsmen in his shop. This in and of itself was innovative for the turn of the century when it was really just a man's world."

Ava glanced back down at her notes. "One of these women

was Alma Pihl. She designed the *Winter Egg*, a stunning piece of art according to the descriptions. It went missing in the 1920s and wasn't found again until 1994, which is crazy." Ava scrolled down and read further.

"Alma also designed the *Mosaic Egg*, another wildly creative design. In fact, Alma's designs are arguably labeled as Fabergé's masterpieces."

Nick leaned forward, his crystal blue eyes boring into Ava's. "That is the beginning of the rabbit trail."

"It is? How do you know for sure?"

"Because you feel it in your gut, and so do I," he said. "Plus, I already had that information." He winked at Ava.

"You already . . ." Ava shut her computer. "What else do you already know?" she demanded.

Nick laughed, which sent his body into a fit of coughing. Carol stood and leaned over the bed, rubbing Nick's back as he heaved and gasped. Ava grabbed a handkerchief next to the bed and handed it to him. Slowly, Nick's shoulders relaxed, and the coughing eased. He sat back on the pillows, taking in slow, ragged breaths.

"Do you need us to leave?" Carol asked.

"No, no," Nick said. "I just need a minute."

Ava reached onto the table next to Nick's bed and grabbed the cup of water that Sylvie had left behind. She handed it to Nick and waited as he took several sips. He gave her back the cup and pushed himself up straighter.

"Boy," he said. "Those fits are the worst."

Carol sat back down slowly, her hand reaching over and clasping Nick's. Ava sat back in her chair.

"So," she said. "You have more information?"

"Ava." Carol shook her head. "Slow down a minute."

"No, no," Nick said. "I'm fine." His voice was weaker now, his breathing a little more labored. He nodded toward her computer. "Did any of the articles you read tell you where Alma was from originally?"

Ava opened up her computer and scanned her notes again, reading quietly under her breath. She stopped short when she got to a sentence buried in the middle of the paragraph she had cut and pasted from the last article she pulled up.

"Alma Pihl was born in Finland," she read slowly. "And in 1921, she and her husband, Nicholas Klee, fled Russia and went back to their native Finland. Alma lived the rest of her days out quietly, never talking of her connection to the former Imperial family."

Ava looked back up at Nick. He stared back at her for a brief moment before turning and locking eyes with Carol.

"So," Carol said. "Finland, huh?"

St. Petersburg, 1905

K arl tied his robe around his waist and walked to the window, pushing aside the embroidered curtain to peer down into the street. The chatter outside had drawn him from his bed earlier than usual, and he'd come to investigate.

The frigid January air left intricate designs of ice across the small window in Karl's apartment, which was situated on the top floor of the building that housed his workshop. He peered through the foggy glass as groups of people, all bundled against the elements, marched down the snowy street.

"It's loud outside for a Sunday morning."

Karl turned to find Augusta entering the kitchen, also in her robe, her hair pinned messily in a low bun at the nape of her neck. Her face was lined, sleep still swelling in her eyes, and her mouth pressed into a thin grimace.

"Indeed," Karl murmured. "It looks a bit ominous out there."

"It's always ominous these days." Augusta shuffled to the small stove and grabbed the teakettle. Pouring water from the bowl on the counter into the kettle, she lit a match and ignited the small burner in the state-of-the-art stove top that Karl had given her. "Will you have some *chai*?"

"Yes, of course," Karl answered. "Let me just go dress. I want to get out and see what is going on."

Augusta pursed her lips and gave a small nod. Karl turned and walked back to his bedroom. It had been some time since he and his wife had shared a bed. They now retreated to their own spaces in the flat, something they claimed was a matter of convenience because of Karl's busy schedule and frequent travels.

Karl dressed quickly, making sure that his crisp suit hung neatly on his frame. Using the comb on his dresser, he carefully arranged what little hair he had left on his head, then brushed his beard, smoothing out the white strands so that he looked elegant and smart. He chuckled as he studied himself. He had a look that elicited stares from many young children when they saw him out and about. Strolling down the street could be quite a delightful experience, especially near the end of the year when wide-eyed little ones were on constant lookout for Father Christmas and his daughter, *Snegurichka*, come to bring cheer and gifts to good little girls and boys.

Karl smiled, his eyes crinkling at the corners. He didn't mind being called Father Christmas. He quite liked the reference, in fact.

Pulling open his door, Karl walked back to the kitchen where Augusta sat at the small table in the corner, her hand wrapped around a steaming mug of hot tea. Karl slid into the seat across from her. He picked up a slice of bread from the plate that Augusta had set in the middle of the table and took a bite. The bread was crunchy, not soft and fresh as he preferred, but times were tough even for the rich, and fresh bread was hard to come by.

"What do you think it is out there?" Augusta asked, jutting her chin toward the window.

Karl drew in a breath and took a sip of his tea. "I don't know," he murmured. "But that many people gathering at this time of day can't possibly be good."

"I suppose not. It is exhausting, isn't it?"

"What is?"

"The constant tension in the air. The rumors. The people forever unhappy and angry with the tsar. Don't you find it all terribly overwhelming?"

Karl sat back and drummed his fingertips on the table. "The people are looking for a strong leader who cares for them." Lowering his voice, he leaned toward her. "I fear they have neither in the tsar."

"I've never heard you speak negatively of him before," Augusta said after a brief pause, her eyes scanning over his face.

"I harbor no ill will toward the man," Karl said, choosing his words carefully. "But I also hold little respect for the way that he governs. He just seems so . . ."

"Distant," Augusta said.

"Yes. But it's more than that." Karl leaned back and took a sip of his chai, relishing the burn of the liquid as he swallowed. "There's an ignorance that I fear dictates most of his decisions. Half the time I'm certain he doesn't have a full understanding of what's happening to the country outside the palace walls. There are too many people in his ear, too many opinions being thrown his way, and he hasn't the fortitude to make up his own mind. It's a problem."

Karl sipped again at his chai. "I do like Empress Marie." He set down his mug and brushed crumbs from his pants. "Working with her has grown increasingly pleasurable over the years. But the tsarina, Alexandra—" He sighed.

"The woman is no more than a mouse," Augusta said. "Timid little thing who just . . . *niggled* her way to the king's table."

Karl paused. "Yes, I suppose that's a reasonable observation. Though I'm not sure it's something we ought to admit out loud." He offered her a wink.

Augusta stared at him for a beat before shifting her eyes downward to look into her mug.

Karl took another bite of bread and finished his tea. "At the end of the day, I suppose it's not too worrisome," he said with a shrug. "At this point, the business is fine enough that we can do without the Imperial family's jewelry orders, though I suppose we will be stuck serving them permanently."

"And the eggs?" Augusta asked, looking back up at her husband.

Karl smiled. "Well, the eggs are just fun. It would be a terrible shame to never make another." He wiped his mouth on the napkin and pushed to his feet. Leaning down, he gave his wife a friendly kiss on the cheek.

Augusta did not react to his daily act of affection, nor did she look him in the eye when he stepped back. She rarely held his gaze for long these days. "Be careful," she said, staring out the window at the gray January sky. "Don't get caught up someplace you shouldn't be."

Karl gave a slight nod, then turned on his heel. Grabbing his hat and coat, he slipped out the door and walked downstairs to the quiet shop below. His employees would start showing up for work soon, but for now he got to enjoy the quiet solitude inside the shop. It was his favorite place to be, especially early in the morning when the day ahead was ripe with design and creativity. Karl could feel in his bones when a good day was coming. There was an energy that buzzed through the shop before anyone else arrived that tipped him off to the productivity to come. This morning, however, he felt something different.

"Ominous, indeed," Karl muttered with a shiver. He pulled on his coat, donned his hat, and stepped outside, the initial blast of icy air taking his breath away.

Pulling the door closed behind him, Karl locked the shop back up and stepped onto the sidewalk of Bolshaya Morskaya, the busy thoroughfare that ran perpendicular to Nevsky Prospekt, connecting Palace Square with St. Isaac's cathedral. Karl drew in a deep breath and took a moment to admire the façade of his building. The Art Nouveau style suited well the street, which had been in existence since the early 1700s. Originally the home of sailors and workers, Bolshaya Morskaya now housed shops and businesses that highlighted luxury items. Karl had even heard the street referred to from time to time as *"Brilliantskaya,"* a thought that brought a smile to his lips.

A group approached, and Karl stepped aside to let them pass. They were mostly women and children, though a few men flanked the outsides. They held up icons, many of the women whispering prayers while the men tossed glares in his direction. He watched them pass silently.

"Where are they going?" he murmured to himself.

"They're marching to the Winter Palace to make demands of the tsar. Father George Gapon is leading a peaceful protest today."

Karl turned to see Albert standing next to him. The two watched in silence as the group disappeared around the corner, making their pilgrimage to the Winter Palace in the hopes of seeing the tsar himself.

"Do they know that the tsar isn't here?" Karl asked.

"I didn't even know that. How do you know?"

"Unfortunately, I am privy to royal gossip," Karl answered wryly. "The tsar is in Tsarskoe Selo with his family."

"Once again missing all the action with his people."

"Indeed. Perhaps the fact that he's gone will cool them off."

He and Albert locked eyes and exchanged a knowing look. Nothing would cool off this growing unrest.

"I don't feel good about this today," Karl murmured.

"I haven't felt good about any of it for some time," Albert said. The two stood silently for a moment watching as more clusters of people walked by.

"Let's open up the shop," Karl finally said.

It was Sunday, so not everyone would be working, but he knew some of his faithful would come in to get started on their weeks. The two turned and slipped back inside the building, not noticing the heated glares of the group of men passing by their windows.

The morning passed in relative quiet. There were no visitors to the showroom, and the craftsmen upstairs kept mostly to themselves as they worked on their commissioned pieces. It was early afternoon when they began to hear rumblings outside on the street again.

Stepping to the window, Karl watched as droves of men and women marched past the front of the building, this time with more anger and urgency in their eyes. They still held up their icons, but now the peaceful prayers of earlier had been replaced by angry cries. Karl turned to his employees.

"Please stay inside, all of you," he said.

Most of them stared back at him with wide eyes, nodding their heads in agreement. Albert stood and walked to the window to join Karl. The day had not warmed at all, nor had the sun offered much grace. It was still cold and gray, matching the faces of those who stormed past them now.

Even the buildings looked dull and lifeless in the backdrop of the winter afternoon. They stood ominously against the gray sky, which looked as if it had been run over with an eraser, all the color snubbed and smeared out.

"They're going to Nevsky Prospekt," Albert murmured.

"Yes," Karl said. "They're still looking for the tsar. Why on earth has he not returned to face them?"

Albert let out a frustrated sigh, turning on his heel to head back to his table. Karl saw Alma stand to greet her uncle, concern lining her young face. He wondered what their family must be thinking as all this began playing out. He worried they would cut ties and head back to their native Finland. Not that he blamed them, of course. But they were some of his most hardworking and talented employees. He would hate to lose them.

As for Alma herself, Karl saw much potential. She had an eye for detail that he appreciated, and her eagerness to learn design and jewelry making set her apart from many of her peers. Having never had any daughters, Karl often found himself drawn to the girl, offering her little words of praise or advice when she came into the office to apprentice under Albert. Karl looked forward to the day when he could employ Alma full time.

He glanced back outside. In the distance, a low hum of voices could be heard now and then, but nothing terribly significant. When curiosity finally got the best of him, Karl ducked out of the workshop and crossed to the coatroom where he donned his coat and hat. It was the uniform of a dignified man, one that would separate him from the men and women on the street who were dressed in the more providential garb of peasants. He meant to stay in the shadows, only to observe the buzzing crowd from afar, but not enter into it.

Pushing out the shop's back door, he lowered his head and walked briskly down Bolshaya Morskaya toward Nevsky Prospekt.

He was almost there when he heard the sound of a bugle pierce the air. A split second later, gunshots rang out followed by panicked screams and shouts. Karl flattened himself against the wall as a mob of people spilled around the corner. Wild-eyed men and women, having tossed their icons in panic, now tore up the street, clutching hands or holding frightened children. Shots continued to fire behind them, wails filling the air and shattering whatever semblance of peace there had been earlier.

"They're shooting at us again! They're shooting at us again!" one woman wailed as she fled with her toddler wrapped tight to her chest.

"First the Winter Palace and now here!"

"There is no God! There is no tsar!"

"Death to the tsar!"

Karl stared in disbelief as people rushed past him. They looked like a pack of deer fleeing from the hunter's barrel. The air around them now smelled like fear and agony, the nip in the air forgotten beneath the cloud of terror. Karl found his heartbeats mirroring the cracks of the gunshots as he remained frozen against the wall and watched the crowd, his countrymen, run in a frantic stampede.

Moments later, the shooting stopped, but the panicked crowd continued to flee. Karl did his best to stay out of the way and remain invisible. He tucked inside the alcove of a nearby building and glanced up. It was building number 2 on the street. He climbed the steps and hid in the shadows as people continued to run past, waiting a long time until he felt it was safe to exit.

He stared at the sidewalk below him where two gas street-lamps stood tall in the gray sky. How modern it had seemed when those lamps were installed. Russia was moving forward, expanding like the rest of the world. Right now, though, he wondered if they weren't, in fact, moving backward. What kind of country would they be when innocent women and children were slain during a peaceful protest?

Fewer people ran by now, and Karl was ready to venture forward to see the damage. With hesitant steps, he made his way to the end of Bolshaya Morskaya, turning onto Nevsky Prospekt and drawing in a sharp breath.

The street was lined with bodies, some still and unmoving, many writhing in pain. Palace police stood to the side, their guns clutched in their hands, as those brave enough to stay behind tended to the wounded. Karl looked in horror at the body of a young child, crumpled and lifeless, lying splayed beneath a tree on the side of the road.

Women wailed as men shouted. Many stood to the sides, stunned, their faces registering the same shock as Karl's.

"What happened?" Karl asked a man who trudged past him, his face streaked with dirt, and his clothes splotched with blood. His wiry, brown hair was slicked back with sweat, and his beard was a tangled mess, gnarled on his face and giving him a look of disheveled panic. His tattered coat hung against a thin frame. He wore the clothes of a farmer, his thin pants long and loose, hanging over shoes so worn that the outline of his toes could be seen through the lining.

The man stopped and looked at Karl. He took in the sight of Karl's expensive coat and hat, his polished shoes and neatly trimmed beard.

"I'll tell you what happened," the man hissed, stepping so close that Karl could smell the hunger on his breath. "We came today in peace. We wanted to be heard by our tsar. We wanted him to know that we are starving and dying while he sits in his warm palace and throws away enough food to feed us all."

The man's eyes narrowed. "We wanted him, and the people like him"—he nearly spat when he said this, his eyes flicking down Karl's frame—"to see us and hear us. And what do they do?" He gestured toward the street behind him. "*Ubili nac,*" he growled. "They killed us. They opened fire on the crowd, and they killed us. Mothers holding their babies. Children watching in the trees. Men carrying icons, not weapons. They didn't care who we were. They just killed us."

He spat on the ground at Karl's feet. "You look like you belong inside those palace walls," he said with disgust. Turning on his heel, he headed back down the street, his shoulders slumped.

Karl watched his retreating figure, then turned back to the street, a lump forming in the base of his throat. A young woman now knelt next to the child's body, racking sobs wrenching from her. She clutched at the child's shirt.

"*Pomogitye! Pomogitye!*" she wailed, begging for help, but no one approached her. There were too many others still alive who needed help.

His stomach lurched, and Karl pushed away from the scene, turning and stumbling back toward his home at number 24. His head stayed down the rest of the way back.

He didn't notice other business members of Bolshaya Morskaya looking out their windows in pity and horror at the men and women leaving the scene. He didn't hear the sound of the ice crunching beneath his feet. He didn't feel the cold that had seeped beneath his skin and settled in his bones. He simply clutched his collar closed and walked as quickly as his feet would take him until he reached the alley that led around to the back of the shop.

Pushing inside, Karl stumbled into the warmth of the back of the storeroom. He closed and locked the door behind him, hung his hat on a peg, then leaned against the wall, his hand still clutching his coat together.

Hearing footsteps, Karl looked up to see Augusta coming down the stairs, her normally stoic face pinched and strained.

"What happened?" she asked quietly.

"They . . . they killed them." His voice sounded tired, old. He was unaccustomed to feeling his age, but today he felt every bit of his fifty-nine years.

"They killed whom?" Augusta asked.

"The tsar's forces. They killed the protestors."

"How many?"

"I don't know." Karl ran his hand over his face, wishing he could wipe away the mother's wails and the image of the crumpled child. "Many," he finally said. "Too many."

Augusta nodded her head, then studied her husband's drawn, tired face. In a moment of tenderness, she crossed the room and wrapped her arms around his shoulders.

"This is only the beginning," he murmured into her shoulder.

"Yes, I know."

Pulling away from her, Karl met his wife's eye. He reached up and brushed a curl off her forehead. "You are a strong woman. Much stronger than I."

Augusta stepped back. "I've had to be." She shifted her eyes away from his. The moment passed as quickly as it had come, and the two stood in awkward silence for a long minute.

"Right," Karl finally said. He shrugged off his coat and hung it on the peg by the door next to his hat. "I must go upstairs and tell everyone to be careful going home."

———— ❈ ————

Augusta moved to the side as her husband walked by. She watched him go, his shoes scraping rhythmically as he trudged up the stairs. She thought of all the years they'd shared together, of the children they had raised and the memories they'd made. She didn't regret any of it, but she did wish it was less complicated. She wished she knew and understood where the divide began. Was it the death of their fourth child? Was it the rapid success of the business?

Was this separation inevitable—an ultimate and inescapable reality that was destined from the start? Rubbing her eyes, Augusta peeked out the back door into the dark alleyway. The cries and sounds had died down, but she believed her husband was right—this was only the beginning.

"The worst is yet to come," she whispered, turning slowly and making her way back to her sitting room.

Present Day

Okay, so hang on," Ava said. She was now pacing at the foot of Nick's bed. "You're saying you already know where we need to start looking? Do you already know where the egg is?"

Nick shook his head. "Nope. That's not how treasure hunting works."

Ava stopped and turned to him. "I feel like you're messing with my head."

He gestured for her to sit back down. "Goodness, she's not the most patient, is she?" he said to Carol.

She smiled in return. "She's improved a little bit with time."

"Ha, ha." Ava made a face at her mom. "Alright, Nick. Fill me in."

He turned to Ava. "Okay, so treasure hunting is all about finding the clues, and they're rarely obvious. They're innocuous and small. There's no real formula to finding lost pieces, but there is a method."

"Which is . . . ," Ava said.

"Well, first you follow the trail that pricks at your interest, like you did in researching Alma Pihl. For whatever reason, her story stuck out to you, and you were compelled to chase it down. That's step one."

"But how do you know if the thing that pricked your interest means anything?" Ava asked. "What if you're being led down the wrong path?"

"Well, that happens, of course," Nick said. "Especially when you're just starting out. But you get better at figuring out what clues to focus on and which details to let go of. Although, I must say I'm pretty impressed at your natural inclination so far."

Ava smiled, his compliment momentarily disarming the shell she'd determined to keep up whenever she was around him. She blinked several times, shaking it off, and retrained her eyes on his, keeping her expression neutral.

"Anyway," he said, "you're on the right track with Alma. She absolutely had something to do with the missing egg. Now we need to find out what that was."

"Okay, so how do we do that?" Ava asked. "What's the next step?"

"Well, how do you two feel about international travel?"

Ava stared at Nick for a long moment before looking over to her mom.

"Excuse me?" Carol asked.

"Come on, girls," Nick said, looking back and forth between the two of them. "You didn't think you were going to be able to find the missing egg sitting in this room with me, did you?"

"No, of course not!" Ava said. "I'm 100 percent in on international travel." She looked at her mom with raised eyebrows.

"Well, I just . . ." Carol hesitated. "I don't see how it's possible. How would we afford it? Ava would lose her job. I only get two weeks of vacation. It just doesn't seem at all feasible."

Ava looked at her hands and drew in a deep breath. "Mom, I'm quitting my job anyway."

"What? Ava!" Carol shook her head and opened her mouth to continue, but Ava held up her hand.

"Mom, I am a hostess at a restaurant. I'm hardly flushing a prolific career down the toilet. I can always get another restaurant job."

Carol cleared her throat. "Well, that still doesn't solve the problem of how you'll afford it."

"I'm paying," Nick said.

Ava looked at him and, for the second time, felt a welling up of gratitude for the father she'd long since written off.

"Nick," Carol said. "That's generous of you, but really." She lowered her voice and looked apologetically at Ava. "I don't know if this is the best idea for either of us . . . or for you."

"Hey, Mom?" Ava leaned forward so that her elbows rested on the bed next to Nick's legs. "I'm going on this trip with or without you."

Carol leaned forward and met her daughter's steady gaze. "And what, exactly, do you hope to find on this little treasure hunt?"

"Uh . . . the missing Imperial Easter egg," Ava replied sarcastically.

"And you're not just doing this to escape? You're not trying to go off on this crazy, nonsensical adventure as a means to not face your current reality?"

"Well, of course I'm trying to do that, Mom! But I am at a point in my life where I *can* do that. There's nothing tethering me to this place—no one that needs me to stay or be present." She flicked her eyes to Nick's face and watched as he picked at the blanket lying over his legs, then looked back at her mom.

"I'm going to do this with Nick . . . and *for* him. And also, I'm doing this for me."

Carol sat back and crossed her arms. She stared at her daughter, then shook her head. "Okay, then. I guess we're in this together."

"You don't have to come," Ava said. "You have more to lose than I do."

"Please," Carol said with a wave of her hand. "I've worked for that company for twenty-five years now and have rarely taken time off. If they aren't willing to grant me an extended leave, then maybe it's time for me to look into new options."

Ava raised her eyebrows in surprise.

"I can be spontaneous too." Carol eyed them both. "Maybe not as easily as you two crazies, but I can do it."

Nick looked at Carol and then at Ava, then shifted his gaze back to Carol again. "Okay, so is that part of the discussion settled, then?"

Carol shot him a look.

"So, what's next?" Ava asked.

"Well, you're going to need passports," he said. "That may set our timeline back a little."

"Nope," Ava said. "We have them. We got them a few years ago in the hopes that we could take an international trip at some point, so we're ready to go there."

"Great!" Nick said. "So, the next step is to assemble your team."

"Our team?" Ava asked.

"Yep," Nick replied. "Nobody does it alone, kiddo." Ava shot him a withering stare and Nick shrank back. "Sorry, not kiddo."

Carol smiled.

"You need a team to help you manage all the pieces. You'll

need someone to run the details and be your lookout. You'll also need protection—a bodyguard."

"A bodyguard? Really?" Ava asked. "Why, just because we're female? Come on, Nick. That's lame."

"Uh, no," Nick shot back. "I always took a bodyguard with me as well. Simmer down, alright?"

Ava clamped her mouth shut and crossed her arms.

"And you'll need a computer wiz to help you with the research, and with the technicalities of searching areas that may be considered . . ." Nick paused and shot a glance at Carol. "Well, places that may be considered off limits."

"Off limits?" Carol crossed her arms. "You mean like breaking and entering? Trespassing? That sort of thing?"

"Only when necessary to gather intel," Nick said. "Never to defame or steal."

"Oh, well in that case I see nothing wrong with it." Carol tossed her hands in the air.

Nick smiled and continued. "Sometimes a hunt requires a little maneuvering around the law. This is why your tech wiz is vital, as is your bodyguard." He raised one eyebrow at Ava.

"So, do you already have a team that we can use?" Ava asked.

"Well, my muscle is available. I've already spoken with him, and he's in. He's young, and a little green in the art of treasure hunting, but he was invaluable on my last hunt, so you'll be in good hands. His dad had been my longtime travel partner, but he got sick about five years ago. Same kind of cancer as me, if you can believe it." Nick paused. "He went pretty quick," he finished quietly.

An uncomfortable pause hung in the air before Ava cleared her throat. "So, what's this muscle man's name?" she asked.

"Xander," Nick answered. "Xander Majors."

"Xander *Majors*?" Ava gaped. "Is that his real name or his made-up name to sound like a fictional character in some kind of spy book?"

Nick threw his head back and laughed. This sent him into another fit of coughing, and Ava and Carol both leaned forward and held his hands until it passed. He fell back on his pillow, spent.

"I'll call Xander this afternoon to confirm," he said, his voice tired and weak. "I'm also going to ask him to line up Anatoly, our Russian muscle and driver." He drew in a careful, shuddering breath. "I never do anything in Russia without Anatoly. Good man. Xander will help . . . us . . . lock that down." He blinked a few times, training his eyes on Ava's, their glassy appearance sending a chill down the back of her neck. "I'll call after I rest," he said, his voice barely above a whisper.

"Sure," Ava said.

Carol blinked heavily as she looked down on him with wide, concerned eyes.

"What about the tech wiz?" Ava asked.

Nick closed his eyes. "We'll have to find someone," he whispered. "My guy quit. I told him to stay home with his wife and kids."

The last sentence was barely audible as Nick drifted to sleep. Ava and Carol silently made their way out of the room and pulled the door closed behind them.

Walking into the kitchen, they stopped and stood wordlessly for a long minute. The midmorning sunshine now streamed through the large, plate-glass window, bathing the room in natural light.

"We'll need to drive home this evening," Carol said. "I need more clothes and supplies, and I'll have to call my boss in the morning and explain my leave of absence."

Ava nodded. "We can drive back tomorrow with all the stuff we'll need to take on our trip."

Carol offered her daughter a sad smile. "This isn't how I envisioned us reconciling with your dad," she said.

"Yeah," Ava replied, her voice steady. "Me either."

———— ✤ ————

Several hours later, Carol and Ava were settled into their car and headed back to Tampa. Ava leaned her head back against the headrest of her mom's Camry and watched the flat Florida horizon slip past them. The drive from Lakeland to Tampa was as bland as it could possibly be, with nothing more than a few palm trees to break up the industrial trail that cut between the two cities. With little to talk about and even less to look at, Ava's mind wandered to Alma Pihl and the missing Imperial egg.

"I wonder why he did it," Ava finally said, cutting through the silence.

"Hmm?"

"I wonder why Fabergé would have created a secret egg and not shown it to anyone?"

"Your guess is as good as mine," Carol said with a shrug.

"The thing is." Ava furrowed her brow. "The only reason that the Fabergé eggs hold such intrinsic value is because they belonged to the Imperial family. They're artifacts with an interesting history. But this egg was never given to the family. And it's not like Fabergé didn't make other eggs. He was known for his jeweled eggs. There were more than just the Imperial eggs in existence, but the Imperial eggs hold so much value because of what happened to the Romanovs."

Ava drummed her hands on her knee and chewed on her bottom lip. "I just don't understand why this fifty-third egg would hold much value if it wasn't ever presented to one of the tsarinas."

"Maybe there was something unique about this egg," Carol said. She exited the highway and merged onto the street that would lead to Ava's apartment complex.

"Like what?"

Carol shrugged. "Oh, I have no idea. That's all I have to contribute to this conversation." She sighed. "Maybe I shouldn't go with you on this trip," she said quietly.

Ava turned and looked at her mom. "Why?"

"Well, I'm not going to be much help, am I? I know nothing about any of this history, I'm terribly concerned about the whole 'breaking and entering' business, and do you really need your mom watching your every move?" She offered Ava a sheepish look.

"Actually, Mom. I think I do need you."

"Oh, stop. You don't have to be nice."

"No, I'm serious! You're good at asking insightful questions. And you're patient, which will probably be good for me since, you know, I tend to be a little impulsive."

"Yeah, well, that's true." Carol smiled.

"And also, please don't leave me alone to travel the world with some guy named Xander Majors. I mean, what kind of name is that! It can't be real. No one would do that to their kid."

Carol snorted. She paused for a moment. "Okay. I'll tag along for no other reason than I am terribly curious about this Xander fellow." She turned into Ava's apartment complex and pulled to a stop in front of Ava's unit.

"Thanks, kiddo." She gave Ava a little wink and chuckled when Ava rolled her eyes.

"Yeah, Nick's really going to have to stop calling me that," she muttered. She glanced out the car window and an idea struck. She grabbed the handle and pushed open the door. "I just thought of something. I'll see you tomorrow morning."

"Sounds good," Carol replied.

Ava closed the door and turned, walking quickly to the apartment below her own and knocking before she lost the nerve.

Zak pulled open the door and Ava almost laughed out loud. It was Sunday afternoon, yet there he stood with his crisp, collared shirt tucked into a pair of jeans that looked like they had been ironed. His dark black hair was slicked to the side, and he had a glass of what appeared to be iced tea in his hand.

"Well, Ava! What a pleasant surprise."

Ava bit her lip and blinked a couple of times before answering. "Hey, Zak, you have a minute? I have a little proposition to run by you."

Zak's eyes lit up. "Yes, of course! Would you like to come in?"

Ava nodded and stepped inside the room. She looked around Zak's apartment and shook her head. It was meticulously clean, though terribly decorated. The brown leather sofa had bright orange pillows stacked neatly on each side and a blue knit blanket slung over the back. In the corner, a dark gray chair sat next to a glass side table on which three magazines were splayed in a semicircle. A large tapestry hung on the wall, brightly colored and patterned in hues that clashed with every other color in the room. His apartment smelled like Pine-Sol, and a vacuum stood against the wall leading into the small kitchen area, which Ava imagined was equally spotless.

"You cleaning today?" she asked jokingly.

"Yes, of course," Zak said, his face sincere. "It's Sunday."

Ava laughed but stopped quickly when she realized that Zak hadn't been joking.

"So, um, what's with the carpet on the wall?" she asked, jutting her chin toward the tapestry hanging behind him.

Zak glanced back at it, then turned back to Ava. "Oh, that was my grandparents'. They immigrated to the US from India fifty years ago, and the only thing they brought with them, besides the clothes on their back and their children, was that tapestry. My dad gave it to me to remind me of my heritage."

"Oh. Cool." She stood with her arms hanging awkwardly at her sides for a long minute, trying to figure out how to redirect the conversation.

Zak motioned her to come in and sit on the couch. Ava lowered herself slowly and sat on the edge while Zak settled into the gray chair across from her, crossing his legs casually.

"What's on your mind, Ava?"

She studied him for a minute before speaking. "So, you work with computers, right?"

Zak nodded. "I do. I work with data analysis and things of that nature."

"Right. So, you're a tech guy then, yeah? Like, would you call yourself a wiz on the computer?"

Zak tilted his head and smiled. "I don't know if I would use that precise term, but yes, I have a very good understanding of technology and how to work with it."

Ava smiled back at him and leaned forward, resting her elbows on her knees.

"Awesome. What would you say if I told you I had a very unique job for you that may or may not pay very much, but could potentially give you the experience of a lifetime? Oh, and it's top secret so you couldn't tell anyone what you were doing."

Zak set his iced tea down on a leather coaster on the table next to his chair and studied Ava. "I'd say you've piqued my interest."

St. Petersburg, 1905

Karl reached over and clicked the light on above his worktable. He yawned and rubbed his eyes as he took in the stillness of the workshop. It was cold tonight, and his fingers felt achy and sore from a long day—a day that wasn't over yet. Not for him, anyway.

Pulling his watch from his pocket, Karl glanced at the time. Midnight. Fatigue and strain tugged at the muscles in his neck and shoulders, but he would brush it all off. There was something he needed to do.

Sitting back in his chair, Karl allowed himself a moment to admire the workshop. He knew he was good at what he did, managing employees and creating fine pieces of art. He'd made it a point to run his shop in such a way that his craftsmen wanted to give their best. His standards were high, but his people didn't mind.

Part of his secret was as simple as showing his employees a little respect. He made it clear that their work was valued and that they were a part of the Fabergé team because they had earned that position. Because of this, his craftsmen willingly worked long hours. He didn't run his company like a factory, utilizing labor as a means to an end. Rather, he approached the House of Fabergé as a family business, where every single person employed held intrinsic value. This meant that their time was valued, and Karl paid handsomely for overtime. It was not uncommon for his jewelers and artists to work until 11:00 at night, which was why he was only now alone at midnight.

Karl opened the box on the table in front of him, pulling out the beginnings of his own project. He'd told no one what he was doing. Truthfully, he didn't even know why he was doing it. He supposed there was something calming about working with his hands, about creating something from start to finish on his own.

The reality that many did not know was that Karl had little to do with the actual creation of most of the pieces in his shop. He was the visionary and the boss. He came up with many of the ideas, and he curated the environment for work, but his craftsmen were the real magic makers. They were the ones bringing the designs to life. With the demands of running the business so high, Karl rarely worked with his hands anymore. There was just too much at stake.

Lately, however, his hands itched to create. Somehow this act of building something from the simple vision in his head offered him the space to process all that had transpired and helped him work out how he felt about it.

He set the egg that he'd begun designing onto the table and leaned forward, studying its shape. He'd placed his creation in the capable hands of Alexander Petroff a few days earlier. His chief enameler had asked no questions about it. Such was the environment Karl had so generously crafted here in his workshop. There was infinite value placed in the skill of each craftsman, and the knowledge that they all brought this skill to the table allowed them to work alongside one another without the need to know or understand the intention for each project brought to life.

Petroff had done what he did so well, expertly covering the golden egg in an opaque enamel so that the gold was visible just beneath the smooth surface. The egg looked so real, as if with a mere tap on the side of the table one could crack it open and see its insides. Karl studied it with great pleasure, the familiar sense of wonder washing over him as he saw a vision begin to take shape.

Gently, Karl pulled the two halves of the egg apart and looked inside at the hollowed-out section he had carved into the gold. His fingers cramped just remembering the process of creating that space. He wasn't as young as he used to be.

Pulling a set of keys from his pocket, Karl reached down to the bottom drawer of the desk and unlocked it. Inside was another metal box, also locked. Using a different key, Karl opened that box and set it on the desk in front of him. Inside the box were diamonds, most of them very small, all clustered together in a mound of enticing sparkle. It was now time to take his design to the next level.

Setting up his magnifying mirror, Karl slowly and methodically picked out the diamonds he would use to create a lattice-work pattern around the exterior of the egg. This part of the work was tedious, with each diamond needing to be evenly spaced and set. Karl knew this part of the process would take him the most time, but time was all he had right now. And he needed to think.

Drawing in a deep breath, Karl placed the first diamond at the base of the egg. All the diamonds would start from this one place, fanning their way out and around the egg with precision and careful attention to detail. This very first stone set the course.

Karl let his mind drift as he gingerly picked up the next stone with his small pliers. He wondered when the first stone of his life had been set—the one that had set the trajectory of his days leading to this quiet moment in the lamplit dark of a workshop he had built into an empire.

Perhaps his course had been set before he was even born. His father had been a jeweler. Gustav Fabergé could never have known how far his son would take the humble company he started. But he'd known his son had a natural talent for the artistry of the jewelry making business. This was why he'd sent Karl, as a young man, to the Dresden Arts and Crafts School.

Karl smiled faintly as he thought back to his years of study, when jewelry making and artistry had been fanciful and thrilling. He'd felt an equal measure of longing to both create something grand and to also please his father.

Gustav Fabergé had been a soft-spoken man. He was kind and quiet, working methodically and with only the smallest amount of pride. Mostly, he was humble about his own gifts and talents. But Karl knew his father was proud of his firstborn son. Gustav tried not to let Karl see how he felt, but every once in a while, Karl would catch a glimpse of his father studying him from the far side of the room, and he could sense Gustav's pleasure.

"Your papa could sit and watch you work all day long," Hiskias used to say to Karl years after Gustav had passed away. Hiskias had been Gustav's dearest friend for many years, and when it came time for Karl to apprentice in the business, Hiskias was the only person Gustav trusted with his talented son.

"Never met a man more taken with his boy in all my life," Hiskias would say with a shake of his head, and Karl would nod stoically in return, but inside he felt his heart do a little turn. There was, perhaps, nothing more thrilling to a young man than to feel the pleasure of his father.

Karl set the second diamond gently, eyeing through his small magnifying glass the exact placement and distance from the first. He sifted through the diamonds to find the perfect stone for the third placement, taking a deep breath as he prepared to set it. A crick in his neck caused him a moment's pause, and he leaned back and closed his eyes. Immediately the image was there, the vision he'd seen that his hands must now somehow bring to fruition.

Karl first caught a glimpse of this vision a few weeks after that wretched Sunday when the bodies lay splayed across Nevsky Prospekt, the image of the crumpled child beneath the tree settling into his subconscious like a terrible nightmare that captured the mind and refused to let go. He'd shot up in bed the first time he saw the vision, his hand clutched to his chest. He waited for the moment to pass, for the picture in his head to fade into obscurity like most dreams are wont to do, but this one never faded away.

It returned, over and over. While he slept, while he ate, while he bathed, sometimes in the middle of conversations, the vision chased him. It was as though he wasn't meant to catch this particular creation so much as it was meant to capture him. He finally gave up trying to fight it and pulled out his sketchpad, capturing each detail with such specifications that it took him by surprise. He hadn't realized how precise the dream had been.

And now here he sat, trying to bring it all to life, but for what, he simply didn't know. Karl sighed, his hand poised over the egg-shaped form before him, wishing desperately that he could talk to his father again.

A rustling sound caused him to freeze, his head turning toward the shadows just beyond where the light over his table reached. In one quick motion, he laid the egg back into the cloth-lined box and shut the lid, pushing it to the side. He tossed another cloth over the diamonds on the table and rested his hands lightly on top of it.

The door below had been locked, he was sure of it. He checked himself before walking upstairs.

"Is somebody there?" he said, his voice coming out like a croak.

"Indeed," came the reply. "It is your wife."

Karl breathed a sigh of relief, his shoulders lowering. Augusta stepped into the edge of the light, her long robe cinched tight around her thick waist. Karl rubbed his eyes as she stepped closer, pushing the cloth-covered diamonds to the side and covering them as best he could with his arm.

"What are you doing down here so late?" Augusta asked. Sleep still lined her eyes as she squinted at her husband in the dim, orange light.

"I'm thinking." He hesitated for a brief moment before reluctantly adding, "And I am working."

"A new design?" Augusta's eyebrows raised as she studied the way her husband shifted in his chair, his arm awkwardly hiding whatever was on the table behind him.

"Yes." He looked at Augusta and felt a pang of regret wash over him. She was a wonderful woman. Early in their courtship and marriage, she had captivated him with her intelligence and wit. He wished he felt a longing for her the way he once had.

She was kind and thoughtful, perhaps a little rough around the edges, but that had been what he'd found most attractive when they were first introduced so many years ago.

Karl glanced back up at Augusta and offered her a gentle smile. He did still care for her. She had given him all of his sons, and she'd been a fine mother, doting on her family without wavering throughout the years. This alone gave him a deep-felt love and respect for her. But it hadn't kept him home.

Amalia's face materialized before him then, blinding him from seeing Augusta, as had been happening for many years now. What he felt for Amalia had also been love, the one his mind and body ached for when they were parted. It wasn't fair to Augusta, he knew this, and he felt terribly for it. Maintaining his relationship with Amalia for so long had not been wise. It had put incredible strain on his relationships with his sons and had compromised his integrity more than once. And yet, he couldn't seem to get his heart back from the Austrian actress who had stolen it right from his chest.

"Who could you possibly be working for this late at night?" Augusta asked. She shivered and crossed her arms over her chest. "Is it something for the tsar?"

Karl sighed. "Eventually, perhaps. But right now, this is something for me."

"Oh, imagine that. You doing something for yourself." The edge in her voice cut through the space between them.

Karl leaned back and looked up at his wife with apologetic eyes. "I'll be there soon, my dear," he said quietly.

She stared back at him, blinking hard, the corners of her eyes glinting in the light. She nodded and turned, her feet whispering back into the shadows and disappearing before Karl's eyes.

He turned slowly back to the box on the edge of the table and opened it, looking at the enamel-covered golden egg.

"Who is it for?" he wondered out loud. "Perhaps the better question is what does it mean?" The words were swallowed up without hint of an answer to follow.

Present Day

Ava stepped outside, pulling her suitcase behind her. She'd packed everything she thought she might need for an extended stay away that may or may not include time spent internationally. Her stomach flipped with nervous excitement at the thought of flying over the ocean, and she found herself smiling as she turned the lock on her door.

She walked down the stairs and drew in a deep breath. It was a perfect Florida morning. The air smelled like fresh rain. The hint of a breeze floated past Ava, and the cool morning nipped at her skin.

"Hey, Ava!"

With a start, Ava turned to see Zak standing in his doorway. He wore a red checkered robe over loose-fitting pants and held in his hand two mugs of coffee. He reached over and handed one to Ava, who took it reluctantly.

"Hey, Zak. You look . . . casual." She took a sip of the coffee and nearly choked. It was strong and scalding hot.

"Yes, well, I spent a lot of time last night thinking about what you told me," Zak said. He leaned against the doorjamb of his apartment and studied her. "I even did my own research on the Imperial family and on Fabergé."

Ava raised her eyebrows. "Wow. And?"

Zak smiled and sipped his coffee. "Well, I've decided I have nothing to lose in helping you."

"You'll lose your job."

Zak shrugged. "I don't like that job. And besides, I can always get another job in data analysis, but I don't think I'll ever be offered the chance to go on a treasure hunt for a lost piece of art by one of the most famous jewelers of all time." He cleared his throat and shifted his eyes to his mug. "I also don't know if I'd ever again have the opportunity to travel the world with a beautiful lady."

Ava sputtered as he spoke those last words. The two stood in awkward silence for a long minute before Ava finally spoke.

"Well, then," she said. "It sounds like you've made up your mind." She offered Zak a stiff smile, and he grinned in return.

"Indeed. I'll call my boss this morning and put in my notice, and I will start making necessary plans."

Ava nodded. "Sounds good. I'm heading back to Lakeland, so I'll start gathering all the info you need to come on board as our tech guy, and I'll keep you posted on timelines. If we need to leave quickly, will you be able to get away?"

"For you, Ava? I will do anything."

"Oh, um, well . . ." She coughed. Turning, she saw her mom's car pull into the parking lot. She turned back to Zak and handed him her coffee mug.

"Thanks for the coffee. I'll be in touch. You have a passport, right?" Ava furrowed her brow, realizing she should have asked him this question earlier.

"Yes, of course. I am ready to leave at your beck and call."
He grinned as Ava backed away.

"Okay, Zak. Thanks for jumping on board!"

Carol slowed to a stop in the parking lot and tossed Ava an inquisitive look. Zak raised his mug up to her in greeting. Carol rolled the window down and waved back.

"Good morning, Zak," she said with a bemused smile.

"And a good morning to you, Miss Carol! Ava and I were just speaking of this wonderful adventure we will all be heading out on soon."

Carol raised her eyebrows. "Oh, really?"

Ava shot her mom a look, then turned back to Zak. "Bye, Zak!" She pulled her suitcase to Carol's car and tossed it in the back seat.

Zak watched with a broad smile. "Alright, partners!" he called out as Ava slid into the car. "I'll see you soon!"

Ava pulled the door shut and offered him an awkward wave.

Carol chuckled as she backed the car up and drove out of the parking lot. "That was your big idea last night, huh?"

Ava groaned. "It seemed like a good idea at the time."

"Oh, he's a nice guy," Carol said with a laugh. "A little strange and clearly smitten with you, but sweet."

Ava glanced at her mom. "Did you call your boss?"

Carol nodded. "I told him I needed to take an extended leave of absence to deal with some personal family matters. He wasn't thrilled, but he ultimately gave me the green light." She glanced at Ava. "I've got a three-month window here, and then I'll have to either return home or quit my job."

"Three months seems like it should be more than enough time."

Carol shrugged. "Nick's trips could last half a year or more."

KELLI STUART

"Do you think you'll ever be able to forgive him, Mom?" Ava asked, leaning her head back against the seat and looking at her mother's profile.

Carol drove in silence for several minutes before answering. "Honestly, honey, I think I *have* forgiven him. I don't harbor any ill feelings toward him." She paused for a moment. "I pity him, really. His travels may have been exciting, and I suppose his work was fulfilling, but he missed out on the most magical parts of his life when he left us behind."

Ava nodded and shifted her gaze out the window as she and her mom merged onto the highway that would take them back to Lakeland. "Yeah," she murmured. "I guess."

They drove in silence the rest of the trip. When they pulled up in front of Sylvie's house, Ava felt her stomach do a flip. She was finally going on the adventure she'd dreamed about since she learned what her father did for a living. She was going to live the dream.

"I wonder who's here," Carol said as she parked the car on the street. A black Mercedes sat in the driveway. Carol and Ava stepped out of the car and stretched for a moment.

"Let's leave our suitcases in here for now," Carol said. "If Sylvie has a guest, she won't like us barging in with our bags, inviting questions from her friends."

Ava nodded.

They walked up the front porch, and Carol knocked tentatively on the front door. Padded footsteps beat a rhythm on the other side, and a moment later the door swung open. Sylvie blinked at the two of them for a brief moment. Her eyes were red-rimmed and watery.

"Sylvie, is everything okay?" Carol asked.

Sylvie shook her head. She opened the door farther and let them step inside.

"Nicky had a bad night," she said, her eyes glancing at Nick's bedroom door. "The doctor is here now with him."

"Is he . . . okay?" Ava asked.

Sylvie turned to her with narrowed eyes. "No, Ava. He's not okay. He's dying."

Ava swallowed and lowered her eyes.

Carol cleared her throat. "Sylvie, we can come back another time. Tomorrow, perhaps?"

Ava looked at her mom with eyebrows raised. She was not planning on going back to Tampa any time soon.

Sylvie sighed and shook her head. "No," she said, frustration humming beneath her words. "He wants to see you both. He's already asked three times this morning if you had arrived." She tossed Carol a glare, then gestured toward the kitchen.

"Just come in and sit quietly until the doctor is finished. There's coffee and pastries on the counter. They're store-bought. I didn't have time this morning to make them fresh."

"We wouldn't have expected that," Carol said gently.

Ava and Carol followed Sylvie into the kitchen and settled at the counter. Neither felt hungry, but Sylvie stared at them with such stern expectation that they both grabbed a pastry and poured themselves cups of coffee, avoiding Sylvie's gaze the whole time.

"I'll go check on Nicky now," she finally said.

Ava and Carol nodded as she turned and retreated silently around the corner.

Sylvie tiptoed up to the bedroom door and leaned in. She could hear the murmur of voices on the other side. She gave a soft tap.

"Come in," Nick's voice rasped from the room.

Sylvie pushed open the door and stepped inside, shutting it behind her. Dr. Tom James sat in the chair next to Nick's bed, writing something on a small white pad. He glanced up at Sylvie, his eyes full of sympathy.

When Nick couldn't stop coughing at 4:00 a.m., Tom was the first person Sylvie called, and he'd been there before the sun rose above the horizon. Now Nick sat up next to him in bed sounding better, if looking weaker than before.

"How are we doing?" Sylvie asked.

Nick offered a weak smile and gave her a thumbs-up.

"Well, I gave him a breathing treatment that's broken up the congestion in his lungs," Tom said, "and I'm writing a prescription for an antibiotic to help with the developing pneumonia, along with a steroid and an anti-inflammatory. This should help make him more comfortable, but . . ." He paused and looked at Nick, who was now studying his hands.

"Nick has agreed that should he have another night like last night, he'll let you take him to the hospital."

Sylvie raised her eyebrows and looked at Nick, who met her gaze and gave a shrug. Tom stood up and walked to Sylvie. He lowered his voice and leaned into her, so close she could smell his Hugo Boss cologne. She drew in a soft breath. She found Tom James quite handsome. Immediately, a sense of guilt washed over her as Hank's face flooded her mind.

"Pneumonia is extremely serious with his type of cancer. Make him rest, and make sure he takes that medicine." Tom studied her. "And call me if you need anything at all."

"Yes, of course," Sylvie whispered.

Tom turned and looked back at Nick. "So, we're agreed, then? You're going to rest, drink a lot of liquids, stay on the meds, and head straight to the hospital if you get worse?"

"Agreed," Nick croaked. His face was drawn, fatigue and pain having aged him even more overnight.

Sylvie turned and followed Tom to the door. "I'll be right back," she said, glancing over her shoulder at her brother.

"Hey, sis?" he said, holding up his hand. Sylvie stopped and turned to him. "I want to see them."

Sylvie sighed and nodded her head. "I know."

Tom and Sylvie stepped into the hallway, Sylvie pulling the door closed behind her.

"What was that all about?" Tom asked.

Sylvie waved her hand. "It's nothing," she said. Anger simmered inside her as she considered her brother's foolhardy plan. "Let me show you to the door."

Tom followed her. Sylvie could feel him watching her as she stepped to the front door and pulled it open.

"Thank you for coming so early," she said, her voice trembling.

"Sylvie," Tom said. "Nick is . . ."

"He's dying," she said, her voice flat. "And did he tell you he wants to reconcile with his daughter by masterminding one last trip? He needs to rest, not be up in the middle of the night surfing the internet and making Excel spreadsheets of some cockamamie artifact he wants them to find."

Tom gave her a small smile. "As your friend, I want you to know I understand how straining this must be."

Sylvie nodded. "And as Nick's doctor?"

Tom shrugged. "I don't have a problem with it. As long as he's resting and taking his meds, it may actually be good for him.

With his mind active and his spirits up, he'll have the energy to fight this off a little longer."

He gave her a quick peck on the cheek. "Call me if you need anything else."

Sylvie blushed and reached over to pull open the front door. She watched as he walked down the stairs and headed toward his car. With a sigh, she closed the door behind his retreating figure and drew in a long, deep breath. She turned and walked to the kitchen.

"Alright," she said to Carol and Ava. "Nicky is chomping at the bit to see you both. Let's go."

Ten minutes later, the three women entered the room where Nick sat up against the pillows, his laptop on his legs, and a pencil between his teeth. A notebook full of scribbled instructions lay by his side. He looked up as they walked in, and a wide smile split his fatigued face.

"Hi, ladies," he rasped.

Carol and Ava stared warily back at him as Sylvie clasped her hands together in frustration.

"I'll leave you guys alone," Sylvie said.

"Hey, sis?" Nick replied, holding up his hand. "Would you stay? I think it would be good for you to know the plans, just in case anything . . ."

Sylvie sighed, her shoulders slumping forward. She shuffled to a large recliner chair in the corner of the room and lowered herself into it, folding her hands in her lap. Nick smiled at her, then shifted his gaze to Ava.

"I've got the plans all set," he said. "We just need to buy the plane tickets."

"Plane tickets to where?" Ava asked.

"You'll start in St. Petersburg, Russia. You're going to retrace Alma Pihl's final steps."

Ava tried to keep her expression neutral as she nodded. "I found us a tech guy. He's my neighbor Zak. He's a total computer wiz, and a little bit of a weirdo, which should keep things interesting."

Nick cracked a smile. "Every team needs a weirdo," he said. "I spoke with Xander last night and he's all in. I've already got his ticket purchased. He'll land in St. Petersburg next Monday."

"So how do we retrace Alma Pihl's last steps if we don't really know what they were?" Ava asked.

"We start with what we do know, and we keep going from there," Nick said.

Ava raised her eyebrows. She glanced at her mom, who looked equally intrigued.

"And what do we know?" Carol asked.

"We know that Alma Pihl had an egg in her possession that the history books have never before recorded."

"How do we know that, though?" Ava asked.

"Because I have a poem written by Alma Pihl that I believe speaks of the egg," Nick replied with a coy smile.

"You . . . you have a poem written by Alma?" Ava asked. She sank down in the chair next to Nick's bed. "How did you get that? How long have you had it? Why didn't you say so right off the bat?" Her eyes narrowed in a demanding glare.

"This is all part of the training, young Padawan," he said with a wan smile. "I found it last year when I went on a familial quest to Finland. I started this search for the missing egg a while back. But cancer is . . ."

Ava swallowed. "Okay. But where did you find it?"

128

"Well . . ." He glanced over at Sylvie, then drew in a slow breath and let it out. "I went to the home where my grandmother grew up and did a little poking around."

"You went to Grandma Lida's house?" Sylvie asked, eyebrows raised. "I thought we sold that years ago."

Nick stared at his hands for a long moment before looking up and meeting her gaze, his expression sheepish. "I held on to it."

"What does your grandmother have to do with Alma Pihl?" Ava said impatiently. "Agh! I feel like I'm talking to Yoda right now! Stop speaking in riddles!"

"Excuse me," Sylvie said from the corner of the room, "but can someone please tell me who Alma Pihl is? And how exactly our family is connected to her? And why you never sold that house when you told me that you did?" She shot her brother a withering stare.

Nick sighed. "If you all would quit interrupting me, I promise I will get there." He looked from Sylvie to Ava, both of whom stared back with pursed lips.

"Okay," he continued. "Alma Pihl was one of Fabergé's master craftsmen. Sylvie, I believe she had in her possession one of Fabergé's eggs, a design that was never shown to anyone, and I believe it's an egg that holds both financial and historical value." He gazed at her for a brief moment before continuing. "Our grandmother knew Alma in Finland. She was Alma Klee then, married to Nicholas Klee. Grandma Lida's older sister was one of Alma's best friends."

"So, how did you find this poem?" Ava asked again.

"While I was in Finland, I met some of the family. One woman in particular was extremely helpful—she was the daughter of Lida's cousin, Veera. She told me all the stories she could remember about our grandmother, who was apparently adventurous in her own right. She said Lida and her sister liked to pretend they were treasure hunters, and that even when they were adults, they would lead the children on grand treasure hunts through the fields and trees near their home. And then she mentioned a little cabin on the property where she said the girls would escape to often. She said there was still a metal box hidden in that cabin with their things in it."

"Seriously? Why would they leave it there and not go through it?" Ava asked.

"It's their way of honoring the sisters. They feel it's a tomb of sorts that's not to be disturbed," Nick said.

"So, you went through it?" Sylvie asked. "Really, Nicky. That's terribly tacky."

Nick smiled sheepishly. "I'm not always proud of this job." He gave an apologetic shrug. "Yes, I went through it. But the only thing I took was this single piece of paper, and I didn't even really know what I had at the time. I just knew it had Russian writing on it. It was my launching point—the hunch I was telling you about." He glanced at Ava. "I left all the other items there in the metal box."

"What else was in there?" Carol asked.

"Mostly little knickknacks and toys, a few more letters and drawings. Nothing terribly interesting other than the poem."

"So, let me make sure I understand what's happening here now," Sylvie said. "You two are going off on some wild search of this mysterious egg that may or may not exist and may or may not hold some kind of value?" She looked from Ava to Carol.

"Yes," Carol answered quietly, a hesitation in her voice.

"And you're dictating this entire trip from your deathbed?" Sylvie asked Nick.

"Yep," he replied.

Sylvie shook her head and leaned back. "I'm in a room full of crazy people," she murmured. An awkward pause filled the room for a brief moment before she continued. "You might as well give me a job in all this. No way you're leaving me out of it."

Nick grinned. "Atta girl, sis. I was hoping you'd be my wingman here stateside so if things get dicey, these guys won't be left out to dry."

It was quiet for a moment as they all pondered the true meaning behind his words.

"So, basically she'd be the Chewy to your Han Solo?" Ava quipped.

Nick snorted. "Yeah," he said, giving her a nod of approval. "That's exactly it. And I like the idea of being Han Solo better than Yoda." He winked at her.

"I'm Chewbacca?" Sylvie asked.

Nick grinned at her as Carol groaned. "You people are going to make me watch *Star Wars*, aren't you?"

"Nah," Nick said. "It's not a prerequisite for the job."

Ava smiled at Nick, and he caught her eye, smiling in return. He swung his computer around to show them the spreadsheet he'd been working on through the night.

"So, here's what we've got so far," he said.

--- ❀ ---

For two hours, the three went over the plans for how they would retrace Alma Pihl's steps, beginning in Russia.

"I still don't really understand why we even need to go to Russia, though," Carol said as they all sat back. "If we know that Alma ended up in Finland, and we know that she had the egg in her possession, then why would we waste our time in St. Petersburg?"

"Well"—Nick turned to face Carol—"we only know that she left Russia for Finland in 1921. We don't know for sure that she had the egg in her possession when she left. This is what you need to find out."

"Are you absolutely positive that she *ever* had an egg in her possession?" Sylvie asked.

Despite her insistence that their mission was a foolish one, she had asked a lot of poignant and guided questions throughout the conversation. Ava had the distinct impression Sylvie was more intrigued than she was willing to let on.

"Actually," Sylvie said, cocking her head to the side. "Are you even sure that there was an egg at all?"

"I'm never positive about anything, sis." Nick crossed his arms over his bony chest and leaned back, drawing in a slow, careful breath. His skin was pasty, like the color of a hazy sky right before it rains. "But I've got a hunch, and in my experience, chasing the hunch has usually worked out."

"Usually, but not always, am I correct?" Sylvie raised one eyebrow. Her eyes flicked over to Carol, then back to Nick so quickly that Ava wondered if she'd imagined it.

An awkward silence hung in the air for one long minute.

Ava let out a small, frustrated sigh. "You have the poem written by Alma, right? Is it here? Can I see it?" she said, cutting through the silence.

"I do." Nick leaned over and pulled open the drawer of his nightstand. Reaching gingerly inside, he grabbed a plastic bag with a single, yellowed piece of paper inside. He held it out to Ava.

Ava took the bag and opened it gently, easing the letter out. The paper felt thin and soft, almost as though it would easily and readily disintegrate between her fingers if she rubbed it hard enough. Carefully, she unfolded it. On the back was a drawing. It had clearly faded and smudged with time, but the detail was still evident. It was an egg, drawn by a master hand, minor strokes of color weaving in and out.

"Do you think this is the egg?" Ava asked.

Nick nodded. "I've done extensive research on Fabergé and his creations, particularly his Easter eggs. There is no record of an egg that looks like that."

"But it looks so ordinary," Ava said, squinting her eyes at the drawing to try and make out more of the detail. "It doesn't look elaborate at all. How do you know this wasn't an egg he made for some wealthy merchant that came passing through? What if it wasn't intended for the Imperial family?"

"Oh, this mystery egg was never intended for the Imperial family," Nick said. "And it wasn't given to a wealthy merchant."

"But how do you know?" Ava asked again.

"Because . . . I just know."

Ava turned the paper over and looked at the writing on the front, scrawling and faded. "What does it say?"

"I've already translated it." He reached into the nightstand and pulled out a small leather-bound book, which he laid in his lap, his wrinkled fingers stroking the cover lightly.

"What's written at the top of the page here?" Ava squinted at the top of the paper in her hands. It looked as though water had splashed on the letter at some pointed, faded ink blotches extending out in sunburst designs, obscuring some of the writing.

"It's unreadable, as are a couple of other words in the poem," Nick replied. "But what I've got is a start. The translation is on the page I've marked."

Ava opened the journal and turned to the page marked with

a scrap of paper. She read through it once silently, then looked up at Nick. "What does this mean?"

"For heaven's sake, Ava, read it out loud to us!" Carol said. Ava turned to her mom with raised eyebrows. "Sorry," Carol said quickly. "You people have me all worked up."

Ava looked back down at the paper and began reading it aloud.

> "'The day I know the secret from the boards
> Hidden beneath the inner chamber of—'"

Ava paused. "That part is missing?" She looked up at Nick. He nodded. She looked down and kept reading.

> "'Held in bondage to the ancient rule,
> Invisible but seen.
> All I knew was stolen then,
> Taken from the watching world.
> The day I know the secret from the boards.
> The day will flee like all that have come before.
> Home is what my heart desires.
> Where the dust settles and the—'"

Ava looked up. "Also missing."

> "'All will be known where the ice doesn't hang.
> The fisted heart of a man now lies
> Not in the light for all to see
> But in the secret chambers of the boards.'"

The room was silent for several moments as they digested the words.

"Gee," Ava said, breaking the quiet. "Too bad that wasn't cryptic or anything."

"Ava," Nick said, "can you get your friend Zak to start doing a little more digging? Actually, you may want to see if he can come here sooner rather than later. I'm going to need to give him specific instructions on how to hack into the files of the Fabergé Museum." His voice trailed off as his eyes closed again. He leaned his head back against the pillow.

"Whoa, whoa. I'm sorry, but what?" Carol leaned forward toward Nick, then shifted her gaze to Ava. "Did he just say Zak would be hacking into the files of the Fabergé Museum?"

Ava nodded. "Um . . . Nick? Can you clarify that for us? Please?"

Nick's breathing grew even and steady, his head lolling to the side and his mouth hanging slightly open. Sylvie pushed to her feet and gestured for Ava and Carol to follow her.

"Alright, Nicky," Sylvie said, her voice barely above a whisper. "It's time for you to rest now."

Nick sighed but otherwise made no response.

"Can I keep this journal with me?" Ava asked.

Sylvie gave an impatient wave of her hand for Ava to leave, and the three women made a hasty retreat from the room, Ava clutching the journal in her hands. They walked to the kitchen and stood around the counter.

"Well, you two might as well go off and do what you need to do," Sylvie finally said with a sigh. "I'll clean up here, then I need to run out for a bit."

"I can clean up for you, Sylvie," Carol said.

Sylvie waved her off and turned toward the sink. "I'm fine."

Carol and Ava glanced at one another, then turned and quickly walked from the kitchen.

"Well," Carol said when they got to the living room. "I guess we should get our stuff out of the car?"

Ava nodded. She gripped the journal between her hands. "And I need to call Zak, then I'm going to sit down and do some more research."

"Of course." Carol nodded. "I'll just find a book to read." She offered Ava a small smile.

"You want to sit with me while you read? That way if I find anything interesting, I can talk through it with you."

"Sure. And, Ava?" She sighed as Ava paused. "What on earth did your father mean about Zak hacking into the museum files?"

Ava shrugged. "I guess it's part of the job."

"I bet they didn't have to hack into Russian files in *Star Wars*," Carol muttered, grabbing her keys from her purse and marching to the front door.

Ava smiled and followed her mom.

Fifteen minutes later, the two had settled on the porch again, the late-morning sunshine warming them as the fans overhead kept the air circulating. It was pleasant and calming, and Ava nestled into the cushions, her laptop propped on her legs as she turned the pages through the journal again.

"Nick's handwriting is the worst," she said. "I can't read half of this. I'm not sure he was even writing in English."

Carol leaned over and squinted at the page Ava was on. "He always did that. When he gets excited, he writes in a weird shorthand that only he can understand."

Ava squinted at the journal again. "I think this symbol here stands for Alma Pihl," she murmured. "And this says something about Bloody Sunday . . ." Her voice trailed off.

"What was that?" Carol asked.

Ava shook her head. "Nothing. I'm just talking to myself."

She rubbed her eyes and set the journal down, opening up her computer and tapping out a few keystrokes.

For the next two hours, the two read to themselves, Ava periodically relaying information to her mom that she found interesting.

"Did you know that the Fabergés had five boys, but the fourth one died after he was born? His name was Nicholas. When they had their fifth boy, they named him Nicholas as well." She raised her eyebrows at her mom. "For someone known to be one of the most creative and artistic minds in history, he wasn't overly original in naming his children."

Carol snorted and returned to her book.

"Oh, this is interesting," Ava said a few minutes later. "In 1905, a group of peaceful protestors was fired upon outside the tsar's palace in St. Petersburg. It happened on Nevsky Prospekt, which wasn't far from Fabergé's workshop. He probably saw the carnage. Several hundred people were killed. They called it Bloody Sunday." She glanced at Nick's journal.

She turned back to her computer screen and continued reading. "This article says that Fabergé was sympathetic to the plight of the people, despite his obvious alliance with the royal family. He even joined the Octobrists in 1906 to show his support for the common man."

"Huh. What were the Octobrists?"

"They were a political movement that formed in 1905 that called for the tsar to fulfill his October Manifesto."

"Right. That's interesting." Carol paused. "And now, for those of us who weren't history majors and who know little to nothing about Russian history, what was the October Manifesto?"

Ava smiled. "It was basically Nicholas the Second's response to the revolution in 1905. It was his attempt to appease the people by ending the autocracy in Russia and granting basic constitutional and civil liberties to the people like free speech and press. It also agreed to create a legislative body that could be elected by the people—the *duma*. The Octobrists were assembled to ensure that the tsar upheld these promises."

"And did he?"

Ava shrugged. "I can't remember all the details. The October Manifesto appeased the people for a time, but it wasn't carried out in a way that made any significant change to how government was conducted in Russia."

"And so, the revolution continued?"

Ava nodded. "All the way until 1917 when the tsar abdicated the throne and was exiled with his family."

"And then was killed, right?"

"Yeah. In 1918."

"Such a tragic story," Carol murmured.

A knock at the front door cut the conversation short. Ava stood up and walked through the kitchen to the front door. She glanced out the window and raised her eyebrows. Pulling open the door, she tried to mask her surprise.

"Hello, hello! Your favorite tech-spert is here!" Zak grinned at Ava, his aviator glasses slipping down his nose as he peered at her above the frames.

Ava blinked, her mouth opening, then shutting, as she formulated a response. "Oh, um . . . hi, Zak. You got here fast. I didn't think you were coming until tomorrow."

She pulled the door open farther so that Zak could wrestle his suitcase into the house. He had a messenger bag slung across his body, a neck pillow around his neck, and a thick coat tucked beneath his arm.

"Well, there's no time to waste, am I right?" he asked. "We need to get our ducks in a row so we can blow this place and find us a treasure."

"Oh, Zak, you're here!" Carol exclaimed as she walked into the room. "How wonderful."

Zak smiled. "Indeed, it is, Miss Carol. And I am ready to work, so let's get cracking, shall we?"

Ava gaped at Zak as Carol reached out and took his coat for him.

"Let me show you to your room." Carol tossed Ava a look over her shoulder.

Ava shook her head and, with an amused half smile, closed the door and followed the two to Zak's room as he remarked repeatedly about the beauty of Sylvie's décor.

"Just stunning," he said over and over.

Ava and Carol stood to the side as Zak turned in circles, a smile stretched wide across his face. He finally stopped and faced them.

"Well, then," he said. "I'd like to sit down and discuss this special project of ours and show you what I've found so far based on the information that Ava gave to me."

"Yeah, sounds good," Ava said. "And when Nick wakes up, he'll want to meet with you and go over your job on this hunt."

"Lovely." Zak clapped his hands. "I will be delighted to meet the great Nick Laine. I found information on him as well. He's quite impressive. His recovery of the Aztec ruins was—"

"Okay, Zak." Ava interrupted, not wanting to discuss Nick. She spun toward the door. "Let's get to it."

They quickly made their way to the kitchen and settled at the table. Zak pulled out his computer and opened up a spreadsheet filled with notes.

"Okay, so I've written down the year that each egg was created by Fabergé and his master craftsmen, and I detailed what the eggs looked like and were named. You'll see in this column, I've listed the eggs that are still missing, and the ones that have been found. I've also tried to list where each found egg is currently being displayed, though there were a few I had a hard time pinpointing, but I'll find them. Oh!"

Ava jumped at Zak's enthusiastic exclamation.

"Did you know that the most recent egg discovered was found by a scrap metal dealer here in the States? It was just a few years ago. The guy bought it for $14,000 and planned to melt it down and sell it. At the last minute, he looked into the details and found that it was the third Imperial egg and was worth $33 million dollars!"

"Wow, Zak," Ava said, eyes widening.

Zak reached into his bag, pulled out a printout of the spreadsheet, and slid it in front of Ava. She looked down at the document, the lines of information spelling out the whereabouts and questions of each of the Imperial Easter eggs. "This is pretty impressive. You did all of this last night?"

Zak nodded. "Anything for you, Ava."

Ava cleared her throat.

"So, one thing that I found in my reading," he continued, "was that Fabergé had three rules for creating eggs, which he established with Alexander the Second when he began this yearly tradition. Each egg had to be shaped like an egg, each creation had to be new and unique, and each egg had to contain a surprise. Outside of those three things, Fabergé's craftsmen had full artistic license to create, and he and his artists did not disappoint."

Ava read over Zak's notes, taking in the detail. "This is amazing. Listen to the detail of some of these eggs." She pulled Zak's computer a little closer and began reading.

"'The *Memory of Azov Egg* was given to Empress Maria in 1891. The surprise was a miniature replica of the ship that her sons were touring on, right down to diamond-encrusted portholes.'" She scrolled down.

"'The *Bay Tree Egg* was made with nephrite'—whatever that is—'diamonds and rubies and looked like a bay tree. When the clockwork animation was wound, a feathered bird appeared, flapped its wings, and sang.'"

"Wow," Carol said.

"Yeah," Ava replied. "No wonder the people found these eggs grotesque. While the common man was starving, the tsar had two of these ornate eggs commissioned every single year. They were so excessive."

"If you look here—" Zak leaned forward and scrolled down, his hand brushing Ava's. He started and stammered as he reached over and pointed at the screen. "Here, um, are the descriptions of the two eggs designed by Alma Pihl, who you asked me to focus on specifically." He glanced at Ava.

"'The *Winter Egg* and the *Mosaic Egg*,'" Ava read. "'They were presented to the tsar in 1913 and 1914.'"

"Yes," Zak answered, "and they were widely regarded as two of the most stunning of all the Easter eggs presented to the tsarina and the empress. It seems that Alma Pihl was incredibly talented."

"Mmmm . . ." Ava scanned his notes. She finally leaned back and looked at him. "This is great, Zak. Really. Thanks for pulling it all together. We're going to start homing in on Alma." She quickly filled him in on what they knew so far, and on the tentative plans for their trip.

"So, we really don't know the exact whereabouts of the egg, then?" Zak asked.

Ava shook her head. "No, but we've got enough to believe that it exists, and that it would either be in St. Petersburg or Finland."

"And what does your gut tell you?" Zak asked.

Ava crossed her arms over her chest. "I don't have a gut feeling on this just yet. But I'm pretty sure Nick does. He's maddeningly slow to share it, though."

"How do you mean?"

Ava shrugged. "He's taking this whole Jedi-Padawan thing a little seriously. It took him forever to show us the poem."

Zak's eyebrows furrowed together, and he looked at Ava curiously.

"Hold on a second." She stood up and walked to the outside couch where she'd left Nick's journal sitting on top of her computer, the baggie with the poem tucked inside the pages. She picked it up gently, then turned and quickly made her way back inside to the table, sliding into her seat next to Zak.

"So, Nick somehow managed to get his hands on one of Alma's poems," Ava said. "Apparently he found it in a cabin in Finland."

Zak looked at her with raised eyebrows.

"Yeah, I know," she said to his unasked question. "It's totally nuts." She gently opened the bag and pulled out the fragile piece of paper. "Alma drew a sketch on the back that we believe could be the missing egg."

Zak leaned forward, brow furrowed, and studied the paper that Ava held open in front of him. "May I?" he asked. She nodded, and he pulled it closer, slowly turning over the page. "Fascinating," he murmured.

"That's a poem that Alma wrote," Ava said. "Nick had it translated." She picked up the journal and held it out to Zak so he could read the translation.

He skimmed over the words quickly. "What does that all mean?"

Ava shrugged. "That's what we're going to need to find out." She leaned over the journal to look at the paper with Alma's poem again, which Zak held in his left hand. Her head nearly touched his, and she heard Zak draw in a quick breath. His hands shook, fumbling the journal and the poem, and they fell to the floor. The journal landed on top of the yellowed paper with a crunch.

"Easy, dude!" Ava reached down to pick the items up. Flecks of paper tumbled to the floor like fall leaves. "This piece of paper is almost a hundred years old." She held it between the tips of two fingers, sighing at the sight of the corner, which had crumbled under the weight of the book. She tossed Zak an annoyed glance, then gingerly folded up Alma's poem and slipped it into the plastic bag.

"I—I'm so s—sorry."

Carol watched him sympathetically. "Zak, let's get you something to eat and drink before Nick wakes up. He'll want to talk with you, and I think he'll be very impressed with your research."

Zak nodded and stood up, tucking his spreadsheet back into his bag. He tossed Ava another look of apology. She swallowed hard and looked away. She hadn't meant to snap at him.

"I'll go grab my stuff and be back in a few minutes," Ava murmured. She walked out to the back porch to grab her computer and papers, sitting down for a brief moment on the couch to gather herself. The door opened, and Ava turned to see her mother step outside. Carol closed the door gently behind her and raised her eyebrows at Ava.

"You are going to have to give that boy a break," Carol whispered.

Ava sighed.

"Ava, he's like a little puppy dog. He follows your every move. You know this, so just be easy on him, okay?"

Ava stood up and followed her mom back into the kitchen where Zak sat at the counter with a plate of cookies and some lemonade. Sylvie had returned and was in the next room getting Nick prepped and ready for another planning session.

"Your aunt made some delicious cookies, Ava," he said.

He slid the plate in her direction and looked at her with a sheepish smile. She grabbed one of the cookies, taking a bite and nodding.

"Yeah, she does that," Ava said. She offered an apologetic smile and hoped he understood the gesture.

"Alright, you two," Carol said. "I'm going to peek my head in to see how Nick is doing. I imagine that as soon as he's up and ready, he'll want you all to sit down with him."

An hour later, the three of them sat around Nick's bed, and Sylvie took her place in the corner chair to observe and interject as needed. He sat up tall, looking better and brighter after having slept.

"Okay, Zak," Nick said. "Your job on this hunt is going to be extremely important, but before I go on, I need you to understand that this job requires a certain level of discretion. You can't share with anyone what you're doing, or how you're going about looking for answers. Are you okay with this?"

Zak paused. "Will I be doing anything illegal?"

Nick shrugged. "Legalities in treasure hunting are blurry.

Technically, there may be a few things required that cross the legal line—"

"Nick!" Carol threw her hands up in the air.

Nick lifted one finger and kept talking. "But ultimately, the way that I hunt makes up for this in the fact that the found treasure is never for personal gain. It's always for the good of others. I've never kept anything I've found. I've given it back to the people to whom it belonged."

"Yeah, but you've profited off your finds," Ava said.

Nick nodded. "Well, a man has to earn a living, doesn't he?" he said with a shrug.

"So, I will be doing something illegal, then?" Zak asked.

"Maybe," Nick said. "Only insomuch as you'll need to do it to find what you're looking for. Also, your job is to protect them. Sometimes, you'll have to bend the rules to do that. How do you feel about this?"

Zak glanced at Ava, then back at Nick. He was silent for only a beat before nodding his head. "Sounds like fun," he said with a smile. "I enjoy a good challenge. I find it gets the blood pumping and makes me feel very alive."

Ava studied Zak, his collared shirt tucked into crisp pants, and she smiled, amusement flashing through her eyes. She turned to see Nick's reaction.

"Yes." Nick grinned. "I can tell you're an adventurous type of guy."

Zak smiled, holding high his head. "I'm ready for my mission then, commander."

"As comfortable as these two might be with everything you just said, Nick," Carol said, "I have some real reservations about it."

"As do I," Sylvie said from her corner where she sat with

a cross-stitch in her lap, quietly sewing as she listened to the plans.

Nick looked back and forth from Carol to Sylvie. "I assumed that you both would. But trust me when I say that if you all do exactly as I tell you to do, you'll be fine."

"And what if things don't go exactly according to plan?" Carol said.

"We'll cross that bridge if we get to it." Nick looked over at Zak. "How are you at hacking into other people's computer files?"

Zak paused. "I know how to do that," he said slowly.

Nick nodded. "I'll need you to find a way to hack into the files of the Fabergé Museum in St. Petersburg, Russia."

Zak's eyes widened. "Okay," he answered, his tone less confident than before. "And what will I be looking for? Assuming I can get into their system at all."

"You'll be looking for any information on Alma Pihl, and on Fabergé himself. Any locked-away photographs or documents, drawings or writings."

"How will we even know what we're looking at, though?" Ava said. "We don't read Russian."

"Xander does," Nick replied.

"Of course he does," Ava muttered under her breath.

"Xander will be there to interpret everything and determine if it's useful or not. He's arriving in St. Petersburg in a couple of days to get your operation headquarters set up. He'll have clothes and wigs and all the tech support you need to make this run as smoothly as possible."

"Um . . . did you say 'wigs'?" Ava asked.

"Yeah." Nick nodded. "You'll need to disguise yourself. Sorry, kiddo, but your look is way too distinctive. You won't get away with anything over there."

Ava ran her hand through her short hair self-consciously.

Nick smiled. "This is the fun part of the job."

"Nicky"—Sylvie leaned forward and stared him down across the room—"you're sending these two kids—and Carol—to Russia with disguises and instructions to hack into the files of a Russian museum. To Russia!" Her eyes widened. "What on earth do you think will happen if they get caught sneaking around in disguise . . . in *Russia*?"

Nick nodded. "I didn't say this wouldn't be dangerous."

Ava swallowed. She avoided eye contact with her mom, knowing what she'd find there. She instead looked at Zak. He stared back at her.

"I'm in if Ava is," Zak said.

"Ava—" Carol began, but Ava waved her off.

"I'm in," she said, shifting her gaze to Nick. "We'll be careful, and we will follow your instructions."

Nick nodded. "And listen." He turned to Carol, who had leaned back in her chair, arms crossed over her chest. "I have Xander on full security detail. If there's even a hint of trouble or danger, he knows the protocol to abort and get you guys out. And he's got Anatoly lined up and ready to go. Anatoly was born and raised in St. Petersburg. He knows the city like the back of his hand. He and Xander will make sure that everything you do is tracked, covered, and traced."

Carol stared back at him, the lines in her face deepening with the skepticism that flashed through her eyes.

"In all my years of hunting," Nick continued, "I've only ever gotten close to being caught once. I know what I'm doing."

"Yes," Carol replied. "And yet, you'll be here in Florida, tucked in your bed, while these two will be essentially operating as spies on Russian soil."

"We will be supremely careful, Miss Carol," Zak said.

Carol sighed. "I'm sure you will, Zak, but I'm still very uncomfortable with all of this."

"Mom?" Ava turned to face her. "It's going to be okay. I really believe that it is. Like Zak said, we'll be careful. And we've got a guy named Xander *Majors* on security detail. I mean, seriously. If this were a book, the guy named Xander would obviously be the hero of the story."

"Well, or the love interest," Nick said. Zak coughed.

Carol shook her head. The corners of her mouth tugged upward as she fought off a smile. "Don't be cute with me right now."

Nick looked back and forth between Ava and Carol, trying to decipher the hidden messages passing between mother and daughter. "Okay, well," he finally said, "let's take a break. I need to rest just a little bit."

"Come on, you three," Sylvie said, standing and walking toward the door. "Let's go make a plan for dinner."

"Uh, Ava?" Nick said.

Ava turned to look at him.

"I'd like a word alone with you for a moment."

"Oh." Ava swallowed hard. "Um, okay."

Sylvie narrowed her eyes, then waved her hand for Carol and Zak to follow her out as Ava sank back down in her chair next to Nick's bed. They stared at one another for a long minute.

"So"—Nick broke the silence—"that was the guy you got to come with you as your tech expert?"

"Well, you only said I needed a computer wiz. You didn't say I needed someone with basic social skills."

Nick chuckled. He picked up the spreadsheet Zak brought and looked it over. Ava glanced at the door. It was the first time she'd been alone with her father in years. He was still a stranger to her. She opened her mouth to speak, then closed it. Then she opened and shut it again.

"Got a question?" Nick put the paper down and turned to Ava.

"Just one?"

He smiled.

"Well, I do have something that I still don't understand."

"Shoot."

"I do believe that your hunch is right, and that there's an egg out there to be found. But I don't understand why this egg would hold any value. It never belonged to the Imperial family. It has no real knowable history. What makes you so sure people will even care about this egg?"

Nick crossed his hands in his lap and looked at Ava for a long moment before answering. "What gives a painting its value? Is the value determined by the particular paint a painter uses on a canvas?"

Ava shrugged. "Not necessarily."

"Is the value determined by the subject matter of the painting, or the weight of the canvas used?" His eyebrows raised. "What *precisely* gives the painting its value?"

Ava paused before answering. "I guess the value comes from the painter itself. It comes from the skill of the one who painted it, and from the value that that particular painter brings to the art."

"Exactly!" Nick snapped his fingers and pointed at Ava.

"Exactly what?"

"Why do you think the *Mona Lisa* is worth an estimated one billion dollars and kept hanging behind bulletproof glass?"

"Because she was painted by da Vinci, and she's regarded to be one of the most unique paintings to come from the Renaissance."

149

Nick nodded. "You know about art."

Ava shrugged. "Again, history major. I took a few classes that dealt specifically with the arts."

Nick studied her, smile fading. He cleared his throat and glanced away. "Okay. So, the *Mona Lisa* gets her value from da Vinci because he is generally regarded to be one of the most masterful painters in history, right?"

Ava nodded.

"So, her intrinsic value isn't found in the paint that was used, or the canvas on which she was painted."

"She was painted on a poplar wood panel, actually," Ava said. "Not canvas. And it's more than da Vinci's name that makes her famous. It's the techniques he used, the way he manipulated shadows to make it seem like her eyes are following you, and the way her smile changes depending on what angle you look at her. That painting was, and still is, cutting edge."

"Yes. But she could only have been such in the capable hands of a master painter. Da Vinci *gave Mona Lisa* her value because he knew how to employ those techniques to create a stunning piece of art."

"Yeah, okay." Ava nodded. "So, you're saying this egg has value because it was created by Fabergé? That the intrinsic value of this egg lies in the fact that it was created by a master craftsman?"

Nick nodded. "The value of an object comes from the one who sculpts it—the one who crafts it with care and skill, and who breathes creative life into it. The master craftsman determines the worth."

"Okay, but still . . . Fabergé created other eggs that aren't nearly as valuable as the Imperial Easter eggs. Why would this one be any different?"

"I just . . . have a hunch," Nick said with a shrug.

"That's it? You just have a hunch?" Ava tossed him a look of exasperation.

"Yes. Fabergé wanted to hide this egg. When the revolution happened in 1917 and everything started falling apart, Fabergé made sure that *this* egg got into the capable hands of someone he trusted. There had to be a reason he didn't want it found. I believe that secret, combined with the fact that Fabergé's initials are on the egg, will give this piece of art immense and extraordinary value."

"But based on Alma's sketch, this egg seems so ordinary. It looks very similar to the very first egg he created for Empress Maria in 1885—the *Hen Egg*."

"You have a good eye for detail," Nick said, a hint of admiration woven in his words.

Ava shrugged, her cheeks flushing.

"My guess," Nick said, "is that the surprise on the inside is going to be a doozy. That's what Fabergé wanted to hide."

Ava leaned back and crossed her arms. They were both silent for a long minute.

"You ready for your first treasure hunt?" Nick finally asked.

Ava nodded. "I've been ready for this for years," she said, her voice soft. Tears pricked at the corners of her eyes, and she blinked hard. She stood quickly, stepping away from Nick's bed. "I should go. You need to get some rest." She turned toward the door.

"Ava," Nick said, his voice cracking.

Ava stopped and looked back at him. He opened his mouth, then shut it. The room had darkened except for the dim light from overhead. Ava watched his eyes flicker from her face to his hands and then back.

"Nothing," he said. "Sleep good. We only have a couple more days before you guys leave. There's still a lot of work to be done."

Ava gave him a single nod, then turned and left the room, closing the door gently behind her.

"Night, Dad," she murmured into the empty hallway, testing out the weight of the word on her tongue. It felt strange and a little uncomfortable. "Nope. Not time for that, yet." She walked up the stairs, her heart thumping, from anticipation or from the almost-connection she had with her father, she could not tell.

St. Petersburg, 1906

A tap at the door made Karl jump, and his eyes flew up in surprise.

Albert stood in the doorway watching him with a mixture of amusement and concern. "Were you sleeping?"

Karl shook his head, then offered a shrug. "Perhaps only for a moment."

Albert stepped into his office and closed the door behind him. "I've just received word that the tsar wants to move forward with his order for an egg this year."

Karl leaned back and let out a long breath. "Really? Now?" He glanced at the calendar on his desk. It was only weeks from Easter. Did the tsar know what he was asking?

"Yes, now. We'll just give him the eggs we prepared two years ago."

"Yes, of course," Karl said absently. He thought of the two eggs that had been sitting unwanted in the safe for the past two years. The future of those eggs had been so uncertain with the war in Japan dragging on and the economic crisis that accompanied it. Karl had wondered how long he could maintain the

153

company under such circumstances, but something had told him to sit tight and wait patiently. He'd continued to pay his employees handsomely when they worked, and he'd also made sure they knew to stay home when the tensions in the street made it too difficult to come to the shop. Albert and Augusta had both encouraged him to make cutbacks in the past two years, but Karl had felt certain the tides would turn. Perhaps this was the moment.

"The *Moscow Kremlin Egg* is one of the finest pieces of art this company has ever designed. It is the perfect way to reintroduce ourselves to the tsarina."

"I don't know," Karl murmured, his brow furrowed. "Perhaps now it will evoke unpleasant memories for her."

"You mean because of the grand duke?"

Karl nodded. Both he and Albert grew silent as they thought of the assassination of Grand Duke Sergei Alexandrovich in 1905. The governor of Moscow, the grand duke had also been the tsar's uncle, and his wife had been the tsarina's sister, Ella.

"He was murdered by an assassin just beyond the Kremlin," Karl said, processing out loud. "His wife watched his carriage explode and picked up pieces of her husband's body in the street. Will an egg that lauds the Upenski Cathedral of Moscow be acceptable given these circumstances?"

Albert was silent for a long moment before answering. "Perhaps not. It may be painful, but what other option do we have? We cannot create another egg in this short amount of time. We'll barely be able to get this egg polished and ready as it is right now."

Karl pinched the bridge of his nose and nodded. "Of course, you're right." He didn't mention the egg he'd been working on in secret through the still hours of the nights. It wasn't near ready either, of course. It was tedious work creating this egg on his own while the rest of his employees slept. He was still working on the diamond trellis design on the outside, having slowed down his progress significantly in order to set each stone just right so that they crisscrossed in a perfect pattern. It wasn't his specialty, setting the stones, so the progress was slow.

"Sir?"

Karl looked up. "Yes?"

Albert studied him for a moment before asking his question again. "I suppose that we will go ahead and prepare the *Swan Egg* to be gifted to the empress as well?"

"Yes, yes," Karl replied with a wave of his hand. "Of course. It's a lovely egg. The empress will adore it."

"Neither of these eggs make mention of the young tsarevitch, though." Albert clasped his hands in front of his body and furrowed his brow. "Will this be a problem?"

Karl leaned back in his chair and mulled it all over. "I think the tsar and his wife will understand. We'll plan a grand surprise for the tsarina next year that hails her son."

If he is still living, Karl thought to himself. Only a few knew of the young heir's disease. It was a secret of the utmost importance, and Karl did not intend to ever speak a word of the horrible truth—that the young tsarevitch would likely not survive childhood due to hemophilia. The rumors had circulated throughout the inner circle of the tsar. Though there had been no official confirmation, Karl had spoken to the family's personal physician out of both curiosity and respect. When the doctor confirmed the suspicions, Karl made the decision to protect the heart of the tsarina in all future designs by avoiding the color red in her eggs.

Connecting with the tsar's young wife had been a challenge.

Alexandra Romanov was quiet and shy. She seemed to want to be a part of the action but didn't at all know how to interject herself fully into the role of tsarina. Though she came off as aloof and snobbish, Karl suspected she was merely unsure of what her place was inside the royal world.

Motherhood suited her well, though. For all her shortcomings as tsarina, Alexandra far made up for them in the way she doted upon and loved her children. It was clear that she much preferred that role to any other.

Her close connection to the self-proclaimed holy man Rasputin was an issue that needed to be resolved, though. Karl thought back to the conversation he'd had with his wife just the day before.

"The tsarina has got to get away from that wicked man," Augusta had clucked. "I'm hearing terrible things about him around town. He's not good, and he is no minister of God. If he were, I'd want nothing to do with that god."

Karl had nodded absently at his wife's ranting, though truth be told, he couldn't agree more. He had wished often that the tsar would put his foot down and remove Rasputin from the royal court, but whatever hold the religious man had on the Romanov family seemed untouchable.

"Ahem."

Karl looked up, surprised to see Albert still standing in his office. How long had he stood there silently?

"Have we decided then?" Albert asked.

Karl nodded. "I suppose we have. Have the eggs polished and prepared for delivery to the tsar."

"The date plates on the eggs still read 1904," Albert replied.

Karl shrugged. "There's nothing to be done about that. There is no time to change it without damaging the eggs."

Albert offered a brief nod. "I'll leave you alone, then. Try to get some rest. You look exhausted."

Karl nodded in return. "I'll be alright."

Albert turned and walked out, quickly ascending the curved staircase and leaving Karl alone once again.

Leaning back, Karl closed his eyes and thought about his secret egg once more. He'd spent the better part of the last few nights working on the secluded place for the egg. Hiding it beneath the floor wasn't ideal, but he'd devised a plan that he felt would preserve the integrity of the precious egg while also keeping it from prying, curious eyes. Using a similar spring mechanism that they'd employed in the *Swan Egg* that would now be given to Empress Maria, Karl figured out how to silently slide the floorboard back and forth so that when closed and latched, it was nearly impossible to detect the difference in the boards.

In the floor, Karl had set an airtight box. Using the same insulation that they used inside the safe to preserve the air temperature, he'd nestled the metal box as deeply as he was able to reach, hiding it beneath the shadows, then sliding the floorboard back into place. The irony of it all was that the secret egg was now buried directly beneath the feet of the men who stood in the gallery and answered questions of interested customers.

Karl felt heavy beneath the weight of being the only one who knew of this egg. It consumed his thoughts day and night. On more than one occasion, he considered telling someone about it, maybe one of his boys or Augusta, but he could never quite bring himself to speak of it out loud. Mostly, he wrestled with what to do with the egg. A few months earlier, he'd nearly convinced himself to give it to the tsar himself. It would be a message of sorts, perhaps even a rebellion. But ultimately, Karl knew he couldn't sacrifice this work of art to the hands of Nicholas Romanov. The moment he'd made the decision, the image of the crumpled boy lying lifeless at the base of the tree on Nevsky Prospekt flooded his mind, and he knew this creation wasn't meant for the royal family—it was meant for Russia.

He needed to preserve it for the people—not the rich and famous who kept him in business, but the poor and the common—the ones who could never afford the pieces in his shop, but who somehow helped revere his name despite their disdain for all that his creations meant for their country. But for this very reason, Karl knew this egg could destroy him. The stakes grew higher as tensions in the country bubbled. If he revealed this secret creation, and the hidden surprises inside, he could very well be accused of inciting violence. His connection to the royal family already set him apart from the common people in his country. This secret would set him apart from everyone.

Karl stood and walked to the window, peering out at the quiet street. He was solemn these days. Gone were his long-ings for excitement and glamour. Now, all he longed for was peace and safety. He missed Amalia, and he missed his wife. He missed raising young children and the thrill of building an empire. He missed it all, but really, he didn't want that life anymore. Now, he only longed for predictability, and life in Russia felt anything but predictable.

Somehow, his secret creation felt like a rebellion. It felt like he was grasping at the younger man he used to be, giving him back a measure of control that had been lost somewhere along the timeline of his life. So he took his time with the secret that plagued him, knowing that there would be a day when he could reveal it to the public. And fearing that that day would come at the cost of his life.

"I am a man at war," he muttered to himself. With a sigh, he turned back to his desk and grabbed his jacket off the back of the chair. It was time to make his rounds in the workshop.

Present Day

A va stepped over the threshold of the building and took in the sights and sounds. She blinked the fatigue from her eyes. Carol put her arm around Ava's shoulders.

"So, this is Russia." Ava looked up at her mom, eyes shining. "I can't believe we're here."

"I can't believe it either," Carol murmured.

Ava closed her eyes for a brief second to capture the image of the city she'd seen an hour before as their plane descended through the clouds. In the distance, she had seen the city's grid-like layout, the rows of buildings all joined together on the banks of the Neva and Fontanka rivers. From the vantage point of the birds, she caught a glimpse of the bright colors that gave St. Petersburg its fairy-tale quality. She'd clutched in her hands the book that she purchased at a used bookstore just before they left a few days earlier. It was a book of translated poems by Alexander Pushkin, one of Russia's literary heroes and a Petersburg man. As they'd made their descent, she read one of Pushkin's most famous stanzas from his poem "The Bronze Horseman: A Petersburg Story."

> I love thee, work of Peter's hand!
> I love thy stern, symmetric form;
> The Neva's calm and queenly flow
> Betwixt her quays of granite-stone.

Ava opened her eyes and blinked, staring up at the sky. It was one of those hazy gray days—the kind that makes you think that the sun wants to push its way through the clouds but just doesn't quite have the strength.

Cars and buses wove in and out on the street before them, men and women dressed in stylish business attire, walking assuredly from the airport to their waiting transportation. Ava pulled the scarf up around her chin to try and stave off the chill as she took it all in, her heart thumping beneath her layers of clothes.

"It's really cold here, isn't it?" Carol asked with a shiver.

Zak stepped up beside the two women, his neck pillow atop his shoulders. He looked around at the bustling street outside the airport, and he drew in a deep breath, then let it out slowly.

"It smells different than I expected," he said.

Carol and Ava turned to him, Carol's mouth turned up in an amused smile. Ava knew her mother had grown fond of Zak's quirky manner. They'd spent hours talking on the plane.

"You expected a smell?" Ava asked.

"Well, sure," Zak said. "Every country has a smell."

"Um . . . what?" Ava asked.

"Yes," Zak continued. "India smells like curry and heat. London smells like baked bread and expectation."

"Heat? Expectation?" Ava gaped at him.

Zak nodded as though what he said was obvious and sensible. "America smells like sugar and potential. And this place smells like . . ." He paused and sniffed the air. "Well, it smells like beets and survival."

"That's very . . . astute of you, Zak." Carol pinched Ava's arm.

"Oh, um . . . yeah. Good observation," Ava said with a nod.

Zak smiled and adjusted his neck pillow. "Thank you. And might I add this morning, Ava, that you look quite ravishing despite our long hours of travel."

Carol tried to cover her laugh as Ava stuttered out a quick thank-you to Zak. The three turned to the right, walked away from the doors, and down the sidewalk outside the bustling airport. They stopped again and looked around.

"Nick said that Xander would already be here and would take us to our place. I want to grab a hot shower and some coffee, then I want to get to work." Ava pulled her phone from her bag and glanced over their itinerary again. They would spend their first day touring the city and formulating their plans to retrace Fabergé's steps.

On their last day of preparations before leaving, Nick had told Ava that she was to visit St. Petersburg under the guise of a writer who was looking to write up a new book on the House of Fabergé.

"Don't let anybody know why you're really there," Nick said. "They'll be wary enough of you as it is, coming in as an American writer. If they suspect you're fishing for information for anything other than writing a book, it could get dicey."

"Dicey how?" Carol asked. Nick had just shrugged his shoulders in response.

"Do we know what this Xander fellow looks like?" Zak asked, scanning the crowd.

Ava shook her head. "All I know is that he's British, and he's meant to be our 'muscle.'"

Zak cleared his throat and straightened his shoulders, attempting to stretch out his height. "Oh, right. The muscle."

"Ava? Carol?"

The three turned toward the honeyed voice that called out their names. A man walked toward them, tall and confident, his broad chest obvious even beneath the puffer jacket he wore. His blue jeans clung to thick thighs, and he wore a skullcap, which only highlighted the sharp features of his face, his dark eyes, strong jaw, and stubbled chin.

"Oh my gosh, you have *got* to be kidding me," Ava muttered as he walked toward them.

"Easy," Carol murmured.

"That guy looks like he stepped out of an Abercrombie and Fitch ad," Ava hissed.

The man stepped up to them and smiled, a single dimple appearing on his right cheek, and held his hand out to Ava.

"I'm Xander Majors," he said, his British accent as perfect and lilting as Colin Firth's.

"Of course you are," Ava said, placing her hand in his and trying not to blush.

Carol reached over and shook Xander's hand next. "It is a pleasure to meet you, Xander. We've heard wonderful things about you and your father from Nick. I'm Carol."

"Yes," Xander replied with a smile. "And I've heard equally lovely things about the pair of you." He turned to Zak and held out his hand. "Hello, mate," he said.

Zak gripped his hand and stood as tall as he could, his head only reaching as far as Xander's chin. "Yes, and hello to you."

Xander eyed Carol's and Ava's bags and held out his hands. "May I carry those for you?"

"Of course." Carol handed him her bag.

"I'm good," Ava answered, chin held high.

Xander nodded. "Right. Well, follow me. I've got the car waiting for us."

They walked several paces down the sidewalk, and Ava watched as just about every single person they passed did a double take when they saw Xander. She shook her head in frustration.

"What is the problem?" Carol whispered in Ava's ear.

Ava turned to her mom and rolled her eyes. "I feel like this is some kind of elaborate prank. How are we supposed to be inconspicuous walking around with someone like him?"

"What are we discussing, ladies?" Zak asked, jogging along-side Carol and Ava, his backpack bouncing on his back as the wheels of his roller bag tapped out a frenetic rhythm behind him.

"Nothing, Zak." Ava glanced at her mom and saw the look in Carol's eyes. It was a look she'd grown accustomed to through the years—the look that said she'd better shape up if she wanted Carol to back off. Ava clamped her mouth shut and sped up her pace behind Xander.

Several minutes later, they approached a black car. Xander tapped the trunk, which popped open, and they all set their bags in the back, then walked around and slid into the back seat of the car. Xander sat in the front seat next to the driver.

"This is Anatoly," he said, looking at them over his shoulder. "He'll be taking us from place to place this week."

"Oh!" Ava smiled. "Um . . . *privyet*, Anatoly. Nick told us a lot about you. He said there wasn't any Russian that he trusted more."

Anatoly nodded from behind the wheel. "Hello." He sat back against the front seat, broad-shouldered and thick, his dark hair thinning in a round patch on the back of his head. He looked at them in the rearview mirror, heavy-lidded eyes over a pockmarked face, cheeks that looked swollen, like he'd spent too much time drinking for too many years. He had a bulbous nose, thick and round. His dark suit stretched tight across his back, and his fat fingers wrapped around the steering wheel.

Ava stared at him curiously for a long moment before shifting her eyes away. Though Nick hadn't described Anatoly to them in detail, he didn't look like the image she had conjured up in her mind of Nick's trusted Russian comrade.

"Right," Xander said. "Why don't we head back to the hotel and let them get freshened up." He glanced down at his watch. "It's nine thirty now," he said, turning around to look at Ava. "Would you like to have some breakfast before we go to the hotel?"

"Is there food at the hotel?" Ava asked.

Anatoly shook his head. "No food left in hotel," he answered in a thick, Russian accent. "Breakfast is finished."

"Oh," Ava said. "Well, I guess if there's someplace we can run into quickly, that would be good."

Xander nodded. "Of course. We'll stop at the supermarket and let you get a few items that you can eat on the go, then we will go to the hotel."

"Okay," Ava answered. She turned and looked out the window, watching as they maneuvered their way from the airport and onto the road. Cars were everywhere, the lines in which they drove less structured than in America. Horns honked endlessly as vehicles weaved in and out. Carol gripped her handbag in her lap while Zak sat next to her smiling at nothing.

"Is this what it's like driving in India?" Carol asked Zak.

"Oh, heavens, no," Zak said. "This isn't nearly as chaotic."

Ava soaked it all in, the sights and sounds. Her heart thumped with excitement, and her mind raced as she thought of all she needed to accomplish. Her number one priority was discovering why Peter Karl Fabergé would have created a secret egg and hidden it. She'd read countless materials in the past week, looking for any clues that would tell her more about this egg and where it could be now, but she'd come up empty every time. All she had was Alma's poem and Nick's hunch.

After a quick but interesting stop at the local supermarket, Anatoly took them to their hotel in the heart of St. Petersburg. Before they turned into the front courtyard, Xander turned in his seat and faced them.

"Grab that bag down there by your feet, please," he said.

Ava pulled a large bag up and handed it to him. Xander opened it and reached inside.

"Put these on," he said. He handed Ava a black hat and a pair of oversized sunglasses. He gave Carol a scarf as well as sunglasses. Finally, he pulled out a fedora for Zak and handed it to him, along with a large scarf.

"Cover your faces as much as possible. When we get inside, I'll trail behind you a few paces. I've already checked you in. Go straight to the elevators and take them to the fifth floor. Don't look at anyone or make eye contact. We want to keep you as hidden as possible."

Ava looked at her mom with wide eyes, pulling the hat onto her head and putting the sunglasses on. "I can hardly see through these things!"

"You'll manage," Xander replied, the smile evident in his voice. He turned to Anatoly and offered a few instructions in

Russian. Anatoly nodded and turned into the courtyard, stop-ping in front of one of the side doors rather than right in front.

"Nick put you all up in one of the best hotels in the city," Xander said, glancing back at them over his shoulder.

Ava squinted through her glasses at the State Hermitage Museum Official Hotel and drew in a deep breath. The pale yellow exterior was lined with grand, white columns. Anatoly pulled the car to a stop and put it in park.

"You all get out here and walk through the lobby like you've been here before and you own the place," Xander said. "Here are your room keys. When you get to the fifth floor, go straight to your rooms and wait for me to get there. I'll bring your bags up."

Ava and Carol nodded. Zak fumbled with his fedora, then wound the scarf around his neck so that it covered the bottom half of his face. The three pushed open the doors and stepped into the frigid air. Ava squared her shoulders and blinked a few times, wishing she could better see the hotel without the barrier of the sunglasses. She walked briskly into the lobby, Carol and Zak on her heels, and took in the opulent interior. High ceilings and an arched entryway showcased a marbled staircase that curved upward. Yellow and gold accents marked the furniture, the details in the ceilings and walls lined in gilt. Ava's mouth fell open as she peered at the dimmed grandeur through the dark lenses of her glasses.

"Well, this beats the Holiday Inn, now, doesn't it?" Carol murmured, stepping up beside Ava.

"I have never seen anything like this," Ava breathed.

"Right then, ladies." Zak walked up next to them. He kept his eyes trained forward and jutted his chin out. "There are the elevators. Shall we?"

The three walked confidently to the elevators and pushed the button. As they waited, they heard the *click-clack* of a woman's heels coming toward them.

"*Izvinite pozhaluysta, a vy kuda?*"

Ava and Carol froze. Zak turned to the woman and offered a broad smile. "I'm so sorry," he answered. "But we do not speak Russian."

"Oh, of course. Please excuse me," the woman said. She wore a crisp uniform, her blond hair pulled into a tight bun at the nape of her neck. "I was curious to know if you were guests at this hotel?" Her thick Russian accent made her words sound exotic and terrifying all at once.

Ava turned and gave her a tight-lipped smile.

"Oh, yes. Of course!" Zak held up his room key and grinned. "We checked in late last night. We just enjoyed our first walk in the city this morning. It is quite lovely here. It's our first time to St. Petersburg."

The elevator dinged and the door opened.

The woman nodded, offering a perfect smile in return. "Yes," she said with a nod of her head. "It is a wonderful city. If you need any suggestions on things to do, please come visit me." She gestured toward her desk across the lobby. She then reached into the elevator and held the door for them as they stepped inside.

"*Spasibo*," Ava said softly.

"You are very welcome here at the State Hermitage Museum Hotel," the woman said. "Thank you for choosing to stay with us." She stepped back and let the door close between them.

Carol let out a long sigh. "Well, that was terrifying," she muttered.

Ava turned to Zak. "Way to think quickly," she said.

Zak grinned at her in return.

The door opened a moment later, and they glanced into the empty hallway. Zak looked at their keys. He handed one to Carol. "It looks like we're across the hall from one another," he said.

Quickly, they made their way down the hall. Ava stopped at her door and unlocked it. Zak did the same behind her.

"See you all in a few moments," Zak whispered. With a grin, he slipped into his room.

Ava pushed the door open, stepping inside with Carol close behind. The room was small, with two full-size beds pushed against the wall. White and yellow accents gave the space an open, airy feel, and the gilt bedposts made it seem ornate.

Carol drew in a deep breath and let it out slowly. "Well, isn't this lovely."

They set down their things, and Ava walked to the window and pushed open the curtains, staring down into the courtyard of the hotel. The St. Petersburg skyline stood proudly in the distance.

"Look." Ava pointed. "There's the Alexander Column. See the angel on top?"

Carol stepped to the window and looked out over Ava's shoulder. "It's beautiful. How did you know that was the Alexander Column?"

"History major, Mom," Ava said. She turned and smirked. "And you thought that would never come in handy."

Carol made a playful face at her in return.

Ava stared at the large, stone angel atop the column that stood in the center of Palace Square. Beyond it, the waters of the Neva lapped in a rhythmic dance. "Did you know that all those buildings used to house the Winter Palace where the

Russian emperors lived from 1763 to 1917? Now the Winter Palace is one of five buildings that make up the State Hermitage Museum, and it houses about three million exhibits." Ava shook her head. "This is so cool. Nick really came through on this one."

Carol looked at Ava quizzically. "Did you think he wouldn't?"

Ava shrugged, opening her mouth to answer, when the sound of a knock stopped her. Walking to the door, she leaned in close. "Yes?" she said.

"It's me."

Recognizing Xander's voice, Ava pulled open the door and he quickly stepped in, dragging their bags behind him.

"Here are your things, ladies," he said. "I'm in the room right next door. When you're ready to come over, simply ring my room—I'm 529. Let it ring once, then hang up. I'll unlock my door for you to slip inside. Make sure no one is in the hallway when you come."

Ava and Carol nodded.

"Right. I'll go tell Zak. We'll be seeing you soon, then." He slipped out into the hall, and the door closed quietly behind him.

Ava turned to her mom and drew in a deep breath. "I'm going to take a shower."

Forty-five minutes later, Ava and Carol leaned out into the bright hallway to find it empty. Across from them, Zak's door opened. The three stepped out and quickly walked to Xander's room next door. They entered quietly, shutting and locking the door behind them. Ava turned to get a good look at Zak. His hair was wet and slicked to the side. He wore a pair of tight, black pants and a bright green sweater, both of which appeared to have been freshly ironed.

"You look refreshed, Zak!" Carol said with a smile.

"Indeed. I feel like a new man!" He looked at Ava, her short blond hair tousled and her face free of makeup. She wore a long-sleeve black T-shirt and faded blue jeans. She looked like the All-American girl next door. Zak gave her a shy smile.

They turned and took in the sight of Xander's room. It was larger, a nook carved out across from the beds where a small couch and two oversized chairs sat in a semicircle. The room was richly designed, with a polished, dark banister separating the hallway leading from the front door to the sleeping quarters.

"Come in, guys!" Xander said with a wave. He stepped out of the bathroom wearing a tight T-shirt and fitted jeans.

Ava's cheeks immediately grew hot. "Oh! Uh . . . Hi! Nice . . . um . . . room." She looked around in an attempt to not stare directly at his chiseled physique.

Xander grinned. "Yeah." He wiped his hands on a small hand towel, then gestured them toward the sitting area. "Nick spared no expense."

The four of them sat down around the small table. "We'll conduct most of our operations from this space," he said. "Zak, you'll want to work here during the days, as I have all the equipment you need to encrypt your computer. Ladies, I've got your clothes set up by day so that we can easily keep track of what you're supposed to be doing and where. There are a couple of different wigs that go with your outfits. I believe Nick mentioned this to you."

"He did." Carol crossed her arms. "I'm still not happy about it."

Xander nodded with a small smile. "He told me you'd say that."

"Can we see the itinerary?" Ava asked.

Xander produced a pile of folders and handed each of them a file with their name on it. "In here, you'll find three different sets of identification papers, including passports. Make sure you always have these IDs on you when you leave. I'll take your real passports and put them in the safe."

"This is awesome," Ava whispered. She glanced up to see Xander staring at her and looked away quickly as her cheeks grew warm.

"Ava, most of the time when we leave this room, you'll be going as Bethany Hansen. You're a language arts teacher from St. Louis. You love Shakespeare and literature and all things design."

"Uh, I know nothing about Shakespeare," Ava said. "I've only read *Romeo and Juliet*, and I didn't understand it until I saw that Leonardo DiCaprio's movie version of the story. What if someone wants to talk about Shakespeare?"

Xander smiled. "We aren't going to actually mention the Shakespeare fact. I just wanted to give you a little history so that you could more easily get into character. Nick used to create entire backgrounds for himself before he headed out in disguise."

"Oh, I see. So . . . I'm a literary nerd?"

Xander chuckled. "Pretty much," he answered. "You're here to do research for a new book on Peter Karl Fabergé. You want to know everything you can about his genius, and your book will highlight all the good things about him, and about the history of Russia. When you speak to the docent at the Fabergé Museum, give her as much praise as you possibly can, and gush about Fabergé's creations."

Xander turned to Zak who was flipping through his file.

"I don't have any identification papers in here," Zak said.

"Yeah, mate," Xander replied. "That's because you won't be leaving the hotel. You stay here and monitor our every move. You're our eyes and ears while we're out." Xander gestured to the laptop on the table in front of them. "This is the computer you'll use. I'll help you set up your own computer with the encryption software for research purposes."

Zak's face fell. "Oh. That's all I do? How will I monitor you all?"

"All of our clothing has tiny cameras pinned to it. You'll be able to see things that we won't, from multiple different angles."

"And what am I looking for?"

"Well, while we're out, you're making sure no one is tracking us. If you see anyone in more than one of the places we visit, you need to alert us. I'll have an earpiece in for communication. We also need you to take screenshots of anything that you feel would be of worth for us to study further. Your position is actually extremely valuable and necessary to the success of this hunt."

Zak nodded, the disappointment in his eyes filtering out slowly. "And what do I do when you're not out and about?"

"You start working on getting access to the files of the Fabergé Museum. We need to know their layout, the security, and everything we possibly can that they don't put out for display in the front. Most importantly, we're looking for secret files that might contain information on Alma Pihl, on Fabergé's involvement in the Russian Revolution, on the dissolution of the House of Fabergé, and on Fabergé's whereabouts after the tsar abdicated the throne."

"I thought we already knew that," Ava said. "Fabergé snuck out of the country on a diplomatic train in 1918 by dressing as a British soldier. He made his way to Switzerland, but never recovered from the events of 1917 and died in 1920."

"Yes, that's what *ultimately* happened to Fabergé," Xander said, "but we don't have much information on how and where he lived during the year between the start of the revolution and when he left. Where was he? What was he doing? Who was he with?"

"Alma Pihl didn't leave the country until 1921," Carol said.

"That's true," Ava said.

Carol smiled. "I remember facts too." She turned to Xander. "Now, what is my role in this ridiculous plot?"

Xander smiled. "Most of the time, you and I will be trailing. We are a wealthy mother and son here on a cultural trip—Mary and Alex Morgan. We'll be with Ava without actually being with her."

Carol narrowed her eyes. "Okay," she said slowly. "But you're British, and I'm American. How will that play into our story?"

"How is your British accent?" Xander crossed his arms and leaned back in his chair.

"Oh . . . um . . ." Carol stammered. "Can I have a spot of tea?" she asked in her best British accent.

Ava snorted. "You sound like a bad version of Mrs. Potts from *Beauty and the Beast*."

Carol gave Ava a playful swat on the arm, her cheeks red. "No one told me I'd need a degree in acting for this job!"

Xander laughed. "Don't worry, Miss Carol. I happen to be able to speak with a near flawless American accent. So, you won't have to become a Brit for this trip," he said, switching to his American accent.

Ava gave a small shake of her head, marveling at the fact

that he somehow sounded just as sexy as an American as he did as a Brit.

"Okay," she said, her voice cracking. She cleared her throat. "We have our identities and costumes—"

"Which I am still uncomfortable with," Carol said.

"And our itinerary," Ava continued. "The goal is to figure out what happened to the egg between the years 1917 and 1921. We believe that Alma Pihl had it in her possession, but we need some proof of that."

Zak turned to Xander. "On the off chance that I do need to leave this hotel for any reason at all, what is it suggested that I do?"

"Dress sharp, mate," Xander replied. "Slick your hair, tuck in your shirt, walk with shoulders back." Xander looked at Zak's combed hair and tucked-in shirt approvingly. "You're already in character, I see! So, the thought is you're a wealthy business-man here to talk with the bigwigs. I have a suit in your size in the closet for the rare time you might need to leave."

Zak nodded. "Okay, so it's possible I might need to leave at some point, then?" he asked, his voice laced with hopeful undertones.

"Look, mate, anything can happen on these trips. This isn't the safest line of work. Nick did warn you all of that, didn't he?"

They nodded, Carol crossing her arms and pursing her lips.

"You're in particularly dangerous territory here for a couple of reasons. This is Russia, and you're from America. There's a history there. You've got to keep your heads up, yeah?"

They all nodded.

"There's also a big prize at stake here," he continued. "Find-ing this egg could have incredible financial repercussions, so this isn't something to be taken lightly. We're on a true mission, one with historical and financial significance. We all need to be on guard, yeah?"

They nodded again. Ava stifled a yawn as she tucked her folder under her arm. Xander glanced at her and smiled, causing her stomach to flip.

"Right. I really need you all to head back to your rooms and rest. It doesn't do us any good for you to start the mission exhausted."

Ava blushed and nodded. She and Carol stood, Zak on their heels.

"Does Nick know we made it?" Ava asked Xander.

"I'm calling him now," Xander said. "I'm sure he'll want to connect with you all later. Today, just plan to rest. This afternoon, we'll head over to the Hermitage if you'd like. That will give you a bit of the feel of the grandeur of this city. Tomorrow, we go to the Fabergé Museum."

"Cool. Thanks." Ava turned to her mom. "I want to talk to Xander alone a minute. I'll meet you back in the room."

Carol nodded. She and Zak opened the door to Xander's room and peered into the hallway. They stepped out quickly and moved toward their rooms.

Xander's door clicked to a close, and Ava turned to face him. "I have something I want you to look at." She reached into her shoulder bag and pulled out Alma's poem. "Nick gave me this before we left. It's a poem written by Alma Pihl."

"Wonderful! Nick told me you'd be bringing this."

Xander gestured for Ava to come sit next to him on the couch. She hesitated for a brief moment, then walked over and sank down beside him. She pulled the paper out of the plastic bag and gently opened it.

"Alma drew a sketch of what we believe to be the missing egg on the back," she began, holding it out so Xander could see.

"Amazing," he whispered. "May I?"

Ava surrendered the poem to him and leaned in a little closer.

"*The secret beneath the boards*," Xander read quietly. "Interesting. Did Nick have any thoughts on what it meant?"

Ava shook her head. "Talking through all of this with Nick was like trying to talk with someone who speaks in riddles." She sighed. "But no, he didn't know what it meant. He felt like that would start to become clearer once we were in the country."

Xander nodded. He turned the page over and looked at the sketch on the back. Leaning forward, he squinted, then he stood up and walked across the room, clutching the poem in his hand. He reached into a black bag on the floor and scrounged around for a moment before pulling out a magnifying glass. He returned to the couch and sat next to Ava, holding the magnifying glass over the text.

"It looks like something has been erased on here," he said. "See there?"

He held the magnifying glass over a small section of the corner and pointed at it. Ava leaned forward and saw what he was pointing at. Faint markings on the page formed the image of something that Ava couldn't quite decipher.

"Is it a drawing or a word?" she asked.

Xander leaned forward. "I think it's a drawing." He pointed at the faint image. "See? Look how it curves around here, and then again down there."

Ava studied it closely and nodded. "Yeah, I see it. There's no way to discern what that is, though."

Xander shook his head. "No, you're right. But it's good to know it's there. Everything is a clue." He smiled at Ava.

She pursed her lips and looked away, annoyed with herself for being at all affected by this handsome man with the ridiculous name.

"Can I keep this right now?" Xander asked. "I'd like to spend a little more time looking at it under the glass, if that's okay."

"Sure, it's fine." Ava stood and turned toward the door of his room. "Well, I should go," she said, her voice a little louder than she'd intended. "I'll see you in a couple of hours?"

Xander stood as well. "You got it."

Ava's heart fluttered as he looked down at her. She pulled open his door and peered into the hallway. Seeing no one, she stepped out and walked quickly to her own room. Xander's door clicked shut behind her.

"Pull it together, weirdo," Ava muttered to herself. She knocked gently, and seconds later Carol pulled open the door. Ava stepped inside and stared at her mom. "So, here we go," she said.

"Here we go," Carol murmured in return.

The next morning, Ava stepped off the elevator, adjusting her bag on her shoulder. She forced herself to keep her hands down, despite the fact that she desperately wanted to reach up and scratch her head underneath the long, thick blond wig she was wearing. The fake hair cascaded down over her shoulders and felt entirely uncomfortable and foreign. She hadn't had long hair in almost a decade for a reason.

The jacket Xander had given her was thick with a fur lining, and it hung to her waist. She wore tight black jeans and a long tunic, which hung out below the bottom of the coat. It was the trendiest outfit she had ever worn, and she had never felt more out of place in her life. She pulled the sunglasses Xander had given her out of the cross-body computer bag she wore and put them on. Catching a glimpse of herself in a nearby mirror, she almost did a double take. She looked nothing like herself.

The ding of the elevator behind her signaled Xander and Carol's exit. Ava turned and glanced at the pair, stifling a cough as she saw Xander step through the doors. He wore a crisp, navy suit, perfectly tailored to fit his body. He had his hair slicked back and wore a pair of dark-rimmed glasses, which somehow made him look even more handsome, like a new and improved version of Clark Kent.

Carol wore a dark pantsuit that made her look ten years younger. Ava had never seen her mother quite so glamorous. She'd put on more makeup than usual, assuming that if she was to be a wealthy American on tour with her son, she'd better look the part. She wore a short, bob-length brown wig and carried a long brown trench coat over her arm. Ava looked away without acknowledging the two. She walked out the front door as confidently as she could in the stiff boots Xander had given her, nodding at the doorman as she passed. Anatoly stood next to the car. When he saw Ava coming, he opened the back door for her. She slid into the car and waited as he walked around to the front and slid behind the driver's seat.

"I will drive around the block and gather Xander and your mother," Anatoly said.

Ava nodded. She let out a long breath and looked out the window as they pulled into traffic. Glancing back up front, she saw Anatoly watching her in the rearview mirror.

"You look good," he said with an approving nod. "You look like stylish Russian girl."

"But I'm supposed to be an American girl," Ava said.

Anatoly shrugged. "Is okay, though. When you look like stylish Russian girl, you blend in better and get more respect. Americans often so sloppy. They do not dress nice enough."

Ava smiled. "Thanks," she said.

Anatoly slowed down and pulled to the side of the road, ignoring the car behind him as the driver laid on his horn. Ava looked back and saw her mother and Xander walking swiftly up the sidewalk. A moment later, the door opened and the two slid into the back seat. Ava blushed as Xander squeezed next to her, the weight of his body pressing into hers.

"It is cold out there!" Carol exclaimed, pulling the door shut. "Floridians have no business trying to walk in such weather."

Xander laughed. He turned to look at Ava. "Well," he said, eyebrows raised. "You look very nice."

Ava cleared her throat. "Yeah, thanks," she said. She felt her cheeks get hot.

Xander leaned forward and said something quietly in Russian to Anatoly.

Ava glanced at her mom behind his back. Carol gave her a good-natured wink. Ava pursed her lips and looked away as Xander leaned back between them.

"Ava," he said, "I sent Anatoly a copy of Alma's poem. He had an interesting observation."

Ava's eyes shifted from Xander to Anatoly's gaze in the rearview of the mirror. "Oh," she said. "What did you think, Anatoly?"

"Are we okay parked here on the side of the road?" Carol asked, shifting nervously in her seat.

"Yes. Is Russia," Anatoly replied with a wave of his hand as he turned in his seat to face them. "May I have copy of poem please?"

Ava reached in her bag and pulled out the copy of Alma's poem that she'd made earlier, not wanting to bring the original out of the hotel. The original Russian was on one side of the paper, and she'd hastily scribbled Nick's translation on the side. She handed it to Anatoly.

"Look here," he said.

Xander leaned forward next to Ava, their shoulders pressed together. She cleared her throat and focused on Anatoly.

"The translation is not accurate." Anatoly pointed at the page. "Is missing correct wording."

"Like what?" Ava asked.

Anatoly pressed his lips together and shook his head. "Well, is missing important . . . uh . . . how you say in English . . ." He looked at Xander and said something in Russian.

"Basically, what he's saying is there's nuance missing in the translation," Xander said.

"Okay," she said. "Where?"

"Well," Anatoly said, "here first line is translated same as seventh line, but there is small variation that is important. See"—he pointed—"first line says, 'The day *I* know the secret from the boards.' But *here*"—he moved his finger down the page—"says 'The day *they* know the secret from the boards.'"

"Interesting. The secret from the boards?" Ava looked at him. "What does that mean?"

He shrugged. "Is all confusing. But I am . . . uh, how you call it? I am man of science. I do not know the poetry." He handed her the paper, and Ava sat back in her seat, reading the poem aloud.

> "'The day I know the secret from the boards,
> Hidden beneath the inner chamber of—' *That part is
>   missing.*
> 'Held in bondage to the ancient rule,
> Invisible but seen.
> All I knew is stolen, then
> Taken from the watching world.
> The day they know the secret from the boards . . .'"

She glanced up at Anatoly's gaze. He gave a small nod. Ava looked back down and continued to read.

"'The day will flee like all that have come before.
Home is what my heart desires,
Where dust settles and the—' *Something* . . .
'All will be known where the ice doesn't hang.
The fisted heart of a man now lies,
Not in the light for all to see,
But in the secret chambers of the boards.'"

Ava looked from the page to Xander and then up to Anatoly. "This is painfully cryptic."

"Seems to me we've got ourselves a treasure map," Xander replied.

"You think?"

Xander nodded. He took the paper from Ava's hand, then pressed his finger to his ear.

"Zak? Can you hear me, mate?" He waited a beat, then nodded. "Good."

"You can talk to Zak?" Ava asked.

"Yeah," Xander replied. "He's all set up in the room and confirmed he sees everything we see, so we're good to go."

"Where's my camera?" Ava asked, glancing down at her outfit. "I don't want to accidentally cover it up."

Xander reached over and tugged on the collar of her shirt. "It's inside this pin here," he said, fingering a small flower pin tucked into the fabric.

Ava's heart fluttered at the nearness of his fingers. She reached up and touched the button on her collar lightly. "Got it. Where's your camera?"

Xander pointed to a diamond-shaped button at the top of his dress shirt. "And your mom's camera is here, inside her brooch." He pointed at the golden flower pin on Carol's jacket.

"What happens when she puts on her coat?" Ava asked.

"I'll be with her, so Zak will still see what he needs to see." He pressed his finger to his ear again. "You hear me then, yeah?" Xander waited a beat. "Cool," he said. "As you're sifting through files, if you come across anything that references the lines in this poem, will you pull it out?" He paused. "Thanks."

He handed the page back to Ava, and she tucked it back into her bag. "So, you think it's a treasure map, then? Really?"

Xander nodded. "Yeah, seems to me that Alma Pihl was leaving us a little message about the egg."

Ava leaned back. "The day I knew the secret from the boards," she murmured. She was silent for a beat, then shot up and turned to Xander.

"Hold on. Zak can see our every move?"

"Yeah."

"So, what do we do if we need to go to the bathroom?"

Xander chuckled. "Just flip up your collar. He won't be able to see anything, and he can't hear you, only me, so all's well."

Ava narrowed her eyes, then slowly leaned back against the seat.

Carol snickered from the other side of Xander. "You've just been dissecting a potential treasure map in cryptic code, and that was the first question you thought to ask?"

Ava shrugged, then turned and looked out the window. The cloud cover from earlier had burned off, leaving the sky vibrant, the cerulean backdrop lighting up the city. Rows of cars snaked their way through the boulevards, but if Ava concentrated, she could dismiss them easily. She imagined what it must have looked like a hundred years earlier when horse-drawn carriages were prevalent. The busy thoroughfare would likely have been crowded with people, most of them dressed elegantly, as it would have been the upper echelon of society who frequented the streets surrounding the Winter Palace.

"*I love thee, work of Peter's hand,*" Ava murmured.

"What was that?" Xander asked.

Ava turned. "I was just thinking of the poem I read by Pushkin." She looked back out the window. "This city is romantic, isn't it?"

"Totally," Xander agreed. "Some of the most famous writers in Russia found their way here, and they never left." He leaned over her and pointed out the window. "See over there? The gilt statue?"

Ava nodded. "That's the spire of the Saints Peter and Paul Cathedral inside the fortress walls."

Xander nodded. "You know your stuff."

"She has a headful of knowledge that hasn't been useful until the last two weeks," Carol piped up from beside him.

Xander chuckled. "Well, Nick did tell me she was much smarter than even she understood." He gave Ava a quick glance. "He also said you had a bit of a stubborn streak."

Ava blinked a few times, shifting her eyes away from Xander and her mother and looking out at the city passing them by. She chewed on her bottom lip for several minutes before turning back to face him.

"So, are we going to visit the fortress while we're here?" she asked Xander.

His eyes locked on hers with an intensity that made her shift in her seat. "If there's time, we should. You can't really understand the unique history of St. Petersburg without visiting the fortress."

Ava glanced back out the window, then turned, a quizzical

look flashing through her eyes. *"Held in bondage by the ancient rule. Hidden beneath the secret chambers,"* she said.

"What?" he asked.

"Alma's poem. Think about it. 'Held in bondage to the ancient rule.' In Alma's time, Russia was held in bondage to the rule of the tsars. Nicholas the Second was widely considered a terrible leader, and the ancient rule crumbled beneath him."

Xander nodded slowly. "Go on."

"In the early twentieth century, St. Petersburg could easily have been considered the heart of Russia." Ava gazed out the window. "I think Alma's clue is pointing us to the city itself."

"Right," Xander said slowly. "Interesting." He looked out the window. "We're quite close to the museum now. Right, Anatoly?"

Anatoly grunted. "Is some traffic."

"See that building over there, across the way?" Xander pointed, and Ava leaned forward.

"That gorgeous palace-looking structure?" she asked.

"Yeah," Xander answered. "That's where the museum is housed."

"My goodness," Carol said. "This city really is magnificent."

"The Fabergé Museum is inside the Shuvalov Palace," Xander said as Ava and Carol gaped at the sight. The marvelous building sat on the bank of the river that ran through St. Petersburg's city center.

"What river is that in front of it?" Carol asked.

"Is the Fontanka River," Anatoly said. He turned the car off the main thoroughfare and wove his way around a short backstreet before turning toward the museum. "Only five more minutes."

"This stretch of the Fontanka used to house much of the Russian nobility," Xander said.

Ava leaned forward to get a better look at the buildings.

"You can see the neoclassical, Baroque style of the buildings, yeah?" Xander continued. "The Shuvalov Palace underwent a huge renovation in 1844 before the wedding of Sofia Naryshkina to Count Pyotr Pavlovich Shuvalov. Their descendants lived in the palace until the revolution. The palace was nationalized in 1918. And now it houses Fabergé's treasures, which is a bit of a fitting end to the palace's history."

Ava blinked up at Xander as he rattled off the historical facts. He smiled in return.

"You're not the only one interested in history," he said with a wink.

Ava looked away quickly, unnerved by how charming he could be.

"Your mother and I will exit the car here and walk," he said as Anatoly pulled to the side of the road and stopped the car. "We'll enter the museum as patrons before you come in, and we will simply begin looking around. You come in and approach the front desk. Ask to see Larissa Pavlovna. Tell the front desk you've got an appointment. Larissa is the docent on duty today and is expecting you. After you introduce yourself, I'll approach and explain that we're here on vacation from America and would love to join in on your tour if that's okay with you. If you concede, Larissa Pavlovna will as well, because then it means she won't have to give two separate tours. From there we'll pretend we know nothing about what you're discussing, and we can all ask questions at will. You have your notebook and pen ready?"

Ava nodded.

"Alright then. Shall we go?" He turned to Carol. She nodded slowly.

"You okay, Mom?" Ava asked.

"Yeah. Just gearing myself up to step out into the cold." Carol tossed them an apologetic look, then grimaced as Xander reached across her and shoved open the door. Carol gasped as the icy cold air hit her face. Ava watched the scene play out with mild amusement.

Xander shut the door behind them, then turned and walked quickly away from the car, his hand on Carol's back. Anatoly merged back onto the road and pulled around the corner to the front of the building, slowing down in front of the large glass doors that opened up into the Fabergé Museum.

"Okay," Ava muttered to herself. "I'm Bethany Hansen. I teach literature. I love Shakespeare. I'm writing a book. I can do this."

She shifted her gaze to Anatoly and nodded. "Um . . . thanks."

"Is fine. You do okay in there."

Ava pushed open the door and stepped out. She took a moment to gather herself before marching up the sidewalk and yanking the door of the building open.

She stepped inside and let the door swing shut behind her. It was warm in the building. She pulled off her scarf and slowly unbuttoned her coat. The long blond wig tickled the back of her neck, and she shook her head a little to try and shake it off. She looked around the quiet lobby, taking a moment to observe her surroundings before she had to fall into character. She looked up and took in the ornate interior, the opulence and grandeur overwhelming, even for a girl from America. She tried to imagine what it must have been like to walk into this same space in the nineteenth century, and immediately found herself as awestruck as she'd been the day before in the Hermitage.

She turned at the sound of footsteps and pasted a smile on her face as a woman approached her. The woman spoke something in Russian. Ava blinked and shook her head.

"I'm looking for Larissa Pavlovna?" she asked.

The woman smiled and extended her hand. "Hello. I'm Larissa. You are Bethany then, yes?"

Ava nodded.

"Wonderful. I am happy to give you your tour, and to answer any questions you have about Fabergé and his creations."

"Thank you," Ava said. She took a moment to observe Larissa. She was petite and pretty, with light brown hair that hung to her shoulders. She wore very little makeup, but she didn't need much anyway. She looked young, perhaps even the same age as Ava herself.

"Thank you for helping me with the research for my book," Ava said with a smile as they climbed the small staircase to the first showroom.

"It is my pleasure," Larissa said. "We are always happy to answer questions about the magnificent history of these pieces. Now, if you'll notice where we begin, you will see that there are many interesting and unique pieces of art. Fabergé created more than just the eggs that most people know about. In fact, the Fabergé eggs were only just a very small piece of what Fabergé and his craftsman made and sold."

Ava nodded. She reached into her bag, pulled out the notebook and pen that Xander had given her, and began jotting down a few notes.

"Excuse me?"

Ava and Larissa turned to see Xander and Carol approaching. Xander's mouth stretched into an impossibly handsome smile as he bowed his head slightly.

"I couldn't help but overhear you both speaking in English, and I wondered if my mother and I might join you for this tour?"

"Oh, well, I am unsure," Larissa said. "This woman has paid for a private tour, so I'm afraid it is up to her."

"I don't mind," Ava said with a shrug.

Larissa offered a nod to Xander and Carol. "Of course," she said, motioning with the swing of an arm for the two to join them.

"Oh, thank you both so much." Xander grabbed Carol's elbow and pulled her forward. "Mother, look. We're going to tag along here."

"Oh, wonderful." Carol smiled. "Thank you both."

Ava nodded at Xander and her mom, trying not to laugh at the ridiculousness of the whole plot.

"I'm Bethany," she said with a smile.

"Alex Morgan. And this is my mother, Mary. We're here on a little cultural excursion." Xander flashed a smile as he held his hand out to Ava. She shook it quickly, then turned back to the guide.

"Well, we will continue then," Larissa said.

They followed her through each room of the tour, Ava taking notes and interjecting questions now and then. Finally, they entered the final room of the tour.

"And here we have the blue room," Larissa said with a smile. "This is usually the part of the museum people are most interested in because it is where we house our collection of Fabergé eggs."

"It is lovely in here," Carol said, her eyes sweeping across the room.

Ava nodded in agreement. Her heart pounded in her chest as she walked to the first display case.

"This is the *Hen Egg*, correct?" she asked, turning to Larissa.

"It is," Larissa replied with a smile. "It was the first egg that Fabergé made for Tsar Alexander the Third, which he presented to his wife, Maria Feodorovna, in 1885. This was the egg that began the long-standing tradition between Fabergé and the tsars."

Ava nodded. She leaned forward and stared at the egg behind the glass. It was displayed in three parts. The outside of the egg sat on one platform, the thick, golden exterior covered in an opaque enamel, giving it the appearance of a real egg.

The platform below held the golden yolk, which had been tucked inside the enameled egg. Ava could tell just by looking at the matte yellow-gold yolk that it was heavy. She wished she could reach in and touch it.

Sitting on a platform next to the egg and yolk was the second surprise from inside the egg. It was a solid gold hen, expertly carved and intricately detailed. Ava leaned closer.

"Amazing," she murmured.

"Indeed," Larissa agreed. "But there was originally more to this egg. If you look at the hen very closely, you see that it, too, opens up. Inside, the tsarina found a small replica of the imperial crown made from diamonds and rubies, as well as a small ruby pendant. Those two surprises have, unfortunately, been lost." Larissa paused to let the group study the hen.

"When Maria Feodorovna saw this egg," she continued, "she was so delighted that Alexander the Second immediately commissioned a second egg for the following year."

"May I ask why an egg was given as a gift in the first place?" Carol asked.

"Yes, of course. This is a very good question." Larissa gestured them forward to look at the next egg on display. It was the

Imperial Coronation Egg. The golden egg had been engraved with sunburst panels on the entirety of its exterior, each of which was covered with a sharp gold enamel. Ava turned to listen to Larissa's explanation.

"The tradition of giving Easter eggs dates back a very long time, nearly a millennium! Eggs were seen as symbols of fertility and protection. They represented new life. When Orthodoxy was introduced in our country, eggs took on an even deeper symbolic meaning, with the color red being used to dye them in honor of the blood of Christ. Of course, when Fabergé began designing the eggs for the Imperial family, these eggs took on a whole new form of symbolism."

"So interesting," Ava said. She turned back to the *Coronation Egg.* "Can you tell me a little about this one?"

Larissa looked through the glass. "The *Imperial Coronation Egg* was prepared for Tsar Nicholas the Second and given to his wife, Tsarina Alexandra Feodorovna, in 1898. It was to commemorate the new tsar's coronation. As you can see, the design is extremely intricate." Larissa pulled a laser pointer from her pocket.

"Do you see the detail between the lattice work here?" she asked, pointing at the golden egg. "Each sunburst was delicately hand carved. And in order to drill the holes for the lattice work, they had to put the egg under water. Extreme care and caution was used in designing this egg. It took a full year to complete it."

"The coach is simply stunning," Ava said, looking at the surprise gift that was displayed beside the egg.

"Yes." Larissa nodded. "The craftsman who designed this egg was Mikhail Perkhin, one of Fabergé's top craftsmen and dearest friends. He designed the coach to be an exact replica of the royal coach that Tsar Nicholas and Alexandra rode in on their coronation day. As you can see, the exterior consists of solid gold and red enamel. The wheels work and can actually even turn the coach. And the door works on a spring hinge, which was very innovative for Fabergé's time. Perhaps the most amazing information of all is the fact that this replica stands at only ten centimeters long."

"Wonderful," Carol breathed.

"The detail of the coach was so intricate," Larissa continued, "that when it came time to try and restore the former Imperial coach many years later, they looked at this model for some of the details."

Ava scribbled in her notebook. She looked eagerly back up at Larissa. "Is it just amazing to work here?" she asked.

Larissa smiled. "It is a great privilege for me to work in this place full of history."

"I can imagine," Ava replied. She walked next to Larissa as they went from case to case, looking at each of the displayed eggs and hearing the detailed history of how the treasures made their way back to Russia.

"As you can see, it is very important for us to see our history displayed and shared about properly," Larissa said as they approached the next case.

Ava nodded, then stopped and caught her breath. "The *Winter Egg*," she said.

Larissa smiled and nodded. "This is one of the most unique eggs to come out of Fabergé's collection. It was designed by Alma Pihl, one of two female master craftsmen in Fabergé's company. She was known to be Fabergé's pet. He took her under his wing and had a fatherly affection for her. More than anything, he admired her talent. She had a very distinct eye for detail. The *Winter Egg* was born out of her study of the ice that would form on her windowpane. She took the designs from nature and turned them into this stunning creation."

"It almost looks like it could melt right before our eyes," Xander said.

Larissa blushed and smiled as he looked down at her. "It does," she said. "You feel that it could be cold when you touch it."

"Larissa, your English is excellent," Carol said as they continued to circle the glass, studying the *Winter Egg* from every angle.

"Thank you," Larissa said with a dip of her head. "My father was a diplomat. We spent some years in the United States when I was younger."

Carol nodded. "Well, that makes sense then. I can barely detect an accent."

"And Bethany," Carol said, turning to Ava with raised eyebrows. "Tell us a little bit about the book you're writing. I'm always so fascinated with people who can write books. I can barely string two sentences together in an email." She let out a little laugh as Xander and Larissa smiled.

"Oh, uh . . ." Ava stuttered, flustered at being drawn away from her study of the *Winter Egg*. "Well, I've always had a fascination with history, and Russian history is particularly interesting to me. The world knows a lot about the Romanovs, of course, and the Fabergé eggs are especially interesting to people, but in my research, I realized there wasn't a lot of information on Fabergé the man. Who was he? What motivated him?" She glanced at Larissa. "I want to paint a portrait of the man behind the eggs."

Larissa nodded her head vigorously. "Oh, yes. I could not

agree more. Fabergé was a very interesting and complicated man."

Ava cocked her head. "Complicated? How do you mean?"

"Well, for starters, he was a family man, known for the way he loved and doted on his four sons when they were young. He was the picture of a good father and husband until it became apparent he had a secret mistress. She was an actress who had a very suspicious background. It is reported that she was ultimately exiled to Siberia and died there, likely in a gulag."

"Interesting," Ava said, jotting down a few notes in her notebook. "He didn't have an affair with Alma Pihl, did he?"

"Oh, no. Definitely not. Fabergé loved Alma, but as a father would love his daughter. He recognized Alma's talent when she was very young. That was one of Fabergé's strengths—seeing the talent in others and drawing it out of them."

Larissa looked around the museum, which was quiet and still. "Have you all visited the site of Fabergé's former workshop yet?"

Ava shook her head.

"You should go there," Larissa said with a smile. "It's an apartment complex now, but it would still be interesting for you to visit and see where he worked. He was very close to Nevsky Prospekt. It might help you get a sense of what he would have seen and felt to be in the place where he walked."

"I think I'd like to do that," Ava said.

"Oh, that would be wonderful, wouldn't it?" Carol said.

Xander smiled. "For her, perhaps, but I'm afraid we won't have the time, Mother."

"Well, that's too bad," Carol replied. She turned to Ava and held out her hand. "It was wonderful to meet you, Bethany.

I wish you much luck with your book on Fabergé. It seems you've gotten some great information today."

Ava shook her hand, biting her lip to keep from smiling at her mother's performance. She nodded at Xander.

He turned to Larissa. "Thank you so much for allowing us to tag along on your tour today. It was fascinating."

"You're welcome," Larissa said. She shook his hand, her cheeks turning a crimson red.

Xander and Carol turned, walking back toward the exit.

"He was very handsome, wasn't he?" Larissa asked, turning to Ava.

Ava offered a tight-lipped smile and nodded her head. "I have just a couple more questions, if you don't mind?" she asked.

Larissa cleared her throat. "Yes, of course."

"Whatever happened to Alma Pihl? She was a woman employed under one of the most decorated artists in Russian history, yet there is little written of her in history books. Where did she go after the revolution?"

Larissa looked around at the nearly empty room, then stepped closer to Ava. "I am equally fascinated with Alma."

She gestured for Ava to follow her to another display case. They looked together at the *Lilies of the Valley Egg* displayed behind the glass. Delicate flowers danced up the side of the Art Nouveau–style egg, guiding the eye to the portraits at the top of the egg of Tsar Nicholas II and his two eldest daughters, Olga and Tatiana.

"There is little information about what happened to Alma in the years after the revolution. There are records showing that she and her husband, Nicholas Klee, left Russia for Finland in 1921. I do not know what happened to her after that. But . . ."

Larissa paused. "I did find something interesting not long ago," she said, her voice almost a whisper.

Ava glanced at her. Larissa offered a small smile, then turned back to the case and observed the egg again. Ava took her cue and trained her eyes forward.

"I found a letter written by Alma Pihl to a friend in Finland." Larissa spoke in a hushed tone. "The letter was dated 1918, and in it she mentioned that she'd had something of great value, which she could discuss with no one."

Ava resisted the urge to pull her pen from behind her ear and write down Larissa's words. Instead, she nodded her head and listened intently.

"The letter had some very strange language in it. It was as though Alma was trying to preserve something. She went on to talk about how the fall of the tsar was desperately sad, though she understood and sympathized with the plight of the people. But right in the center of the letter, she said that she wished Fabergé had never given it to her."

Ava drew in a deep breath. "Given what to her?"

"That is the thing. I don't know," Larissa said. She moved around to the other side of the case, still staring intently at the egg inside. Ava followed her. "I showed the letter to my superior. It had been tucked inside the lining of a jewelry box that was being cleaned and repaired. He took the letter and told me to forget about it, which is very strange."

"Indeed," Ava murmured. "Do you know what he did with the letter?"

"I do not. But it got me thinking about Alma. And now here you are asking questions about her as well. I don't believe in coincidences."

"Me either," Ava said.

Larissa checked her watch. "Oh, it is a pity. I have to go now. My next tour begins in ten minutes."

Ava tossed one more glance around the blue room, reluctant to leave the beautiful art encased inside. "Thanks for all the information."

Larissa smiled. "Perhaps that information will give you questions to seek, which will make your book more unique." She leaned forward and raised her eyebrows. "Most people write the same things about Fabergé over and over. It would be nice to learn something new."

Ava nodded. "Well, I'll do my best." She held out her hand and shook Larissa's. "I'll be going now so you can get to your next tour."

"Yes, of course," Larissa said with a nod. She reached in her pocket and pulled out a business card. "You will let me know when your book is released?"

"Oh," Ava said, taking the card from her awkwardly. "Um . . . sure. It will be a while, of course. The publishing industry moves at a snail's pace."

Larissa laughed. "Yes, I hear this is true. Do you have an email address where I can reach you?"

Ava coughed, then opened up her satchel. She riffled through it for a moment, then looked back up. "I'm so sorry. I don't have any of my cards with me."

"Oh, it is fine," Larissa said with a wave of the hand. "Just send me a message at that address and we can keep in touch. I will answer any other questions you have as they come up, okay?"

"Sure," Ava said. "I'll be in touch." She turned and quickly made her way back through the museum toward the front door, her mind turning with questions.

She pushed out into the street, the winter air burning her cheeks. Just as she rounded the corner, the car pulled up to the curb and stopped. Ava grabbed the door handle and slid inside in one swift move, pushing against Xander and pulling the door shut behind her.

"What took you so long?" Carol asked as Anatoly merged into traffic.

"I'm going to need to call Nick when we get back," Ava said.

St. Petersburg, 1910

K arl ducked his head inside and let the door swing shut behind him. Stomping the dirt from the street off his boots, he unwound his scarf, removed his hat and coat, and hung all three neatly on the coat hanger by the door. He rolled his head around, stretching out the tension that had knotted his shoulders and neck. It was finished, the task accomplished.

He turned toward the stairs and walked up quickly, knowing that his employees were waiting for the news that the eggs had been successfully delivered and received by the royal family. Karl made the trip to Tsarskoe Selo every year to hand-deliver the works of art. There was a buzzing sort of energy in the air this time of year. Holy Week was generally their busiest season, as customers came in looking for last-minute Easter gifts, and sightseers came hoping for a glimpse of the newest eggs prepared for the tsarinas. It was an exhausting, overwhelming, and energetic time, and Karl found that he still enjoyed the thrill of the season, but he was more tired than usual this year. Perhaps it was his age, though he couldn't possibly admit that out loud because it felt like a concession of the winding down of life.

He reached the top of the stairs and startled as his son Eugen popped around the corner.

"How did it go?" Eugen asked. "Were they pleased? Did they like the *Colonnade Egg*? How was the tsarina's mood while you were there?"

Karl smiled and placed his hand on his eldest son's shoulder. "It went fine, son. They seemed quite pleased with their gifts this year, as they have every year."

All four of Karl's sons now worked in the business, a fact that made his heart swell with fatherly pride. They were each gifted differently, and they managed to parlay those gifts in ways that benefited the House of Fabergé.

Eugen and his second-born brother, Agathon, both remained here in St. Petersburg. Karl suppressed a smile at the look of relief that washed over Eugen's face at the news that the tsar had been pleased once again. His oldest child was a people pleaser, and he usually described himself as the public relations man of the company. But everyone knew, Karl included, that Eugen's real talent lay in design. His brain popped with ideas and images that were increasingly incorporated into the pieces made in the workshop.

Agathon helped manage the St. Petersburg store alongside his brother, overseeing the gemology department. An expert gemologist, Agathon had taken this division of the company to new heights.

His third-born son, Alexander, now lived full time in Moscow and ran the store branch in that bustling city. Karl often asked Alexander if he really wanted to stay in Moscow, or if he'd prefer to return to the beauty and serenity of St. Petersburg, but he always turned it down. It appeared his son liked the hustle of Moscow, a fact that was mind-boggling to Karl.

Nicholas, the youngest, had taken over the management of the London office with Henry Bainbridge. Augusta, being particularly fond of her baby, commented often on her displeasure at him living so far away. Karl, however, got the distinct impression that London, and the distance it placed between them, quite suited his free-spirited son with the big ideas, big heart, and even bigger personality.

"Papa? Everything okay?"

Karl shifted his gaze to Eugen and focused his eyes in on his son's face. His child now bore wrinkles in his skin and the peppered strands of gray on his head.

"Yes, of course," Karl replied. "Just lost in thought."

Eugen nodded. "You know, Papa, I've been thinking more about our conversation the other night, and I really think we need to move forward with asking the tsar for a higher title."

Karl waved his hand. "I am not interested in fancy titles that mean nothing. I told you this."

"Just listen," Eugen continued. "The title of Supplier to the Imperial Court, which you claim now, doesn't fully incorporate all that you do, and it diminishes your working relationship with the royal family. They must make you the official Jeweler to the Imperial Court. This is the capacity within which you're already working. You deserve the accolade."

Karl sighed. "But it won't mean anything. It won't change what we do or how we get paid."

"But it will change the way you do business abroad, Papa. I really believe that it will. The change in title brings a measure of importance that allows for further expansion."

Karl pulled his glasses off his face and grabbed a kerchief

from the pocket of his jacket, wiping them slowly as he squinted at his son.

"If I say yes to this, will you leave me alone?" he finally asked.

Eugen smiled. "If I promise to leave you alone, will you grant me permission to write the tsar asking for the title change?"

Karl placed his glasses back on the bridge of his nose and peered at his son. "I'll grant it," he said. "But I don't want you to request the change right away. Wait a few months and let the holidays and summer break settle. Then you may write your letter."

"Fair enough," Eugen said, holding out his hand. Karl shook his head and chuckled, shaking his son's hand. Eugen had always been a dealmaker, from the time he was a little boy. He'd write contracts, asking his parents to sign them, promising that they would uphold all kinds of silly bargains, from not making him eat tomatoes to allowing him to stay up later at night to read his books. Some things never changed.

"Well, let's go in and let everyone know the handoff was a success. These people have been working hard. They deserve a little break."

Eugen nodded. He followed his father into the shop where the two stood silently for a moment, watching the various craftsmen bent over their work. Karl felt a wave of pride wash over him. He loved each of his employees like family, and he was immensely proud of the way that they worked.

"*Ahem.* Attention, everyone!" he called out. The bustle in the workshop quickly died down. Chairs scraped against the floor as they pushed away from their tables and stood up, many pushing magnifying glasses up on the tops of their heads, and turned to face the master craftsman.

"It was a wonderful year for the House of Fabergé. I hand-delivered the eggs to the tsar today, and the tsarinas were delighted with their gifts. Empress Maria was especially moved by hers. The image of her husband seen through the egg brought tears to her eyes."

Karl smiled at the memory of the way the empress had thanked him. She was always so effusive in her praise, and for this egg it was well deserved. The concept had been his own, but Eugen had tweaked the design, and the craftsmen who pulled it all together had brought the vision to life.

They called it the *Alexander III Equestrian Egg*. It had become quickly apparent that any egg they could create that honored the empress's late husband was sure to be a hit. In this one, they had engraved an image of Alexander III on horseback in pure gold and set it on a platform of vibrant blue nephrite. The egg itself was clear, made of rock quartz crystal and polished to look like glass. It was framed in a platinum trellis work with platinum double-headed crowned eagles on either side. The base of the egg was made of platinum cherubs, carved to hold up the platform in the middle. The year 1910 had been set in diamonds of the highest quality. The egg was, indeed, a masterpiece, and it honored the former tsar well.

"And Tsarina Alexandra? How did she feel about her gift?" Eugen asked.

"As usual, the tsarina was more difficult to read, her emotions kept very much in check. But she claimed she was pleased, and I believe I even saw a smile, so it can be seen as a true success."

The *Colonnade Egg* was itself less inspired, but Karl found himself running out of ideas for how to please the young tsarina. The only things that truly made her happy were her children, and so they continued to focus on the royal family in her eggs.

This year's egg was covered in opalescent pink enamel,

which gave it a decidedly feminine appeal. They designed the egg to work as a rotary clock, but it was the base of the egg that gave it its beauty. Six green columns of bowenite upheld the egg, making it resemble a Greek love temple, which Karl had suspected would be pleasing to Alexandra.

Below the columns sat four golden statues of girls, each one representative of the four grand duchesses. On top of the egg knelt a golden winged cupid, its boyish face looking down upon the four below with superiority. Of course, the intention in the egg was quite clear—the young tsarevitch was to be hailed and honored as the future king.

Karl, knowing and understanding the danger in which the young tsarevitch lived daily with his medical condition, felt a small amount of sympathy for the challenge his parents faced. Alexei had to be coddled more than the average child, for the smallest bump or bruise could be his demise. If he was to live to see the throne, he would have to be treated differently. And so, perhaps, his mother's elevation of him was understandable, if it wasn't advisable from a parenting perspective.

"So, what would you have us do now?" Eugen asked, cutting through Karl's quiet thoughts as the rest of the employees looked on expectantly.

"Go home, everybody," Karl said with a smile. "Enjoy your families and your holiday. We will convene next week and begin working again."

Karl swallowed hard at those final words. It would start again in just a few days. The work never stopped, and though he desperately loved what he did, the fact remained that he was terribly tired.

He bid a warm goodbye to each of his employees as they walked past him, then turned and slowly made his way up the stairs where he knew Augusta, ever faithful and present, would be waiting with a meal of celebration for the close of the Easter celebrations. With each step, he felt the weight of the conflict in his soul, and by the time he reached the top, the fatigue had grown so heavy that he could barely lift his feet.

Present Day

Ava tucked herself into the couch as Xander looked on from the chair across from her. He was wearing jeans and a T-shirt, and he looked impossibly, annoyingly handsome. Impatience nipped at Ava as she pressed the phone against her ear. Finally, Nick picked up.

"Well, hello there." His voice was weak and tired.

Ava gripped the phone tighter. "Hey, Nick."

"How'd your first day go?" Nick asked.

Ava let out a small sigh of relief. They would go straight to business and skip any attempt at pleasantries. She quickly filled him in on all that she'd gathered, from Anatoly's assessment of Alma's poem to the conversation she'd had with Larissa.

"Interesting," Nick said when she was finished. "Has Zak managed to get into the back files of the museum yet? We need to see if that letter was filed away."

"He's in, but the files are extensive and in Russian. Xander can read some of them, but the language is complex and old, so he set Zak up with some weird translation tool that decodes most of them, but it's not foolproof. It gives some pretty bizarre translations."

"Tell him I've got some momentum going," Zak whispered from the corner of the room where he was surrounded by computers and held a stack of papers on his lap. He wore giant headphones on his ears, which made him faintly resemble a mouse. "Most of the files are uninteresting and meaningless, and there are thousands of them, but I've come up with a system that I think will help me dig through them more quickly."

Ava nodded. "Zak says he's getting there," she told Nick.

"No—that's not what I said!" Zak protested.

"Here, hang on," Ava continued. "I'm going to put you on speaker." She clicked the button and laid the phone down on the table between them. "Xander and Zak are here with me right now," she said, leaning forward and speaking a little louder.

"Where's your mom?" Nick asked.

"She was tired. According to her, jet lag is harder on people over the age of fifty," Ava replied.

Nick chuckled. "She's probably right. What about Anatoly? Can't he help with the translations? I'd like to talk with him anyway. I haven't caught up with him in several years."

"Anatoly is a busy man these days, Nick," Xander said. "But he and I are meeting tonight to go over some of the things Zak's dug up. I'll make sure to tell him you said hello."

"Sounds good," Nick answered. "Tell him to give me a call soon. I'd like to catch up with the old fart."

"You got it, boss," Xander said.

"And how do you feel about things, Xander?" Nick asked.

"Pretty good. I guess I hoped we would get a little more out of today's visit to the museum, but understanding Alma's poem is something, and the lead Ava got from Larissa was definitely interesting."

"Indeed," Nick said.

"What do you think the poem means, Nick?" Ava asked. She pulled the paper out of her satchel and held it up. "What is the secret from the boards?"

"I think it's a clue, Ava." Nick coughed, a wet, gurgling sound that made Ava wince. It took a moment before he continued. "I think the interpretation of this poem has a lot of potential."

"*Held in bondage to the ancient rule*." Xander read. "We were discussing that line earlier, and Ava thinks that's referring to the tsar. If you dig further into that sentence, the word 'rule' is better translated as 'authority.' The whole of Russia was held in bondage to the authority of the Romanovs."

"Good," Nick said, his voice cracking. "I've been chewing on the same idea."

Ava adjusted herself on the couch, shifting under the knowledge that she and her dad were thinking on the same track.

"And that bondage was invisible in that it wasn't physical bonds that held the people," Nick continued, "but it was seen in the effects of poverty and unrest that arose from the tsar's political power."

"Definitely," Ava said.

"Okay," Nick said. "Tomorrow is another day, and you have more work ahead of you. Zak?"

"Yes, Mr. Laine?"

"First of all, call me Nick, please. Second, keep working. Your job is tedious and exhausting, but it's crucial. Anything you can find that points to Alma and her work and connection to Fabergé is important to save, understand? And please be careful. Are you encrypting everything you do online?"

"Absolutely, sir," Zak said. "I'm covering my tracks."

"Good man. Xander, you need to make sure plans are set for tomorrow's excursion. It's going to be the trickiest, as you'll have to figure out how to do your search undetected."

"Remind me what's up tomorrow?" Ava asked.

"Tomorrow you guys head to 24 Bolshaya Morskaya and look around. It's where Fabergé ran his shop and lived. It's a private residence now, so Xander's got a means to get you in, but searching the complex will be a challenge. Formulate a plan, and be very, very careful in the execution."

Ava nodded. "Sounds good. You . . . um . . . you feeling okay?" she asked, the attempt at small talk feeling awkward on her tongue.

"Never better," Nick said, then coughed as if on cue. "I'm fit as a fiddle."

"Fit as a fiddle?" Ava said. "That's an old-person thing to say."

Nick chuckled. "Well, I've never felt so old in my life. Keep me posted on what you find, okay?"

Ava nodded. "'Kay."

"Gotta go," Nick said. "Sylvie is giving me the stink eye."

"I heard that," Sylvie's voice piped up in the background.

"Bye, Nick." Ava ended the call and leaned back on the couch, tucking her feet up underneath her. She grabbed the paper with Alma's poem on it and read over it slowly. She could feel Xander staring at her.

"What?" she finally asked, looking up at him.

"So, what's the deal with you and Nick?" Xander asked.

Ava shrugged. "Nothing."

Xander cocked his head and stared at her.

Ava squirmed and shifted her gaze away from him. "I mean, it's not really an interesting story. Absent father. Bitter daughter. Working together to find a lost piece of art potentially worth millions of dollars. You know, basic stuff."

"Yeah. Heard that boring story a thousand times." He leaned forward and put his elbows on his knees. "You're a tough nut to crack, Ava Laine."

Zak coughed in the corner, interrupting the banter. He tossed a look at Ava, pulling the headphones off his ears. "I may have found something here."

Ava pushed up off the couch and walked to Zak's little table. She leaned over his shoulder and stared at the screen. Xander walked up and stood beside Ava.

"What are we looking at, mate?" Xander asked.

"I opened a folder labeled 'The Master Craftsman,'" Zak answered. "In it were subfolders, each with the names of the different craftsmen from the shop. See here? There's Mikhail Perkhin. There's Hiskias Pendin. And right there, tucked in the middle, is Alma Pihl, only they've got hers saved under the name Alma Klee."

"That was her married name," Ava murmured.

Zak nodded and clicked the folder. It opened to reveal a handful of files. "Most of these are scanned images of her designs, which you can find in just about any book," he said, clicking one of the files. The image of a sketched snowflake design filled the screen.

"She was really talented," Ava murmured, studying the drawing.

Zak clicked back to the folder's contents and scrolled down. "It gets a little more interesting down here," he said. He clicked another file and the image of a notebook page appeared, scrawled handwriting filling the screen.

"This looks to be a letter," he continued.

"Can you read this, Xander?" Ava asked, glancing over at him.

His eyes were narrowed as he studied the image. He shook his head in frustration. "I can pick out a few words here and there, but cursive writing isn't my strong suit. It's definitely a letter, though. See here where she signed her name at the bottom?" He reached out and pointed to the bottom edge of the page.

Ava nodded. "Maybe this is the letter Larissa told me about. Can your translation tool decode it, Zak?"

Zak shook his head. "The device doesn't work on cursive handwriting."

"Can we get Anatoly over here to read it?"

Xander nodded. "Save that and anything else you find with writing on it. Anatoly and I will work through them this evening when we meet to plan tomorrow's outing and make sure we've got our bases covered."

"Shouldn't I join you two?"

"It isn't necessary," he answered. "We're meeting down in the hotel bar. Anatoly works best with a side of vodka. It would be better if you went to bed early and got a good night's rest. Tomorrow will be a long day."

Ava's shoulders slumped. "Okay."

Xander turned back to Zak's computer screen. Ava tried to study him discreetly from the corner of her eye. His hair was swept back in waves, the golden-brown color lit by the overhead lights.

"Hold up, mate," Xander said, pointing at the screen. Ava turned and looked back over Zak's shoulder.

"Scroll back up."

Zak scrolled up slowly.

"There! Look there. Do you see that?" Xander pointed at a

drawing in the top right corner of what looked to be another letter.

"See what?" Ava asked. She leaned forward and squinted at the grainy picture.

"That drawing. What does it look like to you?"

Zak and Ava looked at it for a long moment.

"It looks like a raised fist," Zak finally said.

"It does!" Ava answered.

"I think so too," Xander said.

"Wait! Hold on," Ava said. She walked to the couch and grabbed her notebook, turning to the page where she'd written down Alma's poem. "Yes," she murmured. She walked back to Zak and Xander and pointed at the page. "The last stanza: '*All will be known where the ice doesn't hang; the fisted heart of a man now lies, not in the light for all to see; but in the secret chambers of the boards.*'"

"The fisted heart," Zak said, turning back to the screen. He moved his cursor over the corner of the file and cropped it, expanding the image until it was larger, grainy, and hard to see, but clearly the image of a raised fist. He pointed. "Look at the date written underneath it."

"September 24, 1919," Ava read, squinting to make out the numbers. She stood up straight. "The House of Fabergé was dissolved in 1917. By 1919, Peter Karl Fabergé was already living in exile in Switzerland."

"Exactly," Xander said, straightening up next to Ava. "Alma Pihl Klee would no longer be an employee at this time because the House of Fabergé no longer existed."

"So why does the Fabergé Museum have a letter and a drawing by Alma in 1919 on file, then?" Zak asked, turning in his seat to look at the two of them.

"We need to find that out," Ava murmured. She turned to Xander. "You and Anatoly need to translate all of these. Are you sure it's safe for you to meet in public to do this? Wouldn't it be better if he came up here?"

Xander gave her a smile. "We'll be safe, I promise. Zak, can you get everything printed out for me?"

Zak nodded.

Ava yawned, her eyes watering, then blinked a few times to try and chase away the fatigue.

"Seriously, Ava," Xander said, turning to face her. "You're no good to me exhausted. You should go to bed now and get a full night's rest. Tomorrow will be packed, and I'll need you at 100 percent. You too, Zak. Finish this up and call it a night, mate."

Ava gave a reluctant sigh, the jet lag suddenly feeling like a weight on top of her. "I guess I'll head back to my room now," she murmured. "But I'll be here at eight o'clock tomorrow morning ready to hear what you and Anatoly discussed."

Xander nodded. "It's a plan. I'll brief you on our meeting, and I'll get you your outfit for tomorrow's meetings."

"Am I still Bethany Hansen tomorrow?"

Xander smiled. "Nah. While that ruse worked well for sightseeing and the museum, we're not going to use it again. This next role will be a little more fun." He raised his eyebrows up and down.

Ava resisted, but ultimately failed and smiled.

Zak looked back and forth between the two with mild annoyance. "Okay, then, I guess it's settled? Ava will head back to her room to go to sleep now. I'll print out these pages and shut everything down, and you'll go meet Anatoly for a nightcap. That's the plan?"

Ava cleared her throat and stepped back, crossing her arms

over her chest. "Sounds good," she said, turning to look at Xander as her cheeks grew warm. "I'll see you guys in the morning."

"Night, Ava," Xander said. "Sleep soundly."

Ava turned and rushed from the room. She pulled open the door and checked the hallway. Seeing it empty, she stepped out, walked the few steps to her own door, and knocked lightly. A moment later, Carol pulled the door open. She was wrapped in the fluffy hotel robe, her wet hair piled in a towel on top of her head. Ava stepped inside and closed the door behind her.

"You okay?" Carol asked. "Your cheeks are all red."

Ava pulled away from her mom's touch. "Fine," she murmured. "Just really tired. I'm gonna get ready and go to bed."

Carol nodded. "There's a solid chance I'll already be asleep when you get out of the bathroom."

Ava nodded.

"Did you guys discuss anything interesting over there?" Carol asked, turning toward her bed.

Ava opened her mouth to recap all that they'd discussed, then closed it again. She was too tired to try to share it all. "Not really. Nothing big, anyway. We should know more tomorrow."

Ava yawned. She walked to the bathroom and rushed through her nightly routine. When she came back out, Carol was already asleep, an eye mask over her eyes and her mouth hanging open. Ava padded to her bed, pulled back the covers, and collapsed on her pillows. Her eyes fluttered, then closed. Exhausted, she didn't have time to register the nagging feeling that something wasn't right before she fell into a deep, dreamless sleep.

———— ❊ ————

Ava awoke with a start the next morning, sitting up quickly and looking around as her brain tried to decipher where she was. She saw her mother in the bed next to her, then remembered they were in Russia on a treasure hunt. She laid back on her pillows slowly. Glancing at the clock, she saw that it was only 4:30 a.m.

For an hour, she tossed and turned, thinking about her conversation with Larissa at the museum, trying to fit pieces of the puzzle together to form some kind of image. Finally, she pushed herself up and leaned back against the headboard of the bed.

"You're awake," Carol murmured from beneath her blankets.

"Yeah," Ava mumbled. "Sorry. Did I wake you?"

"Yes. But it's alright." Carol sat up and pulled the eye mask off, squinting at the bedside clock. "It's five thirty. All those years of trying to drag you out of bed in time to catch the school bus, and now you're up and at 'em at five thirty in the morning?"

Ava smiled. "If only school had been this exciting."

"Mmm . . ." Carol sat back against the headboard and rubbed her eyes. "How do we get coffee up here?"

"We could order room service."

Carol turned. "You're right. We could. I have never ordered room service in a hotel before."

Ava smirked. "Me either." She stood up and crossed the room, pulling the menu off the desk in the corner and flipping through it to the English section. "Thank you, Nick Laine," she murmured as she perused their choices.

An hour later, both of them sat propped up in their beds with trays of food on their laps. Ava had her notebook out, reading over the notes she'd furiously scribbled down on the museum tour.

"So, what do you think the drawing of the raised fist means?" Carol asked. She took a sip of her coffee and grimaced. "Boy, Russians like their coffee strong."

"I'm not totally sure," Ava said. "But a fist thrust in the air seems like a fairly universal symbol of resistance, doesn't it?"

Carol shrugged. "I suppose. The images we saw of Alma Pihl make it hard for me to believe she was a part of some kind of resistance movement, though. She looked so sweet and gentle."

"Maybe she was," Ava replied. "Maybe she was no more than a messenger . . . or a transporter."

Ava took a bite of the thick, black bread on her plate. She chewed for a minute as she thought.

"I'm more convinced than ever that Fabergé gave Alma the egg and asked her to hide it for him. And I think it had something to do with the overall feelings of disquiet and discontent that the country felt toward the tsar."

"Yes, but if Fabergé shared the same feelings as the people of Russia, why wouldn't he let them see that egg? Why would he hide it?"

"I think Fabergé was torn between loyalty to the throne and loyalty to the people. He was a businessman first, a Russian second." She took another bite.

"And besides," she continued. "I don't think it would've mattered. One egg wouldn't have changed his outcome. After so many years serving the Romanovs and selling them expensive items while the country suffered under the tsar's rule, Fabergé's loyalty to the people would have been undeniably tainted. He was destined for his final fate."

Carol glanced at the clock. She pushed her tray aside and

stood up. "I'm going to get ready." She stood up and stretched slowly. "It takes me longer to get presentable than you."

"That's true," Ava said.

Carol made a face at her daughter and stepped around the end of the bed toward the bathroom. She paused a moment, then turned to look back at Ava.

"You like Xander," Carol said.

Ava stopped chewing and looked up at her mom, eyebrows raised. "Huh?"

"You like Xander."

"No, I don't!"

"Yes, you do," Carol said with a smile. "It's okay. It makes sense that you'd like him. I'm not sure I've ever seen a more disturbingly handsome man in real life. Just . . . be careful, okay?"

Ava threw her hands up in the air. "What are you talking about?"

"Honey, it's not a big deal. If you didn't at least find Xander a little attractive, I'd be worried about you. But listen, just be aware of it and be careful. I'm assuming it's obvious how Zak feels about you?"

Ava blushed. "Mom! Do we really have to talk about this? I'm not here to discuss boys. I'm here on a mission."

"I know you are." Carol put her hands on her hips. "Zak adores you, Ava. And he's a sweet kid."

"He's basically a puppy dog," Ava said.

Carol smiled. "Exactly. So just be careful with Xander. Because we don't really know anything about him other than the fact that he is drop-dead gorgeous."

"Oh, Mother. Please don't ever say that again." Ava grabbed the pillow on the bed next to her and put it over her face. She heard Carol sigh, then waited until the bathroom door clicked shut before putting the pillow back down.

"I'm here on a mission," Ava mumbled again. "I am not here for boys."

———❖———

An hour later, Ava was sitting at the table with Carol, Xander, and Zak, mugs of hot tea steaming in front of them. Xander spread out the sheets on the table.

"Alright," he began. "Anatoly was very helpful last night. He said these writings were easier to read than the poem. This first one is a letter that Alma wrote to a friend back in Finland. See here? It's dated 1920. Apparently, Alma and her husband were desperate to get out of Russia and back to Finland, and who can blame them, right?"

"Seriously," Ava said.

"Most of the letter is formalities, but there is one section that's a bit more cryptic."

Xander pointed at a section in the middle of the letter that was highlighted. Above the words, he'd written the English translation. Ava read it aloud slowly.

"My dear friend, there are so many things that you and I must discuss when I return. I cannot go into details, but I need to talk with someone soon or I may grow ill with the secret. I'm being buried by it. I've lied to myself, and my dear, is that not the height of personal loss? As Dostoevsky wrote, 'The man who lies to himself and listens to his own lie comes to a point that he cannot distinguish the truth within him, or around him, and so loses all respect for himself and others. And having no respect ceases to

*love.' Please, if you see I've become that person when I
return, tell me truthfully so that I may deal with it and
move forward. My Nicholas has noticed a change in me.
He's asked, but I cannot tell even him—especially him.
The secret lies in the rubble, and I must leave it there. I
will tell you more when we get home—if we get home!"*

She looked at Xander with raised eyebrows. "'The secret
lies in the rubble'?"

He nodded, his eyes piercing hers. He leaned in a little
closer. "What kind of secret would be so dramatic it would feel
like you were being buried by it?"

"*Ahem.*" Zak coughed.

Ava snapped back away from Xander. "Okay, so what about
the other pages? Were any of the writings the letter that Larissa
told me about?" she asked, shuffling through the papers on the
desk with trembling fingers.

"No," Xander replied. "Larissa told you that letter was dated
1918, correct?"

Ava nodded.

Xander shrugged. "Neither letter we found was written
in 1918." He shuffled through the pages in his hand. "Most
of these pages were pretty useless." He glanced at Zak, then
looked back at Ava. "This was the description of a necklace
she'd made for a client in 1915. This was a letter to her sister
asking about her nephew's health. This last page, though . . ."

He pulled a final page from the stack. "This may be helpful.
It was written in 1921, just before Alma and Nicholas were
able to get out of Russia. She mailed it to the same friend as
this last letter." Xander glanced at the paper. "And here is
the most interesting thing about both of those letters." He

paused a moment for dramatic effect. "The friend's name was Isla Laine."

"Isla Laine?" Ava pulled the paper from his hand and stared at the bottom of the page. She looked at Carol. "Does that name sound familiar to you?"

Carol shook her head. She glanced at her watch. "Why don't we send Nick a message. He can get back to us when he wakes up." She reached for her phone.

"No," Zak interrupted. "Let me be the one to text Nick and ask him. We need to make sure our communications stay encrypted."

Carol nodded.

"So, what's so interesting about this letter?" Ava asked.

"You mean, besides the fact that it's written to someone who shares your same last name?" Leaning forward, Xander pointed to the paragraph in the middle of the letter. "Read this."

Ava read aloud again.

"I apologize for the last letter that I sent you. I was feeling much anguish the day I wrote it. I shouldn't have poured so much of my emotion into it, then not written again for so long. Forgive me, dear friend. As the Russians say, 'Pan ili propal'—to gain everything or nothing at all. I cannot continue to dwell on the things gained or lost. I must master my emotions, not let them master me. I'll tame them, as those who tame the horses remind me daily. I know this is all terribly cryptic now, but I'll make it right when we see one another face to face. You'll be my guide in this endeavor to bury the past. I'll not only tell you what I mean when I return, but I will also show you. I truly cannot wait to be together

*again so that we may share all that has transpired in
our years apart."*

"Isn't that interesting," Carol murmured. "What does she
mean, 'as those who tame the horses'?'"

Ava shrugged. "I was a history major for a reason," she replied. "So, I didn't have to dissect cryptic poetry and writing."

Carol smiled. "You've never had much of an imagination,
my dear."

"In my research," Ava continued, "I did read that Alma went
back to Finland and became a respected art teacher. She never
spoke of her time in Russia or her connections to the royal
family. People were shocked when they found out those details
about her when she was a much older woman."

Zak leaned back. "I sent the message to Nick. I'm sure he
will get back to us as soon as he . . ." He paused and glanced
at his phone when it dinged. "Right now. He'll get back to us
right now. He wants us to call."

"It's one a.m. there," Carol said. Her eyebrows raised. "Sylvie
is not going to be happy about this."

"Should I call?" Zak asked.

"Yep. If Nick says call, you should call," Carol said.

Zak picked up his phone and dialed the number, then put
it on speaker and placed it on the table between them. Nick
answered on the first ring.

"What's up, team?"

"Hey, Nick," Ava said. "What are you doing up?"

"I keep unpredictable hours these days," he replied, a wry
smile evident in his voice. "What's going on?"

"Well, Zak found something in Alma's file. It's a letter—two
letters, actually—that she wrote to a friend in Finland. In them

she mentions that she needs to get out of Russia and away from the secrets."

"Okay. Interesting. Are there any details in the letters about what those secrets are?"

"No." Ava leaned a little closer to the phone. "Zak can send you the translations when we hang up. They're pretty cryptic, all about how Alma felt she was being buried by this secret that she wrote 'lies buried in the rubble.'"

"Buried in the rubble," Nick murmured. "Maybe in the rubble of 24 Bolshaya Morskaya?"

"Perhaps," Xander broke in, leaning over the phone. "But 24 Bolshaya Morskaya was never reduced to rubble."

"True," Nick replied. "But the House of Fabergé was meta-phorically reduced to rubble. By 1918, there was nothing left. No assets, no funds, no glory or accolades."

"You don't think she could have buried the egg somewhere inside 24 Bolshaya Morskaya, do you?" Ava asked with eye-brows raised.

"I think anything is possible, Ava," Nick said. "Although the probability of that seems rather slim to me—especially if this particular letter was on file at the Fabergé Museum."

"There's another thing," Zak said. They all turned to face him. He cleared his throat nervously. "Well, I've—uh—been doing a bit of research myself, and it seems that when the revolution finally occurred in 1917 and Nicholas abdicated the throne, most businesses were swiftly shut down and buildings confiscated. By early 1919, the workshop at 24 Bolshaya Mor-skaya was entirely controlled by the communists. No one was left, and anyone who tried to return to the House of Fabergé after those events would have been arrested, as it was overtaken by the NKVD."

Ava raised her eyebrows in surprise. Zak locked eyes with her before continuing.

"I read the story of a man named Hjalmar Armfelt who was one of the contracted craftsmen that ran a shop from inside the House of Fabergé." Zak paused and took a deep breath. "Anyway, in 1919, he was ready to flee Russia with his family and return to Finland."

"He was also Finnish, then?" Carol said.

"Yes," Zak said. "Many of Fabergé's contractors and employees were. So, this Armfelt fellow needed funds to get back to Finland, having lost most of his savings in the collapse of 1918. I read where he'd hidden shavings of gold and silver dust from his shop in the cellar of the building on Bolshaya Morskaya. Despite being warned, he went back in the hopes of entering the building and gathering his possession. But when he tried to enter, he was arrested and sent to a work camp outside Moscow. He was interned for eighteen months before finally being released, sick and worn down."

"What's this got to do with the letter, mate?" Xander asked.

"Oh, uh . . . well," Zak stammered. "I guess my point was that if the egg had been hidden somewhere in the House of Fabergé, no one would have ever been able to return to retrieve it."

They all sat for a moment, absorbing this information.

"That's good work, Zak," Nick said, finally breaking the silence.

Ava leaned toward the phone again. "That line wasn't the most interesting thing about these letters, Nick. There's more."

"Oh?"

"The most interesting thing about the letters is *who* they're written to. Her friend's name was Isla Laine. Do you know who that is?"

"Alma wrote directly to Isla?" The surprise in Nick's voice was evident.

Ava raised her eyebrows. "Yes. Who is she?"

"She was my grandmother's older sister."

"The one who went on treasure hunts and hid knickknacks in the hidden cabin?" Carol asked.

"Yes." Nick coughed. Ava winced at the sound.

"Nick, do you think the egg could have been in that cabin with everything else?" Zak asked.

"Oh, no. No way. I looked all over that place for anything that might be interesting or of value. Hiding the egg there would have been way too easy and obvious. Plus, if there was something like that hidden in the cabin, it would have been found a long time ago."

"Why would Alma have written to Isla in Russian?" Ava asked.

"The people of Finland were known to speak more than one language," Nick said. "Finnish is the native language spoken, but it's not terribly uncommon to hear Swedish or Russian either."

"So, Isla and Alma were friends, and Alma potentially confessed to Isla that she was in possession of the egg? And Isla happens to be a distant relative of yours?" Xander asked. "Nick, this is crazy stuff, mate."

"It's all par for the course in a treasure hunt, Xander," Nick replied. "When it starts getting crazy, you know you're on the right track."

Xander smiled. "That's what my dad used to say."

"I got it from your dad," Nick said.

Ava cleared her throat. "Okay, then. We need to get ready for our day and you need to go back to bed."

Nick coughed. "Yeah, I suppose you're right. Man, I wish I was there with you guys right now. This is the best part of the hunt, when the little pieces start to fit together."

"Bye, Nick. We'll call again tonight after we get through today."

"See ya—" Nick's voice cut off as Ava hit the end button on the call. The sound of longing in Nick's voice had pierced her in a way that threw her off a little. She felt a pang of sympathy, and maybe longing, for her father, and she didn't have the time to process that now.

"Ava!" Carol narrowed her eyes. "That was rude."

"We need to move on, Mom," Ava said. She brushed her hair back off her forehead with a shaking hand. "We can't just shoot the breeze with Nick all day long." She turned to Xander.

"Okay, so what's the plan for today? Who will I be?"

"Who will *we* be—that's the question you should be asking."

"We?" Ava tossed him a questioning gaze.

Xander grinned. "Today, you and I get to play newlyweds."

Zak sputtered and coughed. Carol reached over and patted him on the back while looking at Ava.

"We're newlyweds?" Ava asked.

"Yep. We're in St. Petersburg on our honeymoon. We are the adventurous sort, always looking to do something different from the norm. We're going to check out the apartment that's for rent on 24 Bolshaya Morskaya."

Ava raised her eyebrows.

"You and I are Jack and Molly Andrews. We met at Oxford when you were doing a study abroad and we instantly fell in love. I was studying linguistics and languages, which will explain why I speak Russian, and you were studying literature."

"Why literature? Why can't it be history?" Ava asked. "You know, the thing I actually studied and can talk about?"

Xander smiled. "Nick said something about keeping you on your toes because you were sharp and could handle it."

She blinked. "Okay, so linguistics and literature. Got it. If anyone asks, I'll start talking about *The Lord of the Rings* or something."

Xander grinned. "You can never go wrong with that."

"So, you two are playing newlyweds today," Carol said. "And what is my role?"

"I'm afraid you're sitting this one out, Carol. You'll stay here with Zak and help him run tech and organize anything else he finds online."

"Oh." Carol's face fell. She blinked a couple of times, then offered a thin smile. "Well, I suppose another day to recover would be nice."

Xander clapped his hands together. "Alright then. I've got your outfit hanging in a bag in the closet. What say we change and meet by the elevator in twenty minutes, okay?"

Ava stood and followed him to the closet, taking the clothing bag from him.

"Can't wait to hit the town with you, Mrs. Andrews," he said.

"Oh, brother," Ava said. "Is it always this way? Did Nick have to assume ridiculous characters for his hunts?"

Xander laughed. "Apparently. My dad once told me that he and Nick dressed as Italian brothers for a cave hunt in the Swiss Alps. They ran into a snag, though, when they met someone who was actually from Italy and began speaking to them in Italian. Apparently, your dad—"

"Nick. I call him Nick."

Xander cocked his head and looked at her curiously. "Okay,"

he said. "Well, apparently Nick"—he shot her a look—"came up with some cock-and-bull story about how they had moved to the United States as children and he had forgotten most of his Italian. He went on to say that his brother, my dad, was deaf and mute. They spent the rest of the day using fake sign language to communicate to one another while your dad faked an accent when he spoke." Xander laughed. "Man," he said with a shake of his head. "I used to love listening to Dad tell that story."

His voice trailed off and Ava shifted uncomfortably. It was increasingly apparent to Ava that Xander had stories of Nick that she had never heard. There was more depth in the relationship between Nick and this stranger than her father and herself.

"Well, I guess I'd better go change," she said with a forced smile.

"Yeah." He cleared his throat. "Meet you in a bit."

He reached over and placed a hand on her shoulder. Ava met his gaze and swallowed hard. There was something in his eyes that gave her pause—a pain that somehow mirrored her own.

Ava turned to leave, but not before she caught Zak eyeing her from across the room. She refused to make eye contact with her mom as she rushed next door and let herself in her own room.

"I'm here on a mission," she mumbled to herself as she crossed the hall, repeating the mantra she'd started earlier that morning. "No way am I falling for some guy named Xander Majors."

St. Petersburg, 1913

Alma pushed back from the table and brushed the hair off her forehead. That one curl was forever coming loose from the pins that she used in an attempt to secure it back away from her face, the way that the dignified women did. Of course, she wasn't one to call herself dignified.

"Alma?"

She turned and stood. "Uncle Albert! How are you today?"

He leaned down and gave her a quick kiss on the cheek. "Very well, my dear," he said. Standing up, he smoothed out his coat, the dark fabric of his black suit jacket snug around his rounded stomach. "How is Nicholas?"

Alma smiled, her cheeks growing warm at the mention of her husband. They'd been married for nearly a year, but she still found herself giggling like a girl whenever she heard his name. She couldn't believe he was hers.

"Very well," she said. "Working hard as always."

Albert nodded like a father satisfied with his child's progress. "I'm happy to hear it."

Albert adored Alma, and she knew it. When her own father

had passed away so young, Albert had been quick to come to their side, rushing to Moscow to be with her and her mother as they grieved. Albert took her under his wing that day, and he had looked after her ever since, making sure she was educated, bringing her to the House of Fabergé, and nurturing her talents every step of the way. It was Uncle Albert who was first to see her artistic ability, and he was the one who told her mother she would be better suited to train as an artist than as a homemaker.

And when Nicholas asked for her hand in marriage, Albert made him promise to never squelch her talent.

"She'll be a better wife when she's creating," he told Nicholas. "You remember that."

Still, Alma had wanted to be a traditional wife, and she tried those first few months after the wedding. It was late at night on their third month as husband and wife when Nicholas had crawled into bed next to her, so handsome in his undershirt and shorts, his face smelling earthy and clean. He snuggled close to her, tickling her neck with his prickly mustache until she giggled and pulled away. He kissed her, then pulled back and looked her in the eyes.

"You need to go back to work," he said.

She stared back at him with eyebrows raised. "Oh, really? And why is that, Mr. Klee?"

"Because, Mrs. Klee," he said with a devilish grin. He kissed her again. "You're better in the design room than you are in the kitchen."

Alma wanted to be angry with him, and she should feel insulted, but he was right. She was a miserable cook, and keeping their apartment neat and tidy brought her little satisfaction. She loved the thrill of design, the act of placing pencil to paper and bringing an image to life. After a long day sitting at her desk, she went home more energized than she'd ever felt during those months waiting for Nicholas to return from his job.

"What are you thinking, my dear?" Albert asked.

Alma cleared her throat and shook her head, chastising herself for slipping away again and not focusing on the conversation at hand. It was a flaw of hers, the constant wandering of the imagination. "Just a memory."

Albert studied her. "We would all do well to fall into the memories that make us smile more often than the ones that make us frown." He gave her a playful tap on the nose, then looked over her shoulder at the pad of paper on the desk. "Did you draw these?"

"Oh, yes." Alma reached down and picked up her drawing pad, handing it to him.

"These are stunning." Albert studied the pencil drawings closely, each stroke woven so perfectly into the next. "Where did you get this inspiration?"

Alma jutted her chin toward the small window beside her desk. Albert turned to looked at the icy crystals that had formed outside the window, cutting a pattern from one corner to the next, an intricate web of winter.

"Very interesting," he murmured.

Alma blushed. "I've had little to do these last few days, and I noticed the ice crystals on the window. They looked so delicate and dainty. I wondered what they would look like as earrings."

Albert smiled down at her. "You know, you've always had a magic eye for detail. Your father noticed it when you were very young."

"He did?" Alma's eyes lit up. She loved to hear stories of her beloved papa.

"Indeed," Albert nodded. "He used to write to me all about your drawings and imagination. He was quite taken with you."

Alma blinked up at him with eager, shining eyes. "I miss him every day," she said softly.

"As do I, my dear."

Albert studied the drawings she had made for a few moments, running his rough thumb over the elaborate designs. "May I borrow your sketch pad?"

"Yes, of course!"

"Good girl, I'll soon return with it." He leaned in and gave her a quick peck on the cheek, then turned and left.

Alma watched him walk away, her brow furrowed as she wondered what he was up to.

Ducking out of the room, Albert quickly descended the stairs to Fabergé's office. The boss had grown increasingly agitated lately. Albert believed it was a series of events frustrating the head of their shop: tensions at home, the pressures of his job, the demands that came with operating several branches remotely, and of course, what Albert suspected caused him the most consternation, the sensitive matter of his mistress marrying another man a few months ago.

It wasn't information that he wanted to know, or perhaps even should have known. But the high society circles were small, and gossip ran rampant, which was why Albert knew that the woman Karl Fabergé took with him on trips as his "assistant" had finally, officially, moved to Russia. Albert suspected she had wanted to come for some time, and that she'd wanted Karl to be the one to marry her. It was the only way she could gain citizenship, after all. Karl, however, flawed as he was, was still a family man, and he would never do that to his wife and sons. Still, Karl was quite bothered by her marriage.

Albert found the whole affair in bad taste, personally. Amalia had married seventy-five-year-old Georgian prince Karamon Tsitsiasov, quite hastily, taking his title and his money but, Albert heard, leaving him the day after the wedding. She'd gotten what she wanted: the title of princess and Russian citizenship. It was all difficult to stomach. Why his employer continued to harbor any feelings for that woman was a mystery to all. Though Albert had not met her, he'd heard stories of her arrogance and demeanor. She was beautiful, yes. But her beauty ended on the surface of her skin.

Augusta, on the other hand, did not possess a physical beauty, though she wasn't terribly homely. But her care for others, the nurturing nature of her personality, the way she loved and doted on her sons and, likewise, cared for the employees inside the House of Fabergé—these made her more beautiful than any fake princess Albert could imagine. For all of his boss's many wonderful qualities, his decision to be with Amalia was a character stain that was difficult to ignore.

Still, Albert loved Karl Fabergé just as his father before had loved him. And as he approached his office with Alma's sketches clutched in hand, he felt that familiar rush of excitement he always got when he knew he was about to please the master craftsman. He raised his fist and knocked gently.

"Come in," came the reply.

Albert pushed open the door and stepped inside. It was cold today, and Karl sat behind his desk with a blanket over his shoulders, hunched over a stack of drawings with a magnifying glass in hand, studying each one with his expert eye. A forgotten mug of chai sat beside him, as did a plate of black bread. Albert knew that Karl would be in a genial mood when he was this intent on working and studying the drawings of his creators.

"Ah, Albert my friend," Karl said glancing up. "Forgive me for not standing. It's too cold and my knees hurt terribly. Augusta says I should stand and walk, but it's more comfortable to stay sitting."

"Your wife may be correct, though."

"Yes, I suppose." Karl set down his magnifying glass. "She often is." He looked up at Albert, who shifted from one foot to the other. "What can I do for you? I trust everything upstairs is running smoothly today?"

"Yes, there are no issues. But I've come to show you some drawings and see what you think we should do with them."

He set the drawing pad on the table in front of Karl, who leaned over them and looked carefully.

"These are stunning," he said, glancing up. "Who drew them?"

Albert cleared his throat. "Well, young Alma did."

Karl leaned back over the drawings. "Of course she did," he said with an affectionate smile. "She is so skilled. Look at the way the shadows move to give the image a quality of realness. It's as though they are laying on top of the paper and could be plucked up and whisked away."

Alma had drawn a series of snowflakes and icicles, all so expertly sketched that they almost looked like they were melting. She had drawn them in patterns so that they could be designed into earrings or brooches, and beneath each sketch she'd written specifications for what materials to use to bring the drawings to life, namely diamonds.

"Do you know who Emanuel Nobel is, Albert?"

"Yes, sir. The nephew of the man who invented dynamite, correct?"

"Indeed." Karl handed the sketch pad back to Albert. "He's incredibly wealthy in his own right, of course. I've just gotten off the phone with him a few hours ago. He's placed an order—a rather pretentious order, if you ask me, but I suppose most such orders could be classified as such—for forty pieces that he can use as gifts. He and I settled on brooches. Those will be the most cost effective. He wants his pieces to be, in his own words, 'of a value so low that cannot be understood as bribes.'"

"What does that mean?" Albert asked.

"He wants to buy his way into high society without looking like he's buying his way into high society," Fabergé replied wryly. "I think Alma's design will suit this occasion perfectly. It's different and unique and will end up in the hands of the elite, which will ensure more orders and requests for her unique style. Tell her we're putting in the order now for forty of her icicle brooches."

Albert gave a slight bow. "She will be delighted."

Karl smiled. "I'd go up and tell her myself, but I'm afraid I'm just too stiff today to make it up the stairs."

"Of course. It's not a problem. I'll go tell her now." Albert turned to leave, then paused and turned back. "Oh, and sir? I would listen to your wife about getting up and moving around. She's a smart woman, and she cares about you."

Karl's eyes softened. He gave Albert a nod.

Albert bowed slightly in return, then turned and slipped through the door and maneuvered across the hall to the stairs. He quickly wove his way back to Alma's desk in the corner. He paused for a moment as he approached her. She'd pulled out another sheet of paper and was bent over, eyebrows furrowed in concentration, as her hand moved in the smallest of strokes over the page. What a gem of a young woman she had turned out to be. Albert felt the familiar pang of sadness wash over him as he thought of his dear brother who had loved his little girl so dearly. What pride he would have in seeing her now. Albert smiled at the drawings in his hand.

Few people would have stopped to study something so simple and unassuming as the ice forming on a windowpane, but of course Alma was not few people. She was the girl with a magic eye for detail. She saw the patterns most everyone else missed. Albert's brother had written him of Alma's talent when she was a young child. He still remembered one of the descriptions perfectly.

"Yesterday, she held a leaf up to the sun and commented on the veins inside the greenery. Before I knew it, she had taken a pencil and drawn a pattern on the page that exactly mirrored the leafy pattern, only she'd drawn the veins alone. It was a haunting, beautiful drawing by a seven-year-old. Dear brother, I must admit I'm quite taken with her gift."

"Well, brother," Albert murmured into the void of the stairwell. "Your girl is making quite the name for herself inside the House of Fabergé."

He entered the artist's room and walked the final steps to her desk, tossing the notebook down on the table in front of her. She jumped and looked up at him, then broke into a wide grin and let out a laugh.

"You scared me!"

"You work too hard," Albert replied.

Alma shrugged. She pulled her sketchbook toward her. "Where did you go?"

"Well"—Albert leaned forward, his broad hands resting on

the desk, and looked in her eyes—"I've just been with Fabergé. He's ordered your design be made into forty brooches to be sent to Emanuel Nobel."

Alma's eyes widened. She pushed back in her chair and stood up, throwing herself into Albert's arms.

"Thank you, Uncle Albert!" she exclaimed. "Is it true?" She pulled back and stood before him. "My design will be made?" Her face lit up and she bounced from foot to foot like a child.

"I'm afraid it's true, my dear," he replied. He leaned forward and kissed her forehead. "I am very proud of you."

"Who is Emanuel Nobel?"

"It's of no real importance," Albert said with a wave of his hand. "He's wealthy, and he wants jewelry, and you're going to give it to him. So, you'd better get to work because you're going to be busy. You need to finish writing the specifications and materials list, and you need to get this over to the jewelry maker to begin building them. There's no time to waste."

"Yes! Yes!" She clapped her hands and turned back to her desk. The light from the window streamed in, illuminating her face. She looked angelic and as happy as Albert had ever seen a person.

He leaned forward and spoke in her ear. "This is only the beginning, my dear. It starts with brooches, but your path is only just now being laid out. Soon, *you* will be the one designing the royal Easter eggs."

Alma sank back into her chair and studied her design carefully. She felt her cheeks grow warm at the thought of being the one in charge of this order. "Imagine," she murmured. "Me—a woman—a master craftsman in the House of Fabergé."

"Imagine that, indeed," Albert replied.

Present Day

A va?"

"I'm in the bathroom, Mom!" Ava adjusted her top and stared at herself again in the mirror, not sure what to think about her reflection. Today's disguise included a red-haired wig that had been cut into a trendy bob with bangs that hung to her eyebrows. The auburn strands framed her small face, and she turned her head from side to side.

Her outfit was even more puzzling. She wore black moto leggings with a crop top, and a long, oversized sweater over top. She looked like a college girl who was trying too hard to convince people she was fashionable.

"Can I come in?" Carol asked, knocking on the bathroom door.

Ava reached over and pulled it open, turning to her mom.

"Oh!" Carol stepped back and took in the sight of her daughter. "Well, this is . . . interesting."

Ava made a face and turned back to the mirror. "This is *weird.*"

Carol smiled. "Actually, I think you look stunning with red hair."

"You have to say that because you're my mom."

"It's true. I am contractually bound to give you compliments, whether they're accurate or not," Carol replied. "I'm serious, though. You look lovely as a redhead. But you need a little more makeup so you don't look so washed out."

"Can you help me?" Ava glanced at her watch. "I need to be downstairs in ten minutes."

Carol pulled the makeup bag toward her and fished around, pulling out powder and blush, eye shadow and mascara, and finally, a tube of nude-colored lipstick.

"It's been a while since you let me do your makeup," she said with a smile.

When Ava was a child, she loved to sit cross-legged on Carol's bed and let her mom do her makeup. Carol had worked part-time in the evenings back then as a beauty consultant behind a makeup counter in a department store, a necessary second job that helped her make ends meet until she finally got a promotion at work that allowed her to stay home in the after-school hours.

Ava had been her willing mannequin, sitting for hours as her mom tried new and different makeup techniques. The tradition had carried over long after Carol quit the department store job, and the two of them had spent many hours together playing with makeup and makeovers.

Sometime around Ava's junior year of high school, which happened to coincide with the last visit she'd had with her father, she'd found the idea of "Makeovers with Mom" less appealing. Ava knew her mom not-so-affectionately referred to that time between the end of high school and college as "the dark years."

"So, you're playing Xander's wife today then, huh?" Carol

murmured, interrupting Ava's thoughts. She tapped a makeup brush on the side of her hand, then gestured for Ava to close her eyes.

Ava sighed. "Yes. This wouldn't be my first choice."

"It's not the worst assignment you've ever had, though, is it?" Carol gave her a little wink.

Ava pursed her lips. Carol put a few finishing touches on the makeup, then stepped back with a satisfied smile.

"There," she said. "Now tell me that this look isn't fantastic on you."

Ava studied herself closely. Her mom had done a good job on the makeup application. It highlighted her cheekbones, made her eyes pop, and yet still looked completely natural.

"Not bad, Mom," she said.

Carol tossed her arms up in a touchdown pose and turned around triumphantly. "Let it be known that on this day, my daughter conceded to not only let me make her look like a lady, but that she even liked my work!" She pumped her fist back and forth victoriously.

"Okay, well," Ava said, rolling her eyes good-naturedly. She kissed her mom on the cheek, then brushed past her, walked to the bedroom, and grabbed her room key and her satchel. She picked up the falsified passport that gave her new identity and glanced at it again.

She held the photo page up to her mom. "How the heck do you think Nick pulled this off?"

Carol leaned forward and studied the page carefully. "That's amazing!"

Somehow, Nick had managed to get a photo of Ava with bob-length red hair into this fake passport.

"He must be some kind of wiz with Photoshop," Ava murmured. "Also, check this out." She turned to a back page in the passport and held up a very official-looking entry stamp. "They even drew a stamp for me."

"It's drawn?" Carol asked.

"Yeah," Ava said. She held it closer for Carol to study. "If you look closely, you can tell this was colored on, not stamped. But it looks exactly like the real stamp! I just hope no one official asks to look at it."

Carol crossed her arms. "I'm still not comfortable with all of this. You be very careful today."

"I will, Mom. I promise." She drew in a deep breath, then let it out slowly. "Guess I'd better head down and meet my husband." She shook her head. "This is so weird."

Carol smiled. "Love you, my little redhead," she said with a wave.

Ava stepped out of their room and walked to the elevator, forcing herself to hold her head up high and walk with steps that exuded more confidence than she actually felt. She pushed the button for the elevator and turned to study herself in the mirror hanging on the wall opposite the elevators. She looked like such a different version of herself, but there was something that she enjoyed about it.

"Red hair," she murmured. "Who would've thought."

She stiffened as a man and woman rounded the corner and stopped at the elevator. Turning, Ava glanced at them quickly out of the corner of her eye. The man wore a sharp, black suit, tight over his paunchy frame. His red tie was tucked into the jacket, but Ava could tell that he'd dressed quickly, as she could see the tie bunched up at his midsection beneath his coat.

His hair was thin at the top, but thicker on the sides, and

he'd slicked it over, dark black strands mixed with wiry silver ones all forced to lay down in submission by an overly generous helping of hair gel.

He clutched the hand of a woman who appeared to be half his age, and who looked less than interested in being his arm candy. She had platinum blond hair, the kind that had probably once been full and beautiful, but that had been chemically treated so often that it now looked fragile and brittle. Her clothes were fashionable, but shabby, like she'd worn them too often and for far too long.

As they waited awkwardly for the elevator to arrive, the man turned and said something to Ava in Russian, and her heart skipped a beat. She shrugged her shoulders, giving them an apologetic look.

"No Russian," she said.

Mercifully, the elevator door dinged in front of them. The man gave her a smile that made her feel uncomfortable.

"You speak English," he said in a heavy accent. The three of them stepped onto the elevator. "American?"

She punched the number 1 for the lobby and nodded again, hands sweating. She thought about Xander's admonishment to stay invisible. She wished he would have given her suggestions for what to do if she wound up on the elevator with people.

"I live in America for little while," the man continued, oblivious to Ava's discomfort.

She glanced at the girl who still clutched his hand. Her eyes stayed trained on the ground.

"In New York," he continued. "Very beautiful in America, but is better in Russia, yes?" He laughed, a low, sickly sound that gurgled in his throat. "What is your name?"

Ava panicked, completely forgetting her alias for the day.

What was her name? She opened her mouth, then shut it as the elevators stopped and the doors slid open.

"Nice to meet you," she murmured, stepping through the doors.

The man followed her, practically pulling the woman behind him.

"But we did not meet," he said.

Ava looked up and saw Xander waiting for her in the lobby. She blinked as she took in the sight of him. He wore a wig today, which gave him a head full of blond curls. On anyone else, that would have looked completely ridiculous, but somehow it made him only look more handsome.

He wore dark skinny jeans and a fitted V-neck sweater. A brown leather jacket completed the look, as did the scarf that he held over his arm. He looked like a trendy millennial who absolutely belonged on the crowded streets of a bustling city. He caught sight of her followers. Ava widened her eyes in a silent cry for help as he rushed forward toward her.

"There you are," he said. He leaned down and kissed her cheek, sending a jolt down her spine. He glanced at the man and woman who had stopped awkwardly behind them and gave a slight nod of the head.

Ava grabbed Xander's hand and turned with him toward the door. "That guy is following me," she hissed.

"Walk confidently," he murmured, his hand clutching hers. "Look up at me and smile right now."

Ava turned her head and looked at Xander, pushing her lips into a smile. He grinned back, squeezing her hand reassuringly. They walked briskly through the expansive lobby, morning light streaming through the windows, illuminating the space with a cheery, opulent glow. Xander's polished shoes clacked on the marble floors as he and Ava made their way through the glass doors.

"Here," Xander said. He put his scarf over her shoulders and wrapped it around her neck twice. He leaned down and kissed her forehead. "He's still watching us," he whispered. "Don't look."

Ava pulled her eyes back to Xander's face, completely at a loss for words with him hovering so near to her. She was going to have to pull herself together if she was going to make it through the day pretending to be his wife.

A black car pulled up in front of them and came to a stop. Xander yanked the back door open and gestured for Ava to get in. He slid in quickly behind her. Seconds later, they pulled away from the front of the hotel toward the bustling street. Ava let out a long sigh and collapsed back into the leather seat.

"What the heck was that?" she asked, turning to look at Xander.

"Well, Mrs. Andrews. You just shared an elevator with Evgeny Lazovsky."

"You speak to Lazovsky?" Anatoly spoke from the front seat. He glanced at Xander in the mirror, eyebrows raised.

"Who is Evgeny Lazovsky?" Ava looked from Xander to Anatoly and back.

"He is bad man," Anatoly answered after a brief pause. "You should . . . how do you say in English . . ." He looked at Xander and said a word in Russian.

Xander nodded. "We should avoid him."

"He just ended up on the elevator with me," Ava replied, feeling a little defensive.

"Of course," Xander said. "You couldn't prevent that. But we should be careful. When we get back today, we'll stay together until we've reached the rooms."

"And what happens when we end up wearing different disguises? What if he runs into us then?"

"This is why we'll be careful." Xander sat back against the seat and shook his head. "Lazovsky was staring at you like a piece of meat."

"Who was that girl with him?" Ava asked.

"Probably his latest mistress," Xander replied.

"Or call girl," Anatoly said.

Ava sighed and leaned back. "Is it always this way?"

"What?"

"Hunting. Is it always so frustrating? Because I've seen the movies and read the books, and this is nothing like those. This is so . . . anticlimactic."

Xander smiled. "This isn't *National Treasure*, Ava. Nicholas Cage isn't going to come strolling out with some bogus history that leads us on a wild, international goose chase."

Ava raised her eyebrows. She looked around, gesturing her hand toward the window. "Bogus history. Wild, international goose chase."

Xander laughed, shaking his head so that the blond curls of his wig bounced stiffly. "Touché. But it's still not the same. This is real life, not some story in a book."

"Feels like a story in a book," Ava responded.

"Oh really?" Xander leaned over so that his face was closer to hers. He studied her eyes beneath the bangs of her red wig. "If this were a book, what part would I be playing?"

Ava's heart thumped. She narrowed her eyes and forced herself to stare back at him. "You'd be the romantic interest turned bad guy in the end," she said, her voice cracking as he continued to gaze at her so intently.

Xander smiled. "Romantic interest turned bad guy? And why, exactly, is that?"

Ava bit her lip and shook her head. "Come on," she said. "You can't look like . . . that"—she waved her hand in his face—"and not be the romantic lead. But the book would be boring without a bad guy, so if *I* were writing the story, I'd give you an ulterior motive to keep things interesting."

Xander laughed. "And I guess you'd be playing the tortured damsel in distress?"

"No way! I'm no damsel, and I'm not in distress. I don't need some macho romantic lead to rescue me."

"Who's your character then?"

"The tortured leading lady with daddy issues who overcomes, cracks the code, and solves one of the greatest mysteries in Soviet history. I'm the female Ethan Hunt." She flashed him a proud smile.

"So, would the female Ethan Hunt make a connection with the dashing romantic interest in this book of yours?"

Ava shook her head. "Nah," she said, forcing her voice to sound cool and even. "She'd be too busy trying to track down the treasure for romance. And besides, he turns into the bad guy. She would figure him out."

Xander chuckled. He reached over and brushed the hair out of her eyes, a simple gesture that sent a shiver down her spine. "Well, it's a good thing you aren't writing the story now, isn't it?"

Ava looked at him for a beat, then turned her head and stared out the window, watching as the streets of St. Petersburg bustled by, a tangle of cars and people, modern and historical, all of it locked together to form a chaotic picture of beauty.

"Oh, hey, Anatoly," she said, in a not-so-subtle attempt to change the subject. "Nick asked us last night to have you give him a call. He said he wanted to catch up with you."

Anatoly glanced at her in the rearview mirror, red-rimmed eyes surrounded by a puffy face. Ava thought about Xander's comment that Anatoly worked best with a side of vodka, and she could see the effects of this in the sallow pallor of his skin.

"Yes, Mr. Xander tell me this," Anatoly said. "I will call Nick soon. I am very busy man right now, so is difficult—"

"Ah, here we are, then," Xander said. "Bolshaya Morskaya. Once a bustling business district for the rich and the bourgeoisie. In Fabergé's day, this would have been the place where the wealthiest spent their time. Just down at the end of this street and around the corner is Nevsky Prospekt and, of course, the palace where Tsar Nicholas and his family spent most of their time."

"It looks so ordinary now," Ava said. She gazed at the busy street, cars weaving and snaking their way past a line of buildings that stretched as far as she could see.

Xander nodded. "It is. Now it's a mixture of tourist shops, apartment buildings, and fancy Airbnbs. You'd hardly know that the top names in Russian history once called this home."

"But you see buildings there?" Anatoly gestured at the buildings in front of them, each one designed in that unique style that made St. Petersburg so different from other Russian cities. "The architecture is very interesting."

Ava liked the sound of his words, how he pronounced *een-ter-est-ing*, and the way he seemed to swallow his *r*s before he finished saying them.

"Was very modern back then, these buildings," Anatoly said. "Very fancy."

"I imagine it was." Ava pointed as they rounded the corner. "What is that building there—the one with the glass globe on top?"

"Is old Singer building," Anatoly said.

Xander nodded. "Yeah, you know Singer sewing machines?"

Ava stared up at the globe, marveling at its design.

"This used to be their manufacturing building. They had the glass and metal globe constructed as a symbol of the spread of their company throughout the world."

"Interesting." Ava took in the sights of Nevsky Prospekt. The sun was shining today, which lit up the city in a way that she could only describe as magnificent.

"It's beautiful, isn't it?" Xander asked.

Ava met his gaze. "This really is a spectacular city."

Xander turned to look out the window. "That this city stands at all after both of the world wars is mind-boggling."

Ava nodded. "It was under siege for nearly 900 days in World War Two. But the Nazis never did manage to get into the city. These buildings were preserved by the lives of tens of thousands of people who fought to protect it. It's just . . ."

"Amazing," Xander said.

Ava glanced at him. "Yeah."

"You know an awful lot about the history of this city for never having been here."

Ava shrugged. "I have a headful of useless knowledge and historical facts."

"I wouldn't say it's useless," Xander said. "History is one of our greatest assets. Knowing where we've been as a human race helps us navigate where we're going."

Ava cocked her head to the side.

"What? Do you find me shallow?"

"No! Of course not. I just didn't . . . expect that from you."
She swallowed and tossed him a sheepish gaze.

"Yeah, well, don't underestimate me." Xander gave her a
playful punch on the arm. "I'm more than just a pretty face."

Ava rolled her eyes. "You did *not* just say that," she said.

Xander laughed.

Anatoly slowed down and pulled to the side of the road.
"You get out here. Number 24 is one more building down."
He gestured out the window in front of him. Xander leaned
forward and murmured something to Anatoly in Russian while
Ava looked out the window and studied her surroundings. She
fiddled with her wig self-consciously, then turned as Xander
leaned back.

"Alright, Mrs. Andrews," he said with a crooked smile. "Shall
we go look at the apartment?"

Ava offered him a tight-lipped smile, steeling herself against
Xander's charm. He opened his door and stepped out onto
the sidewalk. Ava slid across the seat and stepped out next to
him, drawing in a deep breath as the frigid air slapped her in
the face.

"What exactly are we going to do when we get in there?"
Ava asked as they turned down the sidewalk.

"We're going to ask to sit in the apartment for a little while
and discuss whether or not we would like to rent it for an
extended period. With any luck, the landlady will leave completely, at which point we'll do a search."

"A search?" Ava asked. "Surely you guys don't think there's
any way something would be left behind in the apartment after
all these years. The thought of it is absurd."

"Totally absurd," Xander said. "But there's a singular line in
Alma's poem that I think needs to be explored, and Nick agrees."

"What?" Ava stopped and looked at him.

"'*The secret beneath the boards,*'" he said. "We need to figure out what that means. Was something hidden beneath the floorboards or behind a wall? This is our chance to at least make an attempt to look around."

"Yeah, but don't you think something as simple as that would have been discovered already?" Ava asked.

"Not necessarily," Xander replied with a shrug. "We're the only people who have that poem, and from what we've found so far it seems she only wrote that poem inside that one place. Which means, we're the only people with that single clue. And don't forget what Zak said. When they were forced to leave the House of Fabergé, no one was ever allowed to go back in. Who knows what could have been left behind."

She nodded slowly. "Okay," she said.

Xander held out his arm, his elbow bent so that Ava could grab hold of it. She balked for a moment, the gesture so intimate and casual that it threw her off. Then she tucked her hand into the crook of his elbow.

Together they approached the front of 24 Bolshaya Morskaya. She paused for a brief moment to take in the building, the gray façade standing regally before them. So much history haunted the space just beyond those concrete walls. Did the people who walked by here every day know it? Did they feel the weight of the past the way that she did?

It was why she'd ultimately chosen to study history, despite her mother's admonitions that she'd never be able to do anything with that degree. She had always been enamored with the stories of others. It started when she was little, and she read the *Little House on the Prairie* books by Laura Ingalls Wilder. Suddenly, the past came alive inside her mind, and she found herself wishing she could visit it for just a little while.

Somehow, Ava knew that she'd always felt the importance of history more than most kids. She just got it. And it never made sense to her why, until this one, singular moment standing in front of Fabergé's old building. She was made to chase history. She just never knew she might catch a piece of it on the way.

"You ready?" Xander asked.

Drawing in a deep breath, Ava turned and flashed him a smile. "Lead the way," she said.

"*Zdravstvuyte*," Xander said, holding out his hand to the woman who answered the door. He went on to introduce himself in Russian, then pointed at Ava, who flashed as sincere a smile as she could.

The woman nodded, then pulled the door open wider to let them in. She asked Xander a question, and he shook his head, answering in such a genial manner that the woman's face broke into a broad smile.

What do you know, Ava thought. *He's charming in more than one language.*

"You not speak Russian?" the woman asked, turning to Ava and taking her by surprise.

"Oh . . . um . . . no, I don't. I'm sorry," she answered.

"Is okay. I speak in English little bit." She held up her thumb and forefinger, slightly separated, to emphasize her point, then tapped her head above her ear. "I understand much better."

Ava nodded.

The woman looked back and forth between Ava and Xander, both dressed so hip and modern with their trendy hair and clothes. Ava resisted the urge to smooth out her red wig, trusting it looked natural and in place.

"My name is Marina," the woman said. "I live in building and help to rent apartments." She searched for her next words while Ava studied her.

Marina looked to be older than Ava suspected she really was. Her face was lined and worn but laced with kindness, as though she had experienced all the pain of life but had chosen not to let it make her bitter. She wore a wide dress over her stout frame, her brown salt-and-pepper hair pulled into a loose bun at the nape of her neck. A few strands fell around her face, and Ava imagined that in her youth she had been quite pretty.

"You are new married?" Marina asked, looking from Xander to Ava.

"We are," Xander said, grabbing Ava around her waist and pulling her into him.

Ava tried to relax as she offered Marina a stiff smile.

"Is very nice," Marina said. "Very pretty wife," she said, giving Xander a little wink.

He laughed and leaned forward. "I'm the luckiest man alive."

"Please, come in. This is only apartment for rent right now."

"It's lovely," Ava said as they stepped into the first room. The apartment was large and airy, plainly decorated and bare. Two large windows stood on the opposite wall, letting in enough natural light to make the space feel quite open. A tapestry hung on the wall, making Ava think of Zak and his apartment at home. She smiled at the thought.

A short divan sat between the windows, and on the opposite side was a light brown armoire with the cabinets open to reveal a small TV.

"Is very nice apartment here," Marina was saying as she

guided them through the sitting room into the kitchen. "Very quiet from street, and central to all business. You do business in Petersburg?" She looked at Xander.

"I have a job that allows me to work remote from anywhere I like. It's mostly online programming and whatnot," Xander replied. "Molly and I"—he glanced at Ava—"wanted to start our marriage off with an adventure, and we've both been so fascinated with the history of Russia, so we decided we'd start it here."

Marina nodded, the expression on her face knowing, almost as though she couldn't imagine why anyone would consider any other place more worthy of beginning their lives than St. Petersburg.

"Is very good choice," she said. "And this apartment very interesting place for you to begin. There is exciting history that happened in these very rooms."

"Oh really?" Xander said. "What is it?"

"This building was House of Fabergé." Marina stood up taller, clearly pleased to be able to offer the Americans a little taste of her knowledge.

"Like, Fabergé eggs?" Ava asked.

Marina nodded. "Yes, very famous eggs made right here in this building."

"Inside this apartment?" Xander asked.

"No, workshop was upstairs. This apartment was showroom and Fabergé's office. Come, I show you bedroom that used to be place where Fabergé worked."

They followed Marina down a narrow hallway that felt much too enclosed for Ava's liking. Still the apartment was very large. Ava wondered how much an apartment like this rented for, given its size and location.

At the end of the hall were two open doors, one on the right and one on the left. Marina guided them into a plain room with white walls and the same wood flooring as the rest of the apartment. A full-size bed sat against the wall, with two floor lamps on either side. A small dresser stood on the opposite side of the room next to a door that Ava assumed led to a closet. A big window looked outside to a small garden area on a patio.

"Is very nice room, yes?" Marina asked. "Very simple and quiet. Perfect for young love." She flashed a toothy grin as Ava shifted uncomfortably from one foot to the other. Xander laughed good-naturedly as though he and Marina had always been friends and such a joke was not at all awkward or inappropriate.

"It's great," he said enthusiastically.

"And what does young lady think?" Marina asked.

"Oh, um, yes. It's . . . uh . . . lovely," Ava stammered. "Um, Marina, can you tell me about these floors? They're very nice. Are they original?"

"Of course," Marina answered with a nod. "Is little original here because building is so old. All has been repaired and fixed. But the floors"—she tapped her foot twice—"they keep floors to help us preserve history."

"Interesting." Ava tossed a surreptitious look at Xander.

"Come, I show you more," Marina said with a wave of her hand.

Xander shot Ava a raised eyebrow and gave her a quick thumbs-up behind Marina's back as they followed her down the hall.

"You see bathroom here. Is very nice," Marina said, waving her hand to the open door on the right. "And here is coat closet."

She pulled open a door that stood just across the hall from the main sitting room. The closet was narrow and long. Marina pulled a string on an overhead light and lit the enclosed space up to reveal two shelves that stretched the length of the closet. Under those were long bars for hanging coats. Two thin blankets and an extra pillow were stacked on the shelves.

"This space very interesting. Builders made closet to be bigger because they say this is spot where Fabergé's salesmen stood to greet customers."

"Wow," Ava murmured. She leaned down to touch the floor. The wood was definitely aged, dark and worn. There was a heavy grain to the flooring, and Ava could tell it was warped in certain places. She stood back up.

"Old flooring is so beautiful," she said.

Marina nodded. "Yes."

Ava got the impression that Marina would say anything she could to rent this apartment out to Jack and Molly Andrews. They stepped out of the closet and walked back into the sitting room.

"Well, and what do you think?" Marina asked. "Is this nice place to start your life?"

Ava turned to look at Xander, who gave a little shrug in reply. "Could we have a few moments alone in the apartment?" she asked, shifting her gaze back to Marina. "I'd like to just sit here and feel the energy."

Marina nodded her head knowingly, as if that was the most reasonable statement she'd heard all day. "Yes, of course. Very smart. Very wise." She flashed Xander a wide smile, her crooked front teeth exposed. "Take your time. I just go upstairs and have my chai. When ready, come to find me. I am first door at top of stairs." She nodded at them both, then turned and walked out of the apartment, the door clicking shut behind her.

Ava turned to Xander. "So . . ."

"Right." He looked around. "Where to start."

"I'll start in the closet," Ava said.

Xander nodded. "I'll poke around the rest of the place."

They split up, with Ava walking quickly to the closet and pulling open the door. She stood for a moment, staring into the space, watching as tiny flecks of dust danced in the beam of light that radiated out in a fluorescent glow. She ducked inside and got onto her hands and knees, feeling gently along the boards, running her fingers over the seams. About halfway through, she sat up and let out a laugh.

"This is ridiculous," she said out loud. "What would we possibly find here after all these years?"

Xander appeared in the doorway. "What is it?"

Ava turned to him with a shake of her head. "I was just sitting here thinking how silly it is that I'm on my hands and knees looking for some clue that clearly would have been found by now if it was here."

Xander stepped through the doorway and held his hand out to Ava, pulling her to her feet. The two of them were now sandwiched together between the narrow walls, Ava's chin right at Xander's chest. Her heart thumped as she looked up and met Xander's eyes.

"Well, it seems we're a bit stuck, doesn't it?" he said. His voice was softer, a little husky, and his accent almost intoxicating. Instead of pulling away, Ava found herself leaning in. Xander lifted his hand and brushed the red hair out of Ava's eyes, running his finger down her cheek and settling his hand beneath her chin. She tilted her face up, eyes drifting closed as she felt him draw near.

With a start, he pulled back, his hand leaving her chin and

going to his ear. Ava's eyes flew open, and she stared at him in surprise and embarrassment.

"Zak, mate," Xander said. "What was that? Repeat what you just said again."

Suddenly, Ava remembered that Zak and her mother could see and hear everything they did through the cameras on their clothes and the piece in Xander's ear. Her face grew hot as she pushed away from Xander, stumbling back into the hallway outside the closet, hands shaking and throat tight with humiliation.

"Interesting, man," Xander said. "You found that where?"

Ava took in a deep breath and leaned against the wall, crossing her arms over her chest.

"Got it. We'll check right now," Xander said.

He turned to Ava and cleared his throat awkwardly. "So," he began.

"What'd Zak say?" Ava asked, quickly directing him away from any mention of what almost happened between the two of them.

Xander stared at her for a beat, then continued. "He was going through the files under Fabergé's name, and he came across the specifications for hidden levers and spring release mechanisms that Fabergé used in his eggs. They were almost computerized, the way that he was able to get things to move around and spring open. It's what made them so interesting and fascinating at the time."

Ava thought of the *Swan Egg*, in which the small platinum jewel-encrusted swan "floated" on a sea of aquamarine through a spring mechanism designed by Fabergé.

"What does that have to do with us?"

"Zak wondered if Fabergé would have used a similar type of mechanism to hide something within the boards of his home."

Ava looked back inside the closet. *"The secret beneath the boards."*

She stepped around Xander and went back into the closet, sliding her fingers along the seams of the boards again, this time pressing down and releasing pressure repeatedly. Xander watched from behind, careful to stay out of her way.

Slowly, she made her way down the first seam to the back wall, then slid her hand over to the next seam and pressed down. On and on she went down the length of the closet. As she reached the corner farthest back, she looked over her shoulder at Xander and shook her head.

"Nothing in here," she said. As the words disappeared into the space between them, she felt a pinch on her fingers and looked down at the floor. She pushed again, the board moving just slightly. Ava narrowed her eyes and leaned into it a little more, pushing harder.

She saw the slightest separation between the two boards.

"No way," she said.

Xander ducked inside the closet and leaned over her. "What is it?"

"Could be nothing. It very well could be old wood that's warped and separated with time, but . . ."

"It could be more than that," Xander said.

"Exactly."

"Most people would have just assumed that it was old flooring acting up."

Ava pushed again, feeling the give beneath her fingers grow more pronounced.

Placing the heel of her hand on top of the wood, she began to push it up and down, moving her hand backward and forward as she did so. The wood bowed and cricked beneath her, like aging knees being forced to stand after sitting for much too long. With a grunt, Ava gave one last push. The floorboard under her hand slid forward, then dipped down a quarter inch. Ava turned to look at Xander with wide eyes. She pushed the board to the right, sliding it easily beneath the board on top and creating a hole large enough to fit both of her hands inside.

"I do not believe this," she murmured.

"Ava," Xander whispered, his breath hot in her hair. He reached in his pocket and pulled out his phone, swiping down and flipping on the flashlight. Holding it over the black hole, he and Ava peered inside.

"It's pretty deep," Ava said.

"Can you see inside?"

"Not far." Taking a deep breath, she reached tentatively into the hole. "This is freaky. What if there are monster spiders down here just waiting to pounce on me?"

"Like gatekeepers of the treasure?" Xander asked. "Soviet spiders tasked with guarding the secrets of the past? I like it."

"Yeah, you make fun of me, but it won't be funny when one of them bites me, and I turn into a giant spider. And then I eat you."

"Man, it must be fun inside your head."

Ava grimaced, her hand hovering just past the edge of the hole. "Okay, I'm going in," she said. She closed her eyes and leaned down, reaching farther inside. Her hand hit the ground, and she yelped, pulling back briefly.

"What's wrong? What was it?" Xander moved the light around in an attempt to see better.

"Nothing. Sorry," Ava said. "It just scared me when I hit the bottom. Hold on."

She reached back inside, a little more slowly, moving her fingers back and forth until she felt the bottom again. She winced.

"It feels gritty," she said.

"Move your hand around and see if you find anything. How big is the space?"

Heart thumping, Ava moved her hand around in a circular motion. "Please don't be spiders. Please don't be spiders," she whispered. Her fingertips grazed across something cold toward the back corner of the hole. She reached farther in, now laying almost on her stomach, and grasped the corner of what felt like a metal box, so cold it hurt her fingertips to linger on it for long. She pulled her arms out and brushed her hands.

"There's a box down there," she said. "But I can't reach it. My arms aren't long enough." She shifted and shimmied up to her feet, awkwardly sliding past Xander. She took the phone from his hand. "You try."

Xander lowered to his knees and put his hand inside the floorboards. "You're right," he said with a grimace. "This is a little unsettling."

"Thank you! Look out for the Soviet spiders."

Xander leaned forward more and shifted his hand back until he felt the box. He grasped it tightly and pulled it forward until it was just beneath the opening.

"It's too wide to get out of this slot," he said, peering inside.

"What if you stand it up on its side?" Ava asked.

Xander nodded. He reached back in and tried to grip the sides of the box to turn it upward, but his fingers slipped. It took several tries, but he finally got a firm enough hold on the box that he was able to shift it to its side.

Ava peered over his shoulder at the box. "Here, let me try again," she said. "I think I can get it out now."

They switched places again, Ava dropping to her knees and gingerly reaching inside the gap with both hands. She grabbed either side of the box and slowly began pulling it upward, ignoring the way it felt like ice on her fingers. At the opening, the sides of the box scraped against the wood, the space growing tighter and more difficult to navigate.

"I'm almost there," Ava said breathlessly.

When she got the box high enough over the ledge of the flooring, Xander reached over her shoulder and helped, the two of them working together until it popped free and landed with a metallic thud on the floor in front of Ava's knees.

"I cannot *believe* this." Ava brushed dirt from the lid, her fingertips lingering for a moment on the cool material.

The two of them stared at the metal box on the floor. Ava reached down, picked it up, and set it in her lap. It was sturdy and heavy, with a small lock on the side.

She glanced up at Xander. "How will we open it?"

He leaned forward, shining his phone light onto the lock. "That looks easy enough to pick," he said. He reached inside his coat pocket and pulled out what looked like a small, cloth-covered booklet. Flipping it open, he revealed several small tools, each long and pointed but different widths.

"You have a lock-picking kit in your coat?" Ava asked dryly. "For real?"

"This isn't my first rodeo," he replied with a wink. He pulled out one of the tools and took the box from Ava. Sitting down on the floor beside her, he stuck the tool inside the lock and moved it around slowly, his brow furrowed in concentration. After a few moments, a small click echoed between them. Xander turned with a triumphant smile.

"Voilà!" he said.

Ava stared at him. "This is nuts. No one will believe it."

"Here." Xander pushed the box toward her. "You open it."

Ava took the box and stuck her fingernail under the lid, prying it open slowly. She pushed back the top and stared inside, her face falling.

"Empty," she said.

"What?" Xander leaned forward and looked inside. A bed of worn red velvet lay empty and cold, like a coffin that had been robbed of its bedmate. The slightest impression made a dent in the middle of the velvet, but otherwise the box was vacant. Xander reached inside and tugged on the material, the fabric giving way easily beneath his fingertips. He pulled it back and saw a second layer of velvet beneath, also empty. He tugged on that and pulled away what seemed to be a hidden shelf. At the bottom of the box lay a single sheet of paper, folded neatly into a square.

"Whoa," Xander said. He picked up the paper and unfolded it gingerly. He held the paper out for Ava to see.

It was a colored drawing of an egg in minute detail. Beside the egg was a drawing of a crown, clearly encrusted in diamonds and rubies, regal and pointed and resembling the royal crown of the tsar. Notes were written off to the side in elegant Russian script. Below both of those drawings was a third, smaller drawing of a fist, raised in the air, standing on what appeared to be a platform of gold.

"Look at the way the fist sits just below the crown," Xander said.

Ava nodded. She pointed to the bottom right corner of the page. "Look there," she said.

К. Фаберже
Для России

"'K. Fabergé. For Russia,'" Xander said. He turned to Ava. "We were right. The egg is real, and it was here."

Ava's excitement deflated. "But it's not anymore."

"No, but it *was*."

Ava reached her hand out and Xander placed the drawing in her open palm. She held it gingerly between her fingers. It felt fragile, as though it could simply dissolve like salt in water. She turned the page over and squinted.

Astonishment flooded her. "Hold on." The air around them felt thicker, and the room stilled. It was as though time itself had decided to stop for a few brief moments.

"What is it?" Xander asked.

Ava looked up at him. "Can I have your flashlight?"

He flipped up his phone and turned the light back on, holding it above the page. Ava narrowed her eyes once more. Xander peered over the top of the page in an effort to see what she saw.

"There was writing here," Ava said. "Look."

She turned the paper toward Xander, then took the light from his hand so he could study it more closely.

"I see," he said. "It looks like it was erased." He pulled the paper closer to his face, then drew in a deep breath. "This writing was in English."

"I thought so too!" Ava scooted to sit beside him, her shoulder pressed up against his.

"Here, see?" Xander held the page in front of her. "There's the word 'the.' And here. I think this is the word 'bridge.'"

Ava nodded. She held the light closer, trying to make out the faded letters. "That second word starts with an *a*. And I think there's a *k* in there too. See it?"

"Yeah." He ran his fingers over faint letters here and there, most of it faded so badly it was impossible to read. He sighed.

"Let's go back to the hotel and work on this," he said. "We need better lighting."

"Yeah," Ava conceded. "And we need food. I'm starving."

Xander laughed. "Yeah, there's that."

"Seriously," Ava continued. "A girl can't survive on tea and black bread alone. I'm gonna need a real meal at some point."

Xander folded the paper back up carefully and handed it to Ava. "Put this in your bag," he said. She nodded, then jutted her chin out toward the box.

"What do we do with that?"

"Let's put it back."

She took the box from Xander and gingerly slid it back between the space in the floorboards, wincing when it slipped through the opening and fell to the floor below with a clang. She reached in, turned it to lay flat, and slid it as far back as she could. She then reached beneath the opening, found the ledge of the missing board, and pulled it back to the opening, then pushed on it slightly. She watched in amazement as the board slowly raised back up and into place. After shimmying it around a few times until the boards met in perfect order, she sat back and marveled at the design.

"He really was a master," she said. Upon looking at the boards now, you could not discern the break between the two. She pushed on the floor and found that it gave a little easier beneath her fingertips, but it didn't show any indication of the opening.

Ava got to her feet. She dusted her hands off and turned to Xander.

"So, what do we tell Marina?" she asked.

"We'll tell her that we love it, and we will be back tomorrow to sign the paperwork. I'll call her tonight and tell her we've had a family emergency and we need to get back to the States as soon as possible. She'll be disappointed, but she's not going to have a problem renting out this space. It's a cool apartment."

Ava nodded. She reached for her satchel, which she had laid on the floor outside the closet, and she gently placed the drawing into a folder and slid it into the bag.

"I still can't believe this," she said with a shake of her head.

"Mrs. Andrews," Xander replied with a lopsided grin, "I believe you just made your first big breakthrough."

Zak yanked the headphones off his ears and dropped them on the table with a frustrated sigh. Carol looked at him sympathetically.

"You okay?" she asked gently.

"Oh, I will be fine, Miss Carol." He shook his head. "I'm sorry. I'm just not enjoying this treasure hunt as much as I thought that I would." He tossed her an apologetic smile.

"Oh, Zak, you don't need to apologize to me," Carol said with a wave. "I'm not having much fun either. It's pretty clear I wasn't needed on this trip. I think Nick and Ava were just humoring me."

"What happened between Mr. Nick and Ava anyway?" he asked.

"Oh, they're both stubborn," Carol replied with a sigh. "Nick is terribly awkward. He doesn't know how to talk to the people he loves most, and despite my best attempts at keeping that from happening with Ava, I'm afraid she is much the same way. The apple fell right beneath the tree."

Zak nodded. "Ava *can* be awkward."

"Yes, she can," Carol said, her voice tight.

"But she's also incredibly intuitive about how people are feeling," he said.

"What makes you say that?"

"Well," Zak said, "I've just watched the way she reacts to people. She studies them, and her eyes tell a story."

"A story?"

"Yes. There is a lot more going on inside than she lets on. Like there was this one time . . ." Zak paused. "We had gone with a few other people from our apartment complex to volunteer at a local homeless shelter, and Ava sat down next to this older man. He needed someone to talk to, you know? And Ava just sat and listened to him. She didn't interrupt or try to offer some pithy advice that wouldn't mean anything. She just heard him, and I think she really saw him. She had this intuitive understanding that the best gift she could give him was her attention." Zak shook his head. "Maybe she lacks a little bit of mercy, but Ava is so compassionate. She just doesn't seem to want anyone to know it." He offered Carol a sad smile.

Carol studied him closely. "That is incredibly astute, Zak," she said. "And perhaps the best assessment anyone has ever made of my daughter."

Zak sighed. "She's kind of magnetic."

Carol reached over and squeezed his shoulder. "You're a good friend to her," she said.

"Yep," Zak mumbled. "I'm a good friend. Lucky me." He picked up the headphones and put them back on his ears, leaning in to watch the girl he loved take the arm of an impossibly handsome Brit she'd known only a few days. She looked up at Xander, and Zak's heart sank as he realized she had never looked at him that way before.

St. Petersburg, 1914

ello."

Fabergé's voice interrupted her concentration, and Alma jumped with a start, dropping her pencil.

"Oh!" she exclaimed, pushing back her chair and standing up quickly. "Forgive me, sir. I didn't hear you coming."

Fabergé chuckled and shook his head. "It's alright, Alma," he replied. "I love watching my employees get lost in their work." He looked over her shoulder. "And what are you working on so hard this morning?"

Alma glanced back down at her drawing. "A new design."

"Oh, really?" He leaned forward for a closer look. "This looks like another Easter egg."

Alma blushed. "It is, but I'm just doing this as an exercise," she said hastily. "I do not expect to be given next year's egg to design. I am happy to continue designing the simpler pieces—the jewelry and brooches. I don't believe myself to be worthy of more than that." The color in her face deepened to a crimson. How foolish to work on this in the workplace where anyone could see. It was the height of arrogance and pretension for her to assume that she would be tasked as the master craftsman on the next egg, when the finishing touches were only now being placed on this year's egg, which she had been commissioned to design for the tsar's mother.

The *Winter Egg* had been a dream to design, her hands and mind working so furiously to bring it to life that she'd hardly slept for weeks. And as the goldsmiths and gemologists, the enamelers and other designers all worked together to bring her vision to life, she'd felt such a thrill that she wondered if she'd ever come up with another idea as marvelous and wonderful as that one again. Of course, it wasn't Easter yet. The *Winter Egg* was to be delivered in just a few short days. Alma didn't even know if the empress would like the egg, and here she was already drawing a new idea as if she thought she earned the right to do so.

She hadn't really meant to start drawing a new Easter egg, but she'd been at her mother-in-law's house the other day, and as she sat and suffered through an interminably long tea with her husband's dear mama, she began to study the lacework of the doilies on the table. They were beautifully intricate, like woven webs, each one carrying a specific design that was similar, yet unique. When her mother-in-law finally took a breath and announced that she would be retiring to her bedroom for her nap, Alma offered to clean up. As soon as she left the room, Alma laid the lace doily on top of an upturned teacup and marveled at the way the lacework changed the porcelain beneath it. The idea hit her then, and her hands had been itching to grasp her drawing pencils in an attempt to capture the vision in her head. And now her boss, the master craftsman himself, was staring at that drawing, and she felt so embarrassed for being caught.

"How lovely and unique," Fabergé said, straightening up. He pulled a handkerchief from his pocket and mopped his brow. "I'd like to see it when you've finished."

Alma nodded. "Yes," she replied shyly. "Of course."

Fabergé cocked his head to the side and studied her for a moment, watching her hands flutter nervously at her sides. Alma shifted from foot to foot.

"I would like to show you something," he said. "Walk with me?"

Alma fell into step next to her boss and mentor. Fabergé walked with his hands clasped behind his back, shoulders straight and chin up, looking very regal. His face was lined, but in the way that made men look dignified and refined. Alma liked Fabergé very much. Her father would sing his praises when she was a young girl, and she never forgot his descriptions.

"The man is practically a legend," her father would say, eyes all twinkly and alive. "He does business like no other man I've known. Firm but fair, innovative and creative and completely confident in his abilities, but not in a way that makes him arrogant. He simply knows what he's good at, and he does that thing with excellence." He looked at his daughter then, tapping the end of her nose while she giggled. "You remember that, little Alma-girl," he'd say. "Those who work with excellence always stand the tallest."

"Ah," Fabergé said, interrupting her thoughts, "here we are." He stopped abruptly, causing Alma to trip over his feet. She straightened herself, blowing the curl off her forehead and trying to act as if she hadn't just done that. Fabergé, without missing a beat, leaned over the man sitting at the table they had stopped at.

"*Dobryy Utra*, Andrey," he said.

Andrey looked up and gave a nod. He was a quiet man, awkward and aloof. But he was one of the hardest workers in the workshop, bringing many of the designs to life with such precision that the artists would all study them for significant amounts of time, looking for even the smallest of flaws to prove that Andrey was, indeed, a fallible man like the rest of them.

Alma stood to Fabergé's side and gave a shy nod of her head. She never had been very good at talking to the other craftsmen. She didn't know why. She liked them all very much—even Andrey with his long face and angular jaw, his sharp nose, which jutted out over a mustached upper lip, and beady eyes that upon first glance seemed harsh and judgmental, but upon further inspection could be seen as gentle.

"And how is it going today?" Fabergé asked.

Andrey sat back and held up the object he was working on. A master goldsmith, Andrey Gurianov had been with Fabergé since long before Alma arrived. He was independently contracted by Fabergé, another who brought to life designs in such a way that his work stood a head above others in his profession.

Fabergé reached out and gently took the object from Andrey's hand. "Come, Alma," he said. "Look closely."

Alma took a step forward and studied the small picture frame cradled in the palm of Fabergé's weathered hand. It was made of guilloche enamel, the spiral, geometric shapes having been expertly treated in a way Alma couldn't even begin to fathom. They were covered in a thin layer of enamel, which gave the metal pieces a polished appearance, preserving their design perfectly and enhancing the color of the metals.

"You used the silver?" Fabergé asked as he slowly turned

the frame from side to side, taking in each precise, geometrical stroke.

"*Da*," Andrey replied. "Then the aquamarine enamel as you specified in your design and layered it very thin to give it the blue hue."

Fabergé nodded. He held the frame in front of Alma so she could study it more closely. "Look at the expertise and care in the design," he said. "What took me mere minutes to draw took Andrey hours and hours to turn out by hand. He used the guilloche machine, turning it slowly as he looked through the magnifying glass, watching that the pattern stayed even as it inched forward."

Alma shook her head. "It's marvelous," she said, awestruck. She glanced at Andrey. "Truly marvelous."

"And then you see here? Look at the edging, the gold trim that runs the length of the frame, highlighting the guilloche pattern. It was designed with purpose, utterly complex and complicated, but when held in the hand looks so simple and plain. How can this be?" Fabergé turned to Alma with raised eyebrows.

"Well, it was assembled by a master," she replied.

Fabergé nodded. He handed the frame back to Andrey. "It looks wonderful, my friend," Fabergé said. "I'm honored that you brought my vision to life."

Andrey nodded, clearing his throat awkwardly, clearly uncomfortable with such praise, though Alma saw the slightest upturn of the side of his mouth. She followed Fabergé as he continued walking.

"You're right," Fabergé said. "The frame is so stunning because it was assembled by a master—"

"And designed by one as well," Alma hastily cut in, then bit her lip, chastising herself for interrupting him.

Fabergé continued talking with hardly a pause. "But will a frame, though clearly so beautiful, expertly designed and created, hold the same value as one of the Imperial Easter eggs?" He stopped and turned, facing Alma directly.

She opened her mouth to respond, then closed it again, forcing herself to slow down and think before speaking. "Do you mean to ask if it will hold the same monetary value?" she asked. "Or intrinsic value?"

"Both," Fabergé answered. Alma detected the pleasure in his reply.

"It won't hold the same monetary value as the eggs," she said slowly, deliberating over her words, "because its design doesn't possess the same creative prowess and genius that the eggs do." She glanced at Fabergé, waiting a beat to see if he would respond. When he remained silent, staring at her intently, she took a deep breath and continued.

"But the frame will possess a greater monetary value than other frames, even other frames that come out of this workshop, because it was specifically designed by you before being implemented by your craftsman." She took a breath.

"As for whether or not it holds the same intrinsic value, I'm not sure. The method used to design the guilloche is awe-inspiring. It's rare and exciting, which gives it a special beauty and value. But, at the end of the day, it's the same material used in the eggs, only it's used for a less noble purpose. So is its value diminished because of that?"

She stopped, grasping her hands in front of her waist and waiting for him to respond. "I'm finished. That was all I had to say."

Fabergé smiled. "Would you say, then," he replied, "that it is a shame we wasted priceless materials such as silver and the blended enamel on a product that held less intrinsic and monetary value?"

Alma hesitated, unsure of how to answer.

"You can speak honestly, my dear," Fabergé said. "I think I might have something to learn from you."

"Well," Alma began after a brief pause, "I would say that the *craftsman* gets to decide how the materials should be used, and if the craftsman deems the silver and enamel worthy of a frame, in which one would place the photo of a treasured loved one or memory, then those cannot be considered invaluable or common." She took a breath. "Likewise, if the exact same materials are used to fashion an Imperial egg, to be displayed and marveled at for generations to come, those cannot be thought more or less noble than the frame."

"So, would you say that the craftsman, then, wields the power over the materials?" Fabergé asked.

She nodded. "Yes, of course."

"And as the craftsmen, we have the right to decide how each material will be put to use, whether for something simple, like a frame or a bowl, or more complex, like an Easter egg."

"Yes." She nodded again, more vigorously.

Fabergé leaned in. "I agree with you, my dear," he said.

Alma smiled, though inwardly working to decipher the deeper meaning behind their conversation. Fabergé began walking again back toward her desk. When they approached, he leaned down and picked up her drawing, holding it out to her.

"It seems to me," he said, "that a master craftsman is at work on her design here. And whether or not that design comes to fruition doesn't for a moment diminish the value that this crafts-man, *you*," he said with a nod, "brings to each piece created. Whether you're commissioned to design a pendant, a brooch, or the next Imperial egg, you bring value according to your gifts and talents and skills. If you're not willing to diminish the value of the materials used to create pieces, then please, my dear, do not diminish the value that you bring to the art of design."

He gave her a wink, then turned, walking briskly away to finish his morning rounds. Alma stood for a long moment, taking in the words of the man who filled so many of the holes that were left when her father died. How could she question her worth inside this company? She resolved in her heart to no longer do so, choosing to accept his praise and walk confidently in it. Who was she to question his authority? He was, after all the Master Craftsman.

Present Day

W hat do you think?" Ava paced back and forth as Zak and Carol stared at the back of the drawing they found in the apartment.

Zak's eyebrows were furrowed, and he hunched over the page.

Carol rubbed her eyes. "Sorry, but I'm not much help. I only see what you pointed out already."

Ava nodded. "What about you, Zak?"

Zak held up a finger and stared harder. He put the paper down on the table and turned to his computer.

"What is it, mate?" Xander asked.

Zak drew in a deep breath, then let it out in a quick burst. "Okay, so you know how St. Petersburg is built on a series of canals, right?" he asked, his fingers typing in the search engine.

"Yeah," Ava said. "Peter the Great did that on purpose because he loved sailing, so he designed the city to sit on the Neva. It was very forward thinking of him."

"Exactly!" Zak said, pointing at Ava. "The problem was, Peter wanted everyone to love sailing as much as he did, so he originally refused to build bridges, which meant people had to boat across the canals to get around the city."

"Super inconvenient and dangerous, given the unpredictable waters of the Neva throughout the changing seasons," Ava said.

"Mm-hmm," Zak said. He finished typing with a flourish and whirled around to face Ava. "You remember that bridge we crossed when we first got here? The one you commented on?"

"The horse bridge?" Ava asked.

"Yes, that one! It's called the Anichkov Bridge. It was first built in 1715. As the story is told, it took one of the noblemen of Petersburg dying in the canals to convince Peter to start building a series of bridges to connect the city. Anichkov was the first. I mean, obviously the current bridge that's standing isn't the original. That one was constructed in"—he looked back at his screen—"1841, and then reconstructed again from 1906 to 1908."

"Right about the time that Fabergé may have been creating this egg," Ava said.

Zak nodded. "Now, think about that letter Alma wrote to Isla. Remember how she commented that she had to . . ." He paused. "Hang on." He rustled through the stack of papers on his table, pulling out one from the bottom. "Yes, here! Alma wrote that she would *tame her emotions like those who tame the horses.*"

"The statues on the Anichkov," Ava breathed. She thought of the four bronze statues that flanked the bridge they'd crossed to Nevsky Prospekt. The ensemble of sculptures was a grouping of horse tamers, muscular men trying to rein in wild horses. Alma must have crossed that bridge daily.

"Look at this writing one more time, now that you know that information," Zak said. He held the drawing out to Ava.

She crossed the room and took it from him, then studied the erased writing more closely.

"I think it does say 'The Anichkov Bridge,'" she said. "Good work, Zak!" She met his gaze and offered a genuine smile.

Zak grinned in return, his mouth drawing back down when Ava turned to Xander, who now leaned over her shoulder. Both of them had removed their wigs, and Ava found that she suddenly felt exposed without the red hair. Her heart pattered in her chest as Xander looked down at her, his eyes crinkled on the edges with a small smile.

"Yep," he said.

"But why?" Ava asked. "What could the Anichkov Bridge have to do with the missing egg?"

"Well, I think there's only one way to find out," Xander said.

"We're going over there," Ava replied.

"It's only a short walk from here," he continued.

"Perfect." Ava stood and turned to her mom. "You want to come?"

Carol tossed a sideways glance at Zak, then looked back at Ava. "I think I'll stay here. Zak and I have made a good team sleuthing around online today. Plus, there is zero part of me that wants to take a walk in that weather."

Ava nodded. She turned back to Xander. "Do we need to put our outfits from earlier back on?" she asked.

Xander nodded. "It's best if we do."

"Give me ten minutes," Ava said. "I'll meet you at the elevator."

"Cool." Xander reached over and grabbed her hand, giving it a slight squeeze.

She looked up at him and smiled in return, the smallest gesture, but comfortable and sweet.

Carol stood and stretched. "I'll head to the room with you, Ava," she said. "I need to get another pair of socks because I am freezing."

The two quickly headed to their room and shut the door behind them. Carol stopped inside the room and crossed her arms, giving Ava a long stare.

"What?" Ava asked.

"What do you mean, what?" Carol asked. "You are flirting with Xander!"

Ava blushed. "I'm not flirting."

"Oh, please," Carol said. "Of course you are! I had to watch poor Zak keep up with the two of you all day."

"Oh, Mom." Ava threw up her hands.

"Ava," Carol said "You could have a *tiny* bit of compassion on what it must feel like for Zak to watch the girl that he's loved for a long time swoon over someone like Xander. And stop giving me that look! I know you're smart enough to see that Zak has more than a little crush on you. For heaven's sake, I noticed he was in love with you the first time I met him."

Ava sighed in frustration as Carol continued, a little more gently.

"Honey, Zak could never compete with Xander, and he knows it. Try to understand what he must be feeling."

Ava sighed. "Nobody says 'swoon' anymore, Mother," she said, turning to grab her outfit from earlier. "And I'm sorry about how I've made Zak feel. I really am." Her voice softened. "I like Zak," she said. "He's sweet and kind, and I know he's been a better friend to me than I've been to him. I never wanted to lead him on, so I've just tried really hard to keep him at arm's length."

Carol reached out and tousled Ava's hair. "I get it, honey," she said. "Just keep it in mind as you interact with Xander in front of him, okay?"

"I will," Ava said. "I really don't want to hurt him. And besides, my mission here has nothing to do with Zak *or* with Xander. I'm not here for the boys." She gave her mom a small smile, then turned toward the bathroom to change.

"Yes, but my dear—" Carol said to her retreating figure.

Ava stopped and glanced back.

"—it would appear that the boys are here for you."

———— ❀ ————

Ten minutes later, Ava met Xander back at the elevator, red hair in place, makeup freshened, and once again feeling confident and sure of herself.

"Ready?" Xander asked.

Ava nodded. "I just wish we knew what we were looking for. And that it wasn't so cold outside. My next treasure hunt better be in someplace tropical."

Xander laughed. The elevator dinged and the doors opened. Ava and Xander stepped inside and waited for the doors to close. Once they did, Xander reached over and grabbed Ava's hand. She tried to pull it away, but he held tight. She looked up at him, then glanced at the camera on his lapel. She dropped his hand and reached for the pin on her own collar.

"I haven't turned mine on yet," Xander said. He reached over and tugged at the pin on her collarbone, pushing it between his fingers for a couple of seconds and turning it off. He smiled at her. "It's just us right now."

He leaned down, eyes closing, and without thinking, Ava stepped away.

"Nope," she said, then looked up at him, horrified. "Oh, geez. I didn't mean to say that out loud."

Xander looked back at her, eyes registering embarrassment. "I'm sorry," he said. He cleared his throat. "Goodness, I'm so sorry. I just thought . . . after this morning at the apartment . . ."

"This is my fault," Ava said, her cheeks hot. "I mean, you didn't know what you were getting yourself into when you agreed to go on a mission with the most awkward female that ever lived."

They stared at one another, uncomfortable. Xander cleared his throat again, staring up at the lighted buttons as the elevator ticked its way toward the lobby.

"I'm the one who should be sorry," Ava said.

The elevator dinged and the doors slid open to reveal the lobby in all its ornate brightness. It was quiet this afternoon with only a few people walking in the lobby.

"No. It's fine," Xander said in a voice that let Ava know it wasn't really fine.

They stepped out of the elevator. Ava followed Xander as he walked briskly toward the front door. She reached forward and grabbed his hand, pulling him to a stop. She saw a pop of anger flash through his eyes, but they quickly softened.

"Look, I get it, alright?" he said. "That was way inappropriate. It's cool."

Ava nodded. "I really am sorry," she said. "I've made this super uncomfortable and confusing for you. I've never been so good with the opposite sex." She shrugged. "You might say I'm a bit of a mess. And I like you. I do! But I didn't come here for this, and I let myself get caught up in the moment this morning, and that wasn't fair to you. I just . . . you know . . ." She drew in a deep breath. "I want to focus on the mission, is all. And I really want you to interrupt me so I'll stop stumbling all over my words."

Xander smiled. "It's really fine," he said. "You're right. We should stay focused."

Ava gave him a grateful smile in return.

"Let's take a walk," Xander said.

Ava nodded, and the two of them walked briskly through the lobby and out the front door of the Hermitage Hotel. Ava reached in her pocket and pulled out a pair of gloves. Despite the shining sun, the icy air hurt her exposed skin and immediately chilled her to the bone.

Xander stopped, then held out his arm. Ava paused for a moment before Xander leaned down. "I promise, Ava," he said. "No more funny business."

She took a deep breath, tucking her hand inside his elbow and leaning in slightly. "I'll bet you're not the kind of guy who gets turned down very often," she finally said.

Xander laughed. "You'd be surprised," he said. She looked up at him. "You're not the only one who is desperately awkward. I mean, honestly, who tries to kiss a girl he barely knows in an elevator?"

"While dressed in disguise . . . ," Ava said. They both laughed.

"Anyway," Ava said, turning away from his gaze. "I'd really love to see more of the Hermitage Museum while here. One quick tour wasn't enough."

"It's a pretty amazing place," Xander agreed.

"I read somewhere once," Ava continued, "that if you spent one minute gazing at each exhibit inside the Hermitage, it would take you ten years to get through the whole thing."

"I guess you'll just have to come back when you have a decade to spare," Xander said.

Ava chuckled. "How far is it to Anichkov?" she asked, turning to look forward.

"Not far. It's just over there, toward the end of Nevsky Prospekt. If we walk fast, we can get there in fifteen minutes."

"Well, let's walk fast, then," Ava said. She was thankful that her outfit today called for fur-lined boots, attire she'd never worn before in her life. Her feet felt blissfully warm.

"Why do you think both Fabergé and Alma made reference to Anichkov in their writings?" Ava asked.

"No idea. But perhaps there's something there that will give us a clue as to where to look next."

"I just can't imagine what we will find at the bridge."

"You're thinking about it all wrong, though. We're not looking for something big or obvious, because nothing like that would be there. This bridge has seen an insane amount of history in the hundred years since Alma and Fabergé left the city. It's survived the artillery fire of the Nazis. It's watched the rise and fall of the USSR. There won't be a tangible clue, but that's okay. If there's one thing that your dad and mine taught me about treasure hunting, it's that you always chase a possibility, because clues come in all forms, sometimes tangible, and other times through an experience."

"You learned a lot from my father," Ava said after a moment of silence.

Xander paused for a beat. "I take it you didn't learn much from him?"

Ava shrugged. "He wasn't around."

Xander turned to meet her gaze. "My dad talked about Nick a lot, and Nick would stay with us whenever he came to London. I remember my dad describing him as a complicated man, entirely passionate about all the wrong things."

Ava looked out at the busy street, people and cars moving in an almost coordinated dance. "Yeah, sounds about right." She sighed. "The thing is, I've been fascinated with him since I was twelve and I actually learned what he did for a living. My mom used to tell me when I was little that he was an international businessman, which was why he traveled so much. It sounded so boring, and I resented him so much for choosing a boring job over me. But then I found out what he really did, and I suddenly kind of understood him more. I guess I always longed for this kind of adventure. Could this kind of thing be inherited?"

Xander shook his head. "No idea. Although you do remind me a lot of your dad, at least from what I remember of him. He was wicked smart. It used to drive my dad crazy, because your father could spout off facts about any subject. He had this weird photographic memory where he never forgot a thing."

Ava looked away from Xander and blinked back tears that pricked at the corners of her eyes.

"But Nick always seemed a little off to me. Not in an odd way or anything," Xander said hastily. "It just always seemed like he was conflicted. My dad used to say that Nick chased treasure like he was searching for the key to life itself."

Ava stared ahead, silently taking in the sight of the Fontanka River ahead of them. They turned the corner, and in the distance, she could see the four statues of the horse tamers on the Anichkov Bridge. The bustle of cars and people cluttered her mind, forcing out thoughts of Nick and his conflicted treasure hunts. She let herself be swept up in the moment, taking in the sights of St. Petersburg, a city that was equal parts modern and historical, as if the city itself was also conflicted. Past or present? Which to celebrate?

The buildings lining the riverbank were colorful and ornate.

It was as though the entire city had been bathed in a rainbow, from corals and greens to yellows and earthy grays. Peter the Great had been very forward thinking for his time. He'd wanted to create a multicultural city, and so he'd invited in architects from Paris and Italy and London, each of them bringing their own unique flavor to the city itself. The embankments they walked on resembled that of Paris, while the canals reminded one of Amsterdam, a city that Peter had been very fond of and hoped to replicate. The countless bridges and canals were reminiscent of Venice, and the many green parks smacked of London.

Though Ava had never been to any of these places, she'd spent so much time reading books and studying them that she felt the presence of each influence as they walked. She studied the beauty of it and breathed in deeply.

"You okay?" Xander asked.

"Yeah," she said. "It just hit me how amazing this experience is. I can't believe I'm here."

Xander looked at her, his eyes studying hers until she looked away, embarrassed.

"Almost there," she said.

The bridge loomed before them, the first two statues gleaming in the afternoon sunshine. Each of the four bronze statues told a different story. They approached the first, and Ava stopped, studying it closely. The athlete was leaning into the horse as it reared back on its hind legs. The look in the horse's eyes was wild as it bucked against the effort to calm it down.

"You can see the difference in the statues," Xander said. "The athlete is attempting to tame the beast and failing in just about every effort except for the last one, which is at the other end of the bridge. Look at that one over there."

They walked across the width of the bridge to the next statue where the athlete lay on the ground, having fallen in his attempt to calm the horse. His hand gripped the rein, and the horse reared back in protest.

"He didn't want to be tamed," Ava murmured. "I suppose he wasn't even meant to be controlled."

"Yeah. Seems about right." He looked at her. "This horse was wild at heart from the beginning. But"—he paused, studying the statue carefully—"the athlete eventually broke him, and he and that horse went on to become mighty warriors, working as a pair."

Ava cocked her head to the side. "How do you figure that?"

Xander gave her a playful wink. "I can make up stories too."

Ava was quiet as she looked from statue to statue, her thoughts muddled with Nick, the missing treasure, the bustle of the city around them, and Xander. "I like that," she finally said.

Xander drew in a deep breath, then let it out, a puff of cold air forming a cloud burst that immediately dissipated in front of his face. They continued walking down the bridge toward the other two statues.

"Alright," he said. "What can we learn about Alma and Fabergé from this bridge?"

Ava stopped and turned slowly in a circle. "Fabergé wouldn't have had reason to cross this bridge often, would he?" she asked. "If he lived and worked on Bolshaya Morskaya, and his delivery of the Imperial eggs most often took place at the Winter Palace, then he wouldn't have frequented this bridge."

"It's hard to say for sure," Xander replied. "Perhaps Fabergé liked to take evening walks across the bridge. We know he traveled often because of his international position. And, of course, there was that pesky affair."

"Yes," Ava said. "With the Austrian. Seems Fabergé was also a conflicted man."

"History is rife with them."

Ava studied him for a brief moment. "And what about you? Are you a conflicted man?"

Xander looked down at her briefly, then looked away. "I suppose I am," he said.

There was something in his voice that gave Ava pause, an undercurrent that made her wonder if there really was more to Xander than she'd originally imagined.

"It seems like Alma's meaning in her letter is obvious," Xander continued. "She was referencing the bridge in order to say that she needed to tame her emotions much like the horses needed to be tamed."

"Yeah. The symbolism seems kind of obvious there. But what about Fabergé? Why would he write Anichkov on the back of his drawing?"

Ava turned around again, studying the Petersburg skyline from every angle. She stopped and stared off in the distance, then leaned back on the railing of the bridge.

"If Fabergé designed this egg for the people of Russia," she said, "then could he maybe have come here to study the skyline of the city he so clearly loved? Perhaps his conflict went deeper than simply his family life. Maybe he was desperate to honor his country, with all its fallacies and imperfections."

"So, you think the egg could have been designed for both the common man and for the crown?" Xander asked.

Ava nodded slowly. "Yeah. Maybe Fabergé was so desperate for the two halves of the country to come together that he designed an egg that could be interpreted as loyal to both sides."

They were silent for a long moment as they both contemplated the thought. Finally, Xander broke the silence.

"I think we need to go to Finland," he said. Ava turned to look at him. He lifted his shoulders, then dropped them again. "It just seems that everything is pointing to Alma having smuggled the egg out of Russia."

Ava hesitated only a moment. "I think you're right." She looked around the city again, the colors and sights washing over her. "Oh!" Her hand flew up to her collar and her fingers gripped her camera. "We forgot to turn these back on." She fumbled with the pin, then looked up at Xander. "Can you switch it on for me? I want Zak and my mom to see all this."

Xander reached out, his hand closing over hers. Ava met his gaze, startled at the change in his eyes.

"Ava, I—" Xander stopped short as a black car sped up next to them, screeching to a stop. The window rolled down and Anatoly peered up at them.

"Get in," he said, his voice tight. "We go now."

———— ❊ ————

Zak leaned back in his chair and laced his fingers behind his head, staring up at the ceiling.

Carol watched him sympathetically. She put her hand on his shoulder and gave it a squeeze. She looked back at the monitor. "Xander still hasn't turned on his lapel camera or earpiece?"

Zak shook his head. "And I'm not getting a feed from Ava either."

"Oh well," Carol said. "It's probably not a big deal. They aren't likely to find much on the bridge."

Zak nodded. He jumped as his cell phone buzzed on the

table next to him. "It's Nick," he said. He picked it up and
swiped. "Nick? Hello? Yes, of course."

Zak put the phone down and turned on the speaker. "Carol
and I are here, Nick."

"Where are Ava and Xander?" Nick asked.

Something in his voice made Carol sit up a little straighter.
"They walked to the Anichkov Bridge," she said. "They found
something today at Fabergé's apartment."

"Who went with them to the bridge, Carol? Do you know?"

"Nobody, Nick," she said. "They walked. What's going on?"

"So, Anatoly didn't go with them?"

"No, I don't think so," Carol said, a sinking feeling settling
in her stomach. "Nick, what's wrong?"

"I got a call about ten minutes ago from Anatoly," Nick
said. There was an undercurrent of panic and anger running
through his voice.

"Okay," Carol said. "And?"

"And *Anatoly* is in New York right now visiting his daughter
and her family. He was calling to let me know he was in the
States and wondered if he could come down to see me."

"Wait . . . what? I don't understand." Carol and Zak looked
at one another, Zak's eyes widening.

"You mean the man who's been acting as our driver is not
the Anatoly you know and trust?" Zak asked.

"That's exactly what I mean, Zak," Nick replied. "I don't
know who that man is, but he hasn't been vetted by me. What
the hell was Xander thinking?"

Carol stood up. "Nick, Ava and Xander left a half hour ago.
Neither one of their lapel cameras are on right now. We don't
know where they are."

Nick cursed. He drew in a breath, then started coughing,

a wet, hacking sound that burst through the phone's speaker. Carol closed her eyes, clasping her hands under her chin. Zak stood up and put an arm around her shoulders. A moment later another voice came through the phone.

"Carol?"

"Sylvie!" Carol grabbed the phone and held it in her palm. "Sylvie, what do I do? I don't know what to do."

"Give me a minute, Carol. Stay on the line. I'm going to get Nicky calmed down so he can help. He's worked up."

"Okay. Okay." Carol blinked back tears. She turned to look at Zak. "What do we do?" she asked.

He took a step back. "I'm going to the bridge," he said. "I'll run over and tell them that Nick's on the phone and wants to talk. It'll be fine."

Carol wrung her hands at her waist and gave him a nod. "Okay, yes," she said. "Yes, that's a good idea. You go get them, and then we'll deal with this."

She closed her eyes as Zak raced out of the room. She could still hear Nick coughing on the other line, and Sylvie speaking softly to him to calm him down.

"Carol?" Nick's voice came out as a scratchy whisper, his vocal cords sounding as though they'd been sanded down.

"Nick?" Carol blinked back tears. "Nick, what is going on?"

"I don't know, but we're going to figure it out. Where's Zak?"

"He went to find Ava and Xander."

Nick let out a long sigh. "Okay . . . that's not ideal, but it's the best we've got for now. Why weren't they wearing their cameras?"

Carol shrugged. "I thought they were," she said. "They put on their same outfits from this morning." She blinked back tears. "Nick," she continued, her voice tight. "If something happens to her . . ."

"I know," he said.

They were silent for a few minutes as Carol paced back and forth in the room.

"I hate having nothing to do," she said.

"I hate being stuck in this bed," Nick replied. "But Sylvie's on her phone with the real Anatoly right now. Hold on, let me talk with him."

"Don't hang up!" Carol said. "I want to hear your conversation."

"I'll put him on speaker."

Carol sat on the edge of the chair in front of the table, leaning in toward the phone.

"Anatoly?" Nick said. "I'm here, and I have you on speaker so Carol can hear you too. She's in St. Petersburg right now."

"Is okay," Anatoly said, his voice faint and crackling through the line so that Carol had to strain to make out his words. "I am very angry, Nick," he continued, his pronunciation of Nick's name coming out as "*Neek.*" His voice was warm and deep, and Carol immediately liked the sound of him.

"Me too, my friend," Nick said in his garbled whisper. "That's my kid out there."

"How could you not know it wasn't me?" Anatoly asked.

Nick sighed. "I took Xander's word for it. He knew you. He's Jack's kid. I trusted him."

"Is sloppy work, Neek."

There was a long pause, the phone line crackling with static as Carol rubbed her eyes. She glanced at the door periodically, willing it to open and Ava to walk through.

"I know, man," Nick said, his voice weary. "I know."

Anatoly sighed. "Is okay. We figure this out. Where is your daughter now?"

Carol spoke up. "She and Xander walked to the Anichkov Bridge about an hour ago. Zak left to go look for them."

"Who is this Zak?" Anatoly asked.

"He's the tech guy," Nick replied, his voice tight. "He's great with computers, smart kid. But he's no muscle."

"And this Zak," Anatoly continued. "He has a device for communication?"

Carol shook her head, fresh tears springing to the corners of her eyes. "No," she said. "He left in a rush. I'm speaking to you on his cell phone."

"Okay," Anatoly said. "Give me few minutes to make some calls. I will connect with my guys in Petersburg and have them start working on finding Ava and Xander. When we get them back safe, we deal with Xander and this fake Anatoly. Nobody pretend to be me like that."

Carol could tell by Anatoly's voice that he was a big man, and not to be messed with. But there was an undercurrent of gentleness in his words that calmed her. She trusted him.

"What do I do?" Carol asked.

"You have to wait there, Carol," Nick said. "I'm so sorry. I know that's hard, but someone needs to be there when they get back, and I need you close to the phone. Keep monitoring the computer and see if the cameras get turned on, okay?"

Carol turned to the computer where a black screen reminded her of just how disconnected she was from her only child. "I feel so useless," she muttered, a single tear trickling down her cheek.

"You're not, Carol. You've never been useless." Nick spoke

the words softly. There was a swelling pause that filled the room around Carol. Anatoly interrupted it.

"I will go now," he said. "I call you back when I speak to my comrades."

"Okay, Anatoly. Thank you, my friend. I'm sorry about this," Nick said.

The line went quiet. Carol could hear Nick breathing on the other end.

"So, I guess we just wait now?" she asked.

"We wait," Nick said. "Can I wait on the line with you?"

Carol was silent. Her mind drifted back to the Nick she had known so many years ago. Tall and strong, and impossibly handsome, Nick Laine had been the picture of confidence. He strode into a room and owned it. Carol had never known him to be at a loss for words, and charm seeped from his pores in a way that instantly made him the center of attention. She had loved being the one on his arm. She adored the way he looked down at her, eyes twinkling and full of adventure and mischief. She'd wanted to stand by his side for the rest of her life.

She never imagined the great Nick Laine confined to a bed, sapped of energy, defeated, broken, and scared. A lump formed in her throat as a fresh wave of tears filled her eyes. Time and pride had stolen so much.

"Nick?" she choked out.

"Yes?"

"You know I never stopped waiting for you. I waited for twenty-three years. Why didn't you come back?" Her voice broke, and she dropped her face into her hands.

"I was a fool," Nick whispered from the other side of the world. His voice floated through the speaker of the phone and hung in the air between them. Carol cried silently.

They were quiet for a long time. Carol stood back up and walked to the hotel door, then back to the phone.

"I hate this," she said.

"So do I."

The hotel door burst open then, and Zak came in, turning and shutting it quickly behind him. Carol stood up and whirled around.

"Zak!" she cried. Her eyes drifted to the closed door, and then back to his ashen face. "Where are they?"

"They're gone," he said. "I couldn't find them anywhere, but I found these on the bridge."

He held out his hands and Carol's heart sank as she recognized the lapel cameras from Xander's and Ava's coats.

St. Petersburg, 1916

Leaning back in his chair, Karl took a sip of his drink. He let the vodka burn his tongue and throat as he swallowed it slowly. He pulled out his watch and stared at the time. 11:00 p.m. He rubbed his eyes and leaned his head back.

"What are you doing?"

Karl jumped as Augusta appeared in the doorway. Her face was pinched. The declining economy due to the ongoing war had taken its toll on them all. Cutbacks had to be made. The factory was now being used to make syringes, and the Moscow factory had been converted into a manufacturer of hand grenades and casings for artillery shells.

Twenty-three of his employees had been conscripted for service in the war, though Karl had managed to keep some of them from being sent away by pleading with authorities on the grounds that losing those workers would essentially shut his workshop down. He hadn't been able to keep them all from the fighting, though, and the thought of it twisted his stomach in a knot.

Likewise, Amalia was now long gone. His Austrian beauty, the companion who had captivated his thoughts for so long, was arrested a few months before and charged as a spy. He'd done all he could, straining what relationships he had left, to vouch for her, to keep her from being sent away, but it was to no avail. She was sentenced to prison in Siberia, and the truth that kept Karl up at night was the knowledge that at any moment, he could be the next one to disappear.

"I'm thinking," he finally said, turning to his wife. His eyes were rimmed in red. "It all just seems so desperately sad these days, does it not?"

"I suppose that it does," Augusta said. "Although, I would argue that it's all been desperately sad for a long time."

Her words were pointed, and they were directed right at him. Karl stared at her. "I'm so terribly sorry, my dear," he said. "I have not loved you the way that you should have been loved. You're a loyal woman." He blinked back a tear. "And I am a desperate man."

Augusta nodded. "I won't disagree with you," she said.

Karl sighed. "I set some things in motion today."

Augusta stepped into the room, the folds of her skirt swishing in the silence. She walked around his desk and stood beside him, glancing over the papers spread across the surface. "A joint stock partnership?"

Karl nodded. "I'll split the firm up between four partners, with each of them receiving two and a half percent of the company. The boys will each receive five percent of the company, and I'll offer a single share to each of the master craftsmen. I will hold on to the rest."

Augusta perused the documents. "Why now?" she asked.

Karl looked up at her. "Rasputin is dead. The tsar and his

wife are erratic. There's revolution in the air, my dear." He looked back down at the papers. "I only hope it isn't too late."

Augusta stared at the top of her husband's head. She opened her mouth to speak, hesitating for only a moment before letting the words tumble out. "And what about the egg that you're hiding?" she asked.

Karl froze, his hand gripping the empty glass, knuckles going white. He turned slowly. "The what?"

"The egg. The secret one you've made and are now hiding? What's your plan for this?"

"What do you know?" he asked, trying to keep his voice even.

"I know you've made an egg. You asked for help from the enameler, offering him some ridiculous story about it being for a secret client." She raised her eyebrows. "He told me all about it before he left for the front. He told me to watch out for you. He was worried . . . and so am I."

Karl turned. "I have a plan," he said faintly.

"And what does that mean?" Augusta asked. She folded her hands in front of her stomach and stared down at her husband. "I have never questioned you," she said. "I have taken you at your word all these years, never openly disagreeing or doubting your sincerity, even when that woman seemed to magically show up on your international trips."

Karl blinked.

"But you've created something, and I want to know what it is. I believe I've earned the right to understand what's happening right here inside my own home." She leaned down, resting her hand on the desk and lowering her face until it was even with his. "If they come for you, I need to know what to do," she said.

Karl looked in her eyes for a long time. At seventy years

old, he knew that he no longer had any fight left in him. With a sigh, he pushed back from the desk and stood up, wincing at the jab of pain in his knees.

"Follow me," he said.

———— ❁ ————

Augusta hesitated for only a brief moment before following him into the dark hallway. The workshop was silent, as it was more and more often these days. Augusta shivered in the cold, dark building. Fifty years ago, the noise that filled the shop was like a beautiful orchestra of sound. If she closed her eyes long enough, she could almost hear it again. The sound of laughter and hammers, papers rustling while the children ran up and down the shop stairs giggling and laughing, Karl calling behind the boys to slow down and stop making so much noise, though his tone was always affectionate and fond. If Augusta missed anything at all, it was those early days, before the Easter eggs and the Imperial expectations.

Augusta followed Karl into the showroom and watched as he ducked behind the counter. She peered over the counter and saw him down on his knees, nudging at the boards in the floor. She gaped as the floor opened up, the boards moving to the side and revealing a cavernous space below.

"Karl," she gasped, the astonishment in her voice evident even to herself. She stared at his face, illuminated by the stream of moonlight that gave the only light in the room.

Augusta watched Karl lean down, practically on his stomach at this point, and push his arm as far back into the hole as he could. He shivered visibly.

"It's cold," he murmured. He slid back, reached both hands down into the blackness, and then slowly pulled a metal box up into the moonlit room. He pushed to his feet, wincing in pain. His eyes darted from side to side.

"Not here," he said breathlessly.

Augusta nodded. She followed him back down the hall to his office where he closed and locked the door behind them. He set the box on the table under the lamp, then pulled a ring of keys from his pocket and unlocked it.

Augusta reached down and slowly opened the lid. Inside lay a beautiful Easter egg nestled on a bed of velvet.

Karl reached in the box and pulled out the egg, holding it up for her. Augusta took it from him, cupping it in her hand. It truly was remarkable. It looked so much like a real egg that she found herself cradling it lest she crack its outer shell, which of course was impossible because she could see beneath the veneer of the enamel that the egg itself was crafted of gold. And the latticework pattern of diamonds that crossed the outside made it sparkle even in the dim light.

"Where did you get the materials to make this?" she asked.

"There are always gold shavings left over. I merely melted them down and shaped them myself."

"How did you keep this a secret?" She turned the egg over to see the signature on the back side etched out in fine diamonds. *KF.* Beneath his initials was the date *1906.* She looked up at her husband, who nodded in return.

"I made it the year the tsarevitch was born," he said. "The year after Bloody Sunday."

"Why have you not shown this to anyone?" she asked.

Karl reached over and took the egg from her. He set it up on an emerald stand that he'd pulled from the bottom of the box, then unclasped the front clip on the egg, a small, simple diamond button that had taken him far too long to create because he'd wanted to do that much on his own. The top of the egg slowly opened on the spring mechanism that he'd designed under cover of dark and revealed the surprise lying inside on a bed of blood-red velvet. Augusta drew in a deep breath.

Karl pulled the surprise out and set it on the table next to the egg. Augusta leaned forward and studied the replica of the Imperial crown. It was made of gold and encrusted in rubies and diamonds. Even in the dim light, Augusta could see how much it resembled the actual Imperial crown.

"How did you do this?"

Karl shrugged. "It isn't terribly different from the Imperial crown replica we designed for the *Hen Egg*," he said. "I simply followed the design notes and drawings that we had on file, while making a few modifications."

Augusta picked it up gingerly and studied it. "What modifications?"

"I didn't make it from gold. I used a polished metal instead, then overlaid that with a gold finish. And there are fewer diamonds and rubies."

Augusta studied it more closely. It had been thirty-one years since that original egg was created, but Augusta remembered it so clearly. Back then, she and her husband had been a team, him bringing her in often to consult on ideas for jewelry designs. When he'd come up with the concept for the egg to be given to the tsarina, he had asked for her opinion on everything from the design to the materials used. She knew the *Hen Egg* well because she had helped to create it.

"I see," she murmured. She looked at him over the crown, his eyes shifting away from hers. Her husband's decision to use cheaper and fewer materials was not merely economical. It was symbolic as well.

"There's more," Karl said. He reached inside the base of the egg and pulled on a small string, releasing the upper platform on which the crown had lain. Augusta watched curiously as he then pulled out the final surprise. He set it on the table next to the crown and Augusta gasped.

"Karl," she breathed. She lowered herself into the chair at his desk and studied the final surprise.

The ivory fist was thrust upward, the fingers expertly carved so that the fist looked to be clenched in defiance. The knuckles had been polished until they shined a bright white, and there even seemed to be a hint of a vein popping on the back of the hand. Augusta turned to her husband, her face pale.

"What have you done?" she whispered.

He leaned forward and picked up the replica of the crown, gently slipping it over the fist so that the knuckles no longer looked white and bared, but rather now looked as if they gleamed with blood.

Augusta leaned back in the chair, stunned. The fist, thrust into the Imperial crown, stood next to the open mouth of the enameled egg, a symbol of resistance like nothing she had ever before seen.

"Who else have you shown this to?" she asked.

"No one," he said. "And I only had a few of the craftsmen help with the creation, though of course I never told any of them what it was actually for."

"Who designed the fist?"

Karl looked away before answering. "Agathon."

Augusta stood up, pushing the chair back. "You brought our son into this?" Her voice shook with barely restrained anger.

"I'm going to give it to the tsar," Karl said.

August gasped. "What did you just say?" She looked back

down at the egg and its hidden surprises. It was truly masterful, the way he had created the two pieces to fit together, and
she knew why he'd done it the way he had. Her husband,
complicated and introspective, had designed the surprises in
such a way as to leave the interpretation of the fisted crown up
to the viewer. To the tsar, it could represent the throne rising
to quell the people. But to the common man, it looked like an
indictment of the throne.

Karl reached down and slowly removed the crown from the
ivory fist. "For many years, I believed that Nicholas would grow
into his role as tsar," he said as he nestled the ivory fist back
into the base of the egg. He set the velvet platform on top of
it, concealing the rebellious symbol, then picked up the small
crown and laid it atop the velvet.

"But he never really did, did he?" He looked up at her. "And
then it seemed that the people would prevail." He closed the
egg with a small click as the diamond clasp held its secrets tight.

"Now, it seems that no one wins," he said. His hand rested
on top of the egg as he blinked back tears. "I have kept it hidden for so many years because I know, my dear. I understand
that this is dangerous. But the time has come when it can no
longer be hidden. The people need to see it, and so does the
tsar. I plan to travel to him this week."

"You will do no such thing!" Augusta cried. "No one must
ever see this."

Karl looked at her, his eyes swimming with emotion. "My
darling," he began, but Augusta cut him off.

"No one can know that Peter Karl Fabergé, Official Jeweler
to the Royal Court, has designed an egg not for the tsar but for
the revolution," she said. "If you take this to Nicholas Romanov,
it will be the final nail in your coffin. You're already despised

by the people because of your connection to the bourgeoisie. But now, you would make yourself an enemy of the crown as well?" She straightened and stared him down, her mouth pressed into a thin line. "No," she said finally, shaking her head. "I won't have it. What little protection we have left will be gone. You, me, the boys—we will be ruined. And I will not spend my remaining years inside a gulag."

"What would you have me do with this, dear?" Karl asked. He had no fight left, all his energy siphoned away.

"Destroy it," Augusta hissed.

Present Day

Ava shrank into the corner of the car, eyes flitting from Xander to the man sitting next to him. Her heart raced as she drew in slow, deep breaths, forcing herself to calm down and think. She glanced at Xander, who sat upright and rigid in the seat next to her, his brow furrowed.

The man sitting to Xander's left leaned forward, his mouth stretched into a thin, haughty smile.

"Hello," he said. The words dripped from his lips and immediately settled like a knot in Ava's stomach. "Is very good to see you again."

Evgeny Lazovsky was a portly man. His hands rested on his thighs, fat and restless, kneading at the fleshy skin beneath his dark suit pants. He looked different than he had when she had shared the elevator with him and his mystery woman—more sinister and terrifying now that she was trapped in close quarters. Ava stared back at him, her eyes narrowed. She leaned into Xander in an attempt to ward off the chill that had woven its way beneath her skin as soon as she'd slid into the car and Lazovsky had pulled the camera from her collar.

"She is very quiet, yes?" he said with a raspy laugh.

Xander stared forward as Ava studied his profile, willing him to look her way and offer some sense of reassurance. She turned to look at Anatoly, who wove the car through traffic, the waters of the Neva lapping the sides of the thoroughfare outside her window.

"What's going on?" Ava finally asked. Her voice came out higher pitched than she intended and didn't sound as brave as she'd hoped. She stared at Anatoly in the rearview mirror, his eyes meeting hers with cold indifference.

"Is time to move on," Anatoly replied.

Ava crossed her arms. "What does that mean?"

Evgeny laughed again beside Xander. He pulled a small, silver flask from the inside pocket of his coat and took a long drink, sighing contentedly as he screwed the top back on.

"Xander?" Ava asked, turning to him.

He didn't respond at first. His eyes stayed trained ahead, nearly unblinking, almost as though he hadn't heard her. She jutted her elbow into his side.

"I want to talk to Nick," she demanded.

Xander turned to her. He reached up and pulled the blond, curly wig off his head, running his hand through his own short, brown hair. He tossed the wig on the floor, then leaned forward and spoke in Russian to Anatoly, who listened and then offered a small shrug as he gave a short, staccato reply. Xander leaned back with a sigh of frustration.

Ava looked back and forth between the two of them, her arms crossed tight over her chest. "Xander, we need to call Nick right now," she repeated, teeth clenched.

Xander looked at her then, the handsome features of his face having hardened into something less appealing. His eyes looked darker now, and his jaw was clenched in anger.

"Sorry, Ava, but that won't be possible," he said. Even his voice sounded different—angry and cold.

"What do you mean, 'that won't be possible'?" She clenched her fists to keep her fingers from trembling.

"It means that we call Nick later," Lazovsky said. "We call him and tell him we have his daughter, and if he wants her back, he will tell us what he knows about missing Fabergé egg."

Ava's heart skipped a beat. She tilted her head and furrowed her brow, trying to make sense of his words. "What's he talking about, Xander?"

He turned to her and gone was the man who had spent the last few days charming her. This was someone entirely different. Ava shrank back from his gaze.

"It means that Nick already knows where the egg is, and we've got what we need to get it out of him." He paused and looked her straight in the eye. "You."

"What are *you* talking about?" Ava said. "Nick doesn't know where the egg is already." She swallowed over the lump forming in her throat. Her heart raced, and she gripped her hands together in her lap.

Xander shrugged. "We think he's got more information than he's telling us. He's using this time as a training exercise to teach you the art of treasure hunting, but there is no way Nick Laine would have ever begun a hunt on this little bit of evidence and information." He shook his head. "He's been waiting for you to begin to fit the pieces together on your own." He met Anatoly's gaze in the mirror. "Apparently, we've decided we're tired of waiting." Frustration oozed through these last words.

Ava looked from Xander to Anatoly and back. "Wait, you've been planning to do this all along? But . . . why?" Ava looked back at Anatoly. "Nick said you were his most trusted partner here in Russia," she said. "And you"—she turned to Xander—"your father was one of his best friends."

"First of all, that's not Anatoly," Xander said. "His name is Pasha. He's like an upgraded version of Nick's Anatoly."

Ava furrowed her brow. "Not . . . who? What are you talking about?"

Xander shrugged. "And my father may have been loyal to Nick, but he wasn't loyal to me. Your father kept my dad away for most of my life. They just couldn't resist the hunt, and they had to do it together. A couple of times, I heard Dad talking with Nick, trying to back out of a new chase, but your father . . . he always got his way." Xander's eyes darkened again. "My father was missing most of my life because of Nick Laine. And my father died because of Nick Laine."

Ava was silent for a long moment, processing everything Xander had just told her. "How is Nick responsible for your father's death?" she sputtered.

"Oh, come on, Ava," Xander growled. "Both of our dads came down with the exact same form of aggressive cancer. What are the odds of that happening randomly?"

Ava blinked at him.

"They were exposed to something on a hunt that *your* dad persuaded mine to join him on," Xander continued. "If it weren't for Nick, my dad would have been around instead of leaving me to fend for myself with an alcoholic, bitter mother. And he would still be alive."

"So, what," Ava said. "This is your way to get back at Nick? Kidnap me?"

Xander shook his head. "No, getting back at him will be finding that missing egg first and reaping the financial rewards. Using you as collateral is only icing on the cake."

Lazovsky let out a deep, rolling laugh as an icy knot settled in Ava's stomach. Xander turned to her with a crooked smile.

"No hard feelings, Ava," he said. "Really. I hate that you got caught up in this, but there wasn't any other way." He gave her a patronizing pat on the leg. Ava pulled away from him, shrinking back as far as she could.

"Kind of crazy how you almost predicted this, isn't it?" he continued. "Romantic lead turned bad guy?" He turned to the driver, a man actually named Pasha, and barked out an order in Russian.

Pasha nodded, face stoic, as he turned into a parking lot and slowed to a stop. Ava looked out the window. They had pulled to a stop in front of a long building, large, angular glass windows arching upward from the brick exterior. On the front of the building was a long sign reading Санкт-Петербург in large, bold letters.

"Where are we?" she demanded.

"Ladozhsky Railway Station," he answered. "Button up your coat." He jutted his chin toward the building where people rushed in and out through the revolving doors, carrying with them suitcases and travel bags. "Time to take a little ride."

Ava shook her head. "I'm not going anywhere with you." She crossed her arms.

Xander cocked his head to the side and gave her a sickly smile. "You don't have a choice," he said. "You're now playing the part of the damsel in distress."

Ava glared at him. "I don't have my passport with me," she said. "I can't cross the border."

Xander chuckled. "Do you think I'm stupid, Ava?" He reached into his pocket and pulled out her passport, holding it up. "Remember, I had you all lock your things in the safe in my room when you first arrived, right?" He shook his head. "You know," he continued, putting her passport back into his pocket. "Nick went on and on about how smart and capable you were. He was certain you'd step right into his shoes. What was it he called you again?" Xander fixed his eyes on hers. "His padawan, right?" He clucked his tongue. "Seems he was wrong about you after all."

He reached up and grabbed hold of the red wig on her head, yanking it off as she yelped in pain, the pins that had held the wig in place pulling hair from her head. Ava ran her hand over her head self-consciously.

Xander leaned over her and pushed open the door. Before Ava could argue, he had given her a small shove, and she stumbled from the car. He slid out behind her and stepped close.

"Don't try to run," he said, his voice close to her ear.

She fought off a shiver. Lazovsky slid out behind them and opened his coat to reveal a small pistol strapped to his waist.

Ava swallowed. "You'll make it through security with that thing?" she asked, hoping she sounded braver than she felt.

"Is Russia," Lazovsky replied with a shrug and his signature laugh.

Ava turned and looked up at the modern building, uniquely designed with sharp lines and angles. It was noisy on the street, the sounds of cars and people mixing with the hiss and whistles of trains. Xander grabbed the top of Ava's arm and gave it a painful squeeze. She tried to pull away, but he held tight.

"Next stop—Finland," he said.

Lazovsky lit a cigarette, the smoke dancing between them

like a thin veil. His eyes squinted as he drew in a long drag, then pulled it from his lips and blew in her face. Ava turned away, blinking hard as Xander gave her a small push forward. He turned and barked something at Pasha in Russian, then the three of them approached the front of the station. Xander slid his arm around Ava's waist and pulled her close as a blast of hot air hit them. Ava glanced up at him coldly.

"You said you wanted an adventure," he said with a patronizing wink.

Carol paced the room, fighting panic, as Zak spoke with Nick.

"Alright, Zak, here's the plan," Nick was saying. His voice sounded stronger now, adrenaline having pushed out the tremor that had settled in his chest from the cancer. "You and Carol pack your things. Don't take everything, just the basics. Make sure you pack up all the equipment and documents. And search Xander's entire room. I doubt the idiot left anything, but if he did, we need to find it."

Zak was nodding his head, already stacking papers and shoving them into a manila folder. Carol began opening drawers in Xander's room and sifting through the belongings he'd left behind. She pulled open the closet door and looked down. Her face went pale.

"The safe," she whispered. She gave the door a tug, confirming what she already knew—it was locked tight. She turned to Zak. "He put our passports in there."

"What's that?" Nick asked over the speaker.

"Xander took our passports the day we arrived and put them in the safe in his room. The safe is closed and locked."

Nick let out a low, frustrated growl on the other end of the line. "If I could get ahold of that kid, I would wring his neck."

Carol wiped fresh tears off her cheeks.

"Okay, let's see," Nick continued. "Does the safe require a four- or six-digit code?"

"Um," Zak leaned down to look at the top of the safe. "Looks like standard four digit."

"Alright, give me a minute," Nick said. They could hear shuffling and murmuring on the other end of the line as Nick and Sylvie spoke to one another.

"Nick?" Carol asked.

"Hang on," Nick said. "I'm having Sylvie look up a couple of things."

Carol bit her lip. She closed her eyes and massaged her temples, trying to push back the headache that was slowly forming.

"Okay, Zak, try this," Nick said. "1-2-1-6."

Zak punched in the numbers. The safe beeped but didn't open. "That didn't work," he said.

"Okay, try 1-2-6-8," Nick said.

"Nope," Zak replied after trying.

"0-9-2-4," Nick said.

"No," Zak said a moment later.

"2-4-6-5."

Zak punched in the numbers and the door to the safe popped. "That was it!"

"He used his mom's birthdate," Nick said. "Amateur."

Zak peered inside the safe and breathed out a sigh of relief. "Our passports are here!" he said. He handed Carol hers, then tucked his own in the back pocket of his pants. "But Ava's is gone."

"Perfect," Nick said. "This lets me know we are dealing with a dumb kid who has a bad plan."

"Who appears to have kidnapped our daughter," Carol barked in reply.

The phone was silent for a moment. "Alright," Nick continued, clearing his throat, "my guess is Xander will call me at some point. He's gonna need information, and he knows I'm the only one who has it."

Carol froze. She turned toward the phone, her mouth going dry. "What did you say?" she croaked.

There was a slight pause on the other end of the line. "I have more information on the potential whereabouts of the egg than I originally let on."

"What do you mean, more information?" Carol asked, teeth clenched to keep them from chattering as her entire body went cold.

"I knew that Alma had the egg, and I really believe she took it with her to Finland. I wanted Ava to find the trail herself." His voice was tight, almost as though he were speaking through a straw.

Carol leaned forward over the phone, eyes flashing. "Nick, you sent us to Russia to work as spies with a kid who has now apparently turned on us, and you knew all along that the egg wasn't even here?"

"I *supposed* it wasn't there," he said, his voice meek. "I didn't know for sure."

"I . . . I don't even know what to say to you right now." Carol clenched her fists at her side, her fingernails digging into her skin.

"Look, we don't have time to talk about it," Nick said. "I need you two to get everything together and cleaned up and get out of there. There's a train that goes to Helsinki from St.

Petersburg. It's a three-hour ride. The next train leaves at seven thirty tonight, and you need to be on it—"

"Nick," Carol said through gritted teeth.

"I know, Carol." The fight in his voice was gone. She could hear the pain and fatigue in its place. "I'm so sorry."

"This isn't how I ever envisioned my first trip to Finland," she finally said.

Ava stepped off the train onto the platform and pulled her coat tight. She glanced at Xander, who stood next to Lazovsky, towering over the shorter man and registering no sign of emotion.

Ava had spent the entire train ride trying to figure out her next step, wondering what Nick would do in this situation. Should she try to run? Should she play along? Ava was certain her mother was panicking, and she wondered if Nick and Sylvie knew what was going on. Would any of them even think to suspect Xander?

"This way," Xander said, his voice calm.

Ava's face flushed in anger as she followed him. Lazovsky eyed her with a sickening smirk. He had stared at her like a piece of meat the entire ride.

They stepped out of the train station onto the bustling streets of Helsinki. The sun was down, masking the city in streetlights. For a brief moment, Ava forgot the circumstances and let herself soak in the fact that she was standing in Finland. She had heritage in this country.

"Alright," Xander said, turning to her. "Here's how this works. We're heading to the small town where Alma Pihl settled after returning to Finland with her husband in 1921. There's a little

314

house on a lake there that I think you'll find very interesting. From there, you're going to call Nick, and you're going to ask him where the egg is located."

Ava blinked up at him. "Where it's located?"

Xander smirked. "Yeah." He leaned forward. Ava pulled away from him in disgust. "Your dear old dad knew all along that the egg was here in Finland. He knew that Alma took it and hid it here."

"If you knew the egg was here all along, then why'd you wait for me?" Ava spat. "Why didn't you just come find it yourself?"

Xander straightened back up, adjusting his bag on his shoulder. "Because we know that Nick has the missing pieces. Well . . . most of the missing pieces, anyway." He winked at her. "We've got you."

A car pulled up and slowed to a stop in front of them. Lazovsky leaned forward and spoke through the window to the driver, his gravelly, drink-laden voice slurring out words that sounded incoherent to Ava. He turned and nodded at Xander. "We go here."

Lazovsky pulled open the back door and waved his arm, his mouth splitting into a smile as he stared at Ava.

"Your chariot," he said. He laughed, a low, wet, gurgling sort of sound that tumbled into coughing.

Ava glared at him, then stepped forward, sliding into the back seat of the car. Xander climbed in beside her. Lazovsky closed the door behind them, then slid into the front seat next to the driver, to whom he spoke one more time. The driver nodded, then merged into traffic. Lazovsky turned to stare at Xander and Ava.

"This is Maxim."

Ava shifted her gaze to the back of the driver's head. He

wore a newsboy's cap over what looked to be thinning, gray hair. He was long and thin, his arms sticking out of a coat that looked far too small. His car smelled of stale smoke and old food. Ava's stomach rolled. She turned to Xander.

"You know you won't get away with this," she said.

Xander stared straight ahead for a long moment before turning to meet her gaze. "And what makes you say that?" he asked.

"Nick will make sure of it," she replied.

Xander snorted. "How would you know?" he asked. "You admitted you hardly know him."

Ava swallowed hard, his words cutting through whatever confidence she had mustered.

Xander leaned forward. "You know, you could help us," he said. "You play the game and help us find the egg. That'd get back at your old man for all the years he was gone."

Ava turned her face away, feeling as though she'd been punched in the gut.

"I mean, seriously," Xander continued, leaning back against the cold, leather seat. Ava could feel him studying her. "This find would put us on the map and make us millionaires."

Lazovsky shifted and barked something at Xander in Russian. Xander stared at him with cool indifference before responding. Ava kept her eyes averted.

"So, what's your end goal?" she finally asked, turning to look at Xander.

"Sorry?"

"What are you trying to accomplish by finding the egg? What makes you different from Nick?"

"Nothing," Xander answered with a shrug. "I'll just make sure he doesn't get any of the funds from the sale of this find." He smiled. "You'll profit from helping us, though."

Ava waited.

"We won't have to kill you if you cooperate."

"You're not going to kill me either way," she said. "You don't have the guts to kill me."

"I do. I have guts." Lazovsky held up his gun and trained it at Ava's head.

She froze, her hands going numb and body cold.

"I do not like Nick Laine," Lazovsky continued. "He was always one step ahead—always finding the prize just before me. Is now my turn."

"Oh, put the blasted gun away, mate," Xander barked.

Lazovsky narrowed his eyes and glared at Xander. He lowered the gun. Ava, not realizing she'd been holding her breath, let out a long, deep sigh.

"Look," Xander said, turning to Ava. "We're going to find this egg. We are going to beat Nick Laine at the game that he invented. You can be a part of that in one of two ways—willingly, or unwillingly. But choose wisely." He stared hard at her, and Ava suddenly wondered why she had ever found him attractive. "Because each of those options will have a very different outcome for you."

They were quiet for a long time. Xander pulled out his phone and began scrolling through it, as Ava continued to watch the lights of the city, which were quickly fading into the background and giving way to long stretches of open, dark road ahead of them. Finally, she turned to Xander.

"Okay," she said, her voice soft but sure. "I'm in."

Carol leaned back on the seat and stared out the window. It was dark outside now, and the rocking train made her eyelids feel heavy, but each time she nodded off, a vision of Ava popped in her head, and she snapped awake.

Zak sat beside her, upright, back straight as a board. He clutched his phone in his hand, checking it periodically to make sure he still had a signal. They'd packed up everything from the hotel room as quickly as possible, though perhaps not efficiently, and they'd rushed to the train station, making it just in time to hop on board before the train pulled away. Nick had reserved them a private car, and for that Carol was enormously grateful. She rubbed her temples, trying to push away the dull ache that had settled there.

Zak's phone buzzed in his hand and both of them jumped.

"Yes? Nick?" Zak put the phone on speaker and held it between the two of them.

"Hey," Nick replied. His voice sounded far away, like he was closed inside a tin can. Carol leaned forward.

"Nick, have you heard anything else?" she asked.

"Not yet. But I'm certain Xander will call me. He needs what I have in order to move forward, and he knows it."

"And what do you have, Nick?" Carol asked.

"I know the location of the journal that my grandmother kept, in which she details her sister's relationship with Alma, and the secret that the two of them shared. It seemed that Lida was a bit jealous of her sister's friendship with Alma. She overheard a conversation one day. She wrote about how no one knew that Alma designed for the tsar. And then . . ." Static cut through the phone, Nick's voice fading in the distance.

Zak shook the phone in frustration. "Nick?"

". . . wrote about where Alma hid it," Nick finished as the static waned momentarily.

"What?" Carol replied, her voice raised.

"Nick, where is this journal?" Zak asked.

"It's in the attic of the house my grandmother owned," he replied. "The house that's still in my name. I went back there last year with the thought in mind that I would set the place up as a retreat. While I was there, I began digging into my family past and discovered the link between my grandmother and Alma. Oddly enough, that's what led me to start looking for the missing egg. Who knew that one of the greatest treasures in history was buried right under my nose?"

Static cut through the line again. Carol leaned her head back and closed her eyes.

"Nick, are you still there?" Zak asked.

"Yeah . . . still here," Nick replied, his voice cracking and faint.

"Our connection is bad."

"There's one more thing," Nick said.

Carol sighed and pinched the bridge of her nose. "I don't know how much more I can handle."

"I have . . . letter . . . found it . . . written by Fabergé. It speaks of the egg in detail."

His last words were crystal clear as the train burst through a grove of trees into the open air, the moonlight momentarily illuminating the outside as they rocketed toward Finland.

"Did you say you have a letter written by Fabergé?" Carol asked.

"Yes," Nick answered.

"Where did you find this letter?" Carol asked. She couldn't even pretend to soften her words as anger bubbled inside her.

"I was in St. Petersburg . . . at the front end of this search. While there, I met . . . who had a trove of secret documents locked in a safe in his flat. He claimed that he had been collecting these secret . . . for years. Most of them were interesting but . . . old letters from veterans to . . . loved ones during the war years . . . notebooks of military commanders and soldiers, sketches . . . drawings of unknown artists from Russian history. Cool stuff, but didn't . . . you know?"

Zak and Carol were quiet, so Nick continued.

"Anyway," he said, the line between them suddenly more clear and sharp again as the train hurtled out into a clearing, "when I mentioned to him that I was interested in learning more about Fabergé and his missing designs, the guy lit up and told me he had just the thing I needed." Nick paused and coughed, wet and gurgling.

Carol glanced at her watch and realized that it was 2:30 in the morning in Florida. She wondered how Nick was still functioning.

"He opened up a different safe, a smaller one, and he pulled out a stack of papers that he said were much more interesting and would cost me more money. I paid that crook a small fortune, but he gave me exactly what I needed."

There was a pause as Zak and Carol ingested Nick's story.

"Which was?" Carol prompted impatiently.

"A letter that Fabergé wrote to his sons in 1917 detailing the creation of a secret egg with dangerous implications. He said that he'd given the egg to the one he loved dearly, the daughter he'd always wished for, in order to keep it safe."

"Alma," Zak said.

"Yes."

"Do you have that letter with you?" Carol asked.

"No," Nick replied. "He wouldn't let me keep it. I took a photo of it and translated it myself later on. I also printed out a hard copy. Once I saw that letter, I knew I needed to go to Finland to search for Alma's things. It was that trip to Finland that led me to the cabin where I found the poem that I gave to you all."

"Okay, but what about your grandmother's journal? Why didn't you just tell us about it in the beginning and send us straight to Finland?"

Nick sighed. "I made a gross miscalculation," he said. "I sent you all to St. Petersburg in order to use it as a training exercise to look for clues. I wanted Ava to learn the art of finding a treasure on her own. And Xander . . ." He paused and sighed. "Well, his dad was my best friend. I wanted to give Jack's boy the same opportunity that I was giving Ava—the chance to learn the art of the hunt. I didn't follow through, and I didn't know that they weren't with the real Anatoly. Had they been, this would have gone as I planned for it to go. Ava's smart, Carol. She's wicked smart."

"Yeah, I know, Nick," Carol shot back. "I raised her, remember?"

An awkward pause hung in the air.

"I knew she would eventually stumble onto the clues," Nick continued. "I mean, she found things I didn't even find! I had no idea that drawing was buried in Fabergé's old showroom. It was only a matter of time before she ended up figuring out that Alma definitely had the egg in her possession, and you guys would have gone to Finland on your own. At that point, my plan had been to drop hints on where to find the journal. I knew Ava would put the pieces together—I wanted her to have the satisfaction of figuring it out on her own."

Carol sighed and shook her head.

"Where do we need to go when we arrive in Helsinki?" Zak finally asked.

"You'll have to rent a car," Nick replied. His voice broke up as the signal on the phone faltered once again. "I'll send the address of the home you're going to . . ." His voice faded and the line went staticky.

"Nick? Nick?"

"Call when . . ." Nick's voice broke through the static briefly, then the line went dead.

Carol looked up at Zak. "Well," she said, her voice tight.

"Yeah," he replied.

They leaned back and rode on in silence.

St. Petersburg, 1918

I have to go. I have to go now."

Augusta watched him bustle through the room, hands shaking, as he threw a few items into a cloth bag. She walked behind him, nodding her head in agreement.

"Yes, yes," she murmured. "We should all go."

"No. My darling, no."

Augusta stopped and stared at him. "What do you mean, no?"

"It's too dangerous. They've already arrested Agathon and Alexander."

Augusta thought of their sons, currently locked up in a secret prison somewhere in the city, arrested, she believed, for no other reason than they were the sons of the House of Fabergé. Karl's association with the Imperial family had put them all at risk. It was time to get out.

The Bolsheviks had succeeded in their plan to nationalize the country by February of that year. When word of Lenin's urging to the commoners to "loot the looters" reached her husband, Augusta knew the writing was on the wall. Though

323

Karl had already liquidated many of his assets and sent some hard currency abroad, she knew that it was only a matter of time before the company was liquidated for good, and a target was on Karl's back.

The Bolsheviks had renamed themselves the Communist Party of Russia, and word quickly got to them that Karl had been identified by Leon Trotsky, Lenin's right-hand man, as a war profiteer.

"They're coming for you," Albert whispered late one night as the three of them walked across Anichkov Bridge, coats pulled up tight around their necks.

Shortly after that meeting, impossible taxes were levied against the company. They'd had to let most of the employees go, a fact that Augusta knew tormented her husband. Famine had reached them all, with bread being nearly impossible to come by. None of them were immune to its effects. Even their dear friend and chief designer, Francois Birbaum, had been hit, losing his wife to starvation just two months before. Karl closed his eyes and swayed on his feet. Augusta watched her husband with a swirl of emotions, from pity to anger to compassion.

"The officials told me last week that the boys will be released soon," Augusta said, breaking the silence.

Karl shook his head. "How can we know that's true, my dear?" he asked, his eyes wet.

She crossed the room and stood before him, her hands clenched at her waist. "We all need to get out," she said, her voice firm. "None of us are safe."

Karl nodded. "Yes, I agree with you, but I need to go on my own first. The officials will come for me before they come for you. If we're all together, they will immediately take you. I must leave tonight. You and Eugen make arrangements to get out as soon as possible. I will meet you when I can."

Augusta shook her head, her lips pursed. "You're a stubborn man," she said.

Karl's face softened. He leaned forward, placing his forehead against hers.

"Perhaps," he agreed. "But for far too long, I've been a foolish man, and I cannot be that right now. Me leaving is the best way to protect the rest of you."

Augusta grabbed his hand. His fingers were cold, his palm slick. His hand felt bony and frail inside hers. The last year had aged him. The great Peter Karl Fabergé had become an old man nearly overnight, as all that he had ever worked for had been taken right out from beneath him. The company dissolved, all assets confiscated by the communists. They'd been evacuated from their building on Bolshaya Morskaya and had moved in with their oldest son. They were able to keep very few of their possessions, everything else remaining behind to be pillaged by the new leadership. They had sent word to all the employees who had worked at the House of Fabergé to stay away from the building.

"It isn't safe to return," they wrote in a letter that they distributed to each family. *"The building is in the hands of the communists. Leave everything behind. Do not attempt to retrieve your possessions."*

The situation was bleak, and Augusta knew it.

Rumors were flying that the Imperial family, long since exiled to Siberia, would be executed. Other rumors circulated that the family was poised to regain their power and return. Augusta suspected they would never really know the truth, and she had resigned herself to the fact that life as they had known it would never be the same. The weight of it all had taken its toll on everyone, but none more so than her husband whose health was fragile.

"There is a diplomatic train leaving tonight," Karl said, breaking her thoughts. "I need to be on it."

"But you're not a diplomat."

"I can pretend. I will disguise myself as one of the British legation."

Augusta looked at him skeptically.

"I only need to get as far as the border," he continued, defending his plan, "and then I'll get to Riga. The communists haven't taken Latvia yet. I will figure out what to do from there." He looked hard in her eyes. "I'll find you, my darling."

Augusta shook her head. "This plan is crazy."

Karl nodded. "It's the only way."

She pulled back and searched his face, the lines of stress and age having etched a path down his cheeks. "What did you do with it?" she asked quietly.

Karl didn't even try to pretend he didn't know what she was talking about. "I took care of it."

Augusta raised one eyebrow. Karl sighed.

"I wrote it all down in a letter to the boys, which I've put in the pocket of my old trench coat. You may read it after I'm gone."

Augusta blinked back tears. Unaccustomed to seeing his wife show emotion, Karl grabbed her hands and pulled them to his lips.

"You've been my pillar all these years, my darling," he said. "I do not deserve you."

Augusta leaned into him. "I've loved you all along," she said. "And I've loathed you at the same time. I still do."

Karl nodded. They stood together for a long time, years of unspoken confessions and heartaches lingering between them, melting in the familiar embrace that had drawn them together when they were young so many years before.

"We'll find one another," he whispered. "I believe that we will. I'll make it, and I will wait for you. As soon as I settle, I'll send word for you to join me."

"I'm going to Finland," Augusta said. "I need to go back to my family."

Karl searched her face. "I cannot go to Finland. I'll never make it there."

Augusta drew in a deep breath. "I know," she replied softly.

Understanding washed through his eyes. "I see," he finally said. He turned his face from hers and tugged his watch from his pocket. "It's time for me to leave."

Augusta nodded, holding her chin high and meeting his gaze. "I do love you," she whispered, fresh tears pricking her eyelids.

"And I you, my dear," he replied, lips trembling.

He tugged his bag up off the ground, then pulled a hat onto his bald head, low over his eyes.

"I'll be off now," he said. "I'll try to send word when it is safe."

Augusta nodded. She leaned forward and kissed his cheek, her wrinkled lips pressed against his sandpaper skin. He nodded at her once, then turned, trudging out the door. Augusta listened until she could no longer hear his shuffling footsteps. She turned and walked to the small armoire, pulling it open and tugging his old trench coat off the hanger. Her fingers trembled as she dug into the inside pocket, pulling out a piece of paper that had been neatly and symmetrically folded. She dropped the coat on the bed, then sank into her chair in the corner, opening the letter and reading it slowly. When she was finished, she lowered the letter back onto her lap and let out a long sigh.

"Alma."

Present Day

The car slowed to a stop just as Ava felt her eyelids getting heavy, the sound of tires on gravel jolting her awake. The moon was high in the sky, casting down a glow bright enough for her to make out hills on the horizon. The reflection of the moon on the lake left a trail that cut a path across the water. Ava turned to look out the front window of the car at the house they had stopped in front of, its porch illuminated by a yellow light bulb that hung outside the door. The house looked sturdy. It was tall and narrow, stretching back almost like an old barn. It looked dark and cold on the inside, and Ava couldn't quite make out the color in the moonlight.

"Alright," Xander said, turning to face her. "Time to call Nick."

She glanced at her watch. "It's the middle of the night there. He'll be asleep."

Xander cocked his head to the side and looked at her curiously. "Do you really think so? Even though his only daughter has been missing now for about seven hours? Do you really think he won't care at all?"

Ava swallowed. It hadn't even occurred to her that her father might care.

Xander pushed open his door and stepped outside. Lazovsky walked in front of the car, the orange dot of his cigarette dancing before his face.

"Where are we?" Ava asked, stepping out of the car.

"This is your old family home," Xander replied.

Ava turned to look at him, eyebrows raised. "This is where my great-grandmother lived?"

"It is. She grew up here with her sister, Isla."

"Alma's friend," Ava said. She shivered. The air was wetter in Finland, especially on the lake. The cold seeped through her coat and into her bones. Ava crossed her arms over her chest and watched Xander and Lazovsky walk up the steps of the front porch casually, as though they were there for a weekend getaway. Lazovsky had one hand hanging by his side, the gun glinting in the moonlight. Ava closed her eyes and marveled at the quietness that surrounded them. It was as though the entire world had stilled and silenced.

"Let's go," Xander said. He spoke softly, but his words carried through the air as if they had wings.

Ava glanced at Maxim, the driver. He leaned against the side of the car, a cigarette dangling from his lips, arms crossed in front of him. He looked indifferent to the transpiring events, as though this were simply another day at the office.

Ava stepped forward, the sound of her boots on the gravel magnified. Everything sounded louder and brighter, but she couldn't tell if it was because of the circumstance or the environment.

She climbed the steps, stopping beside Lazovsky as Xander glanced over his shoulder. He gave her a little wink, turning her stomach, before he reared his arm back and smashed his elbow into the glass of the front door. Ava jumped as it shattered. Xander reached inside the broken window and unlocked the door, then pushed it open and gestured Ava to step inside.

She was thankful that the house seemed to be warmer than the outside, though clearly there was no heat. It was dark, and Ava stepped to the side as Xander and Lazovsky followed her through the threshold.

Xander reached over and flipped the switch on the wall, illuminating the front room in a dull glow. Ava looked up and took it all in. Three weeks ago, she had been a restaurant hostess with daddy issues and no discernible family history, and now here she was, standing in the Finnish foyer of her great-grandmother.

"How did you know about this place?" she asked Xander, as he stepped into the next room and turned on the light. She followed him in and blinked at how cozy and put-together the space looked. A red-and-gold area rug covered hardwood floors. A small brown couch sat facing the redbrick fireplace, which still had broken pieces of wood in it and ashes in the bottom, showing that it had been used multiple times before. A round table sat next to the couch, which had a coffee table in front of it.

"After my dad died, I found a few letters your dad and my dad had written to one another," Xander said. He walked to the fireplace mantel and glanced at the photos that were scattered across the length of it. "You'd be surprised what the two of them discussed in those letters."

Ava stepped up to the mantel and took in the images. They were photographs of her at various stages of her life. There was the one of her and Nick when she was two, the same picture she had at home. There was a picture of her in second grade when her mother had taken her deep-sea fishing and she'd caught a small blacktip shark. There was her senior portrait, and a photo of her in her Easter dress, wearing the ridiculous straw hat her mother insisted she wear every Easter until she grew old enough to refuse.

Every image was of her. Ava blinked as tears pricked at her eyelids. She swallowed over the lump in her throat and turned to look at Xander, who watched her with an odd sense of glee.

"Almost creepy, isn't it?" he asked. "The way he stalked you all those years but never reached out."

Ava blinked several times, then raised her chin. "So, how do we call him?"

Xander grinned. "That's a good girl."

Ava rolled her eyes. "Seriously, don't talk like that. You're being so quintessential British bad guy right now that I don't even believe you." She hoped she sounded braver than she felt. She shoved her hands in her pockets so that Xander wouldn't see them shaking.

He chuckled. "Still writing that story in your head, are you?"

Ava shrugged.

"Alright, then." Xander turned to Lazovsky and spoke to him in Russian.

Lazovsky nodded. He set his gun down on the coffee table and reached in his pocket, pulling out a phone and turning it on. He looked up at Ava.

"Is special phone for calling Nick," he said.

She hated his voice, the way his words rolled and formed so that he sounded all-powerful. Xander took the phone from him and dialed Nick's number.

"Hello? Ava?" Nick's voice broke through the speaker after

the first ring, and Ava's eyes flew open. She felt a shiver rock through her entire body.

"Hey, Nick," Xander said. He held up his hand toward Ava, then put his finger to his lips.

"Xander, you dumb—"

"Nick, I'm going to stop you right there," Xander said. "I'm the one who is currently holding all the power here, so I guide the conversation, understood?"

The other end of the line was silent, though Ava could hear the faint rattle in Nick's breathing.

"Classic. Now, I'll begin. How are you doing, Nick?" He grinned. It was a petulant, obnoxious smile like that of a child who thought he was getting away with something grand.

"Xander, I have no interest in playing your little mind games," Nick said. "For the record, you're not the first one who has tried to steal a treasure from me, and you're also not the cleverest, so let's drop the pretense that I'm terribly surprised and wringing my hands with worry, okay?"

Xander's eyes flashed as he leaned toward the phone. "There's someone here who wants to say hi, Nick," he said, his teeth clenched.

Ava stepped forward, then stopped as Xander held up his hand again. Instead, he nodded at Lazovsky who stepped forward.

"*Zdravstvuyte*, Nick," he said, his voice low and gravelly.

Nick was quiet for a brief moment before he responded, this time his voice notably more tight. "Lazovsky." Ava could hear the change in Nick's voice. "I should have known," he growled.

Lazovsky chuckled. "I tell you last time that I will beat you at this game someday. Is someday now." He turned to look at

Ava, his eyes cold and distant. "I am looking at your daughter. She is very pretty."

"If you lay a hand on her, Lazovsky, I will kill you."

Lazovsky laughed, this time the sound bold and brash and filling every corner of the room. "How you will kill me? From your deathbed with your mind?" He laughed again.

Xander leaned back into the phone. "So, I'm with you, Nick. Let's drop the pretenses. You don't need to pretend to be surprised, and I won't pretend to care about whether or not you're disappointed in me."

Nick remained silent on the other end of the line. Xander gestured for Ava to step forward.

"Here you go." Xander handed the phone to Ava. She drew in a deep breath.

"Hey, Nick," she said, and then against her better judgment and despite her best efforts to remain in control, she began to cry.

St. Petersburg, December 1918

Alma sat on the edge of the bed, her stomach tight and empty, and she watched her husband move slowly through the room. He caught her eye and gave her a small smile.

"It will be fine, my darling," he said. "I'm working on the paperwork to get us out of here. We just have to continue to remain quiet and keep our heads down."

Alma nodded. Her hair was loose around her shoulders. She caught sight of herself in the mirror on the wall. Her face had grown thin and drawn. She wondered how her husband could even enjoy looking at her these days.

Nicholas crossed the room and knelt before her, grabbing her hands in his. Both of them had lost weight, the famine making it difficult to stay nourished. He still held his job, but every day was tense as he waited for the communists to shut his company down and put them out on the streets permanently. For months, he and Alma had been trying to figure out a way to get out of the country.

"I want to go home," Alma had told him last night as he'd

KELLI STUART

cradled her in bed. Her face was pressed into his neck, wet
with tears. "I want to go back to Finland and forget this place
completely."

Leaving wasn't so easy, though. Trains were limited, and they
needed the correct documents to cross the border. Nicholas
was struggling to get the papers they needed to get them both
out without being detected by the communists controlling the
border. Alma's association with Fabergé was a stain that was
difficult to erase.

"I'll be back this evening," Nicholas told his wife, smoothing
her hair back. "In the meantime, my dear, take care of yourself.
Write a letter home telling them that we are coming. Keep up
your spirits."

Alma gave him a sad smile. "I love you," she said.

Nicholas leaned in and kissed her hard, a desperate sort of
kiss that communicated all his fears and longings to protect
her in a single moment.

He pulled back and reached up, his hands on either side
of her face. "I love you more," he said. He kissed her again,
gentler this time, then pulled away and stood up.

"Be well today," he said. He gave her a wink, then turned,
grabbed his long coat off the hook on the wall, and walked out
the door, closing it quietly behind him.

Alma sat still on the end of the bed for a long time, thinking over all the events that had led her here. She knew that
Fabergé had left three months earlier, and she heard that his
wife and sons had made plans to leave as soon as possible. She
wondered how everyone else was managing to get out, yet
she and Nicholas seemed to be trapped in this place. Even
Uncle Albert had escaped, urging her to leave as soon as she
possibly could.

"*Get home, Alma. Get out of this hellhole,*" he'd written to her in the letter he sent, explaining his plans to go back to Finland. They all made it seem so easy, but for some reason she and Nicholas couldn't fit the pieces together.

Alma felt her heartbeat quicken as she thought of the treasure hidden beneath her. She'd lain awake so many nights since Fabergé gave it to her, wishing she had told him no, wondering why she hadn't refused. The weight of this secret was almost too much.

Sliding off the bed, she laid on her back and shimmied halfway beneath the bed that she shared with her husband. She could see the lump hanging beneath the mattress where she'd tied the egg into a sheet and secured it to the bottom of their bed. It felt red hot having Fabergé's rebellious creation so close to their bodies. She'd wondered often if she should tell Nicholas what she had, but she knew that would be foolish. He would be livid. So, there the secret remained, suspended just below the place where they slept, made love, and dreamed of the family they would start once they got out of Russia.

Alma reached up and ran her fingers over the sheet, feeling the lump of the egg beneath it. She hadn't removed it since she'd hidden it there a year ago. She was too afraid to look at it again.

Sliding back out from beneath the bed, Alma stood up and brushed herself off. She walked to the small stove and lit the fire beneath the teakettle. She needed something in her stomach. She looked at the plate that Nicholas had left with a single stale piece of bread on it for her. How different their lives looked from a year ago when she'd made grand meals for them on this same stovetop.

As the water in the kettle took its time to heat, Alma grabbed a pencil and a piece of paper and sat down at the table beneath the window. She looked outside, noticing the crystalized ice that had formed patterns on the windowpane. Once upon a time, she had created beautiful pieces of jewelry that mirrored those same ice crystals. The jewels had been worn around the neck of the tsarina herself. Once upon a time, she had been a master craftsman.

She blinked back tears as her head bent over the paper and her pencil began to scratch out the heartache in her heart. And as the kettle slowly began to whistle a mournful tune, the words tumbled from the end of her pencil.

> "The day I know the secret from the boards
> Hidden beneath the inner chamber of his heart.
> Held in bondage to the ancient rule,
> Invisible but seen."

Present Day

Zak slid into the seat behind the wheel of the car and drew in a deep breath. He looked out at the black night sky lit up by the lights of Helsinki, and the moon, which hung suspended over them in a sort of frozen dance. He turned the key and let the car start and hum as he and Carol shivered, waiting for the heater to kick in and provide some warmth.

Zak glanced at his watch. It was 12:45 a.m. He rubbed his eyes.

"Zak, are you okay to drive right now?" Carol asked, her voice laced with motherly concern.

"Yes, of course, Miss Carol." He forced a small smile. "I'll be fine."

Grabbing his phone, he pulled up the address that Nick had sent. He typed it into the car's GPS system and waited for the map to appear on the screen. He ran his hands over the steering wheel as the car slowly began to heat up. "This is a nice car."

"Nick always liked cars," Carol murmured.

The map appeared on the screen. "Two hours to our destination," Zak said.

Carol sighed. "I just want to get to my girl."

Zak grabbed her hand and gave it a squeeze. "I know," he said. "So do I."

"Ava, are you okay? Have they hurt you?" Nick's voice was tight, anger and concern braided through each word.

Ava wiped her eyes and took in a deep breath. "Yes, I'm okay. And no, they haven't hurt me." She glanced over at Lazovsky as he tapped his gun on the side of his leg.

"Are you on speaker?"

"Yes."

"Xander," Nick said, his voice low and barely restrained. "What the hell are you thinking?"

Xander shrugged his shoulders. "Just give us the information we need, Nick," he answered.

"I want to talk to Ava privately," Nick replied. "I won't say anything to her on speakerphone."

Xander glanced at Lazovsky, who shrugged and said, "She stays here with us to talk."

"Fine," Xander said. "You can talk to Ava off speaker, but she stays in the room with us."

"Fine," Nick said.

Xander took the phone from Ava's hand and turned off the speaker. He put the phone on mute and turned to her. "Remember," he said. "You help us out, and you get to have a piece of the pie. And also, you don't die tonight. So, no games, got it?"

Ava nodded, wiping her cheeks and drawing in a deep breath. She took the phone from Xander, took it off mute, and put it to her ear. "Nick?"

"Ava! Are you alright?"

"Yes," she answered. "I'm fine." She lowered her head and

turned away from Xander. "I need to know where the egg is, Nick."

Nick sighed. "Ava, if I knew exactly where it was, I would have it already."

"Okay, well then, I need to know where you *think* it is."

"Ava, I can give you the information that I have, but I need you to listen to me very closely. They are not going to let you out alive. I know Lazovsky. The guy is a crook, and he's dangerous. He's been trying to outsmart me for years. He's bad news, but he's also dumb as a post, so all you have to do is outthink him to get away."

Ava remained silent.

"You still there?" Nick asked.

"Yes. I just need to know what to do next," she said.

"Okay, I'm going to tell you something. Just nod your head and say 'okay' every once in a while, but listen very carefully, got it?"

Ava nodded. "Okay."

"In the attic of the house you're in right now there is a journal written by your great-grandmother, Lida. In it, she details a conversation she heard between her sister and Alma in which Alma confides about the treasure she was given."

"Okay," Ava said, trying to keep her voice steady and even.

"I need you to find that journal."

"Okay."

"It's written in Finnish, but I translated it and tucked the translation into the journal, so you'll know what the journal says."

"Um . . . okay," Ava said, a thousand questions swirling in her mind. Nick spoke Finnish?

"My mother spoke to me in Finnish growing up," Nick continued almost as though he'd read her mind.

340

Ava nodded. "Okay."

"Listen, Ava," Nick said. "The journal entry doesn't really pinpoint the location of the egg. It more proves that Alma brought something back with her from Russia. When I found that journal, I'd planned to begin searching myself, but the pain in my chest grew so debilitating that I needed to seek medical treatment. As it turns out, cancer doesn't really care if you're on the brink of a major discovery."

Ava was silent. She could feel Xander and Lazovsky staring at her from behind. She ducked her head, brows furrowed. Nick sighed on the other end of the line.

"The journal entry is your final clue, Ava. There's something there. I could feel it when I read it, but I didn't have the chance to put my finger on it. I need you to figure it out, and I need you to do so before Xander and Lazovsky."

"Um . . ."

"Ava," Nick said. "I'm sorry I sent you to Russia. I'm sorry I didn't just send you there to Finland first. I thought I'd train you for the hunt by having you actually hunt. I'm so sorry I've put you in this position. If Jack knew what his kid was up to right now, he would be devastated."

"Nick," Ava said.

"What's he saying, Ava?" Xander asked, stepping up beside Ava and startling her.

She jumped, nearly dropping the phone. "He's telling me where to find a journal that my great-grandmother kept," she said. "We aren't done."

"I want to know what you're saying, Nick," Xander barked, his mouth tilted toward the phone in her hand.

"Tell him I said to give us one more minute, then I'll talk with him."

Ava looked up at him. "He said he needs one more minute."

Xander stepped back and crossed his arms over his chest, glaring down at her.

"Ava," Nick continued. She pressed the phone against her ear and turned away. "Listen to me. You have to get away from them. I know it's dark out and it's cold. You have to slip out and find your way to the southern end of the lake. Please tell me you didn't get your mother's sense of direction and you know north from south."

"I do," she replied.

"Okay, good. There's a small house there. It was a hideaway house that my great-grandmother would use to escape when she got overwhelmed with her kids. My mother used to talk about it incessantly when I was growing up. She said it was the place her mother loved more than anything else. It was the first place I fixed up when I got to Finland. You'll know you've reached it when you see a little carved post at the end of the lake. Etched on the post are the words *Paikka, jota rakastan eniten.* It means 'the place I love most.' If you go into the kitchen of this little house and pull up the rug, you'll find a hidden cellar. Hide there, and make sure you pull the door down securely. Wait in there until I'm able to get Zak and your mom to you, okay?"

"Okay," she said. The skepticism in her voice was impossible to mask. This sounded like a ridiculous plan.

"Alright, now, the journal is in the attic of the house you're currently in. It's in the back corner, hidden behind the boards of the wall."

"*The secret beneath the boards,*" Ava murmured.

Xander cocked his head to the side and stared at her.

"Ironic, isn't it?" Nick asked. "You'll find five nails, slightly raised, forming an *X*. Pull on the nails and the panel will open. You'll find the journal inside. Make sure you're the one to find it. You get your hands on it first. Can you do that?"

"Okay," she said.

"Good," Nick said. "Put me back on speaker now."

Ava hit the speaker button and held the phone out toward Xander. He stepped forward.

"Nick?"

"Ava knows where to go next," Nick said. "Let her take the lead. And Xander," Nick's voice got lower. "Nothing happens to her. I only gave her enough information to get you to the next step. If you want more after that, she better be the one to call me."

"You got it, boss," Xander said. He gave a mock salute toward the phone.

"Your dad would be so disappointed," Nick said quietly.

"Well, I suppose you would know better than me," Xander replied, "since you're the only person he ever really spent time with."

His words hung in the air for a moment before Xander shrugged them off.

"Oh well. Water under the bridge, yeah?"

"*She* calls me," Nick said. "I won't talk to anyone else."

"Got it, Nick." He tapped the red button, ending the call. Turning to Ava, he arched his eyebrow.

"The crying was a nice touch," he said.

Ava shrugged. "It worked, didn't it? He told me what to do next."

The Border of Russia and Finland
December 1918

M ama, we must go now. We cannot wait any longer.
We'll have to go by foot, and it has to be now before
it gets too dark."

Augusta clutched the bag on her shoulder and looked up
at her son. Eugen's face was etched with worry, deep lines
creasing his forehead. He placed his hands on her elbows and
gently helped her step down.

Augusta swallowed over the lump that had formed in her
throat. She had wanted nothing more than to return home to
Finland, and here they were—so close. Eugen had insisted
on accompanying her. At first, she had resisted, but she was
now quite grateful to have him. They'd made it by train as far
as they could, but the barriers set in place by the communists
made it difficult for them to continue. Eugen had convinced
her to travel by sledge, a rickety horse-drawn *troika*, until they
reached the border. She knew he had hoped to ride the sleigh
all the way into Finland, but they had been turned around

because their papers were deemed insufficient for crossing. Staying in Russia was not an option. They needed to get out, and walking was apparently the only way.

Augusta stared at the tree line ahead of them, snow-blocked and ominous. Her mouth was set in a hard, thin line, lips frozen and cheeks burning from the icy air.

"Mama, please," Eugen said, pulling her a step forward. "We must go. Here, let me carry your bag."

Augusta clutched her satchel closer and shook her head. "I'll carry it myself," she said.

Eugen drew in a deep breath and let it out slowly, the way Augusta used to do when the children were younger, and she was trying to maintain patience.

"I'm not a child, my dear," she said, her voice more tender this time. "And besides, the bag is keeping me warm." She took a step forward, her feet sinking in the snow. She glanced up at Eugen. "Is it a long walk?"

Eugen ran a shaky hand over his head. "I don't really know, Mama," he answered. "But it will be difficult. Are you sure I can't carry that bag for you to lighten your load?"

Augusta pursed her lips and shook her head no. "Well," she said, "let's be off then."

Eugen grabbed his own bag, everything he owned now reduced to that which he could carry on his back, and he stepped in front of his mother.

"Stay close to me, Mama," he said, glancing at her over his shoulder, "and tell me if you are struggling and need help." He gave her a wary look. "Now is not the time to try and be heroic. I'm not a young man either. I won't be able to carry you."

"I promise you will not need to carry me, son," Augusta said, chin lifted proudly.

The two marched forward, Eugen's head moving side to side, scanning the horizon for anyone who might come to stop them.

"Are you sure this will lead us into Finland?" Augusta wheezed from behind him. They were beneath the canopy of the trees now, the wind less biting, but also without any comfort of sunlight.

"I am as sure as I can be, Mama," he said.

"And what happens if we get stuck out here after dark?"

She heard him suck in a sharp breath before answering. "We won't, Mama. I'll make sure of it."

She was quiet then, and for a long time they trudged forward in silence, with only the padded sound of their footsteps moving through the snow-packed forest floor and her labored breathing to keep them company.

"Thank you," Augusta finally said.

Eugen stopped and turned to his mother. She paused, raising her hand to wipe the sweat from her face. She was certain she looked a mess.

"For what?" he asked.

"For not leaving me." She blinked several times, hot tears pricking the corners of her eyes.

Eugen grabbed his mother's gloved hand and gave it a squeeze. "Of course, Mama," he said tenderly. "I wouldn't leave you."

She nodded, then took another step forward, shoulders hunched.

"Mama, please," Eugen begged once more. "I would really feel better if you'd let me carry your bag."

Augusta shook her head and pulled it out of his reach. "I cannot let you do that," she said.

"But why?"

Before she could answer, the sound of sticks cracking pulled both of their attention toward the way they'd just come. A shout could be heard in the distance.

"We need to go now," Eugen whispered.

Augusta nodded and put her head down, stepping into his footprints behind him. Eugen increased his speed, reaching back to grasp her hand as they ducked and maneuvered around the trees.

"Look, Mama. Up ahead."

Augusta raised her eyes and saw, about a hundred meters in front of them, a clearing in the trees.

"Is it . . . ?" Her voice faltered.

Eugen grabbed her hand and pulled her forward, catching her as her feet slipped and she fell to her knees. Behind them a shot rang out. The warbled sounds of Russian words met Augusta's ears, and Eugen tugged her to her feet.

"We must run, Mama," he hissed.

Together they pushed forward, Augusta clutching her bag with one hand and her son with the other.

"STOP!"

The warning rang out behind them, but Eugen did not stop or hesitate. He pulled his mother's arm and swung her in front of him, pushed her forward. Augusta willed her frozen feet to cooperate, putting one in front of the other. The clearing grew brighter.

They were steps away when another shot rang out. The tree beside Eugen's head splintered.

"Run, Mama, run!" he shouted.

Stumbling, Augusta pushed through to the clearing and fell onto the field. She looked back to see Eugen stagger out of the trees behind her. He grabbed her elbow and pulled her to her feet. Looking ahead, she saw two men running toward them. They had guns raised and were shouting something.

"We are Finnish! We are Finnish!" Eugen shouted, holding up his hands in front of him.

Augusta burst into tears and looked at the boys wearing the flag of her homeland on their chest. She grabbed Eugen's hand.

"I'm home," she cried.

Present Day

Ava straightened up and shivered as she looked around the dark attic. She could hear Xander and Lazovsky climbing the ladder behind her. Flicking open the flashlight on Xander's phone, she quickly shone it around the room, looking for nails in the wall. Finally, in the far back corner, she caught the glint of metal, and she rushed toward it just as Xander climbed into the attic behind her.

"What is it?" he asked.

"Nick said there's a journal hidden behind the wall up here," Ava said. She stepped over a box and weaved her way around two old trunks that were stacked on top of one another. She ran her hand over the top of one of them, wondering what was inside. More hidden treasures? Secrets of a family past about which she knew nothing?

She stepped up to the wall and ran her fingers lightly over the five nails hammered to look like an X.

"X marks the spot," she murmured. She tugged on the top nail, but nothing happened. She pulled again, this time noticing that the wood moved a little. Setting the phone down, she grabbed the head of the nail with both hands and began to wiggle it back and forth. Slowly, the board shimmied, loosening the other nails, until they all popped out, with Ava nearly falling backward. Xander caught her shoulders and set her back up.

"Easy now," he said.

Ava shrugged his hands off her and reached inside, grimacing as she felt grit and dirt.

"Worried about those Finnish spiders?" Xander asked.

Ava rolled her eyes. "Stop acting like we're friends."

Xander clucked his tongue. "But we are friends, Ava. We've shared our deepest, darkest secrets and bonded over our daddy issues. You and I are just alike."

Ava was about to shoot back a retort when her hand brushed the corner of a book. She reached farther into the crevice of the wall and pulled out Lida's journal. Lazovsky stepped up behind her and peered over her shoulder.

"What is this?" he asked.

Ava brushed off the top of the book and held it gingerly in her hands. She ran her fingers along the edge of the pages, feeling the indent where a piece of notebook paper was folded inside. She casually slipped her hand into the book, then turned to peer back into the hole in the wall, sheltering the journal from Xander and Lazovsky.

Xander grabbed her elbow and spun her around, pulling the book from her grasp. The loose piece of paper fluttered to the ground. He bent down to pick it up.

"Is this what you're trying to get without us seeing?" he asked.

Ava stood silent.

Xander unfolded the paper and turned it over. He glanced up at Ava. "What is this?"

"It's a translation of Lida's journal in which she writes down a conversation she overheard between Alma and Isla. Alma told Isla about a treasure given to her by Fabergé. She and Isla hid it somewhere on this property."

Xander quickly read the page, then turned it over. "This is a map," he said, his mouth spreading into a grin. "You were going to try and get this out so we wouldn't find it, weren't you?"

Ava shrugged. "That's what Nick told me to do, but I'm on your side now, remember?"

Xander leaned in. "There are no sides, Ava," he said. "It's every man for himself."

"And what does this mean, 'every man for himself'?" Lazovsky asked. He grabbed the paper from Xander's hand and slowly backed up, training the gun at them. "It means this?" he asked. He cocked the gun and pointed it at Ava.

"Oh, sod off, mate," Xander said. "You can't shoot her now. No way Nick has made it that easy on us. He said she had to be the one to call him for the next step, remember?"

Ava stood frozen as she stared, for the second time that night, down the barrel of Lazovsky's gun.

"Is true," Lazovsky replied, lowering the gun just slightly. He then swiftly lifted it, pointed at Xander, and pulled the trigger. Ava yelped, clapping her hand over her mouth as Xander hit the floor, clutching his stomach and gasping.

"Maybe I need her little bit longer," Lazovsky said, lowering the gun to his side, "but I do not need you."

Xander lay panting on the floor as Ava stepped back, her hands shaking.

"Come," Lazovsky barked at Ava.

She looked down at Xander, his face contorted with pain

as his eyes blinked slowly. She reached down and pulled the journal from his hand.

"Try to hold on," she whispered.

He shook his head. "He won't let you live."

Ava stood and weaved her way back to Lazovsky, who grabbed her arm and pushed her toward the opening that led down the ladder. She quickly descended, formulating a plan. When she reached the bottom of the ladder, she moved back, allowing Lazovsky to descend. He stepped into the rugged hallway and turned to face her.

They walked back into the great room, where Maxim now dozed in the corner, his book splayed open in his lap. Ava caught the title and blinked a couple of times. The Russian man escorting them around Finland was reading a tattered copy of *To Kill a Mockingbird*. If she hadn't been so terrified, Ava would have laughed.

Lazovsky laid the map on the table and gestured Ava over. "This is a joke?" he asked.

Ava stared at him. She tried not to think of Xander lying in the attic above their heads with a gunshot wound to the abdomen.

"Tell me what Nick said," Lazovsky growled.

"Let me read the journal entry first," she answered, crossing her arms.

Lazovsky narrowed his eyes, then picked up the paper and handed it to her.

Ava took the paper and read her great-grandmother's journal entry aloud:

"I heard them talking today. I knew Alma had a secret. I knew there was something she hadn't told us. She came

back from Russia changed. She was so quiet and jumpy. She teaches art at the local school, and everyone there loves her. They think she's wonderful, and I suppose she is, yet she still thinks of me as a kid.

"But I know the secret now. Alma brought something back with her from Russia. She didn't go into detail. She told Isla it was too difficult to explain, but that she wanted to show Isla because the secret was eating at her. She asked Isla to help her conceal it. She hasn't even told her husband about this secret, and she told Isla! They were talking in low voices, but I heard where they agreed to meet. Twenty paces beyond the black rock in the center field where they played as children. She and Isla don't know that I heard them, and they don't know that I followed them later. The secret hidden in the dirt. Now I have my own secret. Layered tight beneath the place most loved. That's how you conceal a secret. But nothing stays hidden for long unless you cover it and don't tell a soul. And I won't. It'll stay hidden forever now, because I'll never breathe a word of it to another living being. They think me too young for secrets, but they don't know that I'm better at keeping them than anyone."

Overhead, Ava heard a thump. She looked up, then shifted her gaze back to Lazovsky.

"Your boyfriend is not yet dead," he said with indifference in his eyes.

"He's not my boyfriend."

She turned back to the paper and looked at the drawing on the back side. It was clear Nick had drawn the lake, marking where the house was. Little else was drawn except in the top right corner of the map where he'd drawn a cluster of trees, and in the opening, there was a round figure drawn with the words "black rock" written beneath.

She looked up at Lazovsky and shrugged her shoulders. "It seems easy enough," she said. She knew her voice sounded small, and she loathed the way he looked down on her.

"Is stupid map," he growled.

"Well, we could call Nick and ask him."

Lazovsky shook his head. "No. We don't need Nick. We go on our own. If we don't find the egg before sunrise, you die."

Ava shivered as Lazovsky tossed her a sinister smile. He jutted his chin toward the back door.

"We go now," he said. "Only a few hours until sunrise."

Ava turned and followed him out of the house. They walked past Maxim, who had picked his book back up and was reading once again. Her final vision was of him turning the page, slowly taking in the Great American Novel.

Hello? Nick?" Zak shouted into the phone as he squinted out at the road, which had narrowed into two lanes, barely wide enough to fit two cars. Thankfully, he and Carol appeared to be the only ones on the road.

"Where are you guys?" Nick asked.

Zak glanced at the map on his dashboard. "GPS says we are thirty minutes from the destination."

"I need you to pick up the pace, Zak," Nick said.

"Nick, what's happening now?" Carol asked.

"Ava is with Xander and Evgeny Lazovsky, a crook of a man without a soul. It's not good."

Carol dropped her head in her hands.

"Zak, when you get to the destination, you'll have to abandon the car and follow the path through the trees. It will take you to the place I told Ava to go when she gets away."

"If she gets away," Carol barked, the words spilling from her lips in a half sob. She clapped her hand over her mouth and shook her head.

Nick began coughing again.

"Zak? Carol?" Sylvie's voice came over the speaker as Zak pressed harder on the pedal and sped up.

355

"Sylvie, we're here," Zak said.

"Listen, Nicky isn't doing well," she began.

"Sylvie, so help me, right now I don't care how Nick is doing. My daughter is being held hostage in the middle of Finland because of him."

"I know, Carol. I know."

Sylvie's voice immediately disarmed Carol. She collapsed against the seat. "I'm terrified, Sylvie," she said.

"I know, Carol. And you have every right to be. Hold on a moment."

Zak and Carol could hear Sylvie murmuring in the background. Zak glanced back at the GPS and slowed down to turn onto another road, this one narrower than the last.

"Carol, I've got Tom here with me," Sylvie said.

"Tom?"

"My friend. The doctor. He's working to get Nicky calmed down. Tom just gave him a shot that we're hoping will give him the energy he needs to guide you all through the next couple of hours. In the meantime, I'm going to be Nicky's mouthpiece. He needs to rest and trying to talk is causing his lungs to spasm."

"Okay," Carol said. She stared out into the dark horizon, the light of the moon dancing across the treetops with a gentle glow. More stars than she'd ever seen before dotted a perfectly clear sky. It was so peaceful, yet completely contrasted the icy terror that fought to overwhelm her.

"Nicky says that you have to follow the path to the little house on the south end of the lake. Hold on, he's writing something down." Sylvie paused. "Well, he wants to know if Zak has a better internal compass than you do?"

Carol pursed her lips.

"What does that mean?" Zak asked.

"Nick wants to know if you have a better sense of direction than me, and this is not the time for making jokes," Carol said, raising her voice and leaning toward the dashboard.

"He says he's not trying to be funny," Sylvie said. "He just wants to make sure you go toward the south because he told Ava to go to the same place."

"What do we do once we get there, Sylvie?" Carol asked.

"Nicky says that Ava will hopefully be there hiding in the . . . what, Nicky? The . . . hidden space beneath the floorboards."

Carol pinched the bridge of her nose. "Okay, we'll find the path," she said.

"Carol, you can't give up yet. Ava's smart and she's quick. Don't project an ending for this story, okay?"

Carol was quiet for a moment before responding. "Okay," she said, calmer now. "Thanks."

"The GPS says we'll be there in ten minutes," Zak said. "I feel like we've driven to the middle of nowhere, though. How will we know when we're there?"

Carol and Zak could hear Sylvie's muffled voice as she spoke quietly to Nick.

"He says you'll come to a long driveway. Pass that and drive a half mile down the lane. On the left you'll find a wooden fence. That's the head of the path. Follow that . . ." She paused again. "I can't read that writing, Nicky." A beat later, she spoke back into the phone. "Follow that to the hideaway house to meet Ava."

"Okay, Sylvie," Zak said. "I'll have my phone with me."

"On silent, I hope?"

"Yes, of course."

"Call when you can," Sylvie said.

In the background, they could hear Nick coughing again. Seconds later, the line went dead. Carol and Zak drove on in silence, watching the ETA tick down. Zak slowed as they approached what looked to be the driveway.

"Drive a half mile more," he murmured. Two minutes later, he pulled to a stop and shined his flashlight across the lane at a rickety wooden fence tucked into the high grasses.

"So, we have to follow a path beyond that gate?" he asked.

Carol pushed open the door and stepped out. She didn't notice the cold anymore, nor did she miss a beat as she walked toward the fence, despite the fact that she had been a lifelong, self-declared, indoors girl.

Zak hopped out behind her, rushing to catch up.

"It's terribly dark," he said. "Do you think it's safe to shine our lights?"

"I think it's less safe to try and walk a strange path through the woods without a light," Carol said.

Zak flipped the flashlight of his phone back on and shone it down at their feet. A narrow path, barely visible through the overgrowth, stretched out before them.

"Well," he said. "I suppose the only thing left to do is . . ."

"Follow it," Carol said. She pushed open the gate and marched forward with all the determination of a mother bent on saving her only child.

Lausanne, Switzerland, 1920

Augusta pulled the door closed behind her and made her way down the stairs, pushing out onto the street and inhaling deeply. The morning air caught in her lungs while the cool mist that hung in the sky nipped at her cheeks. It would be a lovely autumn day.

She turned and stepped into the narrow alleyway that would lead her out to the main thoroughfare near the river. She could just barely make out the outline of the distant mountains in the space where the buildings parted. Within moments, she had cleared the buildings and crossed the quiet street, the sun not yet having made its way above the mountaintops but casting its morning light out enough for Augusta to be able to take in the sights of the Swiss town.

Lausanne reminded her of St. Petersburg in many ways. The river cutting a path around the outside of the city gave the appearance of home, though she supposed Lausanne lacked the magic of Petersburg. But still, there was a comfort in being so close to the water. If she closed her eyes and listened to the waves gently lapping against the walls beneath her feet, she could, for the briefest moment, imagine she was back home. She could pretend it was all as it once had been—that she was home in the place where she'd raised her children and built an empire alongside her husband.

Augusta opened her eyes and pulled the shawl tighter around her shoulders. The present came roaring back the instant she saw the skyline, beautiful and pure, but not St. Petersburg. The present was much less sweet than the memories of the past, for behind her in the small flat that she currently shared with her two eldest boys, her husband was dying.

"Mama?"

Augusta jumped at the sound of his voice. She turned to see Eugen stepping up behind her. He wore his suit, the same one he wore nearly every day. It was faded now, no longer crisp and dark like it had been in the days when he ran the House of Fabergé next to his father. Still, he looked dignified standing there against the backdrop of the waking city. Augusta reached out her hand and clasped his, marveling at the way it felt to hold the hand of this man who had once been her little boy. He had aged over the last two years, hair gray and face drawn. He looked more her peer than her son. How strange it was to feel so young inside but to have so many years behind her that her child could be considered an old man.

"How is he doing?" she asked.

Eugen looked away from her, his eyes drifting out to the water. When he was a little boy, he used to run ahead to the very edge of the riverbank and teeter on the side, always so brave and bold. He was never afraid of falling in, and somehow Augusta always knew, despite the fact that he charged forward toward the rushing waters, that he would keep his balance. He'd been steady from very early on.

"He's weak and in and out of consciousness," Eugen said.

Augusta drew in a deep breath and let it out slowly, squeezing his hand. He knew she hated when they tried to sugarcoat things. She looked out over the lake toward the mountains, which were growing more defined by the minute as the morning mist burned away and the crisp, September air showed signs of warming.

"What a journey," she said quietly, her words floating out into the air like a wisp.

Eugen turned and leaned against the railing, facing his mother. "Indeed." The two were silent for many long minutes.

"Thank you for the ways you have stuck with me . . . and your father," Augusta said, breaking the silence.

Eugen put his arm around his mother protectively. "Of course," he said, his voice a hum. "I wouldn't have had it any other way."

Augusta leaned her head against his shoulder and thought back over the last several months. Once Eugen had gotten her safely secured with family in Finland, he had parted her company and gone on to Stockholm in the hopes of finding some work, possibly even reviving the House of Fabergé in a new setting. He'd kept in touch with relatives in Germany who confirmed that his father, after fleeing Riga when the communists invaded, had gone on to Berlin, and then from there to Wiesbaden. Eugen had finally gotten a letter from his father in May of the current year. He sent the letter on to Augusta so that she could advise on what they should do next. It had been a sorrow-filled letter written on Karl's seventy-fourth birthday.

"*I celebrated with fifteen of my closest friends from Petersburg,*" he'd written, "*but today was not a day of happiness for me because everything I ever loved, my work and my family, are gone. This is life no more."*

Augusta had reached out to his relatives to find out how Karl was really doing, and that's when they told her that Karl was in rapid decline. His health was poor.

"If you wish to see your husband again, you must come to him," an old family friend had written.

As soon as Augusta heard the news, she made arrangements to gather Karl and bring him to Lausanne.

"The Swiss air will be healing for him," she'd written, informing Eugen of her plans. She hadn't asked him if he wanted to come, but he had shown up anyway. Of course he had. He was her reliable firstborn.

Nicholas refused to leave London, claiming that the safety of his family required him to remain there, though Augusta suspected his refusal was deeper than that. Agathon was still in Russia, having been unable to escape. Alexander joined Eugen and Augusta as they made all the arrangements, and together the three of them transferred the ailing patriarch of the family to Switzerland, but the move hadn't revived him. It had only tired him out. They were now in the final days.

"Mama, do you still love him?" Eugen asked.

Augusta looked out over the water, mouth set in a straight line. She nodded.

"I do," she said. "I always have. Despite everything that's happened, I love him. He was my love from the very beginning."

Eugen nodded. "Even after all that's happened?" He didn't mention *her* name, but it was an unspoken understanding.

Augusta sighed. "It wasn't a perfect love story, my dear." She turned to look at her son. "And he wasn't a perfect man. Nor was I the perfect wife. We didn't set out to become the House of Fabergé as it was. Somewhere along the way, I suppose we lost one another for a time, but here we are now."

"Would you do it all over again?" Eugen asked.

Augusta turned to look back over the water. "That's a difficult question," she said. "I suppose, no, I would not. Once was enough. I'd rather remember the happy times and forget the sad ones."

He nodded and stood silently for a long moment before straightening as he saw his brother, Alexander, hurrying across the street toward them.

"Mama," Alexander said, stepping up onto the walkway and looking into her eyes. He didn't have to say anything more.

Augusta made a small sound, like the whimper of a child, then gathered her skirt in one hand and rushed past him toward the flat. Eugen and Alexander quickly caught up to her, flanking her sides. Eugen's hand rested lightly on her elbow.

The three made their way up the narrow staircase and rushed into the damp flat where Karl lay on a bed in front of the window that looked out over the water and the mountains. His frail frame was covered in blankets, his bald head resting heavily on the thin pillow. He turned his head slowly as they walked in, his hollow gaze resting on Augusta. She rushed to his side and sank into the chair beside his bed, reaching over and grasping his hand.

"My darling," she said, and though she had rarely cried since all this began, she felt a single tear weave a path down her cheek.

Karl studied her. "It was always you," he whispered. His hand fluttered in hers, as though he was trying to squeeze but couldn't. "The treasure, the art, everything. It was always you. You were my muse."

His words were so soft, and had they been a color, Augusta would have painted them opalescent, like the most translucent shade of enamel that covered one of her husband's famed Easter eggs. She ran her hand over his head, a thousand memories rushing through her in a single moment. She leaned forward and kissed him on the forehead.

"I forgive you," she whispered.

A single breath escaped his lungs, and then he was still. The great and grand Peter Karl Fabergé had breathed his last, his hand clutching that of his greatest treasure, the thing that had been right in front of him the whole time.

His love.

Present Day

Ava shivered as they walked unsteadily around the lake. The moon was a little lower in the sky now, and she wondered what time it was. The impending daylight was a death sentence, and her mind raced with how to get away from Lazovsky, who walked behind her, huffing and wheezing from the strain. She had stamina in her favor. But the gun in his hand kept her from bolting. There was nowhere to hide.

"Over there," he said, pointing his flashlight to the right.

A small path cut away from the lake and headed eastward. Ava turned, following the uneven terrain as quickly as she could in an effort to wear him out. They marched on for what seemed a long time when suddenly the trees parted and opened up to a clearing. Ava stopped and squinted in the dim light.

"Is an open meadow, yes?" Lazovsky panted, crunching up beside her. He shined the flashlight in a broad stroke from left to right, settling finally on a large shape about halfway through the meadow.

"The black rock," Ava said.

"What did letter say?" Lazovsky asked. "Twenty paces from this black rock?"

Ava nodded. "But which direction?" she asked.

Lazovsky coughed beside her, his chest heaving. Ava cut her eyes to the left where a small break in the trees gave way to what she felt like might be her escape. She just needed to get him over there.

Ava turned. "Let's start there," she said, pointing to the section of rock that led to the clearing. "We'll start at the rock and count twenty paces out."

Lazovsky nodded. "You stay in front of me," he said.

Ava sped across the meadow to the rock. It was bigger than she'd realized. As she came upon it, she saw that it was, indeed, black, and it reached almost to her waist. Misshapen and strange, the rock looked almost like a bench cut from stone. She turned her back to it and faced the clearing. Taking in a deep breath, she took the first step, then the second, counting under her breath. Lazovsky watched her from the side, his face masked in the faint moonlight. By fifteen paces out, Ava realized that she was still quite a distance from the clearing. The breakaway was risky, but she didn't see another option. At nineteen paces she took off, shooting forward as fast as she could. Lazovsky let out a snarl of rage, and Ava knew, without looking, that the gun was trained at her back.

Zak and Carol froze. Zak whirled around and stared across the lake. He could hear the sound of someone yelling, the voice carrying through the cold night air and across the water as though much closer.

"Ava?" Carol cried.

Zak held up his finger to his lips as Carol clapped her hand over her mouth, her eyes wide. Zak turned and began rushing toward the lake, with Carol following as quickly as she could, her legs shaking beneath her. A gunshot rang out in the night sky. At the north end of the lake, a large house lit the darkness. Carol saw a man come rushing out the back door and stop, appearing to stare out into the night sky.

Zak followed the lake, the distance between him and Carol lengthening as his legs propelled him forward. Carol tripped and stumbled but didn't fall. Zak turned around and began to rush back toward her.

"No, go." She gestured him on. "I'm fine. Go find her, please!"

Zak turned and took off, much faster than Carol would have assumed he'd be, his thin legs pumping in long, even strides. Across the lake, Carol heard the sound of footsteps hammering the ground, twigs breaking and leaves crunching. Moments later a shape emerged from the trees and Carol's heart leapt.

"Ava!" she cried.

Ava stared across the water, the faintest image of her mother standing on the other side bringing a deep sense of relief.

"Mom!" she cried. "You have to go! Get away from the lake. Please! I'll find you, just go."

Zak, now closing the distance between himself and Ava, surged forward. Ava turned and saw him running.

"Zak? Zak, no!"

Just then, Lazovsky burst through the trees halfway between Ava and Zak. He turned and saw Ava, then looked the other way and saw Zak running toward him. He raised his gun and trained it on Zak, pulling the trigger. Ava screamed as Zak collapsed on the bank of the river.

367

Lazovsky turned to face her, and Ava whirled on her heel, tearing back into the trees. Disoriented and turned around, her heart racing and tears streaming down her cheeks, Ava raised her hands to try and keep the tree branches from knocking her out.

"Come back!" Lazovsky roared. "You cannot escape."

Ava jolted to a stop at the sound of another gunshot followed by Lazovsky letting out a scream of enraged pain. She turned and looked through the dark, her senses on high alert as she listened to the sound of footsteps running through the trees. She could hear Lazovsky writhing and sputtering close by. Slowly and cautiously, she stepped back a few paces, forcing her eyes to make sense of the shapes in the trees. She froze when she saw a figure walking toward her, arms down by his sides. She caught the shape of a gun dangling from one of his hands. She ducked behind a tree. Another gunshot rang out, silencing Lazovsky's moans as Ava clapped her hands over her ears. Then the woods grew frighteningly still.

"Ava?"

The voice called out to her clearly, splitting the silence. She slowly lowered her hands and covered her mouth.

"You can come out now. It is safe."

Footsteps crunched through the trees, the underbrush marking a rhythm that matched her slowing heartbeat. She no longer heard Lazovsky. She heard nothing but the approaching sound of someone new.

"Ava, it is safe now. I promise."

The voice, low and deep, held the whisper of an accent, but the English was otherwise perfect. Ava closed her eyes and drew in a deep breath, then let it out slowly. She stepped out from behind the tree and came face-to-face with Maxim, the driver who'd picked them up at the train station, and who earlier had been sleeping with *To Kill a Mockingbird* splayed across his lap.

He stopped and held up his hands, the gun in his right hand, dangling from his thumb. He slowly leaned forward and laid the gun on the ground, then stood back up and faced her.

"Now you are safe."

Ava took a step toward him, her head cocked to the side. "Who are you?"

"I am friend. A friend," he corrected himself. "I worked with your father many years ago. He was a good man, your father."

"But . . . why?" She glanced behind him where Lazovsky's body lay still in the underbrush.

"Xander called me. He and I knew one another through your father. I agreed to drive for him tonight, but he did not tell me that I would be a part of this terrible plan. I did not agree to this." Maxim shook his head.

Ava blinked slowly. "Is Lazovsky . . ."

"Dead," Maxim replied. He spoke the word so casually that Ava felt a momentary surge of fear once again.

Maxim took a step toward her. "Your friend is down by the water."

"Zak!" Ava turned toward the lake and rushed forward. She stopped and turned back to him. "What about Xander?" she asked.

He was still for a long moment before he shook his head slowly. Ava swallowed, suddenly feeling very sad.

"What do we do . . . about the bodies?" she asked.

"I will handle it," Maxim replied. He glanced up at the sky peeking through the trees, then shifted his gaze back to her face. "I know what to do."

Ava nodded. "Um . . . thank you." She rushed past him and cut through the trees, pushing out into the open and stumbling onto the path that led around the lake. She turned to her right and saw Zak lying on the ground, her mother leaning over him. She rushed forward and stumbled to her knees.

"Ava!" Carol cried. She reached over and grabbed her daughter, pulling her into a fierce embrace.

Ava looked down at Zak, who lay grimacing on the ground, clutching his elbow. "Zak! Are you okay?" She reached for him, gently touching his arm.

"Never better," Zak replied through clenched teeth.

"The bullet grazed his elbow. It took out a chunk of skin but didn't lodge." Carol shined her flashlight on Zak's arm and Ava could see the blood-soaked shirt at his elbow.

"Ava, what happened out there?" Zak asked.

"It's too hard to explain right now," she said. "Can you walk?" Zak nodded.

"Good," Ava said. "Because I think I know where the egg is, and we need to go get it now."

"Wait, what?" Carol sat back and stared at her daughter. "Ava, this is over. We're done."

"I know, Mom. It is over, because I know exactly where the egg is. You have to trust me."

Zak pushed to a sitting position, drawing in a deep breath. "Let's go," he said.

Carol helped him to his feet and looked back and forth between the two of them.

"You've both lost your minds!" she said, throwing her hands up.

Ava nodded. "It would appear that's true," she said.

St. Petersburg, 1921

Alma rolled over in her bed, squinting out the window where the sunlight streamed in. She pulled the small watch that Nicholas had left for her off the side table and sat up, rubbing her eyes. It was 11:00. She had slept all morning.

She hadn't even kissed him goodbye when he left—the first time in all their years of marriage. Though they'd had arguments before, last night's was the worst, and Alma still felt her stomach turn in knots at the things they had said to one another.

She pushed herself from the bed and slid her feet into her *tapochki*, then shuffled across the room to the little table under the window. A bowl of water waited for her there. She quickly splashed her face and washed her hands, standing up to straighten and smooth her hair.

The argument had started with her last night. She closed her eyes and wished that she could take back the accusatory words.

"Are you even trying to get us out of here?" she'd whined as Nicholas gave yet another laundry list of excuses as to why he was unable to obtain travel papers for them to leave the country.

"What do you mean by that?" he asked.

"I think you like that this crisis has forced me to stay home. Now you can have your little wife to take care of the house while you go out and work. This is how you wanted our life to be."

Even as she'd said the words, she knew how unfair they were, and the hurt that flashed through Nicholas's eyes would haunt her for the rest of her life.

"Do you really think this is how I wanted our life to be?" he asked, his voice laced with hurt. "Do you think I wanted to watch my talented wife waste away? Do you think I enjoy being able to provide so little for you?" He paused, blinking rapidly, then leaned down so that his face was close to hers.

"Do you think I enjoy not being able to protect you—not being able to get you away from the hell that we're living so that you can go back to doing the thing that you most love? You're not living here, you're surviving. And that is my fault."

He turned away from her and went to bed then. She tried to speak to him later, desperately wanting to apologize, but his wounded heart couldn't hear her. And he'd been up and out the door this morning before she woke.

Alma brushed the tears from her eyes and stared out the window. Off in the distance, she could see the angel atop the spire of the Peter and Paul Cathedral, its golden wings mocking the city. Where was the protection? What good was a guardian angel if he couldn't stop his people from starving?

The Bolsheviks had become the Communist Party, and the entire country had been nationalized. This wreaked havoc on the economy, with Nicholas's pay being cut to a quarter of what it had once been. Alma had looked for work around St. Petersburg, finding quickly that she needed to hide her affiliation with the House of Fabergé. But jobs were few and far between, and she was unqualified for most work. Nicholas refused to let her go labor in a warehouse for little pay, so she'd stayed home, suffering through long, quiet days, keeping herself busy with nonsense tasks until her mind and her heart felt numb.

She leaned forward and pushed open the window. Standing up, she pushed her head out and craned her neck in an attempt to see the Fontanka River, whose waters lapped the sides of the Anichkov Bridge just beyond their flat. She closed her eyes and thought back to her last public meeting with Karl, three weeks before he'd given her . . . the gift, the secret he'd kept beneath the boards of his workshop. He had offered to walk her home that evening, and together they'd come to a stop on Anichkov Bridge and overlooked the darkening waters of the Fontanka.

"I fear it's all coming to an end, young Alma," he told her that night.

"What do you mean?" Oh, how naive she had been.

Karl turned to her and smiled the way a father would smile at the child he adored. He loved her like a father. She knew that.

"Look at the man in these sculptures," he said.

She turned and took in the four bronze horsemen, focusing on the statue nearest to them. The horse reared up before her, the look in his bronze eyes wild. The man at his side clearly struggled beneath the strain, the muscles in his legs and arms tight and protruding. She had never really studied the statues before, usually keeping her head down as she passed by them and rushed home to meet her husband in their shared flat.

"Notice the way the man wrestles and pulls at the horse. The beast is not going down without a fight."

She studied the statue quietly.

"Russia is the horse, my dear girl," Fabergé said beside her.

"She is putting up a fight now, but she will be subdued." He'd turned to her then and grabbed her hand, squeezing it gently. "Don't let them break you, Alma," he said. "You were meant to be wild and free."

Alma pushed back from the window and shook off the memory. Much had happened in the last three years. She had failed in so many ways, but perhaps the most striking was the fact that she had been broken. She had been tamed, just as he'd feared she would be.

Alma jumped as the door burst open and Nicholas came striding in. His hair, which had grayed at the temples, stood in wild tufts around his head and his eyes, wide behind his round glasses, stared at her. She stood mute beside the table. Nicholas strode over to her in three long steps, sweeping her into his arms and kissing her fiercely.

At first, Alma resisted, pushing against his chest with her fists. But she quickly melted into his embrace, the kiss communicating a thousand things that words could never capture.

"Nicholas—" she began, pushing away from him.

He held up his hand, a set of papers clutched in his fist. "I got them, my darling," he said. "We leave tonight."

"We . . . we leave tonight?" she repeated, her stunned words hollow in her ears.

Nicholas stepped forward and pulled her to his chest, cradling her head in his hand. "We're going home, Alma."

They stood still, clinging to one another for a long time before Nicholas pushed back. "Pack only what you can carry with you," he said. He brushed the curl off her forehead with a smile. "I love you so much," he whispered.

"Nicholas," she answered. "I love you." She stood on her toes and kissed him again. He stepped back and gave her a gentle smile, his eyes soft as he drank her in. She knew she was forgiven.

"I'm going back to the office to gather a few items. I left so quickly I didn't get everything I needed. I will be back in one hour. Be ready, my love."

Alma nodded. "Home," she said, her eyes filling with tears.

"Home." He cupped her cheek softly, then turned and rushed back out of the flat.

Alma wiped her eyes and walked to the bureau, pulling open the top drawer and removing the cloth carpetbag that she would pack to take home. She turned back to the bed and felt her stomach turn into a knot once more. She and Nicholas would be okay. She knew that deep down.

But she also knew that she had a secret, and that she would never be able to share it with him, no matter how much space they put between themselves and this life in Russia.

Present Day

Ava ran as fast as she could around the lake, Zak and her mom straining to keep up. Every once in a while she'd slow, the sound of Zak's gasps giving her enough pause to make sure he was still okay. His shirt was now soaked with blood at the elbow, and his face looked pale in the fading night sky.

"Ava," Carol heaved as she caught up. "What makes you so sure the egg is out here?"

"Something Nick said while we were talking," Ava said. She turned and looked ahead, her eyes straining to see through the impending morning light. The birds had awoken, and they whistled a tune in the trees that surrounded the lake. The water was completely still, without a wisp of wind to move it from its slumber. As the sky lightened above the tree line, Ava took in the sight.

"I think the little hideaway house is just over there," she motioned. She followed the path, slower this time, until the hazy image of a wooden post jutting up from the ground became evident before them.

"That's it," she whispered.

"What?" Zak breathed behind her.

Ava pointed at the post. "Nick said there would be a wooden post that marked where the little house stood behind the lake." She jogged ahead of them and knelt down before the post, running her fingers over the inscription carved into the side.

Paikka, jota rakastan eniten.

"What does it say?" Carol asked, kneeling down beside Ava.

"It says 'the place I love most,'" she answered. Using her hands, she reached down and began digging at the ground. It was hard and cold and her fingers immediately began to ache, but she pushed them into the dirt, pulling and moving it aside.

"Ava?"

"Nick told me that this was the place his grandmother loved to escape to when his mother was young. He said it was the place she loved more than any place in the world." Ava grunted as she continued to dig around the base of the post, her fingers finally breaking through the hard earth. The soil was softer farther down.

"In her journal, Lida wrote that she overheard Isla and Alma talking about how they buried Alma's secret in the meadow with the black rock. But she goes on to say that she followed them there, and she now has a secret of her own."

Ava paused, sitting back on her heels and looking from her mother to Zak, who had slumped down beside them and leaned heavily against the post.

"She wrote that the way to keep a secret was layered beneath the place most loved."

"You think Lida reburied the egg here?" Zak asked.

Ava leaned forward and began digging again, her hands moving quickly now as the hole at the base of the post grew deeper. Ava shoved her hands into the ground and yelped as her finger jammed against something hard and cold. She looked down and caught the glint of metal, then looked up at her mom and Zak.

"I think she did," she said, her breath coming out in frozen puffs.

Quickly, they dug more dirt out of the way, Zak using his good arm to push the mounds of dirt to the side so they wouldn't fall back into the hole. Minutes later, Ava dragged out a square metal box, dented and cold. She turned it to the side and breathed a sigh of relief when she saw no lock. Drawing in a deep breath, she pulled open the lid and looked inside. She fell back against the post, the air shooting from her lungs as though she'd been punched.

"Ava?"

Ava looked up at her mom, then at Zak, the blood from her face having drained slowly. She reached inside the box and pulled out a single sheet of paper, opening it up slowly.

It was the most detailed picture of the egg they'd seen so far, minutely drawn by someone who had clearly studied the object closely. Beneath the egg was the drawing of a fist thrust upward in defiance. A crown had been drawn over the fist, colored red, though the markings were now faded. It looked like a bloody hand raised in revolution.

Ava looked back into the box. At the bottom, on a worn piece of red velvet, lay a pair of diamond earrings shaped like frozen icicles against glass.

"The egg isn't here," Ava gasped.

They stared at one another, stunned, the juxtaposition of the rising sun and singing birds stark against their ashen faces.

"What do you mean, it's not there?" Carol asked. She peered

inside the box and gingerly pulled out the earrings, laying them in her palm and holding them up.

"Are those the earrings that Alma designed?" Zak asked.

Ava sat heavily into the cold, wet grass, fatigue crashing down on her as the adrenaline siphoned out of her body. She opened her mouth to answer, when the phone in Zak's pocket began to buzz.

Carol placed the earrings back in the box and reached into Zak's pocket for the phone. "Nick?" she said. "Nick, you're not going to believe this."

"Carol, it's Sylvie." The voice on the other line tremored.

"Sylvie?"

"Do you have Ava? Is she alright?"

"Yes, Sylvie." Carol looked at her daughter. "We got her, and you're not going to believe this. We need to talk to Nick."

A long pause swelled before them.

"Carol," Sylvie finally said, "you all need to get back now. Nicky doesn't have much time."

Finland, 1925

Lida dug her hands into the soft earth, glancing over her shoulder as the air in her lungs pushed in and out in short bursts. She'd done it, and there was no going back now.

She dug until the skin beneath her fingernails grew raw and tight. A worm wriggled its way out of the clump of dirt in her palm and plopped on the ground at her knees, where her skirt splayed out around her, muddy and soiled. Isla would surely give her grief for that.

Lida paused, thinking about her older sister. Isla was ten years her senior, and it made her act more like a mother. Still, Lida loved her and looked up to her, if perhaps she resented her at the same time.

Beautiful Isla who still lived at home. For a long time, she had been the most eligible bachelorette in town, with scores of young men coming by to squire her away. But Isla was a wild spirit, longing for freedom and afraid of commitment. She'd never been one to take on the role of housewife, so she remained at home, now the subject of much gossip as the elder ladies in the town clucked their tongues when she walked past without a single care, her long blond hair braided and swinging side to side.

"Such a waste. A beautiful girl like that, now doomed to be a spinster. I suppose the family's only hope is in the younger one, a homely little thing, but perhaps better suited for a family." Lida could hear their whispers, and she knew they spoke of her.

When Alma returned, she and Isla had taken up where they'd left off as children, whispering and giggling together like schoolgirls. Alma, already married, was different from Isla in many ways. She was more genteel and shy. Somehow, their differences worked, though, and Lida envied their friendship.

Alma had hired her to come clean her house periodically, as she had gone back to work as an art teacher at the local school. In that way, Alma and Isla were identical—neither much cared for the traditional womanly roles that defined most of their peers. They far preferred their independence and autonomy. Lida wished she could be like that but knew what was expected of her. Father would be sending her to Helsinki next week. When she had complained to her mother about being sent away, the truth of her situation had been revealed.

"Getting an education is only a means to an end, my dear," her mother had explained. "The hope is you will find a nice man who will love you and make you a wife."

She stopped digging and looked up across the lake at her parents' house. She wished she loved that home as much as they did. She supposed she would have to learn to love it, as the expectation was that someday she and Isla would maintain it and "fill it with children," her mother would say periodically.

Behind her, down the little path and tucked away in the woods, was the real treasure. It was the little house her father had built for her and Isla when they were children. It was there that Lida followed Isla like a puppy dog, giggling at her big sister's stories of adventure and treasure hunts. Isla used to hide knickknacks and objects all over the woods surrounding the little house, then give Lida treasure maps and tell her to go find them.

"Someday, the people who come behind us will discover these treasures of ours. A historical treasure trove," Isla would say, eyes dancing.

Of course, that had been when they were younger. Somewhere along the way, they'd grown up enough to stop playing silly games.

Lida turned and picked up the metal box that she'd taken from the meadow where the black rock lay. She'd followed Alma and Isla that day and watched them quietly and methodically bury it beneath the dirt. After they left, she dug it up.

She didn't know why she'd done it. Perhaps she'd been jealous of the way they seemed so intent on keeping that secret from her, as though she didn't deserve to know about it. Whatever the case, she'd impulsively gone back out, by light of the moon, and unearthed the box. And now, it sat in her lap.

She laid it gently back in the dirt, then grabbed a clump of earth and dropped it on top of the metal box with a thud. She'd looked inside the box. She knew the secret. It frustrated her, however, that she didn't understand why it was so important—why Alma was so frightened and intent on hiding it. Even Isla, who treated just about everything in life as though it were a grand joke, seemed somber and nervous when they buried the box together.

Lida knew there had to be more to the secret, but she didn't dare ask Isla or Alma. Whatever it was, Alma was afraid for anyone to know she had it. She was so frightened she would bury it. And now, Lida had her own secret, and she would guard it better than anyone else.

Lida quickly finished burying the box, pushing the dirt around until it no longer rolled into a mound but lay flush with the earth surrounding it. Then she grabbed the post that she'd carved out earlier with the knife she took from Father's shed. Soon, she would be sent to Helsinki to begin a new life, but she would mark this day and this place before she left.

She dug another hole in front of the first, then stood up, pushing and shimmying the post into the ground, sweat gathering on her upper lip as her mud-caked hands twisted it into place. She filled in the places around the post until it stood upright, then she stepped back admiring her work.

"The place I love most," the post read, and it was true. She really did love this little spot of lake that led to the treasure trove in the trees more than any other place in all the world. She turned and walked away with her eyes trained forward, knowing somehow that her treasures were there, preserving what little freedom she'd ever possessed.

Present Day

Carol reached over and grabbed Nick's hand, pulling it to her chest. He turned his face to hers, his labored breathing coming out in small gasps. Anatoly had managed to get them a flight out of Helsinki the same day that Sylvie called, flying them home to Tampa, where they jumped in their car and drove to Lakeland, all while the sun remained high in the sky. It was as though they had been chasing time itself, trying to catch it before it slipped away. Ava sat on the other side of Nick, her hands clasped under her chin as she leaned against the bed.

Sylvie stood at the foot of the bed, silent tears coursing down her cheeks as she gently rubbed the feet of her brother. Zak had come in briefly, then gone to the other room with Dr. Tom to have his wound cleaned and better treated.

"Carol." Nick's voice came out like a ragged gasp.

"I'm here, Nick," she said.

He turned toward her, his eyes sunk into his head, hollow and gray. It took a moment before they focused. "Ava?"

Carol nodded. "Yes, she's here too."

Ava reached down and grabbed Nick's hand. He turned to look at her, the corner of his mouth turning up in the faintest smile.

"Hey, kiddo," he breathed. "Good to see you."

"We didn't find the egg," Ava said, her voice breaking. "It wasn't in the box."

Nick turned his head and stared up at the ceiling. "It doesn't matter," he whispered. Turning, he looked back at Carol.

"I was . . . such a fool. I'm so sorry."

Tears filled her eyes. She kissed his hand and shook her head. He drew in a slow breath.

"I spent . . . so much time . . . trying to find the perfect . . . treasure." He shifted his gaze from her face to Ava's. "It was . . . right there in front . . . of me. The . . . whole time."

Ava squeezed his hand tighter and leaned forward, resting her head on the top of his hand, hating how cold and lifeless it felt. Tears pricked the corners of her eyes. Nick moved his hand slightly, pushing her chin up so she would face him.

"You," he whispered. "You were . . . the treasure. You are my . . . ." He gasped and grimaced as a wave of pain washed over him. "You're my treasure," he wheezed.

"Dad," Ava cried. She squeezed his hand. "Daddy, no. Please. Stay here, okay? Don't leave yet. Please." She leaned forward, pressing her lips against his sallow cheek.

"Oh, kiddo," he breathed. "I wish I could stay. I wish . . . I would have stayed." He gasped again.

Ava pushed up and studied him. "I'll keep searching," she said. "I'll find it, I promise."

Nick let go of Carol's hand and slowly reached over, running his hand down Ava's cheek.

"You have . . . the gift," he gasped. "But don't . . . let it . . . steal your life."

Ava nodded. Nick pushed the corners of his mouth up in a smile as tears dripped onto the pillow behind him.

"I . . . love you, kiddo," he said. He shifted his eyes to Carol. "And you . . . ," he breathed. "It was always you."

She dropped her head and covered her face with her hands. Nick drew in a breath, then let it out.

"It was . . ."

His hand went limp in Ava's, and the room grew still. Sylvie leaned forward and shook Nick's foot.

"Nicky?" she asked, her voice shaky. "Nicky? Nicky?"

She rushed to the side of the bed and placed her hands on his cheeks, turning his face to hers. His eyes were half closed, his body still. Sylvie fell on the bed in a heap of sobs, as Ava slowly stood up and backed away, her throat burning. She tripped over the dresser and turned, running from the room.

"Ava?" Carol called, but Ava didn't stop. She pushed open the back door and stumbled down the porch steps, through the immaculately kept grass, and into the grapefruit trees at the back of Sylvie's property. It was dusk, the setting sun giving way to a spectacular sky. From the horizon and across the dome above, the air was painted a vibrant pink. Ava stared at it, her chest heaving up and down. She dropped to her knees and let out a long, guttural cry. Leaning forward, she put her face in her hands, folding into herself.

She didn't resist when Zak knelt beside her and pulled her to his chest. He gripped her with his good arm, his wounded elbow wrapped against his chest in a tight sling. He held her for a long time, until the sky faded from pink to orange to gray.

When she finally sat up, she turned to him, the dim night air barely illuminating his face.

"He's gone," she whispered.

Zak nodded. He winced as he shifted his weight.

"We didn't find the treasure, and Nick is gone," she said. "My dad is dead."

"I'm so sorry, Ava," Zak said gently. "Truly. I am terribly, terribly sorry about your dad."

She turned to him, pain swimming in the center of her eyes. "What do I do now?"

Zak drew in a deep breath, then let it out slowly. "I suppose you need to feel this for a little bit," he said. "The pain. You need to just *feel* it."

"I don't want to," she whimpered, fresh tears falling on her face. Ava laid her head on his shoulder and closed her eyes.

"See, the thing is, Ava," Zak said. "I think maybe you did find the treasure you were looking for. I mean—you found your dad."

Ava sighed. "Nick . . . *Dad* . . . said something similar right before . . ." She pushed up and turned to Zak. It was almost completely black outside now.

"You're a good friend to me, Zak," she said.

He gazed back at her. "Am I only a friend?"

She heard the hope in his voice, and for the first time she paused at the thought. There was a feeling there that she wasn't sure she understood just yet, but it was enough to make her slow down before responding.

She reached down and grabbed his hand. "For now," she said.

He smiled. They were quiet for a long time, the Florida air dancing around them, balmy and comfortable.

"You know, the egg is still out there somewhere," Zak finally said, breaking the silence.

Ava pushed her head back and looked up at him, eyebrows raised. He shrugged, then winced.

"Does it hurt?" Ava touched his bandaged arm gently.

"I'll be okay," Zak said. He stared at Ava, a small smile turning his mouth up. "You and I could be a good team," he said.

Ava nodded, then leaned her head back onto his shoulder. "We really could."

They sat for a long time as the world around them fell asleep. Beyond the shadow of trees, Ava could see Sylvie's house, the orange glow of the lights giving a deceptively inviting view. She knew she should go back inside. She should help her mom and Sylvie prepare for the funeral home to come remove her dad's body. But she felt heavy and tired.

Zak nudged her head off his shoulder. He stood up and reached down with his good arm, offering her his hand.

"Let's go," he said gently. "It's getting chilly out here."

Ava grabbed his hand and let him pull her up. She thought about how different Zak was from Xander. As if reading her thoughts, Zak spoke again.

"I saw a news article about a missing British man whose body was found in the woods of Finland next to that of Evgeny Lazovsky, a notorious Russian mob leader. It was the body of Alexander Majors, son of the famed British treasure hunter, Jack Majors."

Ava drew in a deep breath.

"The deaths are under investigation, but the article makes the initial assumption that the two were part of a treasure hunt gone wrong. No one else was placed at the scene of the crime."

Ava let out the air that she'd held in her lungs. "It's terribly sad, isn't it?"

Zak nodded. Ava grabbed his hand again and walked with him toward the house.

"I don't want to go in there," she said quietly.

Zak squeezed her hand. "I know," he said. "You don't have to be strong about this. I've got your back. Okay?"

She looked up and smiled. "Okay."

Lausanne, 1920

A ugusta sat silently on the small divan in the flat over-looking the mountains. The bed where her husband had died just a few short days before had now been moved, and the room suddenly felt empty and cold. Her hands were folded in her lap as she stared at the box that sat before her on the coffee table. It was made of a thick cedarwood, planked and stained so that it appeared to be a bold decoration. The top of the box had a lid that could slide open and shut. She had asked specifically that it be easy to open.

"I may choose to spread his remains," she told Eugen when making her request. "I want the freedom to make that choice."

Eugen and Alexander sat across from their mother, watching her as she stoically stared at the box that held their father's ashes. They were already making plans to transfer Augusta to France, where she wished to go visit family who had settled in Cannes.

"I am ready to leave this place," she'd told them right after Karl breathed his last. Now, they stared at her, giving her the emotional distance she needed to process all that had transpired.

"I'd like a moment alone," Augusta finally said. She looked up at her boys, each of whom nodded.

"Of course, Mama," Alexander said. He stood and walked over to her, leaning down and giving her a quick kiss on the cheek. Eugen followed suit.

"We'll go for a short walk and clear our heads," Eugen said.

Augusta nodded. She grabbed each of them by the hand and squeezed them tight.

"You've been good to me," she said, looking from one to the other.

They nodded and quickly retreated from the apartment. Augusta waited until their footsteps faded beyond the door, then she slowly rose to her feet and walked to the other room. She opened the armoire and pulled out the cloth bag that she had carried with her from Russia to Finland and on to Lausanne when she heard Karl was sick. Reaching a shaking hand inside, she pulled out the cloth-wrapped treasure she'd been hiding for two years. It was the reason she refused to let Eugen carry her bag when they traipsed through the trees on their escape to Finland. It was the thing that had kept her up at night for years.

She slowly unwrapped the cloth that she'd hastily wound around the treasure, and when the final strip was removed, she pulled it to her chest and walked slowly back to the sitting room, setting the egg on the table next to Karl's remains.

She closed her eyes and thought back to the day she'd gone to Alma's flat and demanded the girl give it to her. The poor thing had tried to pretend she didn't know what Augusta was talking about, but ultimately, she'd broken down into tears and dropped to the floor, sliding beneath the bed and producing the egg that Karl had asked her to hide.

"He told me to keep it safe," Alma whimpered.

Augusta grabbed her by the shoulders then and pulled her into a tight embrace.

"And you have," she whispered, as Alma wept against her shoulder. "But this shouldn't be your burden to bear. It wasn't fair of him to put this on you."

Augusta stepped back, reaching into her pocket and pulling out a pair of earrings that Karl had given to her for Christmas many years before.

"Please," she said, laying the earrings in Alma's hand. "Take these. I believe you designed them."

"No, I couldn't." Alma held them out to Augusta.

"No, I insist that you take them," she said, closing Alma's fingers around them and pushing her hand back. "Keep them and remember that you were loved and respected by my husband. He used to tell me that of all his master craftsmen, you were the finest. I want you to have these. But you must not let anyone see them until after you escape. It's not safe to possess anything from the House of Fabergé."

"What will you do?" Alma asked. Her eyes shifted to the egg in Augusta's hand.

"I will protect my husband," Augusta had said.

She opened her eyes now and reached down, sliding the top of the box out to reveal the ashes inside. Drawing in a deep breath, she slowly lowered her hand into the sandy matter, the flutter of her heart pattering against her chest as she sensed the presence of him near. She took the egg from the table and wrapped it back in the cloth, then she wedged it deep into the box, covering it with the ashes until she was certain it was stuck tight and completely hidden.

Taking the lid, she slid it slowly back into place, then rested her hands atop the wood, closing her eyes and letting out her breath.

"There, my love," she whispered. "The secret stays safe with you, concealed beneath the boards. Guard the treasure well."

Note from the Author

Writing historical fiction is a funny business. As an author, I feel the weight of making sure I get the history right, while as a storyteller I long to weave in a little imagination. Blending the two—history and imagination—is not a task to be taken lightly.

This is a work of fiction, but it's grown from the pages of history. Peter Karl Fabergé was a master craftsman whose creativity and vision is almost unparalleled in history. Beyond his depth of creativity, however, was also an astute businessman who was very forward thinking for his time.

Fabergé was known to be a tough but good employer, pushing his employees to rise to every challenge he set before them. His standards were high, but he made sure that the work environment was conducive to meeting such standards. And, of course, the results of Fabergé's vision captured the hearts and imagination of the world.

In 1917, the Russian Revolution exploded in St. Petersburg, leading to the fall of the Romanov family and, ultimately, the establishment of the Soviet Union. In the whirlwind of events that occurred after the revolution took hold, most of the tsar's possessions were confiscated and squired away, including all of the fifty-two eggs designed for the tsar, his wife, and his mother over the course of two decades.

To date, only forty-one of those eggs have been recovered, the latest of which was found by a scrap metal dealer in the US in 2014 when he purchased the egg for $14,000, only to find out later he'd acquired the third Imperial Easter egg, which was worth an estimated $33 million. Not a bad day at work!

This story sparked an idea—a question, really. And all good fiction starts with a question.

Where were the other Imperial eggs? Who was searching for them? And could there possibly have been more than just the fifty-two the history books have recorded?

It was from this place that *The Master Craftsman* was born. A few questions without any real answers. And here is where imagination met history and attempted to bring it to life. So, were there more than fifty-two eggs? We don't really know for sure. We do know, however, that Fabergé was a creative, complicated man—a Master Craftsman—so anything is possible.

Acknowledgments

If no man is an island, then no book can be written in seclusion. All books are collaborative, and this one is no less. From the genesis of the idea to the final product, I've had a team of people rallying behind me to create as polished a work as possible.

Rachel McMillan was the first to hear my crazy idea. I shot her an email one afternoon with a simple question—what if there are more eggs? Should I write about it? To which she responded, "YES!" And then she followed up her early encouragement by helping me get the manuscript in front of the right team of people to bring it to market.

The team at Revell immediately jumped on board with enthusiasm, and all an author could really hope for in a publisher is one who catches the vision and rallies behind it. So, thank you to Rachel McRae and team for your enthusiastic support from the very beginning.

I don't release any words out into the world without first having them looked at by my dear friend, and editor extraordinaire, Bethany Hockenbury. She's the one who tells it to me straight—the good, the bad, and the ugly—and because of her I don't release ridiculous novels full of misplaced commas and unnecessary superlatives.

To my fellow authors in Her Novel Collective: you all started as business partners and have grown into friends. You encourage me, build me up, make me smile, and challenge me with your knowledge of the craft of writing. I could not be more grateful.

To my family: my parents, who put me on a plane to Russia when I was fifteen and told me to go have an adventure, not realizing that that trip would forever alter the course of my life—thank you! My husband, Lee, hardly bats an eye anymore when I start talking about new stories and bizarre characters as if they are real people. He listens, even though he doesn't understand fiction, and he tells me to keep going. I'm here because he wouldn't let me quit.

And of course, my children: Sloan, Tia, Landon, Annika, and Sawyer. You guys make me want to be better. You make me want to try harder and not give up when things get hard. Thank you for putting up with a mom who probably doesn't sleep enough, who isn't a very good cook, and who is always a step behind on the laundry. But we have some fun, don't we? Thanks for keeping my imagination fresh, and for bringing me joy on a daily basis.

And finally—thank YOU, Reader, for picking up this book and taking the time to read the story. I can only do what I do because you take the time to dive into a story. I am grateful for the chance to weave these tales every single day.

Kelli Stuart is the award-winning author of the novels *Like a River from Its Course* (2016), *A Silver Willow by the Shore* (2019), and *The Fabulous Freaks of Monsieur Beaumont* (2021). Fluent in the Russian language, Kelli has spent the last twenty years studying the culture and history of the former Soviet Union. Kelli writes from her home in Tampa, Florida, where she lives with her husband and five children. To learn more about Kelli and her work, follow her at KelliStuart.com.

Meet Kelli

Find Kelli online at

KelliStuart.com

to sign up for her newsletter and keep up-to-date
on book releases and events.

Follow Kelli on social media at

KelliStuartAuthor

KelliStuart

KelliStuartAuthor